DARK EMPATHY

by Katy Morgan

Dedication

To Jenny, because I promised. (It only took 28 years!)

To the betas: AJ Brown, Bryan Hinds, Meredith Lowe, Sarah Mayes, Ben Strauss, and the parentals.

And with extra thanks to Peanut, who explained to me why punching someone in the face is a really bad idea.

Prologue

"TELL ME WHY you did it."

Snyder is trying to hide his trembling hands. Pointless, since they're shackled to the table, but it's a reflex, even after hours of this. Bastian feels the fear-frustration-disdain rolling off him, still at the same level it's been since the officers brought him into the interrogation room for this interview.

("Interview," Valentine calls them, like a polite name will make it sound better.)

"I swear, I didn't do anything!"

Snyder's practically blasting the emotional signature Bastian felt at the crime scene, but without getting it directly from him as well, the case won't hold up. Since Bastian's game has been off lately, the original read wasn't definitive. And Valentine will want definitive.

"Sebastian," she says in his earpiece. "We don't have all day."

Speak of the devil.

"What would you suggest?" Bastian mutters. "I'm sure the black coats would be pleased to beat a confession out of him."

He can feel her amusement-exasperation-irritation through the two-way mirror on the far side of the room. "Security isn't going to do your job for you. Stop dawdling and take care of this, please."

Ah, the please that isn't a please.

Snyder is still babbling about his innocence—obviously an act, since it's accompanied by a slimy smug-contempt-scorn that makes Bastian's skin crawl.

Enough. Bastian sighs and takes off his gloves. He leans forward and grabs Snyder's wrists mid-sentence, pinning them to the table, ignoring his squawk.

"Hey! What are you—?"

Bastian half closes his eyes against the wave, but it's strong—sweaty, stinking fear, getting louder as Snyder realizes Bastian's not listening to his protests.

The surface stuff is what Bastian expected: everything he's already felt during the interrogation, now with a little more focus. Conspicuously absent is any sense of regret or remorse. Not unusual. Bastian is amused to feel the animosity and fear specifically directed at him. Also not unusual.

But none of this is what she wants.

Bastian presses his lips together, closes his eyes completely, and *pushes*.

He doesn't realize anything's wrong at first. Going deeper isn't so strange; most people he interrogates end up requiring it.

(He hates it, though, having to touch them, feeling the increase in sensitivity of his power, their emotions seeping into him, past the shield he's spent so long perfecting. But if he can't match the interrogation read to the crime scene read, she'll make him do it again, and the more he does it, the worse it gets, especially lately—)

This time is the worst yet.

It's like tripping when you put all your weight down where a step is supposed to be but isn't. He's not just feeling Snyder's emotions; he can connect them to specific actions like *the echo of the urge that rose up in him that day, the desire to feel his hands around her neck, to hold her down, the pleasure of having that kind of control over someone's life. She was helpless against him, especially after he dazed her with a blow to the head. The fierce joy as he held her under the water, the sense of control returning, the triumph over a world that thought he couldn't have her, that he wasn't good enough—*

Bastian breathes in sharply, opens his eyes, and lets go of Snyder's wrists. His stomach is roiling as he puts his gloves back on and gets to his feet, nearly stumbling like an idiot. He goes to the two-way glass and taps once to let Valentine know it's over. Out of the corner of his eye, he sees Snyder has gone strangely still.

Officer Michaels wheels in the machine while another officer holds open the door for her. Bastian rolls up his sleeve to the elbow so she can attach the wires to his arm. She's meticulous and focused on her task like always, so it takes a moment before she looks up at him and frowns.

"Would you like to sit down, Mr. Lucas?" she asks.

Bastian glares at her, fighting not to wobble on his feet, and she doesn't press it.

When Michaels turns the machine on, he feels the jolt run through the wires and into his blood. It's unpleasant on the best of days but particularly disgusting today.

"What…?" Over at the table, Snyder sounds dazed but is starting to function again.

The intercom crackles to life. "Your guilt is being recorded, Mr. Snyder," Valentine says, getting a word in just like always.

"But I didn't—"

"Verbal confirmation is unnecessary. Circumstantial evidence, combined with the work of the gentleman in the room with you—"

"Oh, I'm a gentleman today, am I?" Bastian mutters.

"—make your confession moot. It would be helpful, certainly, but we can still hold you emotionally culpable for the murder of Ms. Ramsay."

Out of the corner of his eye, Bastian sees Snyder blanch. "That's—but you—"

"The impulses being recorded by Officer Michaels are coded to your emotions. Their particular signature will, I'm certain, match the signatures of emotional disturbance left at the scene of the crime."

"I...." Snyder seems to lose his train of thought. Then he locks gazes with Bastian, who gets hit with a tremendous wave of fear-disgust-confusion underneath the machine's recording.

"I've heard rumors about you," Snyder says, his lip curling. "A whole facility of freaks, government pets who make people disappear. I thought it was just an urban legend, you know, something to scare little kids...."

His eyes go glassy for a moment; then he shakes his head and sneers at Bastian. "What kind of freak are you? The kind who tricks people into confessions?"

Officer Michaels switches off the machine, and in the same moment, Bastian is ripping the electrodes from his skin, trying not to shudder.

"The official term is 'empath,'" Valentine says.

"Freak," Snyder insists. "It'll never hold up in court."

"Actually, you'll find the courts quite amenable to data retrieved from this facility. I'd start thinking about what you'd like for your last meal. Officer Michaels, please escort Mr. Snyder to his cell."

Bastian leans against one of the dull gray walls, arms crossed, and watches them go. His stomach is still protesting, and now his head is getting in on the action. So it's particularly delightful to see that it's Valentine herself who holds open the door for Michaels and Snyder before entering the interrogation room. He steels himself for...he doesn't know what. Certainly not being given a handful of antacids and painkillers, as well as a glass of water.

He stares at her, and she smiles back. "You looked unwell."

She waits while he takes them, then nods. "You did a good job here, Sebastian. But there's more to do." She pauses, looking him up and down. "Unless you'd like to see Dr. Wright before we move on?"

"No," he says quickly (too quickly).

She smiles. "Good. Then let's get to work."

Chapter 1

One year later

THE RAIN IS picking up when their vehicle reaches the ravine. Henry checks the GPS to confirm: the potential is there at the bottom, which happens to be the nexus of the growing storm. Of course.

He shuts the engine off and turns around to address his team. "No heroics today, folks. Let's do this like we always do."

"With unbearable amounts of aplomb and style?" Johnson calls. His seatmates snicker.

Henry rolls his eyes. "How about with the proper respect for your commanding officer?"

"Sir, yessir!" Johnson salutes, elbowing the officer to his right when he raises his hand to do it.

Henry sighs. "As I was saying: Follow the plan. Use the serum sparingly; we're running low. And let's try not to alarm the stormmaker, shall we? I don't want to send any of you to medical for massive head trauma due to hail."

The team exits out the rear of the vehicle while Henry uses the driver-side door. They're immediately drenched with rain as they break up according to subteams: surveillance staying back, taking measurements of the ravine and the surrounding area; distance making their way carefully around the lip, out of sight, positioning themselves to be able to take a shot if needed; contact geared up and awaiting his order to go down into the ravine.

Once everyone is ready, he puts in his earpiece and takes a quick look down.

She's young—fourteen, according to her file—and sitting in a pool of water, her back to them. The rain is starting to lift a bit, but it's still going. That, along with the hunched-over body language, spells fear.

He signals for the contact team to follow him down the side of the ravine to where she's sitting. They're well trained enough not to have their guns drawn but to have them close enough that they can shoot her with serum if they have to.

(He hates the serum, hates when they have to use it, even though he knows it doesn't hurt the potentials, just cancels out their powers and makes them a bit sleepy. Easier to transport back to the compound. Still. Better to have the opportunity to explain.)

It's slow going with all of them trying not to slip on the wet rock. Despite that, they manage to do it quietly enough so that when they finally get down there, she isn't immediately aware of their presence.

Now for the tricky part.

"Mariah?"

She whips around and scoots backward.

Henry raises his arms and keeps his voice level. "Sorry, didn't mean to frighten you."

"Who are you?" she demands.

"My name's Henry. I—"

"Where did you come from?"

"My team and I work for a place that helps people like you. I'm going to get my ID to show you, all right?"

She narrows her eyes at him, then nods.

Henry retrieves his identification card from his shirt pocket and holds it out to her. For a moment, he thinks she's going to keep sitting there and refuse to look at it, but then she gets to her feet, walks slowly over, and takes it out of his hand.

"Captain Henry Mortimer," Mariah reads out loud. She looks up. "What's a compound?"

"It's an organization that helps people with gifts like yours."

"Helps? How?"

Henry pauses. "It can be difficult when you're different. Other people might not understand. They might not treat you well. The people at the compound understand what you're going through. There are people like you there, and they can teach you how to control what you can do."

"Are you like me?" she asks in a small voice.

Henry smiles. "No. But I help people who are."

Mariah hands back his ID. "I—"

There's a noise from the upper part of the ravine—a rock falling. Henry shoots a glance upward and sees Valdez hastily fading back into the shadows. So much for staying well hidden.

Mariah immediately tenses.

"Captain!" says a voice in his ear. "Permission to fire?"

"*No.*" Henry grits his teeth. "Mariah—"

"Why are all those people up there?" Mariah asks, an edge to her voice. "Are you helping me or abducting me?"

"We're not—"

"You're a liar," she says, face flushed. "Do you go around tricking people into going back with you to your creepy base? Act like you're all nice and stuff, then shoot them in the back?"

"That's—" (Closer to accurate than it should be. Damn.)

"I won't let you!" She raises her hands, palms up, obviously about to use her power. "I'll—"

She stops, confused.

The shot comes so quickly, he's not even sure he saw it until Mariah crumples to the ground with a needle in her neck.

"Who fired that?" Henry says furiously into his comm.

Nothing for a moment. Then Smith, from the distance team, steps forward. "She was going to attack, Captain. I had to—"

"Directly disobey an order?"

"You and the contact team were in danger."

"Not your call, Officer Smith. We'll discuss your inability to follow orders when we get back." He turns to Johnson, who's standing next to him. "Get her loaded. Gently."

"Yessir." Johnson hesitates. "Captain…she was having trouble using her power even before Smith hit her with the serum."

"I know."

"And Smith, she only—"

"Too much, Johnson."

"Yessir."

There's another voice in his ear. "Captain? Message from Major Valentine. She wants to speak with you right away."

"Copy."

He watches Johnson and the rest of the contact team carry Mariah, eyes now closed, over to the vehicle. They'll make sure she's strapped in properly and delivered to medical when they get back.

Henry won't see her again after this, but he knows she'll be all right.

That's what he always tells himself, anyway, and now doesn't seem like a good time to stop.

***

Henry's not often called to Major Valentine's office, but like everyone who lives and works at the compound, he knows where it is. If the compound has a hub—or, if you want to be poetic, a heart—it's the major's office, which is at the center of everything.

According to some, it's also where all the top secret agendas get plotted. Henry doesn't spend much time on that kind of baseless rumor, though.

Even so, he finds himself hesitating in front of her door for a moment and realizes he's a bit jittery. Frowning, he forces himself to knock and, once he has the go-ahead, enter.

The major's enormous oak desk is the focal point of the room, mostly because there's nothing else to challenge it. A window behind her with a terribly exciting view of the vehicle loading dock. Nothing on the walls. No chair for visitors—they'd be expected to stand anyway. Even the floor is nondescript: concrete, dull gray, and lifeless.

Major Valentine herself, however, is about as far from lifeless as you can get. As her severe blue eyes look up at him, the movement measured and calculating, he straightens up involuntarily.

"Captain," she says, nodding. "I understand there were some complications with the potential retrieval today."

"Not…as such, ma'am."

He did speak strongly with Smith when they got back, though, and her excuse was a repeat of what she said on-site: She thought the contact team was in imminent danger and acted on instinct. She'd been too far away to see that Mariah was having trouble with her power and was therefore unlikely to hurt anyone.

"You disobeyed an order," he'd reminded her.

"I know." She looked a little abashed, but only a little. "The team was in danger, sir. *You* were in danger."

"Were you even paying attention during training? Our job is to bring in the potentials—consciously and willingly, when we can. Full stop. That *has* to be your number one objective."

Seeing her face, brazen but concerned, he'd softened a bit. "I appreciate that you care about the rest of the team, but I need to know you'll follow orders in the field. I need to know I can rely on you."

"Sir." She hesitated, then added, "Seems to me…I'm not the one you should be worrying about."

He raised his eyebrows at her.

"The potentials we bring in. The assets they become. Whatever they are, however they do what they do, they're dangerous. We bring them here, and who knows what happens after that? Who's to say there isn't one down there in the basement with that crazy scientist guy plotting to murder us all in our sleep?"

Henry sighed. This wasn't the first time he'd heard the secret-plot-to-kill-us-all argument from Smith. "Enough. Get to training. Sounds like you could use it."

Now, confronted in the major's office, he tries to stay calm while meeting her piercing gaze. He can't help but wonder how much she knows about that discussion, if anything.

To his surprise (and relief), she drops it entirely. Instead, she hands him a tablet. "I need you to bring in an asset."

Henry takes the tablet automatically before he realizes what she just said. "An asset? Not a potential?"

Her look says she's doubting his basic intelligence. "As I said, Captain."

"We've only ever brought in people with the potential to be part of the asset program. I've never heard of an actual asset escaping the compound."

"That's because it rarely happens. So you can imagine the importance of this mission. And the need for discretion."

"Yes, ma'am."

He flips through the file, but there's not much there. Name, age, description, last known location. An image of the man, a few years younger than Henry, glaring at the camera. Henry can easily imagine this guy causing problems for everyone involved with him.

He also looks a bit…sad? The file says he's been in the program for most of his life. Of course, the asset program exists to help people like him, but if he was admitted, it probably means he had nowhere else to go. Henry's heard it said that Major Valentine collects potentials like strays, gives them someplace safe to develop their powers, to do some good. Not unlike how she collects officers.

He skims the file again and realizes there's something important missing. "What's his power? I'll need to apprise my team so they can take precautions."

"That's classified," Major Valentine says. "His power won't impede your ability to bring him in. It could make things a bit…challenging, though. He'll very likely know you're there even before you show yourselves. But he isn't a threat."

Henry wants to ask, of course—he's never seen this kind of secrecy around an asset—but he keeps his mouth shut on that topic, since she obviously doesn't want to talk about it. "Understood," he says instead.

"I'll expect you to report back as soon as the mission is complete. You may go."

He's turned on his heel and is about to leave when her voice comes again. "Captain."

"Ma'am?"

"No more dissent from the ranks. A team is only as strong as its leader."

He grits his teeth. (She's not wrong.) "Yes, ma'am."

"That's all."

He nods, tucks the tablet under his arm, and lets himself out.

Chapter 2

BASTIAN CAN FEEL them coming before they get to the clearing. Excited-nervous-energized, trying to remain calm and failing, a sense of purpose stuffed in there somewhere, difficult to feel through everything on the surface, and then—

Nothing.

It's the nothing that makes him sit up and take note. He knows what he felt, but suddenly there's just…a space. It's weirdly relaxing, if he lets himself think about it. Quiet in a way things are never quiet.

It's also extremely disconcerting. Because there's *always* some sort of noise, and if he can't feel it, that means…something. He's not sure what.

"Bastian?" Laurel's wandered over from her garden, brushing dirt from her hands and looking concerned. Which he can't feel, either. (Why can't he feel it?)

"I know." He gets to his feet and turns toward where he felt the last wave of incoming emotions. "You might want to—"

"Stay here and make sure everything's okay? Thanks, I will."

Bastian rolls his eyes but doesn't have time to discourage her before a man enters the clearing.

He's not armed, but there's something off about him. He looks unassuming. Not like he's there to cause any trouble or to inconvenience anyone. He looks like the kind of person who's content to stand around in the background and not take up any space. Like he wanders into presumably uninhabited clearings all the time.

The most important thing, though, is that Bastian can't feel him. At all.

It's like being suddenly blindfolded—or just knocked senseless. Some people are harder to read than others, of course, but Bastian's never met someone he couldn't read at all.

(Does he know what he's doing? Why is he here? He has to be from the compound, but why did Valentine send him *now*?)

"Sebastian Lucas?" says the man. "I'm—"

"Yeah, who are you?" Laurel demands, putting herself in front of Bastian before he can stop her. "Are you here to take Bastian back? Because that's not gonna happen. Just so you know."

"Laurel," Bastian says in a low voice, "I really think you should—"

She ignores him, puts her hands on her hips, and glares at the intruder. "Well?"

"My name's Henry Mortimer." To his credit, he stays calm and polite about it.

Bastian sighs. "What is it? Officer? No, Captain; there's a team somewhere around here."

Mortimer seems surprised, but Bastian doesn't have time for it. "Why did she send you? I mean, obviously to bring me back, but why?"

Mortimer has the good grace to look a little abashed (not that Bastian can really tell—this is so weird). "If you mean Major Valentine, she wasn't specific. Presumably, she values you as an asset and wants you to come back to the compound, where you can be safe."

Bastian snorts. "Yes. Because an asset's safety is so important to her." He sees the look on the captain's face. "Really? You still believe her? You must be new."

Mortimer frowns. "I've been stationed at the compound for fifteen years."

"Oh. You're just an idiot, then. An idiot who's never had anything to do with the asset program, since I've never seen you before. First time out of a cushy desk job?"

"Bastian." Laurel looks at him disapprovingly.

"What? He's trying to—"

"You're being rude."

"I'm always rude. And anyway, you're the one who was just demanding—"

"It's my clearing, so I get to demand. You're just a guest, so you get to hush." She eyes Mortimer. "I haven't decided about you yet, so watch it."

His mouth twitches, but he manages to keep a straight face, clasping his hands behind his back. "Noted."

Bastian frowns, then turns to Laurel. "He's not here for you. You should get out before—"

"I don't even understand how you got in," Laurel says loudly, glaring at Mortimer. "The trees and I set up traps and everything."

"Let's maybe not tell the nice compound officer about all of our defenses," Bastian suggests. Not that it matters. Apparently, this guy is impervious to Laurel's power.

"Oh, don't worry. Henry isn't going to hurt us, are you, Henry?" Laurel smiles daggers at him.

Mortimer smiles back tentatively, which means Bastian knows what's coming.

"I think you should go," he says. Last-ditch effort. For all the good it'll do.

Mortimer almost looks sympathetic. Valentine's trained him well. "I'm afraid I can't do that. Not unless you agree to come back with me."

"Hand in hand, skipping down the lane? Or in a body bag?"

Laurel looks alarmed now. Her fingers twitch, and then she frowns. (Tried to use her power and couldn't. So it's definitely not just him.)

"I'd prefer willingly," Mortimer says.

"That would be convenient for you, wouldn't it?" Bastian narrows his eyes. "No."

Mortimer nods once. "I figured. For what it's worth, I'm really sorry about this."

He's not sure what he was expecting—a rifle butt to the head? A bullet? Not what he gets, exactly, which is a sudden, sharp pain in his neck, like a dart or a syringe, and then his legs give out—

(Why can't he feel anything, why didn't he know someone was nearby, why is he suddenly groggy and tired, why…?)

He's blinking and on the ground, and from somewhere off, he hears Laurel say his name in a panicked voice, and he hears footsteps getting closer—

"Laurel—go—"

Then he can't talk anymore, and he closes his eyes without meaning to. And then there's nothing.

One year ago

"HEY. ARE YOU alive?"

Bastian's honestly not sure. He tries opening his eyes, which works, to his surprise.

The girl bending over him makes him start. Bad idea; now he remembers that everything hurts. Either she'll put an end to it, or the sunlight will.

He hears a groan, and it takes him a moment to realize he made it.

The girl frowns at him, pushing a strand of hair behind her ear. (Concern-confusion-surprise—no desire to hurt, as far as he can tell, but he really shouldn't have made the effort to focus because now the pain is coming back, and he's thinking about Dr. Wright and the scalpel and the harsh lights of the experimentation room and—)

"None of that," says the girl sternly. She touches his arm, sees him flinch, and removes her hand immediately. She looks over her shoulder at something, then back at him. "Do you think you could not die for a few more minutes? Since the trees let you in, they must think you're worth saving. So I need some supplies."

He wants to ask why she'd bother trying to save him—or maybe he just wants to laugh—but when he manages to open his mouth, all that comes out is, "No promises."

She frowns, then makes some sort of movement with her fingers. "Can I get a little help, please?"

He blinks at her. "Uh—"

"Not you." She's looking at the ground. "He needs—I dunno, a pillow? Elevate his head a little."

He feels something move. There's something coming from her, too—a respect-affection-appreciation that's directed at…the grass? Which is growing? So she's a—

"Sorry." She reaches over and lifts his head slightly (hurts, but everything hurts, and at least she's gentle about it). His head is now resting on something that does feel a bit like a pillow—one that smells like grass.

She smiles reassuringly, then goes serious and shakes a finger at him. "No dying. I'll be right back." She gets to her feet.

He doesn't understand. Why is she doing this? Does she expect something from him? How is there an asset out here in the forest anyway? How has she kept hidden? Does Valentine know about her?

"Who are you?" he asks.

She turns back and grins. "I'm Laurel. What's your name?"

"Bastian."

"Hello, Bastian! Nice to meet you. I'm going to save your life, and then I'll show you my garden if you want. Anyway, the beeches say we have about a week before it rains again, so you should be all right out here for a while. That's good because I don't want to move you, and—" She shakes her head. "Right. Life saving first. Hang on."

She doesn't exactly skip away, but it's pretty close.

Chapter 3

BASTIAN WAKES WITH a chill running through him but no damage, as far as he can tell. Whatever they hit him with, it wasn't meant to hurt him; just knock him out. He's never had cause to know what they use to bring people in, but it looks like Valentine's found something effective.

The room he's in is dark except for a small blue light—part of a monitoring machine. The kind he's extremely familiar with.

He's on Level 13.

He squashes the panic (pathetic) and focuses on getting his bearings. The wrist and ankle restraints will be easy enough to get out of—he's basically perfected the art after years of dealing with them. They've taken his clothes (and his gloves, he notes with irritation) and given him a stylish hospital gown instead. Underneath, he can feel where the restraints have bitten into his skin.

He works himself free, which takes longer than it used to, since he's out of practice. Then he sits on the bed for a few moments, feeling out to see if anyone's nearby. When he's sure the coast is clear, he jumps down and sticks a hand out. Usually, there's a drawer near the beds, and...there it is.

Doing all of this by touch instead of sight adds a delightfully frustrating element, but it's better to be quick than to waste time searching for a light switch.

He finds clothes in the drawer and changes into them. His size, so they were meaning to move him soon rather than keep him here.

Here being the compound.

If he's back—if Valentine went to all the trouble of having one of her minions bring him in—then she must need something from him. If she cared simply because of the embarrassment of losing an asset, she would have sent someone a long time ago. As it is, he's had nearly a year on his own—well, with Laurel—in the clearing. He hasn't had to use his power for anything other than feeling things like dim-witted animals and Laurel's incessant, strangely soothing cheeriness.

Naturally, it wasn't going to last.

Voices in the hall, and two sets of emotions: curious-irritated-frustrated and pleased-plotting-disdain. He doesn't recognize the first one, but the second one is definitely Dr. Wright.

"Is this really necessary?" asks a voice. The captain.

"You've done well to bring him back so quickly," says Wright, completely ignoring the question. His voice is thin and slippery, a slimier version of fingernails on a chalkboard.

Bastian clenches his jaw and briefly considers hiding.

"Major Valentine said it was important. She also said we were to report back to her as soon as we brought the asset in." The captain does a remarkably good job of being pointed while still maintaining some semblance of respect for the other man. He also must have gotten in front of Wright, because their movement stops.

"Major Valentine won't object to a brief intake exam," says Wright. "After all, we need the asset in good shape for—"

"Yes, for what, exactly? What could possibly be more important than following the major's orders?"

Bastian is weirdly relieved to hear Mortimer trying to pull rank. Not that it'll help, since Wright's always thought himself above all that. Still, it means he followed Wright here on purpose. Which means he's concerned about fulfilling his orders. Which means he won't leave Bastian alone with the doctor when he's supposed to be bringing the asset to Major Valentine, apparently.

This shouldn't be a relief. Mortimer dragged Bastian back here—not exactly something in his favor. But if he hates Wright as much as Bastian does—or just doesn't trust him—that might be enough to help Bastian temporarily avoid unpleasantness.

"I believe that's above your pay grade, Captain," Wright says. His emotional signature starts coming closer again.

"Questioning authority is, too," Mortimer counters, the edge in his voice increasing as he follows. "And authority told me to bring the asset in, not stick him indefinitely in an observation room. Can you tell me why I should disobey those orders?"

They're right outside the door now, and apparently the proximity is enough for Mortimer's whatever-it-is to be acting on Bastian's power again. (Took longer for it to impact Bastian's power this time. Does Mortimer's range change depending on some particular circumstance?)

So Bastian can't actually feel it, but he can almost hear Wright deflate. "Oh, very well," the doctor says with a sigh as he opens the door.

Bastian hisses against the bright light of the hallway, which makes him stumble back a step or two. When he can see again, he realizes that Mortimer looks surprised that he's up and dressed. Wright isn't, of course, having dealt with it before.

"How are you feeling, Sebastian?" Wright asks.

"Like I was shot with a dart or something."

Mortimer looks a little embarrassed. "Sorry about that."

"No, you're not," Bastian says. "Just doing your job."

"Yes. Well. The serum doesn't cause any lasting damage, but if you'd like to have the doctor take a look—"

"No," Bastian says quickly (too quickly, and he feels his skin crawl at the thought, weak and stupid, but he can't stop it).

Mortimer gives him a penetrating look but backs off without saying anything. "All right. Then come with me, please. Major Valentine would like to speak with you."

Bastian snorts. "Yes, I suppose she would." He holds out his hands.

The captain blinks at them, then at him.

"Cuffs?" Bastian prompts.

"Why would I cuff you?"

"Because I'm a dangerous, recently escaped asset who could wreak havoc if not properly restrained?"

"Are you planning to try to escape between here and the major's office? Or harm anyone in the compound?"

"Not particularly."

"Then I think we're good." He stands aside and gestures for Bastian to precede him out.

It's Bastian's turn to blink stupidly. "You know that's how assets are handled in the compound, right? Treated like criminals and test subjects, ushered around corridors with massive cohorts of black coats to keep everyone else safe, all that?" He frowns. "Have you ever even met an asset, Captain? Aren't you concerned you'll be overpowered or injured?"

Mortimer gives him a smile that could almost be called cocky. "Not at all."

The thing is, looking at him even without being able to feel him, Bastian's pretty sure he's right. Mortimer looks unassuming, easy to pass over. But he also walked unarmed into an unknown location and had no trouble subduing a powerful asset. (That still rankles.)

Add to that this thing he can do where he…negates? Dampens? Makes it impossible for an asset to use their power? He may not be consciously using it with any sort of precision, but that doesn't mean he isn't dangerous.

Bastian realizes he wants to smile back, but he cuts it off.

Mortimer turns to Wright. "Thank you for your assistance, Doctor. I'll be taking Mr. Lucas to the major now."

Wright sighs and shakes his head. "I do hope you haven't ruined our chances for further scientific insight, Captain," he says, laying it on thick. "It would be a shame to miss out on important research that could enhance our assets."

"I'm sure if further study is warranted, the major will be in touch." Mortimer is pleasant but firm.

"Goodbye for now, then, Sebastian," says Wright. "I'm sure I'll be seeing you again soon."

Bastian clenches his jaw hard enough to hurt. He pretends not to notice that Mortimer keeps himself between Bastian and the doctor until they're safely out into the hall.

Chapter 4

BRINGING POTENTIALS BACK to the compound is fairly easy. Figuring out what to say to a full-blown asset you're marching down the hall? Not so much.

Henry considers a few options: Do you know why the hell the Level 13 beds have restraints? Are assets really herded around the compound like prisoners? What's your power, and why did the major refuse to tell me about it?

He can't actually ask any of that, of course. He has his orders, and they don't involve interrogating Lucas or questioning what happens on Level 13. Officers who ask those sorts of things get demoted into obscurity, and while their teams get reassigned, there's a stigma that never goes away. Henry isn't about to let his idle curiosity endanger his team's future. Still….

He's saved from his thoughts by a small, dark-haired officer who hails them as they turn a corner.

"Captain," she says, nodding to him. "It will be a pleasure working with you."

Henry has no idea how she even knows who he is, since they've never met. Lucas, on the other hand, obviously knows her.

"Michaels!" he says, sounding almost…happy? Amused?

She nods to him. "Mr. Lucas."

Lucas frowns at her. "Please try to be a little more reserved, Michaels. Your emotions are all over the place."

"I'll endeavor to try, sir."

"Really, it's very unseemly."

"I understand, sir."

Lucas catches Henry's eye, and Henry realizes with some surprise that he's about three seconds away from grinning.

"Now," Lucas continues, "what's this about working together?"

Officer Michaels hesitates. "I suspect the major will fill you in on the particulars."

"Of course she will." Lucas's face goes dark.

"Please excuse me." Michaels nods and continues down the hall.

"Friend of yours?" Henry says when she's gone.

Lucas shakes himself, and they continue walking. "We used to work together. And yes, she's always that formal. With everyone. I never once saw her smile or come within five miles of laughing. Trying to crack her was my project for about six months." He catches Henry's look. "What? I got bored."

It's just as well that Lucas is facing the other way. Henry's pretty sure he shouldn't be trying not to laugh at an asset.

There are no further interruptions on the trip to the major's office. Lucas knows the way better than Henry, whose work keeps him on a specific set of levels, none of which is 13. Whatever Lucas used to do, it gave him a much wider range of access than the captain of a retrieval team gets.

When they reach the office, Henry raises a hand to knock on the door, but Lucas steps around him, pushes it open, and walks right on through.

Major Valentine doesn't seem particularly surprised about the intrusion. "Hello, Sebastian."

"Valentine." His voice is artificially pleasant—much different than it was with Michaels a few minutes ago.

Well. This isn't going to be awkward.

"Gentlemen," says the major. "I have a mission for you."

Lucas crosses his arms over his chest. "This is why you dragged me back? Don't you have enough minions?"

"This mission involves the investigation of a series of murders. Your old purview, Sebastian."

Henry clears his throat. "Major, if I may. I lead a retrieval team. I don't see how we can be of service in an investigation unless it somehow involves potentials."

"No potentials or assets are involved," says Major Valentine, "so far as I know."

"Then why bring it to the compound?" Lucas demands. "Can't the police handle it?"

"Special request from the Compound Council," the major says. She turns back to Henry. "I won't be requiring your team, Captain. Just you."

That makes even less sense. "I—"

"She wants you to babysit me," Lucas says, rolling his eyes. "What, you don't think Michaels will be enough?"

"I think you've shown dedication and ingenuity when it comes to abandoning your duties, Sebastian. The captain should be a sufficient deterrent."

"Abandoning my duties?" Lucas laughs humorlessly. "That's ridiculous. You know exactly why I left."

The major sighs and waves a hand. "I'm afraid I don't have time for one of your tantrums, Sebastian." She looks at Henry. "I'll have the case files sent to you this evening, Captain. You'll need to review them so you can brief the others. You'll be leaving from the vehicle loading dock at 0700 tomorrow. Officer Michaels will accompany you."

"Yes, ma'am."

"Oh, and one more thing."

"Ma'am?"

"Please cuff the asset and remit him to the prison officer on Level 15."

"What?" It's out of Henry's mouth before he can stop it. He backpedals immediately. "With all due respect, Major, he hasn't—"

"The asset is recently escaped and could be dangerous, Captain," Major Valentine says, her eyes still on Lucas, who is…smirking? "Within the confines of the compound, he might easily wreak havoc if not restrained."

Definitely smirking. And now turning to Henry, holding out his arms like he did in the observation room. "You heard the major," he says. "Can't have a dangerous asset wreaking havoc."

Henry glances at Major Valentine, but she's already gone back to working on something at her desk, no doubt assuming her orders will be carried out without anyone needing a reminder about who's in charge.

He turns back to Lucas. With only slight hesitation, he takes the cuffs from his belt and puts them on Lucas's wrists. This close, he notices a pair of faint scars, but he doesn't have time to get a good look before the major is speaking again.

"Thank you for bringing the asset in, Captain," she says. "That will be all."

It's not just that no one's telling him anything, Henry thinks irritably as they leave the major's office and walk to the elevators. It's that he can't possibly be expected to do his job if he doesn't know a damned thing about what he's doing.

It's common knowledge that there's a whole contingent in the compound focused on law enforcement. And he's heard there are more assets in that division than in any other.

But Henry's in retrieval, and that's completely different. He's never even been to a crime scene, and now he's expected to hang out on the edges of a serial killer case? What's the major thinking?

And what does Lucas have to do with any of it?

"What kind of work did you do?" Henry asks as they get on the elevator. "Before. Obviously something with investigations."

"Obviously."

Henry gives him the side eye as the elevator starts to descend, but Lucas doesn't say anything else until they've gone down a few levels. Then he looks at Henry and raises his eyebrows. "Should you really be engaging in conversation with a dangerous asset, Captain?"

"We *could* go the rest of the way in total silence. Or you could tell me something about what you do so I can figure out whether you'll be useful tomorrow or if I should just let the prison officer keep you locked up."

Lucas snorts. "You'll do whatever Valentine tells you to do, and she said for both of us to investigate."

"Sure. And she also assigned me to be your babysitter. Which means if you don't behave, I can put you in time-out. In a jail cell."

He looks at Henry for a few moments, his expression unreadable. Henry has no trouble matching it.

Lucas is the first to look away. "My power is…useful at a crime scene. Officer Michaels can record my read there and compare it with reads I get from interviews with suspects. If they match, it can help the authorities get a conviction."

"Read? What kind of read?"

The elevator doors open on an older woman who takes one look at them and starts.

"Bastian!"

"Hello, Catherine. Still locked in the basement, I see."

Henry raises his eyebrows at Lucas. "Another one of your friends?"

"Ah, sorry, you must be Captain Mortimer," the woman says. "I'm Prison Officer Templeton. Bastian used to work down here with Officer Michaels."

She turns to Lucas. "You gave us all quite a scare, running off like that. I heard you were dead."

"Not quite."

"Still getting into trouble, though, if the major wants you down here."

"She likes to lock everyone up. You know that."

Henry frowns. "This won't be a conflict of interest, will it, Templeton?"

"I promise not to seduce the jailer, Captain!" Lucas calls. He's moved on down the hall, obviously aware of where the jail is—though it's still unclear to Henry if that's because he worked with Templeton or because he got himself locked up all the time. Henry suspects it's some of both.

He and Templeton catch up at the jail block entryway, where Lucas is leaning against the intake desk like he owns the place, despite being shackled. "Do you have a good cell ready for me, Catherine? I'll take the one where the bed's got Egyptian cotton sheets and a fleece throw."

Templeton rolls her eyes and turns to Henry. "I can take it from here, Captain."

She gestures for Lucas to follow her down the hall, which he does. Henry comes along, too—just to make sure everything gets taken care of properly. It definitely has nothing to do with his curiosity or his discomfort with the idea that an asset could be locked up just for existing.

When they get to the far end of the jail block, Lucas bounds around Templeton and stands in front of one of the cells. "I'll take this one. Smells slightly less of urine than the others."

"I'll have you know I keep every cell in pristine condition," Templeton says, taking a key from the large ring on her belt. She uses it to remove the cuffs (not concerned he'll make a dash for it, apparently), then takes up another one and opens the cell door.

Lucas brushes past her and flops onto the bed, kicking up a small cloud of dust. "Pristine," he says around a cough. "Clearly."

Templeton shakes her head and locks the door. She returns the key ring to her belt and the cuffs to Henry. "There's really no need to worry, Captain. When the major is ready for him, I'll make sure he's here."

"Do you have a deck of cards?" Lucas asks. "And maybe a hat? I could get bored in here waiting for Valentine to get her head out of her—"

"Behave yourself, young man." She turns back to Henry. "Anything else I can do for you, Captain?"

Henry decides he probably shouldn't wait to get his brain wrapped around all of this. His team needs to be debriefed, after all. "No, thank you. Just let me know if there are any problems."

"There won't be any problems," Lucas says cheerfully. "I'm an excellent prisoner. Ask anyone."

Henry tries very hard not to laugh. Or to think about what that comment actually means. "Right. Well. As you were, Templeton."

"Yes, sir. Oh, and one more thing," she adds as she walks him out. "The work room just over there is available if you need it. To go over case notes and such."

Henry frowns. "Is that how it was before? When you were all working together?"

"Certainly, when there was that sort of work to do. If Bastian and Officer Michaels weren't on site, they were here."

"And L—Bastian stayed here? He didn't have, I don't know, a room or something?"

Templeton blinks at him. "A room? Of course not. The major didn't want to chance him ever being out of range of security." She nods toward the cameras in the ceiling, then smiles slightly. "Bastian's not like the other assets, as I'm sure you can tell. He's a dear, but he does like to get in trouble. It was worse when he was younger."

There's a mental image Henry didn't need: a little boy locked up in a jail cell every night, only let out to do whatever his trick is.

(Did he get taken to crime scenes as a child? Another thing Henry doesn't want to think about.)

"Thank you," he says. "I'll come get him at 0630 tomorrow."

"Very good, Captain."

Henry looks back down the dimly lit jail block hall. Then he nods at Templeton and heads back upstairs to see to his team.

Chapter 5

BASTIAN THINKS HE'S dreaming at first.

Well. He sort of is. He knows he was on the brink of waking up for the fourth time (cot springs digging into his back, the smell of a musty blanket that's been washed within an inch of its life, clouds of dust in the air—definitely not conducive to a restful night).

But mostly, he just feels enveloped by calm and darkness. And…something else. Some*one* else.

Hey! Is this working? Can you hear me?

Worried-anxious-amused in his head, but he's alone. Catherine left a long time ago for her bunk, so…?

Okay, promise me you're not gonna freak out, Bastian. (worry-frustration-caution) *I'm pretty sure I've got it, but it'd be helpful if you told me it's working on your end.*

"Laurel." His voice sounds too loud in the silence of the jail block.

(delight-relief-pride) *Yes! That's—oh. Please don't be angry. I was just worried about you, and I thought an empath link would be the best way to keep in touch with you until you get out again.*

He can read her, even from so far away. And she can read him? How—? "Empath what?"

Her exasperation pokes him in the temples. *What, didn't your compound teach you about that?*

"Laurel, I'm the only empath in hundreds of years. Why would they teach me how to do whatever you're doing? How *are* you doing what you're doing, by the way?"

Oh, you know, experiments. I was only born with one power, but they liked to try…splicing.

She's lying, but she's also not lying. He feels sick. "You—"

Anyway, the mental link is basically, um, me piggybacking off your power. You can feel me from there, right? It's sort of like…I reach out and grab on, and your power keeps us connected. If I let go, we're disconnected. Neat, right? Only it'd be easier if I could latch onto more things, make the connection stronger. Do you have any plants over there?

"In an underground facility? I'll ask maintenance to put in a few more if I'm ever not incarcerated."

I'm really sorry about that. If it helps, I don't think the captain really wanted to—

"If there isn't an important reason for you to be in my head, can you please get out? It's…I don't like it." He shudders.

I know. I'm sorry. I just wanted to—it seemed like it was really bad last time, and I thought this would be the easiest way to plan how I can get there to help spring you.

"No." He chokes down the alarm. "Promise me you won't come here."

She's never said what happened to her, but he's seen her power, and while it may not be on the level of an empath, it's enough that Valentine would be interested, particularly with this splicing thing. Valentine would have a field day researching that, and Bastian is *not* going to let her—

I thought you might say that. (amusement-fondness-concern) *Listen, I won't come break you out if you don't want me to, but I'm not leaving you alone in there, either.* (A pause.) *I want to be able to communicate, and I'm not going to go rooting around in your mind or anything, but if this really makes you uncomfortable….*

He sighs. "No, it's—okay. And…thanks. Are you all right?"

I'm fine. When they came in from the woods, I kicked one in the shin and ran. I thought they'd come after me, but I heard the captain tell them not to. I wanted to stay and make sure you were okay, only….

"No, you did the right thing. No reason for both of us to—" He frowns at the feeling coming from her. "What?"

You didn't ask.

"About what?"

The captain.

"Why would I ask about him?"

He let me go. And there's that thing he does.

"You couldn't use your power, either."

Nope.

Bastian digs his palms into his eyes. "Look, one thing at a time. You need to get out of the clearing. Valentine obviously knows where it is. If she sends more troops, they'll find you."

(indignation-confidence-determination) *No way. I'm not leaving.*

"Laurel—"

Why did they want you back, anyway? I mean, why now?

"There's some sort of murder case. Serial killer. I don't know what's so different about it that she wants me and the captain on it, but—"

The captain's working with you?

"Yeah. Why?"

No reason. Continue.

"That's all I know. Unless Valentine just missed locking me up."

No…experiments?

He tenses, then forces himself to relax. "Not yet."

Good. Because if there were—

"Laurel, I told you, stay away. The last thing Valentine needs is a wild asset to play with. Just stay in the clearing for now, I guess, and go deeper into the forest if you have to. My caches should—"

You realize you're not the boss of me, right?

"Laurel—"

Yes, okay, I get it. (concern-worry-hesitation) *Is this really all right with you? This link? I meant it; I can sever it if it makes you too uncomfortable.*

He'll never understand it, this thing where she asks if something bothers him instead of just doing it, like how he feels about it actually matters. "No, it's…just let me get used to it. You can do this anytime? Anywhere?"

Well. Probably not with the captain around, if he's doing that thing. And when you're closer to sleep, it's easier—your mind's sort of more…open, I guess. And it really would be better if there were some plants. But basically, yes.

He nods. "Okay. I don't know what kind of security they have now in terms of monitoring powers, so we should keep it short."

I'll go, then. You need to get some sleep. Good night, Bastian.

"Night."

He can feel it when she leaves, but it's not as unpleasant as he was expecting. It even comes with a lingering sense of calm that lulls him back to sleep for the rest of the night.

Chapter 6

HENRY CAN'T SLEEP.

He's usually a light sleeper anyway—something that's saved his team more than once in the field. It's also meant he's been able to catch them at the occasional illegal poker game and admonish them to at least *try* to make it a challenge for him.

Tonight, though, he only got into bed at the usual time out of habit, and now that it's several hours later, he's basically given it up as a lost cause.

For a little light reading earlier, he went over the case notes Major Valentine sent him. Two senators murdered in as many weeks on the grounds of the Hall. No leads. The compound was asked specifically to review the case and investigate—presumably because the city police got nowhere, and there might be an asset involved, though it's unclear from the notes.

That request to investigate, Henry suspects, is what led Major Valentine to want to bring in an asset who apparently has a background in law enforcement.

Of course, that's what's really keeping him up: this asset who escaped. Who, according to his file, basically grew up in the compound but was still compelled to run away. Who has some sort of fraught personal relationship with the major.

And now Henry's supposed to help him find a serial killer.

Henry sighs, sits up, and rubs his eyes. His tablet is still on the bedside table. He's thinking he'll go over the case notes one more time, but when his finger hovers over the file, he changes his mind.

This is incredibly stupid. If he's not careful, it'll look too much like unwarranted curiosity—the kind he's already very sternly told himself not to have. If snooping comes back to bite him in the ass, that's his problem; but if it affects his team….

Never mind. It's not unusual for an officer to review a potential's file after a mission. An asset shouldn't be any different.

He'll be quick about it. Just in case.

Henry has slightly more access to the asset database than most, given his role in retrieval. Only Dr. Wright and Major Valentine have complete access, though, so he really doesn't know what he's expecting to find.

It takes a bit of digging to even bring up Lucas's file—it isn't tagged to be easily found like the other asset and potential files. When Henry gets there, he realizes it's mostly classified (warning bells) except for the basic information the major shared with him earlier when he got the assignment.

There are a few things he didn't see before, though. Notes that Lucas's blood is on file—Henry has to squint and reread it several times to be sure—with more than a hundred vials of it in various vaults throughout the compound. (Why the hell would they need so much?) Something about significant tissue samples and experiments as well, though there aren't any details on that beyond a few dates.

There's another brief note at the end, probably added by Dr. Wright, that makes very little sense:

> *Latest observations include rapid deterioration of brain cells, epistaxis, hallucinations, heart palpitations, migraines, violent mood swings. Prognosis: 13 months or less if power used at current capacity.*

It's dated twelve months ago. About the time Lucas escaped from the compound.

Henry swallows and closes out of the file as quickly as possible. Of course, he doesn't really know what it means, not without the context of the whole file. But it's obvious that whatever Lucas was doing, whatever his power is, it was—and maybe still is—killing him.

Henry shakes his head. He can't worry about this. He has his orders. The only way any of this is relevant is if it keeps Lucas from doing his job.

(Who is he kidding? It doesn't matter if it's not relevant. If this were about someone on his team or one of the potentials he brought in, he'd be concerned. He's responsible for Lucas now, so of course he's concerned about this, too.)

Not that there's anything he can do about it.

Henry doesn't sleep much the rest of the night.

Chapter 7

CAPTAIN MORTIMER LOOKS tired, Bastian thinks. He comes to Bastian's cell that morning with bruised shadows under his eyes and his mouth set in a firm line. Doesn't seem like the type to get nervous before a mission, but then again, he's never worked a murder case, has he?

On the other hand, the nervousness could be because he's in formal uniform for reasons Bastian can't fathom. If that's it, he doesn't have anything to be nervous about because he looks very—

Mortimer gives Bastian a small smile and hands over a pair of black leather gloves as Catherine opens the cell door. "I was told to give you these before we head out. It's not that cold, though, so I'm not sure why you'd need them."

Bastian makes a face and puts them on. It feels much better with the buffer between his skin and everything else. She'd know that, of course. "Valentine?"

"That's what the message said."

Which means she expects him to be doing his "best" work, shifting between intensity of reads. Which probably means headaches and then some, depending on how deep he needs to go. Great.

"I didn't realize we were attending a gala," Bastian says as they head up to the vehicle loading dock. "And me without anything to wear."

Mortimer sighs. "I'll explain in the car."

Michaels is as calm and unflappable as always, giving them a perfunctory greeting as she loads the machine into the back of the vehicle. The driver doesn't talk much, either; just holds the doors for them and then gets on with the driving.

Not that Bastian minds. He's busy trying to figure out how he's supposed to do a read if Mortimer is hanging around. With such an uncertain range for his power, would it be best to just tell him to take a walk? Would it be better to tell him what he's doing and see if he knows?

But if Mortimer goes around telling—or showing—people what he can do, he'll get thrown into the asset program in two seconds flat. Obviously, Bastian couldn't care less about that. But it might make Valentine happy, and that should be avoided at all costs.

"Hey." Bastian realizes Mortimer has turned around in the front seat and is trying to hand him a tablet.

Bastian shakes himself inwardly and takes it. "Mission details?"

Mortimer nods. "Two deaths on Hall grounds, one last week and the other the week before. Both senators. No connections otherwise. The city police are ruling them suicides—one drowning, one carbon monoxide poisoning. Despite that, the Compound Council wants us to look into it."

"Why would the Council care about suicides?" Bastian asks.

Mortimer shrugs. "Presumably because they suspect an asset is involved. Or they just want to make a good show to the city government. And if they're not actually suicides…."

"What are our orders, Captain?" asks Michaels.

"We're supposed to talk to Senator Haldis. Most of the senators seem to agree with the police that the incidents were suicides, so they don't want to waste their time with voluntary interviews. Senator Haldis has been a bit more agreeable and didn't balk when the Council asked him to be an initial resource. We're also supposed to do a read of the grounds where the apparent murders took place."

Mortimer looks up from his screen. "This would be a good time for one of you to tell me what a 'read' is."

Well, it's not like Bastian can do one now. He glances at Michaels, who, of course, is just going to sit there and let him handle this.

"It's related to my power," Bastian says at last. "It'll be easier to show you when we get there." Assuming he can figure out a way to do that.

They've all gone back to reviewing the case notes when something occurs to Bastian. "Captain…you said we're supposed to talk to a senator?"

"Yes."

"When you say 'we'…."

Mortimer sighs. "I am. As a representative of the compound."

"Which is why Valentine ordered you to polish your shoes and—"

"Yes, okay, I feel ridiculous. Can we move on?"

"Absolutely, Captain." Bastian smothers a smile.

When they get to the bridge security station just outside of the city, the driver rolls down the window and hands over their IDs. The inside of the vehicle instantly gets hit with the smell of smog and polluted water from the nearby tributaries. Bastian wrinkles his nose; the pleasantness of the city is something he was happy to forget after a year away.

The officer doing the ID check matches faces to plastic, then frowns when he brilliantly realizes there are four people in the vehicle, and he only has three IDs.

"He doesn't have an ID," the guard says, pointing at Bastian.

"He's a special operative," Mortimer explains. "You can check with the Compound Council. Or the Hall."

"I'm sorry, sir, but I can't—"

Bastian rolls his eyes and leans forward. "AP367284."

The guard blinks at him. "Sorry?"

"Put it into your ID database."

The guard looks dubious but asks Bastian to repeat it and types it into the tablet he's holding. When Bastian's file comes up, he squints at it for several moments, then looks up, now slightly uncomfortable. "Uh. Right. You have till curfew at 2 AM. Go ahead."

They always look nervous. Do they think he can read their minds or something? Just as well Mortimer's blocking everything—nothing more boring than a checkpoint officer's emotions.

"Why *don't* you have an ID?" Mortimer asks as the car starts again. "It'd make things easier."

"If assets had IDs, we'd lose the secretive mystique Valentine tries so hard to cultivate around the program. By which I mean if we lost our ID cards, anyone who found them would know who we are and what we can do. Can't have information free-flowing and readily available. Better to give us an impersonal number that goes into a secure system and only hands out the minimum amount of information required to get us into and out of the city."

It doesn't take long to get to the Hall after that. It's located in the precise center of the city, as if politicians needed any more reasons to see themselves as the center of the universe. The grounds are expansive and beautiful, and the Hall itself is immense, marble, and old.

And there are people. A *lot* of people.

Bastian grits his teeth as the car comes to a stop after yet another security check, this time to get into the Hall area. He'll be able to block some of it by shielding, but he's rusty with big crowds after a year in the forest. (And people have so many emotions, flinging them into the ether without even thinking about it, noisy and messy and complicated and—)

"We should have free access to the grounds," Mortimer is saying, "so you two can do your read while I check in with Senator Haldis. The senators are on break now, which means it shouldn't take too long to get hold of him. The reflecting pool where the drowning took place is on the south side, and the parking garage where the poisoning happened is on the north. Start with the pool, and I'll meet you there when I'm done with Haldis." He sets his shoulders like he's headed off to war.

Mortimer and Michaels get out of the car, which means Bastian has to as well.

It's fine at first. Mortimer's still close enough that he's blocking Bastian's power, so it's almost like being normal for a while. At least, what Bastian assumes normal is like.

Then Mortimer heads up the steps and into the Hall, and Bastian immediately gets an excruciating headache.

(There aren't that many people here, really, but he can feel them in the Hall, in the chambers and the rotunda, happy-sad-afraid-angry and the other ones politicians are so good at, conniving-plotting-smug, and he tries to remember how to breathe, how to block it out, how to make it a small stream filtered through his shield rather than an enormous wave—)

"Mr. Lucas? Are you all right?"

It's as close to concern as Bastian's ever seen on Michaels's taciturn face.

"Yes," he says, managing to keep the shakiness more or less out of his voice (pathetic). "Fine. Let's go."

Chapter 8

HENRY FINDS SENATOR Haldis standing just outside the chamber doors with several aides and what looks like a reporter—she has the mic and the shoes, anyway. Haldis doesn't seem particularly interested in any of them, judging by his frequent looks anywhere but at the people he's presumably talking to. It's evasive maneuvering if Henry's ever seen it: make them think you don't care to hide the fact that you do. Plenty of potentials, not to mention members of his team, do it.

"Senator?"

Haldis and the others turn toward him. It's obvious that they're wondering who the hell he is, what the hell he's doing there, and how the hell they can have security get rid of him even though the rotunda is theoretically open to the public.

(This is why he hates the dress uniform—makes it look like he's trying to fit in with these people, when everyone knows he never will and doesn't want to. Still. Orders.)

Henry plasters on a smile. "Senator, my name is—"

"I know who you are." Haldis pushes through his little throng and gives Henry a once-over. Then, to his flock: "We'll finish up later. I have an appointment."

Sending Henry murderous glances, the others move off down the hall. One of the aides immediately begins a not-very-surreptitious conversation with the reporter.

The senator turns back to Henry. "We can talk in my office."

Henry's been inside the Hall before, but not often. The giant rotunda and the never-ending click of shoes on marble make him feel small and insignificant. He supposes he can see the appeal if you're into grandiose architecture, but it's not the sort of place Henry would ever want to work. Even if having windows and being above ground seem nice.

It's not far to Senator Haldis's office. When they get there, he swipes his security card, lets Henry in, and sits down behind his desk. He gestures to Henry to take a seat. Unlike Major Valentine, the senator apparently takes pity on his visitors' feet.

"What can I do for you…Captain, isn't it? The Compound Council's liaison committee said someone would be stopping by, but they weren't specific about what you need."

Henry sits and tries not to look uncomfortable. "How familiar are you with the recent deaths of your colleagues, Senator?"

Haldis shakes his head. "Such a shame. Suicides, weren't they?"

"That's the official story, yes."

"But you people only get called in when there's not enough evidence for a conviction. Why would there need to be a conviction in a suicide case?"

"There's some question of whether or not they actually were suicides."

Senator Haldis raises his eyebrows. "The Council thinks they weren't? Despite the determination of the police? Is there evidence?"

Awkward. "Not that I'm aware of. I believe that's why Major Valentine sent us here today—to see if there's any evidence to be found."

"And what's her interest in these specific cases? Neither Anderson nor Goldsmith were on the liaison committee, so there's no connection to your compound."

"I only know that the Council requested we investigate. I'll need to ask you some questions, if I may?"

Haldis sizes him up. Henry doesn't look away and keeps his face pleasant.

After a moment, the senator leans back in his chair and crosses his fingers over his belly. "Very well, Captain. Ask away."

"Have you seen anything out of the ordinary around the Hall the last few weeks?"

"No. Some of the speeches have gotten a bit more long-winded than usual, but that's it."

"Were you on the grounds on Thursday last week or Tuesday the week before? After the last session?"

"The police have already asked me these questions. Is this really necessary?"

"Sorry for the repetition, Senator, but yes."

Haldis gives him a tight smile. "In that case...I have a strict work/life balance philosophy, Captain. When my day is over, it's over. I leave promptly every day at six o'clock, barring emergencies."

"And there weren't any emergencies those days?"

"No."

"I understand you're generally the first to arrive when there's a session."

The senator's smile goes a bit thin. "I'm not sure I understand where you're going with this."

"The first incident with Senator Goldsmith drowning in the pool took place early in the morning before the start of the first session. The second with Senator Anderson in the parking garage happened late at night after the last session. If you don't stay late, it's unlikely that you would've seen anything related to that incident. If you're usually here earlier in the morning, you might have seen something before Senator Goldsmith drowned."

"But I didn't." Haldis stands up. "I'm happy to assist the liaison committee in this matter, Captain—I believe cooperation between our legislature and the Compound Network is vital to both of our communities. However, I'm also very busy. Please give my regards to Major Valentine."

Haldis starts for the door, but Henry stays where he is. "Could I trouble you for access to the security feeds, then? Since they cover the grounds at all times, they might've caught something."

The senator sighs. "Again, the police have been over this already. But you're welcome to talk to security on level 5 if you don't think it would be a waste of time."

"I'm sure it won't be. Thank you." Henry stands as well.

Haldis lets him out and doesn't bother to say goodbye before walking down the corridor and away.

Security is a little more solicitous than the senator. The officer is suspicious at first, but once she sees his ID, she's happy enough to let him behind the desk for a look at the cameras.

The video of Senator Goldsmith is tricky because of all the trees obscuring the view. Still, it looks pretty clear cut: Goldsmith walks up to the pool, stands there for a moment, and then steps over the stone edge and into the water, moving forward until her head goes under. A few bubbles, then nothing. The police report in the case file said she filled her pockets with rocks.

The parking garage video is basically the same. Henry can see Senator Anderson go to his car, methodically stuff something in the tailpipe, get in, and turn it on. No hesitation. No one else on camera. No reason to think it's anything other than a suicide.

Henry goes back to Goldsmith's video one more time, and that's when he sees it: a slight blip in the recording, like it's missing a few frames. He squints and looks at the time stamp: no break. Still…her left foot is raised, then on the ground, no movement in between. Less than a second, but….

"Captain?" The security guard is looking at him.

"I'd like copies of these," Henry says.

Chapter 9

WHEN THEY REACH the reflecting pool, Michaels sets down the bag containing the machine and goes to clear out the few aides hoping to enjoy their session break by the water. Bastian leaves her to it and takes a look around.

In preparation for their arrival, or just for appearance's sake, there's no police tape. No indication that anything unusual happened here. Just a placid pool surrounded by a perfectly clean stone walkway on all sides and a few trees here and there.

Bastian recognizes some of the trees as red oak—only because Laurel tried to teach him how to identify them ages ago. He wasn't even aware he was listening.

Reading a location instead of a person is harder, since all that's left are echoes rather than the live emotions themselves. Emotions leave residue, though; sometimes a cloying amount. Bastian will have to concentrate harder to get anything out of the pool and the surrounding area, and the read will be slightly less clear.

He crouches down by the water, taking a few deep breaths and just trying to be open to anything that comes up. Michaels has the area cleared out now, but he can feel echoes of calm-worry-anxious from people who passed by recently, along with a bunch of other emotions he has to sift through. Not unusual for a public space with a lot of traffic.

The next step, actually touching the stone walkway, nets him something a bit more specific: Goldsmith was here, and…something's not right about it. He can't feel anything at all.

It's not like it is with Mortimer. That's a sort of comforting nothing, like curling up under a blanket on a cold night. This is…nothing. Everything is muted unnaturally, like someone's strangling it, holding it back. If Goldsmith were here and contemplating suicide—or about to get murdered—she would've felt *something*.

Grimacing, Bastian takes off his gloves and puts his hands, palms down, on the concrete.

It hits him like a slap in the face: a mind reaching out, *pushing*; the senator, dead eyes and muffled mind, devoid of emotion except for a dull throb of nothing, walking slowly toward the water, pockets weighed down with rocks; the other mind pushing harder as she goes under the water, *keeping her mind down, the power of it, making someone do what you want, all the air in her lungs being replaced with water, I did that, only I can do that, because I'm just that strong, she did it because I—*

(He knows that *push*, it's like when he—)

It stops abruptly, and he almost falls over into the pool, except someone grabs his arm just as he loses his balance.

"Hey. What happened? Are you all right?"

The captain is crouched next to him, hand still on his arm. Bastian doesn't need to be able to read him to see the concern and confusion in his eyes.

(He wants to read him anyway—and doesn't. Doesn't understand the concern. Mortimer obviously doesn't get this asset thing, how no one is supposed to waste time caring about an asset, they're just there to do a job, no one actually—)

"Please step aside, Captain." Officer Michaels is there with the machine, which she puts down and begins to set up.

Mortimer frowns at her. "Whatever you're going to do, it can wait. I'm pretty sure he's not supposed to be green in the face."

"It's fine." Bastian gets to his feet with minimal wobbling. "Michaels is right. We need to get a recording before it's too late."

"Recording?"

Mortimer lets go of Bastian's arm, allowing him to walk over to Michaels, who's finished setting things up. With cool efficiency, she attaches all the electrodes without giving Bastian a chance to do it—she must see he's a bit unsteady, too—and turns the machine on.

Bastian manages to hold still. The slight discomfort of the machine is nothing compared to whatever it was he just felt.

When it's done, and Michaels is putting things away, Mortimer comes up and hands Bastian his gloves. "Okay," he says. "What was that?"

Bastian sighs and rubs his temples. "What did Valentine tell you before you brought me in?"

"Not much. That you were an asset who made a break for it. That you weren't dangerous, but your power might make my team's job more difficult." He pauses. "You were using your power just now, weren't you? Is it always that—?"

"No." Bastian looks out over the pool. Of course it's placid now; not like what he felt, with the senator's nothingness, the murderer's glee. Does it count as murder if you manipulate someone into killing herself? "That was…different."

"What was Officer Michaels recording?"

"The readings I picked up. I can…feel things. Emotions from people near me. But also the residue left by emotions felt in a specific place. Valentine would have us record what I felt at a crime scene and then compare it with what I felt in the presence of a suspect. People leave emotional traces, like signatures. If you can match them, you can determine whether or not a person was in a place—and sometimes what they did there. It's not an exact science, but if the police couldn't prove someone did something, they'd bring the suspects to the compound and use our data."

He doesn't say anything about what else Valentine had him doing. What it looks like the murderer can do.

"You're an empath." The captain's face is unreadable. "There hasn't been an empath in hundreds of years."

"No." Bastian smiles slightly. "Can't have someone running around who knows what you're feeling, especially if they can use that to tell if you're lying. Awkward when your entire organization is built on deception and keeping secrets."

Mortimer skips that part. "Have you always—? I mean, did you manifest at the compound? Or did a team bring you in?"

"Valentine found me when I was a child. I don't remember ever not being like this."

"Can you read anyone? Whenever?"

There it is. "Yes. Some people have really good shields, so that makes it more difficult, but—yes."

"Can you read me?"

Bastian forces himself to meet Mortimer's eyes—and is immediately confused. He doesn't see the usual disgust or fear; only a little wariness. Mostly it's curiosity.

Why isn't he scared? People are usually frightened and uncomfortable when they find out what Bastian can do. Like that city guard. Maybe the captain was hit over the head as a kid.

"I—"

"Captain? Mr. Lucas?" Officer Michaels is standing a few feet away. "Would you like to get a read from the second location?"

Mortimer nods to her. "Yes, sorry. The session break is almost over, and we'll want to be done here before then so we're not in the way."

"And your meeting with the senator was successful, sir?"

Mortimer smiles ruefully. "Sort of. But we can talk about that on the way back. Lead the way, Officer Michaels."

"Yes, sir."

Bastian puts his gloves back on as they walk. "You know, honorifics are just a method of brainwashing conceived by the military hive mind."

Mortimer blinks at him. "What?"

"Michaels insists on being overly polite about it, but that's only because she's bought into their insipid lies. If she had any interest in standing up to the corruption inherent in the system, she'd call everyone by their first names."

Mortimer's mouth twitches. "Is that what I should call you, then? Your first name?"

"Only if you want to make a bold statement against the establishment."

"Well, clearly I wouldn't want to be in the same class as Officer Michaels, at any rate. She's too competent and task oriented. What's her first name, anyway?"

"No idea. I've always suspected she doesn't have one."

"I believe the parking garage is through here, Captain," says Michaels, a little ahead of them.

Bastian catches Mortimer's eye, and they snicker.

Michaels stops and looks between them. "Perhaps the most competent and task-oriented thing to do at this juncture would be to hurry it up?"

"Well!" Bastian says. "I guess we'd better get on with it if we don't want to get grounded." He looks at the captain again and smirks. And definitely doesn't feel anything stupid like his heart skipping a beat at the answering grin.

Chapter 10

HENRY INTENDS TO stay close during the second read, but Bastian shoos him away to talk to the garage security guards, who turn out to be extremely unhelpful. Apparently, everything with Senator Anderson went down while the guards were on break—and they didn't break in shifts, like they were supposed to.

"We've already been reprimanded," one guard says gloomily. "I guess it's better than being dismissed. Anyway, I don't know what happened that night, honest. It was the only time we've ever not gone in shifts."

His partner shrugs at further questions.

If they're hiding something, it's not the sort of thing spending a night in the police station could get out of them, so it doesn't seem likely that Henry can.

By the time he gets back to Bastian and Michaels, they're packing up.

"Anything?" Henry asks.

Bastian shakes his head slowly, putting his gloves back on. "Nothing, except that it's like the other one. I have to…sort through it."

Speaking of hiding something. Henry doesn't press it. "I might've found something on the security footage that could help. I'll need one of the compound hackers to take a look, though."

Bastian gets a mischievous look in his eye. "I know just the one. I can hit him up tomorrow." Then his face goes dark. "First I need to talk to Valentine, though."

Other than a brief summary of Henry's exciting visit with Senator Haldis, there's not much talking on the way back. Once they arrive at the vehicle loading dock, Michaels heads off to analyze the recordings, and Bastian goes in the opposite direction, accompanied by several black coats, to…do something. Probably talk to the major. (He wasn't kidding about assets being marched around flanked by security, then.)

Just as well. Henry's team has been without him long enough to have gotten into trouble if they're inclined toward it today. He told them to train, but their definition of "train" could easily include playing pranks on black coats that will earn them neighboring cells to Bastian for a night.

That said, he's not actually expecting any real trouble. Which is why the yelling coming from the training room is disturbing, to say the least.

Henry breaks into a sprint and bursts into the room just in time to have to duck to avoid a bolt of electricity that hits the wall where his head was a moment before. His gun is in his hands without him having to think about it—but he nearly lowers it when he sees what's happening in the room.

Everyone has stopped what they're doing to stare at Johnson and Smith, who were apparently sparring at the back of the room. Smith is frozen on the ground, muted terror in her eyes, while Johnson stands over her, breathing heavily.

And shot through with sparks of electricity all over his body.

"Captain?" he says shakily, looking up at the doorway. The electricity enveloping him dims. "I don't know what—"

Henry does lower his gun a bit then, holding out his other hand. "I know. Just…take a few breaths. We'll figure this out. Can you step away from Officer Smith, please?"

"We'll handle this."

Henry tenses at the voice, tightening his grip on his gun and praying he won't have to use it.

He flicks a quick glance to one side—three black coats, terrific—then back to Johnson. "It's okay. I'm sure they didn't mean to startle you. If you'll just—"

"Your assistance isn't required, Captain," says one of the black coats. She steps around him right into his line of sight—and fire. "Cuff the asset and take him to Level 12," she instructs one of her cohorts.

Henry remembers what Bastian said about cuffing assets. Right; Johnson will be considered an asset now. The irony of someone on a retrieval team manifesting isn't lost on Henry.

"Captain?" Johnson is slightly calmer now, and the electricity around him has faded entirely.

Henry puts his gun away and turns to the black coat who spoke to him. "It might be better if I—"

"Stand down, Captain. That's an order."

Of course, there's nothing he can say to that. Henry clenches his jaw, nods once, and steps aside as they cuff Johnson and lead him out of the room.

Johnson catches Henry's eye as they go, and Henry tries to exude some sort of reassurance, but he doubts it does much good.

Everyone else is still standing around. Or sitting around, in Smith's case.

"Welcome back, Captain," she says awkwardly. The others give half-hearted laughs.

"Yeah, thanks." Henry's voice sounds tired in his own ears. "Why don't you all take five?"

As they file out quietly, Henry finds a chair in the corner of the room and sits down.

It's not as though manifestations never happen in the compound. It's rare, since most potentials manifest as children, but it's not unheard of. Henry's just never considered what it would mean if it happened to one of his team. That he'd have to give them up to the black coats. That he'd probably never see them again.

(That he'd see that look on Johnson's face, confused and scared, expecting Henry to have some sort of explanation, except Henry doesn't, just like he doesn't know all sorts of things, and he can't ask if it would put his team at risk—not that that's going very well, is it, because Johnson's just—)

Henry sits there until his team starts to trickle back in, purposefully not looking at him.

What he should do now, of course, is go check in with Major Valentine and see how she'd like him to proceed. Instead, he sits there for a little while, watching his team train, before getting up and leaving.

He goes back to his room and changes out of the dress uniform—no need to be uncomfortable while dealing with an existential crisis. Then he wanders aimlessly up and down the Level 1 halls, mostly to avoid paperwork, trying not to think about anything at all.

Until he realizes he's stopped in front of the elevators.

Chapter 11

"THERE'S ANOTHER ONE."

Valentine looks up from her usual pile of paperwork and raises her eyebrows at Bastian. "You'll have to be more specific. Preferably quickly. I have a lot to do."

"Major!" A panting black coat bursts through the door. "I'm sorry, he got away from—"

Valentine waves a hand. "Never mind. Sebastian and I need to talk anyway. Close the door on your way out."

The black coat nods and exits, closing the door as asked.

Valentine turns back to him. "Well?"

"You sent me there because there's another empath. That's why you had Hen—Captain Mortimer bring me back, isn't it? To deal with your little problem?"

"If there's evidence of what you're suggesting, I'm sure it will turn up in the recordings. But you realize how unlikely that is, don't you?"

"I know what I felt."

Valentine leans forward and laces her fingers together. "Sebastian. You know there hasn't been another empath for a very long time. I monitor the situation closely with the best of the compound's technology." She smiles slightly. "I would have thought you'd be pleased to be unique."

Bastian rolls his eyes and tries (and fails) to hide his agitation. "Fine. Let's say I have no idea what I'm talking about, which you know for a fact isn't true. You also know that if there *is* another empath out there, particularly one who's taken it upon themself to kill people, it's worse than just a manifesting you missed." He hesitates, then forces himself to say it: "They can do what I can do."

"And you think this is why I brought you back." (Curiosity-amusement-something else he can't read. Her shield is good, maybe even better than before.)

"I know it is. What I don't understand is why you didn't do it sooner. And why you'd bring the captain into it. Doesn't he have a team to train and lead?"

She's definitely smiling now. "Are you concerned about him, Sebastian? How very unlike you."

"I'm not," Bastian says quickly. "I just want to know what's going on."

There's a long pause before Valentine says, "You no doubt have your suspicions regarding Captain Mortimer. Don't you think it would be helpful to have him around in case you meet someone who can do what you're suggesting?"

Keep it in the land of supposition. Admit nothing. He doesn't know what he was expecting, really.

"I assure you," Valentine adds, "Captain Mortimer is quite capable of taking care of himself."

"Not against an empath."

"Are you referring to yourself? Or the murderer?"

He doesn't have an answer to that, so he says nothing. Just stands there and hates her amused smile.

She stands and comes around to his side of the desk. "Sebastian," she says quietly, "I think you forget the good we do here. The good we were able to accomplish with your help. All those criminals we put away. By doing as I asked, you made a difference in so many lives. Helped so many people. I still don't understand why you would run away from that."

"Oh, I don't know. Maybe because your pet scientist was trying to kill me?"

She smiles sadly and shakes her head (disappointment-hurt-resignation). "I'm sorry you were never able to understand how much we helped you. How much more we wanted to help you.

"And speaking of helping people," Valentine continues, "I read the report on your retrieval while you were out. Very interesting."

Bastian tenses. "Why? Just your goons doing their job."

"It appears that there was someone else in the clearing with you that morning. Someone the captain's team was unable to recover."

"I have no idea what you're talking about."

"Of course not." Valentine sighs. "If you *did* know what I'm talking about, though, I'm sure you'd want to be on your best behavior so that nothing unfortunate happens to that person."

He keeps standing there, fuming like an idiot, while she goes to the door to get the black coat. "Please escort Sebastian to his quarters."

"'Quarters' is a nice word for a jail cell," Bastian says. "Don't I warrant a suite yet?"

Valentine goes back to her desk and sits down. "When you've proven you're not going to leave us again, we'll see about more permanent accommodations."

Since of course he's going to escape the compound as soon as he figures out how, there's not much he can say to that. Instead, he turns on his heel and lets the black coat drag him back to his cell.

Chapter 12

HENRY NODS TO Templeton when he enters the jail block. She looks completely unsurprised to see him—probably assumes he's here to talk to Bastian about the mission. Not an unreasonable assumption. Also not an accurate one.

He didn't mean to come here, exactly. But if anyone knows what's going to happen to Johnson....

Henry walks down the hall to Bastian's cell and doesn't see him in the semi-darkness at first. He's sitting on the bed, completely still, knees drawn up to his chin and arms wrapped around his shins.

Then he sees Henry, and his demeanor immediately becomes cold. "What do you want?"

Henry's taken aback. After the mission today, he'd thought...he doesn't know what. That Bastian has a mischievous side and a nice laugh he probably doesn't use as much as he should, and come to think of it, he never did answer Henry's question about—

"Well? If you don't need anything, go away. I'm busy trying to figure out how to save a friend you endangered with your stupid report."

Henry stares at him. "My what now?"

"*Someone*," Bastian says, getting to his feet, "wrote a report that included mentioning that a girl got away when you came to the clearing and shot me. You can imagine how interested Valentine was to hear about that."

"There's always a report after a mission with all the details. I didn't think—"

"Obviously."

"Why would the major even care?" Henry says, frowning. "My team's job is to bring in potentials who have just manifested and might need help. Your friend isn't—"

He looks at Bastian's furious face and sighs. "She's an asset, too."

"Brilliant."

"The major told me an asset hasn't escaped from the compound in ages."

"Who said Laurel's from this compound?"

"Then which one is she from?"

Bastian hesitates. "I don't know. She never said."

"Anyhow, the major's in regular contact with the Compound Council. How would none of them know about another escaped asset? And why wouldn't Major Valentine have ordered us to bring her in, too?"

"Maybe Valentine's holding out on the Council. Wouldn't be the first time she's hidden something from someone." He runs his hands through his hair in irritation. "The point is, Laurel's in danger because of that report, and there's nothing I can do about it locked up in here. So thanks very much for that."

"I'm sorry."

Bastian gives him an odd look, then sighs and rubs his eyes. "What do you want, Henry?"

Now Henry feels like shit for even bringing this up, but…."I need to ask you something."

He pauses long enough that Bastian starts sliding back into annoyance. "Are you going to get to the point, or—?"

"One of my team manifested today."

Bastian blinks at him for a moment. Then: "How far away were you?"

"What?"

"When they manifested. How far away were you?"

"Down the hall. I mean, that's where I was when I heard the commotion and came running. But I don't see what this has to do with—"

"What power was it?"

"Electrocutor. He had sparks coming off of every part of him. It looked like they got worse when he was agitated, but they dissipated when he calmed down."

"Which he did when you got there, I'm guessing."

"Yeah, I think so."

Bastian snorts. "Valentine will love this one. Channel the electricity once he's trained and use it to power the compound for months. A giant battery." He notices the look on Henry's face. "Not what you wanted to hear?"

Henry forces himself to stay calm. "I just need you to tell me what's going to happen to him."

"I'm sure you could get a reassuring lie from Valentine. Or just by reviewing your training. Poor helpless assets get entered into the program when they manifest because they need saving, right?"

Okay, calm can go die in a fire. "I don't want a lie; I want the *truth*. Look, I know you're pissed at me about the report, but I need your help. Johnson's my responsibility. He was scared, and I just let the black coats take him away. I need to know if he's all right. I need to—"

He cuts himself off and pinches the bridge of his nose. "You know what, never mind. This is stupid. I shouldn't have bothered you." He turns to go.

"They'll take him through testing," Bastian says after a moment. "Wright does most of that. Assuming he survives it and his power isn't considered dangerous, he'll be entered into the asset program and given assignments that match his new abilities. You probably won't see him again."

Henry stands there for a moment, then turns back. He doesn't envy Johnson the extended interactions with Dr. Wright, but all things considered, that doesn't sound so bad. (Try not to think about the "assuming he survives it" comment). Anyway, the team will get by. And it sounds like he'll be able to make himself useful—good for a guy whose mouth gets him into trouble regularly.

But he can't get Johnson's terrified face out of his mind—the black coats cuffing him like a prisoner, the same way they treat Bastian—and if that's how all the assets are treated, and no one knows about it...he can't just let it go, can he?

"Thank you," Henry says.

Bastian gives him that same odd look from earlier, like he doesn't understand the concept of politeness.

"For telling me," Henry clarifies. "I didn't want to just…not know."

Bastian's eyes narrow. "You're going after him, aren't you?"

Henry wasn't planning to, exactly, but—"What makes you think that?"

"Look, it's a bad idea. There's no telling what level he's on. And let's say you did find him—what then? Sneak him out of the compound?"

"I know of at least one person who's managed it before."

"Yeah, but I had—"

Bastian pauses. "I wouldn't recommend actually trying to break your man out. But I might know a way you can find him, at least. And we can get some information for the case at the same time."

Henry raises his eyebrows. "And you'd help me with that? Even though my report—?"

"I'm not helping," Bastian says quickly. "I'm…jumping on the opportunity to irritate Valentine by giving her officers information they shouldn't have."

He turns away. "As for Laurel, I'll figure something out. Or she will. It's not like she's defenseless out there."

Chapter 13

BASTIAN TELLS HENRY to come back down in the morning. For a moment, Henry acts like he's going to demand to be let in on whatever Bastian has in mind, but in the end, he just nods and leaves.

Once he's gone, Bastian paces the cell and considers. He couldn't read Henry, of course, but all the rest of the evidence was there in his agitated body language and frustrated tone of voice. That ridiculous *earnestness*.

Henry really thinks there's something he can do about his manifested officer.

That doesn't mean Bastian should have (sort of) offered to help. But it really will annoy Valentine, and they need the evidence analyzed anyway. If that does something good for Henry at the same time, that's just a fortunate side effect.

Sometime later, Catherine brings him dinner, which he barely touches. Instead, he suggests she consider getting a few plants to liven up the place. She looks at him like he's lost his mind but doesn't veto the idea.

She comes back after a while to take the tray and frowns at him. "You need to eat, young man."

"The human body can survive three weeks without food."

"I don't see how starving yourself is going to help anything."

"Maybe if the meals were more edible...."

"I'll have you know the cafeteria is run by extremely reputable, hard-working—"

"—people who can't cook. I know."

Catherine sighs and picks up the tray.

"Maybe...."

She turns around (wary-worried-curious).

Bastian puts on his most innocent face. "Maybe if I could walk around a bit, I could work up an appetite. Even for this slop."

Catherine gives him a half-smile. "Do you really think I'm going to fall for that, Bastian?"

"It's not like I could escape," he says, shrugging. "There's only one exit, and it goes right past your desk. And if there are areas you don't want me to get into, you can just close them off. As for colluding with other prisoners, that's not an issue on this side of the jail block, since there aren't any."

"How do you—?"

"No one emoting over here besides you and me."

Catherine looks at him awhile longer, debating. Then she shakes her head and goes for the door. "I'm sorry, Bastian. My orders don't include facilitating field trips."

She steps out into the hall and closes the door.

And doesn't lock it.

"There would be consequences, of course, if a prisoner got out of their cell," she says. "But it would take me at least fifteen minutes to find them and put everything back in order. If a prisoner *were* to get out, given all that, they'd probably be able to have a decent, uninterrupted walk if they were careful about the security cameras and stayed out of row F."

Good old Catherine. This means he can leave the lock picking till next time. "Completely understandable, Prison Officer."

She gives him a last warning look, then heads back down the hall to her desk.

He slips out of his cell as soon as he's sure she's gone. He does his best to avoid the most obvious cameras for now and heads around the corner to row F. If he's going to get caught—and it's only a matter of time—might as well go big.

***

He doesn't notice at first.

It starts as an itch in the back of his mind (bored-bored-bored), dim enough to explain why he'd thought he and Catherine were the only ones on this side of the jail block. He knows it's an emotion since he's feeling it, but it's like it's coming through a thick barrier. Like he's not quite hearing the whole thing because it's being muffled. A bad connection.

Most minds are a whirlwind of emotions, soft and strong, quick and slow. This one's just…gray. Something he's never felt before.

Except that's not true, is it? There are the murder scenes.

(And he felt it back when—but the people he did that to wouldn't be here. Valentine would have sent them on to the authorities. Unless she didn't.)

There's one of the gray minds in row F, and Bastian's feet take him to the cell without informing him that that's where they're headed. He peers through the bars but can't see anything.

The grayness is still there. "Hello?" Bastian calls.

The feeling coalesces into a body, weirdly devoid of any emotion except for the slight bored-bored-bored that repeats itself irritatingly at the same pitch. The body shifts, making the shadows shift along with it.

Someone steps forward. Someone Bastian recognizes.

Not that it's easy. Snyder's eyes are two sunken holes housing eyeballs that are all white. His skin sags off his bones like he's been starved for years. Most of his hair has fallen out. He has none of the smugness of the suspect Bastian interrogated a year ago.

"You," Snyder says, pointing a bony finger at him. "*You.* I know you. You're the freak who did this to me." He begins to laugh.

"What are you doing down here?" Bastian demands.

"What are *you* doing down here, freak?" he responds between giggles. "They finally locked you up, did they? Decided they didn't need you anymore? Found themselves a new freak to follow orders?" He laughs louder, throwing his head back so violently, Bastian half expects it to fall off.

A new freak. The other empath? The one who killed the senators? How would Snyder know about that?

Snyder grins. "They didn't tell you, did they? Wouldn't want you to get jealous. Especially her. You're her little pet, aren't you? That's why she had you do this to me. Mindless little pet."

"I didn't do this to you," Bastian says, mouth dry.

"Didn't you? You didn't rip into my head, scramble my brains, get what you needed, and throw me away?"

"I—"

Snyder bolts forward with startling quickness, hands clenching around the bars, his breath in Bastian's face. "You know exactly what you did. Just because someone else told you to do it doesn't make it okay." He locks gazes with Bastian.

(Should look away, can't look away, the gray nothing is so loud, pounding in Bastian's ears, inexplicable and *wrong*—)

"There were others like me, you know," Snyder says. "So many others. Sometimes they came through here. Sometimes they were worse than me, even. Brains so addled, they couldn't stand up straight. Sometimes they came in wheelchairs, and they crawled around or sat very still until they died."

He licks his lips. "We hear things, we call for help, but no one listens. She even sends someone to make us forget, but I don't. No matter what she does, I never forget."

"That's not—" Not what? Not what Valentine told him would happen to the people he interrogated? When has she ever told him the truth about anything? She tells people what they need to hear. He needed to hear that what she made him do wasn't really hurting anyone, that it was just another annoying little way she had him use his power. Not that there were real consequences. That people were dying.

He forces himself to focus on something else for the moment. "Who did she send to make you forget?"

Snyder rolls his eyes—particularly creepy when they're so white in the dark. "Your master sends her. She's no one; she's just the way it gets done. Only it doesn't always work on us, does it? You've broken us so much, we can't break anymore." He grins. "We should thank you."

"An asset who makes you forget?" Bastian presses. "What does she look like? Where does she come from?"

Snyder goes pale and backs away into partial shadow. "You going to do it again? Make me give up information? Nothing left to give, freak. You're not touching me. Nothing left! All gone!"

"Snyder—"

But he's already melted back into the darkness. And Bastian realizes he has bigger issues: a mess of angry-disappointed-concerned-embarrassed is headed his way, and—

"Sebastian."

Valentine is there when he turns around, followed by Catherine and a small contingent of black coats.

Catherine was supposed to catch him, not Valentine. Shit.

"Out for an evening stroll?" Bastian asks cheerfully.

She ignores it. "I was made aware that the security cameras caught a prisoner outside his cell. It's not at all surprising to discover that it's you." She looks over her shoulder. "It *is* surprising to see such a lax effort from you, Prison Officer Templeton."

"I'm sorry, Major," says Catherine, face flushed. "It won't happen again."

"No, it won't. My security detail will discuss options for future safekeeping of the jail block with you."

The black coats march Catherine off. She doesn't look at Bastian as she goes.

Valentine turns back to him. "Explain."

"You first." He jerks a thumb at Snyder's cell. "You lied to me. The people I interrogated—you said they went to the authorities. But you actually locked them up down here and left them to rot."

She smiles his least favorite smile. Which is saying a lot, since he hates all of them. "Come now, Sebastian," she says. "If you're here, you must have seen the state of poor Mr. Snyder. How could I let criminals who had that kind of reaction get stuck in the penal system?"

"You needed to hide your failures, you mean."

"It's a bit immature to blame others for your own actions."

"I only did it because you ordered me to!"

"Is that so? Blindly following orders? You've never done as I asked without second-guessing me, Sebastian. If you'd wanted to know more about what happened to the suspects, you would have found a way."

"I—"

"Besides, I thought you didn't care about that sort of thing. You always said people were a waste of time."

"That isn't—"

"The truth, Sebastian, is that you have no interest in the consequences of your actions. What will happen to Prison Officer Templeton now, for instance, after this infraction? Which, incidentally, I have no doubt you instigated?"

Valentine sighs. "You've only ever cared about what you want, not what this compound stands for or the work we're trying to do. If I didn't tell you what happened to suspects like Mr. Snyder, it's because I honestly thought you didn't care. I was trying to make things easier for you, just like I always do."

"Easy," Bastian spits. "Like ordering me to use my power in a way that would've killed me, not to mention other people."

"And there's the real issue: your inability to sacrifice for the greater good. Think of how many murderers we put away because of your power. It's unfortunate that some of them didn't come out of interrogation entirely intact, but that was a small number. Ultimately, the program was effective. We were doing good work. And then you ran away."

"*Because it was killing me!*"

(He shouldn't do this, it'll go nowhere, and it's pathetic and stupid to think she'll show any kind of remorse, he can't care about this, can't think about what she's done, can't give her more ammunition to use against him—)

"I remember a time when you cared about doing good in the world," Valentine says quietly. "When you begged me to let you help. I remember a lost little boy hiding in a dirty alley because he couldn't control his power and didn't understand what he was. Do you remember that?"

Damn her. "Yes."

"Because it seems to me you've forgotten. Everything I did for you, everything you asked of me. I could have left you there, let you suffer alone. But I saw something in you, a capacity to do good, even after you'd closed yourself off to me."

She shakes her head sadly. "I always thought the work was important to you. It wasn't easy work, but it was important work. And while the things we do here at the compound have many positive outcomes, there can also be negative consequences. I thought you understood that. But it seems I was wrong."

The black coats are back. "Please take Sebastian to his cell," Valentine says. "And make sure it's locked this time."

Bastian clenches his jaw and follows them silently.

Chapter 14

IT MIGHT BE Henry's imagination, but it seems like Bastian is even more stonily silent than usual this morning. Maybe he's still worried about his friend—Laurel, was it?

He notices Templeton is quieter as well. Possibly because of the black coats posted at the end of every cell row. And the one behind the desk with her. She nods at Henry when he comes in and then immediately goes back to her paperwork, obviously on her best behavior.

"Something happen I should know about?" Henry asks lightly when he and Bastian are out in the hall.

"No." Bastian brushes past him and makes for the elevators.

Okay, then.

Henry follows and watches him press the button for Level 4. "You want to tell me where we're going?"

"Hacker ops."

"Makes sense for looking at that video footage I found. But what about—?"

"Not here."

Henry briefly considers shooting Bastian until he stops being cryptic but decides against it. If Henry starts shooting, he might not be able to stop.

Hacker ops takes up the entirety of Level 4. There are hundreds of rooms of coders working on different projects—overseeing security, finding potentials, creating algorithms to track asset progress and capabilities. Henry knew it existed, of course, but he's never been on this floor and had no idea their HQ was so big.

Bastian seems to know where he's going, though. He walks to the end of the hall and pushes open a door with a series of nonsensical numbers on it.

This room is dimly lit and full of computer servers. The rest of the space is taken up by long tables of hackers typing at breakneck speed. No one looks up as they enter.

"Where's Kent?" Bastian asks loudly.

A few heads pop up at that, but most of them lose interest right away and dip back down. The one head that stays up has a blueish face in the light of her computer screen and large, owlish eyes.

"Kent's on break," she says. "He just got off an all-nighter. Should be back soon, though. Something I can help you with?" She sounds as if helping them with something is the last thing she wants to do.

"Yes, actually." Henry goes over and hands her the disc he got from the Hall security officer. "I need you to take a look at these recordings and tell me if they've been tampered with."

The hacker frowns at the disc but takes it from him, turning it over. "I'll need to see if we even have a computer with a disc drive anymore." She looks directly at him for the first time—more specifically, at his ID—and blinks, suddenly embarrassed. "Um. I'll just—go do that. Right now. Captain."

"Thanks."

She disappears quickly behind the servers.

A moment later, the door opens, and both Henry and Bastian turn to find a gangly hacker with bags under his eyes entering the room. He sees Bastian, stops to cross his arms over his chest, and says a single word: "Nope."

This doesn't deter Bastian at all. "Hello, Kent. Nice to see you, too."

"Four letters, one syllable, Lucas: n-o-p-e. Get out of here before I call the black coats."

Henry opens his mouth but can't get a word in before Bastian responds. "What's the matter? We had fun last time, didn't we?"

"Fun?" Kent gives him a particularly vicious glare. "You remember what *happened* last time? Oh, no, you don't because you weren't here. You'd already—" He glances at Henry and cuts himself off. "You'd already, um. Done something. About which I have no knowledge whatsoever. Because I wouldn't. Have knowledge, I mean. About that. Something I can help you with, uh, Captain?"

Bastian rolls his eyes. "Honestly, when did you become such a killjoy?"

"Killjoy?" Kent glares at Bastian, immediately forgetting Henry. "I'll show you the killing part, anyway—"

"All right, enough of that." Henry inserts himself between them and turns to Kent. "Look, I know you're tired, but we need your help."

"Right. Yes. Of course you do. I mean, of course you do, *sir*. And I'm happy to oblige because I am a model employee. Follow me."

Henry considers asking why Kent is taking them someplace before he even knows what they need, but Kent and Bastian are already heading out the back door. Henry follows them into the rear hallway, which is empty for the moment. A little way down, the corridor is blocked by a security door, which Kent lets them through using his ID card. As soon as they're all past it, he stands up straighter, and his eyes get sharper. He turns to Bastian.

"You really want to do this in front of an officer, Lucas?"

"Never mind that. How long do we have?"

"Five minutes. What is it? Jammer again?"

"At least two—one for me and one for the captain here. Data access as well."

Kent snorts. "You're going to have to be more specific. Security's tightened since you got out. Which reminds me, why are you back here again? You hate this place."

"Not how I want to spend my five minutes, Kent."

"More like four minutes and thirty seconds now."

Henry frowns. "Is one of you going to tell me—?"

"Not how I want to spend my four minutes." Bastian looks over at him. "I'll explain later."

Kent grins. "All you need to know, Captain, is that I'm very good at my job, and that thing I told you I had no knowledge of is actually something I have a lot of knowledge of." He pauses, then adds, "Which I am only telling you because Lucas says you're trustworthy. And so you can fully appreciate the artistry of my work."

Bastian snorts. "Yeah, we got all that from the artistry of your dissembling back there."

"Hey, I'm a hacker, not a people person. And we hardly ever get visitors. I can't be expected to—"

"Data access. I'm not sure how deep we'll need to go, but at least to level 3. You can do that, right?"

"Theoretically, yes. In practice, no. Well. Not easily."

"I didn't say anything about easily."

Henry scans the ceiling and the door while they're talking. "You realize that all of this is being recorded, right? The black coats are going to know everything you're talking about, and they'll likely lock us all up." He eyes Bastian. "Those of us who aren't already spending most of our time locked up, that is."

"No, it isn't. Being recorded, I mean." Kent jerks a thumb at the cameras in the ceiling, looking extremely pleased with himself. "See the little black boxes to either side of the cameras? Say hello to my stationary jammers. They'll play the cameras a nice little ditty about a clear hallway for five minutes, after which we'll need to scram, or we *will* be recorded conspiring against the enemy." He pauses. "Uh. By which I mean other officers. Not you. I think. Sir."

Bastian rolls his eyes. "Focus. Level 3—yes or no?"

"Yes. It'll take some time, though."

"Do it. How long for the mobile jammers?"

"A few days. I'll put them in the usual place. Don't tell me what you're going to do with them, either; plausible deniability helps me sleep at night."

"And you'll let us know when the codes for level 3 access are ready?"

"If it's possible, it shall be done." Kent takes out a phone and looks at the time. "You guys'd better get out of here. Keep going down the hall, and you'll end up at a door that leads back to the main corridor. This conversation never happened."

"I have no idea what you're talking about." Bastian turns to Henry. "Let's go."

"Oh, Captain?" Kent calls after them. "I'll have Sybil send you that information as soon as she's able to put it together."

"How did you—?"

Kent waves his phone and grins. "All-seeing eyes. Well. All-seeing eyes that monitor the work order queue. Now move, before you get us all in trouble."

When they're back in the main hallway, Henry notices that the area they just came through is unobtrusive, almost invisible. Not the sort of thing you'd pay much attention to if you were just walking around minding your own business.

"So. Do I need to be concerned about how easily compound security can be hacked?" Henry asks, keeping his voice low.

"Hmm? Oh, don't worry about it. Kent just likes the challenge. He's not about to actually endanger anyone."

"Yeah. Kent. That was a pretty drastic turnaround he had there."

Bastian shrugs. "Security's tight in the main hacker banks. He had to make it look good." Bastian seems pretty nonchalant for having just broken who knows how many compound rules. (At least six, Henry's trained mind offers.)

"He really helped you last time? I mean, when you...?"

"I can neither confirm nor deny. And we really shouldn't be talking about this here."

Henry's a bit startled that his first instinct is to tell Bastian to cut the crap and just say it. Not because Henry wants to report him—although he should, and Kent, too—but because he wants to know how the hell Bastian managed it.

They shouldn't be doing any of this, Henry thinks grimly. All that counseling himself to stay away from curiosity, and the minute it affects his team, he jumps right in. Even though it could mean worse consequences for everyone.

But he remembers the terrified look on Johnson's face and knows there's no question he'll do whatever it takes to make sure Johnson's all right.

"I get the advantage of being able to run around without having to worry about security," Henry says when they're back on the elevator and headed down. "But I don't see how that helps with Johnson. I mean, I can sneak all I want, but it's useless if I don't actually know where he is."

"That's why we need the data access. If it's good enough, we can coordinate with Kent to figure out where he's being held and where he is in the process of being admitted into the asset program. It's not necessarily accurate up to the minute, but it's a good place to start." Bastian looks over at Henry. "What?"

Henry smothers a smile. "You said 'we.'"

"Yeah, well." Bastian turns away awkwardly. "I told you; I like causing trouble for Valentine. Hard to beat corrupting a captain."

The smile turns into a full-blown grin. "Is that what you're doing? Corrupting me?"

"Well, I'm certainly not helping you."

"Of course not."

"I don't help people. I don't even like people."

"Seems like a wise policy."

"Especially people who shoot me."

Ouch. "Okay, strictly speaking, it wasn't me who—no, you know what, I ordered it, so it's on me. For what it's worth, I really do think we need your help with this case. And I'm grateful you're…not helping with the whole Johnson thing. I hope being back here hasn't been entirely awful for you, although I'd understand if it were."

The elevator comes to a stop, and they get off and head for the jail block.

Henry hesitates, not wanting to push it, but: "Bastian…what you said at the Hall, about how your power lets you read anyone. You never said if you can—"

"No, I didn't."

Henry gives him a sideways glance but doesn't say anything else about it.

When they get back to the jail block, Templeton greets them, still subdued but with a little more of the usual bounce in her step. She gets her keys out and starts to herd Bastian past the black coats and back to his cell, but he stops and turns.

"It's not," he says.

Henry raises his eyebrows.

"Entirely awful."

"Oh. Good." Henry gives him a small smile that lasts slightly longer than he intended it to. And does his best to ignore the feeling in his chest when Bastian smiles tentatively back.

***

Henry doesn't see Bastian for a few days, in large part because he and his team are sent to bring in several more potentials. It's just as well, since there's been no news from Kent or Sybil or any other hacker.

So he's back to the usual day to day, which never used to bother him before. Now, of course, it does. Because somewhere out there, a murderer is running free. And somewhere in here, Johnson is doing who knows what. And there's nothing Henry can do about any of it.

There's one thing he *can* do, though: make sure the rest of his team is all right in the aftermath of Johnson's manifestation. At a glance, everyone seems okay, but it doesn't sit right. They're…*too* okay. Especially Smith.

He takes it upon himself during one morning training to go over to where she's using a weight machine. She notices him almost at once and sits up. "Sir?"

No really good way to do this, and even if there were, he wouldn't know how. "I wanted to see how you were doing."

She looks confused. "I'm fine, Captain."

"Good. I know you were friends with Johnson, so—"

"Who?"

He should reprimand her for interrupting a superior officer, but he's distracted by her response. "Teammate. Johnson. Skinny guy with red hair? You used to tease him about his freckles? Manifested in here a few weeks ago? Electricity everywhere?"

She looks dumbfounded. "I don't understand."

"Look, if this is a joke—"

"I'm sorry, Captain. I have no idea what you're talking about."

He turns to the officer on the mat next to her. "Alexander, you remember what happened in here the other day, don't you?"

"Sir?"

Henry rolls his eyes. "All right, this is just—Hey, listen up!"

Everyone stops what they're doing and turns to him.

"This is cute, but it's beginning to get on my nerves. What's with the caginess about Johnson? Let's have a real answer, please."

They all look at him like he's sprouted wings. "Is that…someone in accounting, sir?" Valdez calls from the back of the room.

"Done being patient here, people," Henry says firmly. "Play time is over. Someone answer me. *Now.*"

There are quick looks back and forth and a general growing air of concern.

Ohtani finally speaks up. "Sorry, sir, but we don't know who you're talking about."

Can his entire team be having some sort of mass delusion? Does that even happen?

Henry doesn't say anything else, just walks out of the training room and back to the barracks, trying not to snarl at anyone who gets in his way. It doesn't make any *sense*. How could they all forget Johnson? And why hasn't he?

His mind immediately goes to an asset, of course, but he's never heard of one who could make people forget things. And why would someone want his team to forget Johnson, anyway?

He's civil, if somewhat curt, during the next mission: a potential with psionic powers who nearly knocks them all out. They manage to bring him back—not willingly, and only after he gives them all temporary migraines.

Henry doesn't linger after everyone is checked back in and the med techs have taken the potential away.

(Don't think about where he'll end up or what will happen to him or if he'll come across Johnson or—)

Walking down a Level 1 corridor, Henry doesn't even have time to draw his gun before someone grabs his arm and pulls him around a corner.

"Probably best to avoid the cameras," says a voice next to his ear.

"What are you—?" Henry realizes it's Bastian holding his arm and peering around him at the same time. "How—?"

"Two excellent questions. I'll answer them later. Come on."

Bastian lets go of his arm and heads down the corridor, sticking close to the wall, obviously expecting Henry to follow. He has something in his hand: a little black device with a screen Henry can't read from this angle.

His better judgment having apparently fled, Henry finds himself following.

When they reach the end of the hall, Bastian holds up a hand to stop. That gives Henry a chance to take a better look at the device. It's made of metal and has some sort of countdown clock on it.

Frowning, Bastian looks around the corner…and immediately pulls back, finger to his lips.

A small group of black coats walks by the intersection, silent and imposing. And apparently unaware of Bastian and Henry standing right there.

Once they're gone, Bastian motions for movement. They go down several more hallways, zigzagging from one direction to another, until Bastian looks at the timer and, without preamble, shoves Henry into a broom closet and shuts the door.

"Five minutes exactly," he says. "Would've preferred ten, but maybe Kent can work up some modifications as we go."

"That's the jammer, then?" Henry asks.

Bastian passes it over. "Kent just got them to me today. I've been testing them out. So far, so good—on fourteen floors, at least."

Henry turns it over in his hand. "And you're not concerned about getting caught wandering around outside your cell? Templeton might get in trouble for that, you know."

Bastian goes quiet for a moment. "She and the black coats were busy with prisoners on the other side of the block. I'll be back before they notice." He sounds a little uncertain about it. "Anyway, it's important."

Henry hands the jammer back to him. "How did you even get out?"

"Jammer to avoid detection. Kent was good enough to deliver them in a bigger cache of supplies, so no one knows I have them. And then there's this." He holds up a pin and grins, obviously pleased with himself.

"I didn't realize you were so fancy about your hair."

Bastian rolls his eyes. "I've been in that cell before. There are reasons I chose it."

"So, what, you've got a hidden stash in there?"

"Plenty of things a long-term prisoner might need to save for a rainy day."

Henry shakes his head. "Okay, I'm suitably impressed with your ingenuity. But you should really get back down to Level 15 before—"

"Don't be ridiculous. There are plenty of floors left to test, and—"

There's a knock at the door.

Henry and Bastian look at each other. "Expecting someone?" Henry asks.

"No. And who knocks on a broom closet door, anyway?"

Henry opens the door and somehow isn't surprised by the officer standing there.

"Captain? Mr. Lucas? There's been another murder," says Michaels.

Chapter 15

THERE ARE TWO bridges over the river and into the city. Both are heavily patrolled, which makes it that much odder that Senator O'Connell could jump off of one without anyone noticing.

"She actually died from hitting her head on the rock, not from drowning," the bridge guard says helpfully. He's not the same one who challenged Bastian for his ID last time they were here, but Bastian's always found the guards pretty interchangeable, so he might as well be.

"Police ruled it a suicide, of course," Henry says to Bastian as they look over the side. "They were pretty quick about it, too."

He turns to the guard. "Thanks for your help. We'll let you know when we're done so you can let traffic through again."

"Yessir. Oh, but you should probably know—there was a witness."

Bastian frowns. "That wasn't in the file."

"It's only just come to light. She wasn't on any of the security feeds. Must've found a blind spot."

"You should go talk to her," Bastian says quickly to Henry.

"Won't you want to…do what you do with her, too? Not just the location?"

Logic. Dammit. "Where is she?"

"The police took her back to the station for questioning," says the guard. "I can have them bring her—"

"No, you can take Captain Mortimer to talk to her there. Michaels and I will come when we're done."

Henry gives him a funny look but agrees, following the guard back to the far side of the bridge. Bastian's bought himself a little time, but he'll have to hurry.

It's going to be incredibly obvious that he doesn't want Henry around when he does reads, but what else can he do? He still doesn't want to be the one to tell Henry about his power. It's safer not knowing. Because if he became aware of it, Valentine would become aware that he's aware. And if Valentine knew, Wright would know, and that would mean….

"Mr. Lucas?" Michaels's voice is mild, but the almost imperceptible impatient-restless-edgy gives her away.

"Yeah. Right." He moves over to the point on the railing where the senator went over. He takes a deep breath, blows it out, and wraps his hands around the metal of the railing.

The gloves help a bit, but it's still an overwhelming burst when it comes, *a mind* pushing *while the senator stands there for a moment, then slowly climbs over.*

(There should be guards. Why aren't there—?)

He feels them then, turned away from the monitors, missing all the fun. (Fun?) *Dulled but not as gray as the senator; just encouraged to feel like looking the other way.* (Like the guards at the Hall.)

The senator's over the railing now, looking at the stinking river below. Her mind is numb, no emotion, like—

(Like Snyder in the cell, his mind gradually destroying itself because Bastian—)

There's something else there, too: another mind full of fear-curiosity-excitement— the witness, getting eyes on all of this so she can…what? She wants to pass on the information, get back at the senators who only ever ask her to bring them coffee and answer their phones—she'll show them, when she has this information and passes it along to the right people, like that reporter she's already been talking to. And when the story's out about a mentally unstable senator, when all the senator's votes come into doubt after this, they'll know they can't underestimate her—

(No desire to actually help Senator O'Connell, Bastian notes with disgust.)

The senator is jumping now, finally, and there's a feeling behind it then, while she's falling: glee-amusement-pride, he's done it again—

Bastian starts and tries to remember where he is, how much time has passed. After a moment, he registers a sound: ringing. Michaels's phone.

"Yes, Captain? I see. Please excuse me." She puts the call on hold and slips the phone into her shirt pocket. "Ready, sir?"

In some ways, this one is easier. He got to keep the gloves on, for once— unusual since he started being able to do this kind of intense read. The emotions here are recent and strong, easy to pick up. And the machine already has the basic emotional signature of the murderer, based on what Bastian's felt before. So it doesn't take long to get the latest read recorded.

When it's done, Bastian removes the electrodes and hands them back to Michaels, who gives him her phone.

"Henry? You found the witness?"

"No." His voice is terse. "She's gone. They realized it about an hour ago."

"Interesting time for a vacation."

"No one saw her leave the station. It's not on any of the security cameras, either."

Bastian makes a face. "Let me guess: the security guards suddenly found their attention somewhere else for exactly the amount of time she would've spent leaving."

"Yup. And the footage looks like it's been doctored—just like the footage from the Hall. I'll need to run it by Sybil or Kent to be sure, though."

"The scene feels similar to the other ones, too. I think the murderer has settled on an MO."

"Great."

"We'll come get you. There's work to do."

***

"Sybil got back to me—the security footage has definitely been altered," Henry says. "Not by a professional; just someone with a basic program and the right kind of access. Probably only took a few minutes. Enough to fool anyone who's not paying close attention."

"That must be what happened at the police station, too," Bastian says. "And since I doubt any of these security guards are aiming to get themselves fired, it was probably the murderer manipulating them."

Bastian, Henry, and Michaels have set up in the jail work room. It's about as clammy and claustrophobic as Bastian remembers, but there's also enough space to spread out and a decent chance of not being disturbed.

"You're sure it's another empath?" Henry asks.

Bastian frowns. "If you don't believe me—"

"No, it's just…there *aren't* any other empaths, right? So how can the murderer be one?"

"The last empath manifested two hundred sixteen years ago," Michaels says. "It seems unlikely that that empath would still be around and murdering people."

Bastian and Henry stare at her.

"Research is very important in order to maximize efficiency," Michaels says, going back to reviewing the case files on her tablet.

"Sybil couldn't determine what was actually cut from the footage, either," Henry continues. "It was only a few seconds each time, but it could be anything."

Bastian narrows his eyes at his screen. "Three murders, all of which look like suicides: drowning, carbon monoxide poisoning, and now jumping off a bridge. All senators with nothing in common in terms of age, race, ethnicity, or political viewpoints."

"Were any of them on the same committees? Or working on the same bills?" Henry asks.

"Not according to any of the Hall proceedings available to us," Bastian says. "They knew each other; that's it."

"Mr. Lucas's reads indicate that the suspect…coerced the victims to commit suicide," Michaels notes. "Of course, that's impossible to prove just by looking at the security footage. They look like suicides."

"Maybe that's what he had them cut," Bastian suggests. "If the murderer were close enough to get on camera, it would be proof—or at least an indication—that these *weren't* suicides. That someone else was there. And depending on the range of his power, he probably had to get fairly close to make sure the murders went according to plan."

"And you're sure they are? Murders, I mean?"

"*Yes*," Bastian says. "I could feel it when they—"

Henry looks at him expectantly.

(Ignore it, never mind what they think, they don't have to know what it means—)

He forces himself to say it calmly. "Empaths can do more than just feel other people's emotions or the echoes of emotions in a place. The more powerful ones can convince people to feel things. And to act on those feelings."

Henry frowns. "So this empath just…convinced the senators they felt like killing themselves?"

"The processed reads do show some indication of that kind of manipulation," Michaels admits. "And after all, Mr. Lucas would know—"

Bastian looks up sharply, and she immediately shuts her mouth.

The awkward silence doesn't have much time to settle before there's a knock at the door, and Catherine pops her head in. "Can I get you all anything? I'm heading to the cafeteria, and…."

Michaels clears her throat and stands. "Excuse me. I'll just go and make sure the major received our last report."

Catherine moves aside to let her pass, then hesitates for a moment. "Well. I'll leave you to it," she says at last, her voice laden with forced cheerfulness. She shuts the work room door behind her.

"Can you do that?" Henry asks quietly. "What the murderer did? Make people feel like…doing things?"

Bastian considers lying or yelling or playing dumb, pretending it's all theoretical, there's so much that's not known about empaths, maybe he was wrong….

"Yes," he says instead.

Henry's face closes off. "Have you?"

"Yes."

"Within the last few weeks?"

"*No.*" Bastian frowns. "You think *I* might be the murderer?"

"No. I just—it seems really unlikely that there would suddenly be two empaths, doesn't it?"

"New potentials manifest all the time." Even he can hear how stung he sounds. Stupid.

"Hey." Henry waits until Bastian is looking at him. "I didn't mean to imply anything. I'm just grasping at straws here."

"Yeah, well. That's a stupid straw."

Bastian pretends to look at his copy of the files for a while. (Don't say anything, let it go, you'll only make it worse—) "You didn't ask."

"Hmm?" Henry's gone back to his own screen, probably looking at the same data.

"What Michaels said. What I just told you. About how I—you didn't ask why I did it. Or when."

Henry shrugs. "If it wasn't in the last few weeks since the murders started, it doesn't matter."

"Seriously?" Bastian stares at him. "How can you—?"

(This is dangerous and pointless, and he needs to stop now, there's no reason to pursue this and make Henry think…whatever he'd think if he knew what Bastian did, all those interrogations like Snyder's, pushing past shields until they broke, making suspects feel the contrition so they'd confess—then the nausea and headaches and nosebleeds that got so bad, Valentine made him see Wright, and—)

Henry's looking at him, eyes wary and confused.

"You don't ask questions," Bastian says, his voice sharper than he meant it to be. "You just sit there and do your job and let yourself *not know* things. You take the first answer someone gives you and never bother to think about whether or not they're lying to you. It gets a little hard, and you back off, like you're too much of a coward to find out what's really going on."

Henry is silent, just looking at him. Then, with forced calm: "Unlike you, I have to think about the people who depend on me. I'm not happy about it, but I have to pick and choose my battles. If I get out of line, other people suffer. And since I actually give a shit about other people—"

"Okay, fine, you care about them. Good for you. But while you're busy caring, you're not thinking critically, and—"

"Who says I can't do both?"

Bastian scoffs. "No one does both. It's like the myth of multitasking—you're never actually doing two things at once; you're doing one thing and then the other thing really quickly."

"So? What's wrong with that?"

"Emotions are powerful. Dangerous. They bleed all over everything else. They *affect* everything else. You can't afford to have them, especially here. Better to have nothing at all so it can't be used against you."

"Is that what you've done? Just decided not to have feelings?"

"Yes."

Henry lets out a bark of a laugh. "Even if I hadn't seen proof to the contrary, that's not possible. Human beings feel things. That's how we work. It's not always pretty, and yeah, sometimes it means we make stupid decisions, but that doesn't mean you can just turn it off."

Bastian looks at him.

"You really think you—?" Henry pinches the bridge of his nose. "Bastian, you can't—"

"Maybe *you* can't. Maybe that's the real reason you haven't bothered to ask the big questions about what Valentine has you and your team doing. You say it's to keep your team safe, but maybe instead of worrying about people you've supposedly trained to take care of themselves, you should be asking why you use your *feelings* to keep yourself from having to deal with what this place is and what it does."

"And what does it do?"

Bastian looks directly at the security camera instead of at Henry. "It kills people. It collects them off the street, does horrible things to them, then spits them out to be Valentine's lackeys—assuming they survive. There's nothing noble or helpful or *good* about the compound or what your happy little retrieval team is doing. It's just your feelings that are deluding you into thinking you're some sort of hero."

Henry falls silent for a long time. Then he nods once, clipped and efficient. "You might be right," he says. "Maybe I am a coward for not asking. But at least I'm not a hypocrite who can't admit he's afraid."

Bastian opens his mouth to offer a good retort, but Henry rolls right over him. "You asked why I didn't demand to know what Michaels meant? It's because I'm not going to force a confidence. If it's not relevant to the case, you don't have to tell me. It's a question I don't need the answer to right now. I'm not interrogating you because I actually give a damn about not being an asshole. You should try it sometime."

He collects his things, gets to his feet, and walks out of the room.

***

Bastian wakes, groggy, to a tapping on the door of his cell. He feels like it's only been five minutes since he managed to close his eyes.

"Mr. Lucas?"

He grunts and sits up, rubbing his eyes. Michaels is at the cell door, looking as pristine as always.

"Ah, good, you're awake. I've received a report from the city police—they found the witness in a hotel on the south side of the city. They're going to move her into protective custody, but we've been invited to speak to her if we can arrive there within the hour."

"And what hour is that, exactly?"

Michaels checks her watch. "One AM."

It's been slightly less than five minutes since he closed his eyes, then.

He frowns. "City curfew is two o'clock. They'll close the entry points on us."

"I expressed that concern when this intelligence was given to me, and apparently it's possible for a compound officer to get special dispensation from the local police force if the situation warrants it."

"So you or Henry could...?"

Michaels hesitates. "I could try, but it would be better for the captain to request it."

"We'll have him do it, then." Bastian gets to his feet and notices her caution-worry-confusion. "What?"

"I was...unable to find Captain Mortimer to inform him of these developments."

"Did you try looking behind the couch?"

Michaels must be worried since she doesn't even try to acknowledge his brilliance. "I checked the barracks, his room, the cafeteria, the training room—all the places he's been known to spend his time, according to his file."

"And he's normally at those places at one in the morning?"

"Sometimes. But not now."

Bastian frowns. It's odd that Henry would just disappear. So that means... what, exactly? Is he angry with Bastian because of their argument? Henry doesn't seem like the kind of person who would be petty enough to sit out a mission just because he's had an argument with a...coworker? Friend? Whatever Bastian is? But then again, Henry just said he'd basically do anything for his team, including not asking questions, so maybe bailing on a mission is on that list for some reason.

Should Bastian try to find him? How would he even get permission for that? "Hey, Catherine, I need you to get the black coats to babysit me while I go track down the captain and see if he's still angry with me"? Probably better not to tempt fate by trying to sneak past them again, either—he barely managed it to test the jammers. But if something's really wrong....

So much for not having emotions. He *is* a hypocrite.

Anyway, this is a more efficient way to do it, right? If Henry's not around, he can't negate, and Bastian doesn't have to deal with the issue of whether or not to tell him what he can do in the first place.

"I'm afraid if we wait too long, we'll miss our window of opportunity to speak with the witness," Michaels says.

"The police are with her?" Bastian asks.

"They have a detail on her, yes, and she's agreed to stay put till we get there." Michaels pauses. "They're worried she'll figure out how to escape from their protection, though. She's shown interest in doing so. They want to move her to a more secure location as soon as possible."

"Escape from their protection" sounds like something Valentine would say. Bastian grimaces. "Okay. We'd better not wait for Henry, then."

As Michaels is letting him out, she clears her throat. "I'd like to apologize for being out of line earlier. I never meant to share information you weren't prepared to—"

"It's not a problem. Let's go."

She instantly drops it. "Certainly."

The loading dock is mostly devoid of people at this time of night. The quiet is actually relaxing—he can feel some techs nearby, but they're far enough away that it's not overwhelming. Michaels and the driver are calm enough that their emotions aren't too annoying, either.

Bastian watches Michaels load the machine into the back of the car, but before they can get in, the sound of boots on pavement interrupts them. Bastian turns and is in no way relieved to see Henry hurrying toward them.

"Sorry," he says, slightly out of breath when he gets in the car. "I lost track of time, and—never mind, I know we're in a hurry. Let's just go."

Bastian wants to ask, but that would be going back to the conversation from earlier, when to ask and when not to ask, and he'd rather avoid that particular minefield, especially on next to no sleep.

He still notices that Henry won't meet his eyes.

Chapter 16

HENRY SPENDS THE ride into the city on the phone, trying to get hold of someone on the police force who can grant them permission to leave after curfew. It takes him most of the trip to find someone even vaguely related to the request, at which point he gets an earful about security and the safety of millions and why he should be ashamed to want special accommodations when plenty of others, from dishwashers to senators, follow the rules with no complaints, and why do the compounds think they're somehow above the law, etc. etc. etc.

Then he has the great pleasure of being stuck in the hall, still navigating the phone tree, while Michaels and Bastian go in to see about the witness.

It doesn't help that he has a headache and can't remember anything that happened between leaving Bastian in the work room and waking up in his room five minutes after his phone pinged with the mission alert. It's happened before, but not often, and he should probably see a med tech about it. But there's no time, and at this rate, they'll be stuck in the city overnight, which will likely mean a stern talking-to from the major. Just the sort of confrontation Henry doesn't want after…but he's decided he's not going to think about anything Bastian said, so—

"Captain." Michaels is at his elbow. "You should see this."

That sounds ominous. Henry signs off with yet another unhelpful official he was trying as a last-ditch effort and gestures to Michaels to lead the way.

One of the hotel staff shows them through a back entrance to the kitchen not far from the lobby. Given the number of police officers milling around, Henry suspects he already knows what happened.

Michaels takes him to a door leading down into a dimly lit storage area. There's a long, narrow set of stairs. And a body at the bottom.

"They were withholding her information for security reasons, but they've agreed to pass on what they have, given the situation," Michaels tells him, handing over a tablet. "As I mentioned earlier to Mr. Lucas, Ms. Cambridge gave the police the very distinct impression that she feared for her safety. She mentioned several times that she thought they were being watched."

Michaels nods to the stairs. "It's unclear how Ms. Cambridge got out of her secure hotel room to begin with, but obviously, she ended up here. No one heard anything, and there aren't any security cameras in this area. The police are ruling it an accident for now. She fell down the stairs and broke her neck."

"See what she did for a living," Bastian calls, stepping around the scene markers and coming up the stairs.

Henry looks at the tablet. "Political aide to—Senator Reginald Haldis." He frowns. "I saw her with the senator when we visited the Hall. Seemed pretty interested in talking to a reporter. So, what, she just happened to be hanging around the bridge when O'Connell jumped, ran away from the police station, wound up here, and then fell down the stairs and died?"

Bastian snorts. "Of course not. She was murdered."

"You can confirm that with the read?"

"The read seemed…inconclusive when we were recording," Michaels admits. "Once it's properly rendered back at the compound, we'll know more."

"Inconclusive?" Henry raises his eyebrows.

"Interference," Bastian says, not looking at him.

"From the murderer somehow?"

"Maybe. There are a lot of reasons a read might be unclear. We done here?"

"Er. About that." Henry sighs. "No one would give us permission to leave after curfew. Maybe because we got to them so late."

Michaels checks her watch. "It *is* three o'clock."

"So?" Bastian sounds impatient.

"We'll have to hole up here overnight. I talked to the concierge, and they don't have any free rooms in this hotel, but they knew a place and called ahead for us. Not luxurious, but it was the best I could do."

"Are the rooms better than a jail cell?" Bastian asks dryly.

"I guess we'll see."

They leave the hotel and head for the car. Other than the street lights and a few signs, everything is dark and quiet. A few police are still around the building, but there aren't many pedestrians on the sidewalks. This isn't the sort of neighborhood where people loiter in alleys late at night.

Henry is reaching out to open the car door when Bastian stops suddenly. "I need you to go across the street."

Henry blinks at him. "What?"

"And have your gun ready."

"Bastian, I'm not going to—"

"Never mind." He starts walking away quickly, then breaks into a run.

"Captain?" Michaels has stopped on the other side of Henry, the bag with the machine in her hand.

"Stay here." Henry gets out his gun and runs down the street after Bastian.

Henry can't catch up right away, but when Bastian turns sharply into an alley, Henry nearly barrels into him.

The alley is empty.

"What was *that* all about?" Henry demands. "You could've—"

"Shut up. Stay behind me. Or better yet, do the going across the street thing."

Henry rolls his eyes. "I told you, I'm not going to—"

"Hello, Bastian."

A man materializes out of the shadows, a huge grin on his gaunt face. He's wearing a suit and fedora, but they don't fit well. In the meager light, Henry thinks they're probably secondhand. Or fifth-hand.

So much for no late-night alley loiterers in this neighborhood.

"Who are you?" Bastian demands.

The man looks over Bastian's shoulder at Henry, and his grin widens. "Well. That makes your life a bit harder, doesn't it?"

"Answer the question."

The man takes a step closer, and Henry raises his gun. "I don't think so."

That makes him laugh. "That's useless, you know. And just because your little thing works on Bastian here doesn't mean it'll work on me. He's a lot weaker than I am."

He looks over at Bastian, apparently unperturbed about having a weapon pointed at his head. "I'm version 2.0. But I'm betting you don't know anything about that, do you? The project didn't really pick up until you left."

"Start making sense," Bastian says. "Quickly."

Henry has most of his attention on the potential threat in front of them, but he can't help but notice that not only is Bastian tenser than Henry's ever seen him, he has sweat at his temples and looks like he's either going to take this guy down or turn and run the other way.

"Did you tell him what he is?" the man asks, nodding at Henry. "I bet you didn't. Wouldn't want Valentine figuring out he knows. We're no good to her if we have minds of our own, are we? He's neat, though. Not scared at all, even though I could make him kill himself in less than five seconds. It's helpful when they bring their own weapons, isn't it?"

"What's he talking about?" Henry asks under his breath.

Bastian doesn't answer. He's only got eyes for this man, and at the moment, those eyes are confused. "You can feel him."

"Have you told him you can't?"

Henry frowns. "You're the empath. The other one. The one who's been killing people."

The man gives him a pitying look before turning back to Bastian. "He's not very smart, is he?"

"Why are you killing them?" Bastian asks. "What's the point?"

The man shrugs. "I'm just the experiment, following orders. You know all about that, don't you, Bastian?"

"How do you know my name?"

The man laughs. "You think I didn't go through the files when Valentine wasn't looking? Only she probably *was* looking. She's always looking. She must've thought it wouldn't matter, but of course it did. Anyway, what I couldn't reach myself, I convinced other people to reach for me. And that's how I figured out what she was doing with me. Why she made me."

"She…made you?"

The man gives Bastian an ugly look. "We can't all be born with it. Not like you. Hundreds of years since the last of us…do you think that one was made, too? Or were they *special*, like you?"

"Anytime someone wants to explain what the hell is going on," Henry says pointedly.

The man turns to him and smiles. "Sorry, Captain. Didn't mean to leave you out. But this part's not really about you, so you can just—"

"Why are you killing the senators?" Bastian demands again.

"I told you: just following orders. Have to get as many of them in as I can before…." He leers at Henry. "Well, ask Bastian. He knows."

(Henry remembers the note on Bastian's file—"13 months or less if power used at current capacity"—)

"Enough." Henry steps out in front so he has a clear shot. "If you've done what you say you've done, the major will want to speak with you. Come with us." It isn't a request.

The man holds up his hands. "Don't shoot! I'll go quietly. Except obviously I won't. I'm not like Bastian, giving up my freedom at the first sign of a pretty face."

Henry tightens his trigger finger. "You'll want to stop talking now."

"Henry, don't—"

Whatever Bastian was going to say gets cut off when the man looks back at Henry, and suddenly Henry just…doesn't feel like doing anything. He lowers the gun slightly—but only slightly because some part of him still thinks it might be a good idea to keep it handy. He can't remember why, though. In fact, he's a little bit sleepy. (It's the middle of the night; shouldn't he be in bed?) Maybe he should sit down somewhere. The ground seems like a nice place to sit. (Only he's not supposed to be sitting, right? He's supposed to be…something.) The gun is heavy, and he's not sure how much longer he'll be able to hold it steady. Why did he get it out again…?

"Stop." He hears it from far off. "You shouldn't even be able to—How are you—?"

"Oh, come on. I don't even have to catch my breath. Not everyone's as weak as you are, you know." A pause. A grunt of effort. "Okay, he *may* be holding out better than the others did. I bet Valentine will want to know that."

"Don't—the longer you—"

"Scramble his brain?"

"*Stop.*"

"Hmm…nope. I think you're going to have to make me."

Henry realizes he's not on his feet anymore, but he can't remember when that happened. He's also pretty sure the person next to him is distressed, and he doesn't much like that, but a bigger part of him doesn't care and doesn't feel like doing anything about it. He's still holding the gun, but it's at his side now. He feels like dropping it altogether.

He's sitting in what appears to be a puddle when the person next to him suddenly leaps forward and punches the other man in the stomach. Then he kicks the guy's feet out from under him as well, sending him crashing to the pavement. The man on the ground is laughing and wheezing.

"You can't do it right, can you?" he says. "Can't even use your power when it matters. Have to rely on these crass, unrefined—"

Bastian (that's his name, right) kicks the man again, then turns to Henry. "Come on."

He grabs Henry's arm and hauls him to his feet. Henry leans on him as they hobble away from the alley in a bit of a rush. His head seems to be clearing up, but he's still confused.

"You're a coward!" yells the man in the alley.

Bastian's mouth is set in a firm line, but he doesn't say anything.

When they're closer to the crime scene, Henry comes back to himself, shaking his head and standing up straighter. "What…the *hell*…was *that?*"

Bastian lets go and hands him back his gun. (Henry doesn't remember losing it.) He looks grim and stays silent as they turn the corner, and the hotel comes into view. Henry's arm is still warm from where Bastian was holding it.

(Focus. Bastian doesn't think he asks enough questions? Okay. Question time.)

"*Hey.*" Henry stops and refuses to move until Bastian turns and faces him. "What just happened? Did we let a murderer go free?"

"You think you were in any state to bring him in?"

"Point. Still not explaining." And when he gets nothing in response to that: "We're well into the realm of things I need to know for the case, Bastian. Start talking."

Bastian flinches slightly and looks over at Michaels and the few remaining police officers just down the street. "I…all right. But not here. We're stuck in a hotel for the night, right? I'll explain there."

***

It's an awkward, though brief, drive to the hotel. Henry gives Michaels a quick summary of their encounter and promises to go over it again before they submit their report. There's a lot he doesn't understand, so he summarizes by saying they might've met the perp but were unable to secure him.

The clerk doesn't look particularly pleased to see them, but when Henry mentions he can arrange with the compound to get her some sort of financial reward for her hospitality on such short notice, she brightens up. She even takes time out of her busy evening managing a completely empty lobby to personally escort them to their adjacent rooms—the only two that were still available.

After reminding them all that they should be ready to leave at 0600, Michaels wishes them goodnight and follows the driver into their room.

Bastian goes right into the other room, which ends up being even less luxurious than Henry expected: brown carpet, brown walls with ugly paintings, one stiff-looking chair, and one bed.

Henry sits in the chair and crosses his arms. "Okay. What was all that? What did he do to me?"

Bastian flops onto the bed and sighs. "I told you. Some empaths can do more than just feel. They can make other people feel things, too. And do things."

"And that's what he was doing to me."

Bastian looks away. "Yes."

"You seemed surprised. That he could, I mean."

"He shouldn't have been able to."

"Why?"

"Because of what you can do."

Henry frowns. "What I can…?"

"You're an asset. Or you would be, if you were ever officially processed."

Henry stares at him. "I think I'd know if I manifested."

"Not if no one told you."

"People don't *tell* assets when they manifest. It's kind of hard to miss."

"Depends on the asset. Have you ever seen anyone use their power around you?"

"That guy did."

"Besides him."

"Of course. All the potentials—"

(He remembers Mariah, how the storm she made lessened when he got closer, how the team didn't even have to hit her with the serum before she couldn't use her power....)

"And Johnson—"

(But he didn't actually see Johnson manifest, and by the time Henry got there, things were calming down....)

"And you—"

(But when did Bastian actually use his power in Henry's presence? Henry's always been somewhere else during the reads. He was a little closer tonight with Stacey Cambridge, but he still didn't actually see it, and didn't Bastian say the read was muddled somehow...?)

Bastian raises his eyebrows.

Henry sighs. "Okay, no, not really. Not lately, anyway. But—"

"Why do you think I told you to go across the street earlier?"

"Because you were being an ass?"

Bastian's mouth twitches into something that's almost a smirk, but he doesn't say anything.

"Because…you were trying to use your power. To figure out where the murderer was. And you couldn't do it while I was around."

"Right in one."

"You can't use your power at all if I'm around?"

"I haven't quite figured out proximity—it seems to change—but yes. If you're too close, I can't feel anything."

"But that man, he—"

"I know."

"So is it just you?" Henry remembers the man saying Bastian was weak. Is it possible that someone's…whatever-it-is Henry's supposed to be able to do could only work on one person?

"No. It worked on Laurel, too. And anyway, Valentine's interest makes more sense if you can negate more than just one asset's power."

"Her interest?"

"You said you've been at the compound fifteen years, right?"

"Yeah."

"Where did you train?"

"With Major Alexis."

"So halfway across the country. Why would Valentine have Alexis transfer one of his men to her? She prefers to raise her own minions so she can mold them into whatever she needs them to be. If she scouted you, it was for a reason."

"But even if I can—what, negate?—assets' powers, I haven't always been able to do it. I can't even really do it now. I mean, I can't control it. So how would she have known? And what good would it be to her?"

Another thought occurs to him. "You knew," he says, almost accusingly. "It's not just that the major didn't tell me—you didn't, either. Why?"

Bastian fidgets with the duvet. "It's…complicated."

"I don't mind complicated. I mind people lying to me."

Bastian snorts. "If that's true, you're in the wrong profession."

This is close to the conversation in the work room, the not-asking-questions-and-being-a-coward bit. Bastian's not entirely wrong about all of that. Henry *doesn't* ask questions, not till recently, anyway, and even now, he'd never bring something like this to Major Valentine. Not when it might come back on his team.

But why didn't she want him to know? His whole career, his whole *life* might hinge on this thing he didn't even know he could do. So how can he not ask about it?

"I don't know why Valentine didn't tell you," Bastian says after a moment. "Maybe she wasn't sure until you manifested. Maybe your official blood tests showed something, but she wanted to wait and see what happened. Maybe she figured if you don't know, she can direct you toward who does and doesn't get negated."

"Like assigning me to babysit an empath so he can't use his power to escape again."

Bastian smiles slightly and says nothing.

"Okay, but what about you? Why didn't *you* tell me?"

The pause is longer this time, long enough that Henry doesn't think he's going to speak at all. But then: "If you know, if you use your power consciously and someone sees it, they'll admit you into the asset program."

"So? You said it yourself about Johnson—there'd be testing, sure, but wouldn't that help me learn how to use this power? How to help people and—what?"

"That's not how the program works."

"What do you mean?"

"The asset program, it's an experiment. A scientific study. So yes, you get trained, but not how you're thinking. Valentine likes to catch manifestations early, preferably in childhood, so she can observe over long periods of time. Adults have to be caught quickly because their window of opportunity is shorter."

"Shorter how?"

"There's an optimal testing period, right after the manifestation happens. Kids tend to have more resilience for the testing. Adults, not so much."

"So what happens to them? The ones without the resilience?"

"They die."

Henry stares at him. "You're saying the major kills assets?" Smith would have a field day with this.

"Not directly. She'd much rather we survive so we can be assigned tasks and make ourselves useful. But the testing doesn't always turn out that way. Dr. Wright isn't always…kind. He has more important things on his mind than keeping his subjects alive."

"That's why you hate him," Henry says quietly. "The testing."

Bastian grimaces. "He was…particularly interested in me. There were quite a few tests, and they weren't pleasant."

"Because you were the first empath they'd seen in hundreds of years."

"But not the only one, apparently."

Henry frowns. "What do you think he meant? That the major 'made' him?"

"Another experiment, I suppose. Something to create and augment his powers? He's stronger than me. And you."

They fall silent. Henry can hear faint car noises from the road and some murmuring voices from a few rooms down. The city may be relatively quiet after curfew, but it's never silent.

"You wanted to keep me out of the asset program," he says. "So I wouldn't be in danger."

"Yes," Bastian says irritably. "Weren't you listening the last five minutes?"

"And when I asked you if you could read me, and you wouldn't answer, it was because you didn't want me to know what I can do, since it might—"

"*Yes.* Are we going to rehash this whole conversation now?"

"I'm sorry."

Bastian blinks at him. "What?"

"Before, in the work room, when I said—I made it sound like you were selfish, like you didn't give a shit about other people, when really, you were…."

"Yeah. Well." Bastian looks uncomfortable. "I might have said some things about you that aren't completely accurate. I mean. You did try to hold a murderer at gunpoint to protect someone else. And you just grilled me on something I'd been keeping from you. Those aren't things a coward would do."

Henry shakes his head and smiles. "Maybe not a coward, but an idiot might. Try to point a gun at a massively powerful asset, I mean. Or demand another one tell me things he'd rather not."

Bastian sits up and meets his gaze. "You're not an idiot, Henry."

Henry finds he can't look away for a few heartbeats. (Stop it, there are more important things to focus on, like how the team forgot Johnson or how Henry lost time or what the hell he's supposed to do now that he knows what he knows, not—)

"Get some sleep," he says after an awkward silence.

Bastian makes a face. "I'm not—" A yawn interrupts the rest of his sentence. "Oh, shut up."

"We only have a few hours before we have to get up and head back to the compound. Sleep while you can."

"You're not my—"

"What, babysitter? I think you'll find that I am."

Bastian huffs and rolls over to one side of the bed, facing the wall. He kicks his shoes off and curls up on top of the covers like a cat. It's…cute. Which is something Henry will never tell him because being glared to death doesn't sound appealing.

Henry gets up to shut off the light, then goes back to the chair. He shifts around a bit, trying to get comfortable. He's slept in worse places on missions, so he's not too concerned about it. Even just twenty minutes would be—

"What are you doing?"

In the dark, he can only make out the vague outline of a lump on the bed. "Sleeping?"

"Not in that chair. Unless you prefer to sleep while being tortured."

"It's fine."

Is it possible to hear an eye roll? "Forget what I just said. You *are* an idiot. Come take the other half of the bed so we can shut up about it and get some sleep."

Henry hesitates, realizes he's hesitating, and sternly tells himself not to be stupid. He drags himself over to the bed, discarding his shoes and jacket, and gets under the covers, putting an extremely respectable distance between them.

"I kick in my sleep," he says for absolutely no reason.

"Not a deal breaker." Bastian yawns again. "Good night."

"Night."

Chapter 17

HEY, CAN YOU hear me?

Obviously, Bastian thinks, he just needs to give up sleep entirely, since the universe isn't about to work in his favor, as far as that's concerned. "Laurel?"

Oh, good! It's easier to reach you now. Where are you?

"I'm in the city." He rolls over and looks at Henry, who's on his side with his back to Bastian. His shoulder is moving regularly up and down, so he's probably asleep.

What, you got out? I'll come—

"No, it's not like that." He tries to keep his voice as low as possible so he doesn't wake Henry. "Look, now isn't a good—"

(surprise-amusement-glee) *Oh! OH! You're—*

Bastian stuffs down his embarrassment. "Whatever you think I am, I'm not. What do you want?"

Okay, we're going to talk about this when I see you again because I can't tell what's going on, but you're projecting a lot of—

"Laurel!"

Right, sorry. I just wanted to tell you about things that have been happening at the clearing. I think they may have something to do with your compound.

"What things?"

Disturbances. My plants are getting ripped up, only not by animals. The trees are telling me about seeing someone in the forest they haven't seen before. Yesterday, there was a man rooting around like he was looking for something or maybe just trying to get through the barriers I set up. The skunk cabbage didn't like him much.

"Just one guy?"

Yeah, that's what's so weird. Would your compound authorize only one person to go sniffing around like that? I wouldn't say it's a compound thing at all except the trees said he smelled like compound.

"What did he look like?"

Plants aren't good at describing people, but...tall? Thin? Weird top?

"Top?"

Like a hat, I think.

Bastian's chest tightens. "A fedora?"

Is that a hat?

"Never mind. Anything else you can tell me?"

Only that they viewed him as a threat—and not just because he tore up some brush. I think the plants are worried he'll do more to upset their environment. And if he's messing around in the forest like that, it's only a matter of time before he finds the clearing.

"Laurel, I really think you should leave there."

(determination-loyalty...love?) *I can't do that, Bastian. There are things here I have to protect.*

That's more serious than she's ever been about the clearing and her reasons for staying. He's always known there's more going on with her and that place, but if the murderer is closing in, for whatever reason....

"Are the things you have to protect things you can take with you? Because if the man in the forest is who I think he is, he's already killed four people and shows no sign of stopping."

There's a long pause, long enough that Bastian thinks Laurel might have severed the connection. But then: *The forest will protect me for as long as it can. But if this man is someone you know, I think you should come get him. Soon.*

"Yeah, I think we should, too."

I mean, he's not always here. Sometimes he's away for days on end. The trees have only spotted him here and there, anyway. But he always comes back, so—

She stops. *You* do *know this guy, don't you?*

Bastian hesitates, then says, "Yeah. Henry and I saw him for the first time today, but we've known he's around. Or suspected, at least."

It's Henry now, is it?

"Okay, how do I terminate this thing?"

No, wait! I'm sorry, I really am. I shouldn't tease you about this. If there's someone there looking after you, then I'm really—

"He's not *looking after* me. I'm not a child."

He's pretty sure she just thought *could have fooled me*, but he may have imagined it.

It's not a bad thing, you know, Laurel says. *Having someone care about you. Caring about someone else.*

(It is, though. It's weak and painful, and it gives them one more thing to use against you, and if there's anything he's learned about emotions by being an empath, it's that emotions are *worthless*, they're the perfect excuse for idiotic behavior, just like he was telling Henry, and if you let yourself be swayed by them, you deserve whatever you get—)

He chokes it all down; no need to have this argument with Laurel, too. "Do what you need to do to stay safe, all right? This guy leaves a mess wherever he goes, and I don't want to have to deal with yours."

He can feel her smile. *I'm worried about you, too, Bastian. Take care of yourself, and I'll check in again soon.*

Of course that's not at all what he meant, but she's gone from his mind, so all he can do is try to go back to sleep.

Nineteen years ago

THE BLACK EYE *still smarts, but the dog got away, and that's all that matters. Dad will get angry and maybe give him another black eye, but so what? Henry did the right thing. Why can't people just* do the right thing? *It's not that hard; all you have to do is not be an asshole. And it helps to not care about anything else, even if it hurts.*

(It usually hurts.)

Anyway, it's done, and if there are consequences, he can deal with them when his parents get home. The school's probably already called them, and they'll be pissed.

He does feel bad about causing trouble, but who kicks a dog? And the teacher just standing there…what sort of grown-up doesn't do anything about something like that?

He puts down his backpack in the hall and realizes his shoulders are sore, too. Guess shoving Adams into the mud and wailing on him wasn't the best idea. Worth it, though. Worth it to see the dog who wandered onto school grounds look at him once, then scurry off, only limping a little, its tail even wagging a bit.

He always wanted a dog, but Dad never let him. Said Henry couldn't handle the responsibility, that he wouldn't know how to take care of it. Henry would, though. Or he could learn. It'd be something to keep him company, since his parents are away so much. Something to tell his thoughts to. Something that would actually listen. Something to play with. To protect.

The doorbell rings.

His parents never ring the bell, since they live here and all. And no one ever comes for a visit. So…someone from school?

He goes back to the door, opens it, and finds a man and a woman on the doorstep. They're dressed in something like army fatigues, and they're wearing sunglasses.

"Henry?" says the woman, smiling at him. She takes off her glasses, and he can see her pale blue eyes. The smile is a bit stiff, like she's happy to see him but not used to smiling about things.

"Yes?"

She holds her hand out to shake. "My name is Major Valentine, and this is Major Alexis. May we come in?"

Henry ignores the hand and eyes them warily. "I'll need to see some ID."

"Sensible," says Major Alexis. They both hand over their IDs. Henry opens the door a bit more so he can take them.

They look like the police badges on TV, only there's way less information on them: just names, pictures, a seal, and a number—two letters and a series of digits. He can't tell if they're real or not, but better safe than sorry.

"Talking like this is fine," Henry says. "What do you want?"

"We'll only take up a moment of your time," Major Alexis says as Henry hands back the IDs. He doesn't take off his sunglasses, but he smiles as well. "We'd like to offer you an opportunity."

"What kind of opportunity?"

"Major Alexis and I run a school system of sorts," says Major Valentine. "A collection of training facilities for people like you with extraordinary abilities."

Henry snorts. "I'm not—"

"It's not only magic and flying saucers that are extraordinary, Henry," says Major Alexis. "Even normal, everyday people can do extraordinary things. Stand up for people who can't stand up for themselves. Maybe not just people; maybe animals, too."

So they know about school today. Somehow. "I—"

"We know you've attended a lot of schools over the past few years," says Major Valentine, sounding sympathetic. "It's probably been very difficult. But we believe we can help. We can train you in ways that will help you help others. Give you a place to truly belong."

It sounds good, if cheesy. And impossible. Whoever these people are, there's no way they really want him at their school or whatever—this is obviously a mistake. He's not special. And there's another thing, too.

"You'll have to talk to my parents," he says.

"Your parents have already been informed, actually," says Major Valentine. She takes a folded piece of paper from her breast pocket and hands it over to him. "They've left the final decision up to you, of course. But you have their approval."

Henry stares at the paper, which has both of his parents' signatures on it. "How—?"

"We spoke with your school a few days ago and had them get in touch with your parents before they returned from their last trip. I apologize that we're only informing you just now, but it took us some time to make the final arrangements."

"*The decision is yours, Henry,*" *says Major Alexis.* "*But I'd be pleased to have you at my facility. We believe you have aptitude for this kind of work.*"

Henry tries to imagine what that would be like: being somewhere people actually want him. Where he could do some good. Where doing the right thing wouldn't be so unusual.

"*I…as long as it's all right with my parents, I'll just—um—get my things.*"

"*No need.*" *Major Valentine smiles at him.* "*We'll have them sent to you. I want you to know you're making an excellent choice, Henry. We'll make sure we're worthy of your trust.*"

She holds out her hand again, and this time he shakes it.

Chapter 18

A FEW HOURS later, they're in the car on the way back to the compound. Bastian is oddly silent while Henry runs Michaels through their encounter with a little more detail.

He doesn't say anything about how he's apparently an asset himself. (He also definitely doesn't think about waking up to the warmth of Bastian curled up against his back or how he'd suddenly wanted to turn around and—)

"So we know who the murderer is," Michaels says.

"Sort of," Henry agrees. "We can give a description to the hackers and see if they can have the police distribute it in case he shows up in the city. But he's still a John Doe in terms of identity, and we don't really have proof that he's the murderer beyond what he told us, which wouldn't hold up. Bastian wasn't able to do an actual read on him; we were a bit busy."

"You're certain he's an empath, though?"

"Yes." It's the first thing Bastian's said since they got in the car. It's the only thing he says, too.

Henry and Michaels eye each other. "I'll talk to the hackers when we get back," Henry says.

"I'll file the recording from the Stacey Cambridge scene and report to the major on our progress."

That's not quite the way it goes, though.

As the car pulls into the vehicle loading dock, Henry sees several black coats waiting for them. They let Michaels go on her way, which she does—with a quick look back at Bastian and Henry before the black coats close ranks.

"Captain. Mr. Lucas. Follow us, please," says the leader.

The black coats take them to Major Valentine's office. Kind of overkill to send them an escort, since they both know perfectly well how to get there, so it must be a show of force. But why bother?

The black coats don't leave when they get to the major's office, either. Instead, they follow Henry and Bastian inside, where the major herself is standing behind her desk.

"Gentlemen," she says, nodding to them. "I trust the case is going well?"

"Four people are dead, so you'd have to have an interesting definition of 'well,'" Bastian says.

"We're following a few leads," Henry adds quickly. "We should have more to report once Michaels has finished going through the recordings."

"Good. Now, Captain, I wanted to let you know that you'll be down a man for the next few days, but I expect you and Officer Michaels to remain on top of the mission." She turns to one of the black coats. "Corbett, please escort Sebastian to Dr. Wright on Level 13."

Out of the corner of his eye, Henry sees Bastian freeze.

"Is that necessary, ma'am?" Henry asks carefully. "I haven't seen any evidence of medical concerns—"

"Merely routine, I assure you both." She smiles at Henry in a way that might be called patronizing. "I appreciate your concern for your charge, Captain, but this is hardly your area of expertise. You should stick to your assignments: assisting Officer Michaels and dealing with any missions that may come up in the meantime regarding potentials."

She turns back to Bastian, who is silent, his face completely blank. "I'd suggest being cooperative. It tends to make things run more smoothly, wouldn't you agree?" She nods over his shoulder. "You can take him down now."

The black coat comes forward, cuffs in hand, but Valentine shakes her head, a hint of a smile still on her face. "That won't be necessary, will it, Sebastian?"

"No." His voice is dull but even.

(You can't take him, Henry wants to scream. You already took Johnson to who-knows-where, you'd have to be blind not to see how much Bastian hates the doctor, stop taking people away from me, people I'm supposed to look after, stop making me watch this and know there's nothing I can do—)

He tries to catch Bastian's eye as the black coats lead him away, but Bastian's too busy looking straight forward and keeping his face empty. Maybe he really can shut off his emotions.

"Captain? I believe you have duties to attend to," says Major Valentine.

Henry swallows, then nods to her. "Yes, ma'am."

He leaves the office and wonders what the hell he's supposed to do now.

***

Kent glances up from his screen and sighs when Henry enters. "Look, Captain, I don't have anything new to tell you since yesterday."

Henry comes over to his station. "No more hits on that image I had you put together?"

"The same number there were yesterday and the day before." Kent switches off his monitor before Henry can see the screen—not that he'd understand any of it. "That number's zero, in case you forgot."

"Okay. But you'll let me know?"

"Yes, sir."

"Good. And the other project?"

"Ah, that one." Kent gets to his feet. "Let me show you."

They go out the back entrance and through the security door, where Kent pauses a moment before turning to Henry. "Five minutes, Captain."

"It's been two weeks. Nothing?"

"What, the brilliant way I pulled off level 3 data access for us isn't enough?"

"I'm sure unfinished maps for unlabeled levels will come in handy at some point, but none of that does me any good if I don't know where I'm trying to go."

Kent sighs again. "I have every bit of software hitting the dark areas of the compound, but I haven't found either Lucas or Johnson. I'm only scratching the surface here—I can't just go around hacking cameras in an area that closely guarded."

"I know." Henry rubs his eyes. "And the jammers?"

"I've gotten one up to fifteen minutes, but any more and it overheats."

"Fifteen minutes isn't going to cut it. I need at least an hour, Kent—probably more, depending on what's down there."

"Just give me more time—"

"They may not *have* time."

Kent looks at him silently for a moment, then rubs his neck. "I can't do better than I'm already doing on enhancing the jammers, but as for the search algorithm…it might go faster if I only searched for one of them instead of both."

Henry's stomach sinks. "There's no way I'd get more than one chance to go down there."

"I know."

"I'd have to choose one."

Kent says nothing.

"I can't do that. I can't just leave one of them to—" He stops, pulls himself together. "Make it happen, Kent. Soon." He turns to go.

"Captain? I did find something odd. Hard to get a good look, since security is more intense there than anywhere else, but…."

"But?"

"There's a room on the south side of Level 20. Huge, open, filled with… something. Small boxes or old videos or books, maybe? It's some sort of storage facility. Doesn't seem like it's related to your objective, but it's weird. If you got down there and needed information, that might be a good place to start."

Henry can't see how anything that won't definitely help him find Johnson and Bastian could be useful at this point, but at least it sounds like Kent's been able to find abnormal locations, which is probably good.

"Thanks." He pauses. "Were you being straight about the image?"

"Yeah. Whoever your John Doe is, he's not in any database, and no one's reported seeing him."

"Great." Henry blows out a breath. "Thanks, Kent. I appreciate all of this."

"No problem. Well. It *is* a problem, but come on, it's boring around here without Lucas to stir up trouble, isn't it?"

Henry gives him a half-hearted smile. "Something like that."

Two weeks, Henry thinks as he heads back down the hall. Two weeks and four missions to bring in potentials. No evidence beyond his own eyes and Bastian's reads that this John Doe even exists. Major Valentine has been extremely unimpressed with their status reports, claiming that they'll need much more if they're going to bring in the murderer.

Henry asked Michaels about the reads—he'd assumed that they constituted solid evidence in past cases—but she mentioned, with some concern, that the recordings had turned out unusually vague. Henry assumes that's his fault. One more frustration.

At least he understands what's going on with the potential retrievals in terms of his power. The closer he gets, the less often they need to use the serum. He's considered not going in with the contact team so he can see what happens when he's farther away, but in the heat of a possibly catastrophic encounter seems like a bad time to experiment. And his team would notice.

He hasn't brought up Johnson again, and no one else has, either. For all intents and purposes, Johnson has stopped existing, and the team seems fine with that.

Henry knows he should leave all of this alone. Definitely shouldn't involve Kent, who could get into serious trouble for trying to breach security. But not doing anything is just as bad as doing something. He's started asking questions, and now he can't stop.

The elevator doors have barely opened on Level 1 when he's intercepted by Michaels. "Captain, the major would like to see you."

For a split second, Henry wonders how Major Valentine could possibly know about his visit to Kent, particularly the part in the jammed hallway. Then he realizes he's being paranoid, and this must be about something else.

"Thanks, Michaels. I'll go now."

"Anything new from Kent?"

Okay, maybe not paranoid. "Not yet."

She nods and heads off down the hallway in the opposite direction. Henry squares his shoulders and proceeds to the major's office.

She answers after his first knock, and when he goes in, she's seated behind the desk but looking up. "Captain, thank you for coming. You can close the door behind you."

That's not ominous. (Not unusual, either. Calm down.)

He stands there at parade rest until she continues speaking. "How have your missions been going?"

He's thrown again. She never asks about routine missions. "Fine, ma'am. All of the potentials were brought in without difficulty."

"And without having to use the serum, if these notes are correct." She's flipping through files on a tablet. "Would you say that's unusual?"

"Not particularly. My team tries to avoid using it if possible."

"Why?"

"Well…because it can be a jarring experience for the potential. We prefer to encourage potentials to come with us of their own free will. It conserves the serum for more difficult acquisitions, too."

"But not using the serum would be more dangerous for your team, wouldn't you say?"

"Actually—"

Major Valentine puts down the tablet and laces her fingers together. "The serum was created to protect our teams from potential- and asset-based threats. A potential, as I'm sure you'll remember, hasn't been trained and may not even be aware of their power. That means any interaction with them could end with an altercation in which people get hurt. I'm sure you don't want anyone on your team to be hurt, Captain."

Don't think of Johnson. "No, ma'am."

"I thought not. Then why expose them to danger by not using the serum? Are you not provided with enough at the beginning of each mission?"

"We receive an adequate supply, thank you. I just thought the best method for bringing in a potential would be one where—"

"Perhaps you should leave the strategic thinking of this nature to your superiors and focus on following orders. If you truly care about your team, I know you'll want to protect them, particularly when you're given everything you need to do so."

He clenches his jaw, then forces himself to relax. "Of course, ma'am."

"Very good." She gives him an odd (disappointed?) look. "That will be all."

He nods and turns toward the door.

"Oh, one more thing."

"Ma'am?"

"I understand you had an incident with your team a few weeks ago. A manifestation."

"Yes, that's correct."

"That kind of disruption can be difficult for everyone involved," she says sympathetically. "I wanted to offer my assurances that Officer Johnson is being taken care of in the asset program. There's no need to worry about him any further."

He wants to believe her, that Johnson is doing all right, that there's no need to worry. But he can't. Not till he's seen it with his own eyes.

"Thank you, ma'am."

"If you find yourself with…lingering issues regarding what happened, please let me know. I have access to a resource that could smooth things over."

Smooth things—? "What sort of resource?"

"The particulars aren't essential for you to know. But it could certainly make your life easier and lead to fewer problems on missions. It's already been administered to your team, and they seem to be performing admirably, given their leadership."

He digs his fingernails into his palms and is suddenly extremely glad he's got his hands behind his back where she can't see them. "You dosed my team with something without telling me?"

"No, Captain," she says, voice suddenly steely. "I initiated a protocol that helped them. And you'd do well to remember to whom you're speaking."

He deflates slightly. "Excuse me, ma'am. I'm just…confused."

"Obviously." She sighs. "I wouldn't even have brought it up, except I know you're having trouble with your duties, so I thought perhaps—"

"I'm not having trouble with—"

"—you might benefit from the same treatment your team has already gotten."

"Would that be a treatment that made them forget Johnson ever existed? How exactly does that help them?"

The room is suddenly very quiet. Then: "Have a care, Captain."

(They're my team, they're my responsibility, you can't just do something to them and not tell them, not tell *me*, accuse me of not caring about their safety when all the while you're doing things behind my back with consequences I don't even know about, how *would* I know, no one tells me anything, do you really expect me to just shut up and—?)

"I'm sorry, Major," Henry says, struggling to keep his voice even. "I appreciate your advice, and I'll definitely take it under consideration."

She eyes him steadily for a moment, then nods. "Good. You may leave."

He does, and he even manages not to punch anyone when he's back out in the hall.

Chapter 19

BASTIAN'S DREAMING. AT least, he thinks he is. Everything has a weirdly muddled tinge to it, the edges soft and blurry.

He thinks he's in the clearing—all the green is a bit of a giveaway—but he can't feel Laurel anywhere. It suddenly seems really important to find her, but he's lying on his back and can't move.

"Don't worry about it," says a voice. "In fact, you don't need to worry about any of it anymore. She made me to replace you, you know. Right here, somewhere around here, that's where it started. I just need to find it."

Bastian tries to crane his neck to see where the voice is coming from, but he immediately hurts everywhere *and has to stop.*

(He's felt this before, only one time this bad, when they'd had to strap him to the gurney, and his throat was raw from screaming, and he doesn't remember how he made it to where he'd stashed Kent's jammer, how he made it out of the compound and to the clearing and Laurel and—)

"Hey, can we focus here? We were talking about me."

"You were…talking about you," Bastian mutters. Every word is a struggle.

Someone crouches down next to him. He sees the fedora out of the corner of his eye. "You're calling me John Doe, huh? Like I don't even have a name. I suppose that's true. If I had one, I forgot. You can forget a lot when Wright gets out his scalpel, can't you?" Bastian can only see half the grin at this angle, but it's more than enough.

"There's something human about it, right? Wanting to know who you are? I've been just slipping a little suggestion to one of those hackers, and whoop! Off they run to find me what I need."

His voice goes dark. "Only they can't find it, can they? So much good stuff about the asset program in that library, but nothing about me, not that I've found yet. And Valentine's not even paying attention. I put in all this effort to find what she doesn't want me to find, and she just ignores it."

"How...do you know her?" Bastian manages. "What is...she to you?"

"She's Mom," says John Doe. "Obviously. Just like she is to you."

Bastian frowns. (Even that hurts. Fun.) "She's not...my mother."

"She made you, right? Not like she made me, but close enough. She took you in when you had nowhere to go and taught you how to be her tool. Nothing more motherly than that. Then you ran away, and she had to think of something else—me. Only I wasn't going to sit around, either."

"How...are you even...?"

"What, inside your dream? Do you like it? I rummaged around a bit in your head and saw that you've done this kind of thing with that plant girl of yours. So think of it like that, only much better because we're both full-on empaths. And I'm strong enough to give you visuals, see?"

He waves a hand, then sighs when Bastian doesn't look impressed. "There's so much you don't know about being an empath. So much you can do. Like making people kill themselves. Oh, wait, you already know that one."

"I...didn't...."

"Well. Not like I did. Not with my level of showmanship. But you did. Just think of poor Snyder! He's dead now, in case you were wondering. The last hacker I controlled looked it up for me, all the people who died because of you. They're not all on file, of course, but that one is. See, I make them feel like they want to die. You just destroy their minds so there's nothing left. Which of us is worse, I wonder?"

Now Bastian hurts everywhere, and he feels sick. "Get...out of my...head."

John Doe laughs. "But it's so much fun! You have all these dinky little shields set up in here because you're afraid of your own feelings—which are really pathetic, by the way; I can see why you want to avoid them. The captain? Really?"

Bastian grits his teeth. "Get. Out."

"What do you think she'd do if she knew about him? If she knew that he knows what he can do? I mean, he was always going into the asset program eventually, but if he knows about his power and she knows he's a weakness for you, well—"

"Shut. Up."

"Anyway, you should know that I'll probably kill him. Not because she tells me to, but just for the fun of it. Your little friends at the compound, too—you know, for someone who claims not to like people, you sure care about lots of them. Oh, and the plant girl, that'll be fun—"

"GET OUT."

The clearing is silent then. He throws every bit of strength he has left (not much) into shielding, but he doesn't know if it works because he's already drifting.

Chapter 20

HENRY'S LEAVING HIS room to meet his team for a retrieval mission when someone grabs his arm and pulls him around the corner. He has his gun out and pointed at their face before he realizes it's Kent.

"Good way to get shot," Henry says irritably, putting his weapon away and wondering why this keeps happening to him.

Kent looks like a bleary-eyed mole just emerging from underground, but he doesn't seem particularly alarmed about having just had a close encounter with a firearm.

"I have something," he says.

Henry glances at the camera near the ceiling. "You want to talk about this here?"

Kent holds up a jammer, hiding it partially between his body and the wall. He looks around, making sure they're alone, then grabs Henry's hand and puts a similar device into it. "Thirty minutes. It's the best I could do. And before you get all grouchy, I made a modification so it can recharge faster. When the timer runs out, all you have to do is hide for five minutes to avoid the cameras, and then it'll restart."

"Hide? Where?"

"How should I know? I've never been to Level 19."

"You found them there?"

"Not exactly."

"Kent—"

"There are heat signatures, database evidence that people matching their descriptions were brought down there around the correct times. And that level

3 data access let me decode a bit of one of the maps, which shows that Level 19 has a bunch of experiment rooms. Your jammer has that info on it now, for what it's worth. But security down there is intense, so I can't tell you anything for sure." He gives Henry an odd look. "You're really going after them?"

Henry runs his thumb over the device he's holding, then hides it in his jacket pocket. "Yeah. I really am."

It feels weird to say it, like he's crossing some sort of line—which he is. If he's caught, he could very well end up in the jail block for the rest of his life.

So not unlike an asset, then.

"One more thing." Kent pulls a gray, rectangular object from his pocket and hands it over. "I assume you're going to want to get in places, not just peep through windows. This beauty is an earth magnet, courtesy of one of the computers in the hacker bay. It'll confuse the electronic doors into opening."

Once Henry's got that stowed as well, Kent nods. "You didn't get any of this tech from me, of course," he begins.

"I know. But thank you."

Kent shakes his head. "Just—if you find Lucas, tell him I know what I want as compensation. Though obviously now I'll need to add a few more things for all the emotional and psychological damage this is causing me."

Henry stifles a smile. "Noted."

Kent starts to switch his jammer off, then pauses. "I really hope you find them."

"Yeah. Me, too."

Kent nods again and flips the switch. His face and demeanor change immediately. "Captain, I swear, there haven't been any hits on that John Doe image," he says loudly. "Calling me up here doesn't change that."

"I need answers, Kent," Henry says, playing along. "Do whatever you have to do to get results. People are dying. It's our job to find this guy and put a stop to it."

Kent rolls his eyes. "Sure, fine. Just don't call me up here again. Too much light makes my skin break out. Sir." He nods almost imperceptibly and hurries back down the hall to the elevators.

After the mission, then, Henry thinks, forcing himself not to keep touching the jammer to make sure it's still there. After the mission, he'll figure out what's going on.

Or put an end to his career for good.

***

The area on the far side of the city is drier, but it's not a full-blown desert. Or it wasn't until today.

They're only able to take the vehicle about halfway there before having to abandon it by the side of the road so it will still have all its parts to take them home. Smith grumbles a little, but when Valdez points out she'll get to stay back and won't have to directly interact with the sandmaker potential, Smith goes quiet. Probably grateful she won't have to fish as much sand out of every nook and cranny once this is over.

Henry isn't looking forward to interacting with someone who can do this, either. His eyes are already stinging with the sunlight and the sand in his face, despite the protective coverings he's wearing.

And it's going to take awhile, his brain helpfully points out. Unless this potential is remarkably agreeable—which pretty much never happens—there's no way Henry's getting back in time to go on his other mission tonight. He'll have to wait until at least tomorrow and hope that Bastian and Johnson can hold on that long.

The walk feels ten times as long as it actually is, according to their instruments. Henry tries to keep it slow to avoid alarming the potential, but there's nowhere to hide, so they were probably spotted ages ago.

The sand begins to kick up as they get closer. Not a sandstorm, exactly, but definite agitation. The distance team sets up a perimeter with Smith organizing things, while others fan out to see to their duties as well. Contact team follows Henry in closer to the potential: a man in black, standing quietly and looking out at the horizon.

Henry tries not to notice, but he can't help it. As his boots sink into the sand with each step, the swirl of not-quite-storm around him quiets. It's subsiding for everyone, but especially around him. No one looking could think for even a moment that he doesn't have something to do with it.

"I've heard about you," says the man in black, turning around to face Henry. "Stories saying that no matter how strong we get, there'll always be someone who could take us down. A fail-safe."

He peers at Henry like he's assessing a threat. "I thought it was a secret, shady organization. Government operatives working behind the scenes, something like that. Not just some"—he tips his head, a slight smirk taking up residence at the corner of his mouth—"I don't know, some guy in fatigues who looks like he's in a B-grade war movie."

"You really know how to build up someone's ego, don't you?" Henry mutters. Then, louder: "Alex Barrett?"

"That's me. Who are you? I mean, besides the obvious."

Henry glances at the rest of the contact team. They're watching the potential—and him. But he can see their tension; they know something's up, even if they don't know what. This isn't the usual potential chatter.

"Captain Henry Mortimer," he tells Barrett. "I'm going to reach into my pocket and get my—"

"I don't need to see ID, Captain. I get why you're here. There are rumors in the city, sometimes even warnings about where to go to avoid you people. I'm not really into all that stuff, though. I just want to be left alone to do what I do and be who I am."

"Doing what you do has turned miles of this area into sand dunes. Pretty sure you don't have permission to redecorate. Or force people out of their homes."

Barrett shrugs. "Testing. Calibrating. You know how it is."

"I don't."

"Really?" Barrett takes a few steps toward him, and there's an immediate buzz in Henry's ear. He motions for the distance team to stand down for now.

Barrett looks around and nods. "I get it. You don't want them to know what you can do. That's okay; a lot of people hide it at first."

Henry skips it. "Alex, if you know who we are, then you know we're not here to hurt you. We just want to—"

"Jury's out on what exactly you want. You know what the stories say? Some say you have a secret facility where you take us and lock us up. Some say you tag us and release us back into the wild." He laughs. "I don't think anyone really knows. But I'm guessing whatever comes out of your mouth will be a lie, so I'm not really interested, thanks."

He turns his back on them again. "The rumors say I shouldn't be able to use my power around you, but I'm willing to test that out. Maybe if I push hard enough—"

"Now," Henry murmurs into his comm.

"Captain," says Smith in his earpiece, "He hasn't actually—"

"*Now.*"

Smith takes the shot, and Barrett crumples instantly, kicking up a tiny cloud of sand. Henry hurries to his side, taking his pulse and feeling it slow. Henry can also feel Barrett looking at him, confused.

"You didn't need to," Barrett says, his voice already slurring. "What you can do—"

"Don't," Henry says quietly. He already feels sick.

(The major said this was how he could protect his team, how he was *required* to protect his team, but he hates it, he's always hated using the serum, and the startled—and quickly hidden—looks from his team, who are so used to him trying to find some other way and only using the serum as a last resort…he hates that, too.)

"We'll have to carry him back to the vehicle," Henry tells the contact team. "And he's not in any state to help us. Valdez, with me."

Between the two of them, they carry Barrett, with the rest of the team trailing behind.

It's a long ride home in silence.

***

Watching his team unload several hours later, Henry can't deny that they seem…content. They're a little confused about what exactly just went down, of course, but not even Smith is asking questions. Yet.

Even so, he can't bring himself to think what the major did to them—the "protocol"—was a good idea. Or that it was okay to do it behind his back.

But he also can't see that it's hurting anyone.

In fact, while Henry spends the next day debriefing and putting together reports and filing data, he doesn't have to track down any errant team members or referee any fights. Everyone's doing what they should be doing.

So maybe he was wrong. Maybe there's nothing sinister here; just the major doing her job, too: keeping people safe in whatever way she thinks is best. It's completely reasonable that she would know things other officers don't and that she would make decisions based on that information that might seem odd to someone who doesn't know the details.

But it still doesn't sit right. There's something wrong with it. Or just wrong with him.

He's exhausted by the end of the day—and still finding sand between his teeth—but it doesn't matter. He needs to get down to Level 19 before he gets caught up in another mission and before something bad happens to…well. He's not going to think about that.

Night is going to be the best time to avoid the most black coats, so that evening is when he sets out.

Level 1 is easy enough. He doesn't even have to use the jammer here, since it's normal that he'd be wandering around the halls at any hour, given that the barracks, his room, and the training facilities are all on this floor. The tricky part will be once he tries to go lower than he has security clearance for.

He's just about made it to the stairs when his jammer pings loudly. Henry starts and ducks into an empty corridor. It's unlikely he'll get much company here, given the time of night, but he's careful anyway about taking the jammer out of his pocket and glaring at it.

The device isn't jamming, but it's turned itself on. As far as Henry can tell, based on the icon at the bottom corner, it's picking up some sort of signal. Kent must've thought he was doing Henry a favor by upgrading the jammer with some additional sensitivity, but it would've been helpful if he'd actually taken a moment to explain what the hell he was trying to do. Is this part of the level 3 data access? Or just Kent thinking up a neat way to give him a heart attack?

Then the voices start.

"We have some concerns about your handling of the situation, Major," says one—slightly tinny, like it's coming through a phone or a video conferencing program. Even as Henry scrambles to turn the volume down to a safer level, he also realizes he recognizes that voice from somewhere.

"I assure you they're unwarranted," says Major Valentine. Her voice is a little more clear but also seems to be coming from far away.

"These assets of yours are extremely powerful," the first voice continues. "We know we don't have to remind you that you've already lost control of one. And now—"

"Senator, I have everything in hand," Major Valentine says firmly. "There's no need for the committee to worry. In fact, I should have an updated report for you within the week on the next round of experiments."

"See that you do. We warned you about the issues inherent in fighting fire with fire, and so far, it would appear we were correct. Should the situation get out of hand, of course we would deny knowledge of this project."

"With all due respect, Senator, you're not in the field or here at the compound. You're not seeing how these assets are performing and what we're learning from them. This work is vital to the security of—"

"So long as you're aware that if you should encounter insurmountable difficulties, we will be recommending the implementation of the fail-safe."

The way the voice says "recommending" makes it obvious that it wouldn't be a recommendation.

"Of course." Major Valentine's attempt to be appeasing is ruined by the fact that she sounds like she's talking around clenched teeth. "And may I remind the committee that I have many years of experience with this work and far more success than any other compound has seen in our lifetimes? But naturally I defer to the committee's wishes, as always."

"Very good, Major."

Haldis, Henry realizes. What's this committee he's talking about? Some group of senators that works directly with Major Valentine? Henry's never heard of that sort of arrangement. Sure, there's the Compound Council's liaison committee, the one that promotes cooperation between the city legislature and the compounds. But that sort of committee is always tightly controlled by the Compound Council, not individual officers.

And this "fighting fire with fire"? That sounds like pitting two people against each other. Two assets?

Two empaths?

The voices stop, and the squiggly lines on the jammer indicating audio go still. Henry frowns and heads for the stairs.

His knees are happy to remind him that going down eighteen flights isn't something they're excited about, but he'd rather that than be caught on an elevator going someplace he shouldn't be going. A jammer wouldn't be much help if someone else got on an elevator with him at a restricted area.

It gets dimmer the lower he goes. By the time he reaches the door to Level 19, he's only making out details in the stairwell via flickering, intermittent lights above.

He hasn't had to use the jammer for its intended purpose till now—there are few enough cameras in the stairwell, and they're easy to avoid. Once he opens this door, though, he'll have to start the countdown. Thirty minutes to find something or hide.

It's an electronic door, so Kent's magnet comes in handy. Henry starts the jammer at the same time he opens the door. Then, despite the proverbial ticking clock, he pauses.

No screaming alarms. No black coats. Nothing.

The hall is lit only by the occasional blue light—an energy-saving tactic for this far down in the compound, where few people come on a regular basis. His movements would probably be triggering brighter motion-sensitive lights if he weren't jamming the security system.

There are doors on either side of the hall stretching both ways, none with any sort of signage. Henry blows out a breath in annoyance and looks at the map data Kent found. Not terribly helpful, although it does show that the floor is arranged so that clusters of doors open to the same large room. So he'll only have to check every third door or so.

He turns right and hugs the wall, peering into windows as quickly and quietly as he can. For all the good it does: everything is dark.

He loses about ten minutes to this before he hits the emergency exit at the end of the hall. Grimacing, he turns and starts on the opposite side.

Better luck here. A few doors down, he can see a blueish light through the glass and hear a faint hum. The door looks similar to the one he faked out with the magnet, so he gives it a try...and it slides open.

The room is full of precisely positioned beds. A bit like barracks but without the little touches that make it obvious a group of people lives there. Next to each bed is a machine with wires coming out of it, sitting on top of a white drawer. Every machine is shut off, and the beds are empty.

Except one.

That's where the little blue light and the hum are coming from: the machine blinking near the one occupied bed. There's someone lying there, mostly covered by a thin blanket except for his right arm, which is out, palm up. Even from the entrance, Henry can see the needle in his skin, connected to the machine.

Henry feels his stomach clench.

(He feels something else, too: familiarity. Has he been here before?)

He isn't even aware he's walked over to the bed until he's standing there at the foot of it, staring down at Bastian. Even in the dim light, Henry can tell Bastian's skin is paler than normal, and he's lying completely still in a way that makes Henry want to shake him just to be sure he's not—

There's a monitor at the end of the bed where Henry's standing. He's not a doctor, so he doesn't understand all the notes and statistics, but one thing stands out: the amount of blood taken. Nearly thirty percent. Holy shit.

Henry barely resists the urge to rip the needle out of Bastian's arm immediately. He has no idea what's going on with the setup, he reminds himself, and touching it could make things worse.

He remembers what he saw in Bastian's file—the large amounts of blood drawn. Henry had assumed they were small amounts taken over time along with the other samples mentioned, but if they were basically bleeding him dry repeatedly…well. No wonder he hates Dr. Wright.

And what do they need that much blood for, anyway?

Forcing himself to stay calm, he takes Bastian's hand, trying to ignore how cold his skin is. Henry also does his best to ignore the better look he gets at the scar on Bastian's wrist. (Obvious how it got there, no doubt there's one on the other wrist as well, but it's useless to think about wanting to hurt whoever or whatever made Bastian think that was a good idea. More important things now. Focus on the mission.)

"Hey." Henry fights to keep his voice steady and reassuring. "Bastian? Can you hear me?"

Nothing for a long moment. Then Bastian slowly opens his eyes—and immediately frowns. "Told you…get out of my head," he says in a scratchy voice barely above a whisper. "Don't show me what I…doesn't matter, I won't let you…." He trails off into mumbling and starts to close his eyes again.

"Wait!" Henry sits awkwardly on the narrow bed. "Don't go to sleep."

Bastian manages to look up at Henry, confused but slightly more lucid. "You…you're not here."

"Yes, I am, and it took a hell of a lot of work to pull it off." He swallows around the lump in his throat and holds Bastian's hand a little tighter than he probably should. "Look, I'm sorry. I should have come sooner. I tried, only—"

Bastian shifts his gaze downward at a glacial pace and looks at their hands. Then he looks back up, and Henry instantly hates the expression on his face: confused, like he doesn't understand why anyone would have gone to all the effort to come for him.

"You *are* here."

"Yeah." Henry gives him a small smile. "Kent helped me look for you and Johnson—"

"You…your officer. That's why you…." Bastian closes his eyes briefly, then opens them again. "At the end of the room…left side."

Henry feels his heart sink. If it's dark, and there aren't any other machines running, that has to mean…. "Johnson's here?"

"Yes." Bastian looks away and doesn't say anything else. He lets go of Henry's hand. Reluctantly, Henry thinks.

(Don't think that. He's here to save people, not to think things.)

With more than a little trepidation, Henry gets up and walks down the row of beds to the corner Bastian mentioned. The beds here are all empty, the machines turned off, until he gets to the end of the row.

Johnson is in the last bed, looking a bit like Bastian does, only somehow even more still. He's not breathing, Henry realizes. That sends Henry to Johnson's side in an instant, but of course it's too late. Johnson's machine is off, his eyes closed, his arms completely underneath the blanket. Henry draws it back a bit and touches Johnson's hand: he's been dead for somewhere between eight and twelve hours, judging by rigor mortis, though it's hard to know for sure.

Henry looks down at Johnson's calm, pale face and swallows once. Then he puts the blanket back, turns on his heel, and marches back to Bastian's bed.

Bastian still isn't looking at him. "I've been…in and out, but…I think they brought him in earlier today. Tests probably…didn't go well. The last step is to… get as much blood and samples as possible for…testing. Salvage the situation."

"Is that what they're doing to you?"

Bastian smiles humorlessly, though it seems to pain him. "No. This is just… standard for me."

"This—they've done this to you before? Regularly?"

"Yes."

The matter-of-fact way he says it makes Henry want to punch someone. Or something. Possibly several someones or somethings. He takes a few breaths to steady himself.

"All right, listen. My jammer's going to run out of juice in a minute, so I have to hide for a bit while it recharges. Once that's done, you're going to tell me how to unhook this thing and get you out of here."

Bastian looks at him like he's crazy. "That's—you can't—"

"I am *not* leaving you here," Henry says firmly. He looks at the jammer's timer. "I *am* going to hide under your bed, though, so maybe don't jump on it for the next five minutes."

It's quite possibly the longest five minutes of his life. There's not much room under the bed, turns out, and the concrete floor is cold enough to bite through his shirt and into his skin. But the worst part is that he can't feel or hear or see any movement from Bastian above, so his mind starts playing tricks on him, telling him Bastian's dead, too, that he was too late for both of them, that he's failed everyone he was supposed to look after, including someone he—

The jammer finally blinks at him, and he turns it back on and shuffles out from underneath the bed. Bastian is awake and looking at him.

"Okay," Henry says. "How do I—?" He pauses. "What?"

The corner of Bastian's mouth twitches. "You've got…." He moves the first finger on his left hand to his nose.

At least motor functions aren't in doubt. "I don't—"

"Come here."

He leans down, feeling silly. Bastian reaches out and rubs at Henry's nose. "Guess there's no…top secret custodial staff," Bastian says, almost smiling.

Henry thinks he should probably say something, but he gets distracted for a moment by Bastian's hand brushing dust out of his hair. (Painfully slowly—he's only capable of minimal movement right now, and touching Henry's hair is what he wants to be doing?)

Henry shakes himself inwardly and clears his throat. "How do I unhook this machine?" he asks again.

Bastian hesitates, dropping his hand. "You really shouldn't—"

"We're getting you out of here. Tell me how."

There's another pause. Then: "Two cords. In the back. Make sure it's…off. Then I can…take the IV out."

Henry does it and turns around to find Bastian wincing as he pulls the needle out of his arm. Then he tries to sit up far too quickly. Henry grabs him around the shoulders and holds him still for a moment while he shudders and looks like he might be sick.

"I won't be able to…keep up," Bastian says quietly into Henry's arm. "You should—"

"Shut up. Let's try moving, okay?"

With help, Bastian manages to swing his legs over the side of the bed. He's breathing a bit heavily, but even just this little movement seems to put more color into his face. Which he's keeping hidden as much as possible. Henry thinks he might be embarrassed.

"What about…?" Bastian nods toward the end of the room and the bed where Johnson is lying.

Henry sets his mouth in a thin line and shakes his head. "There's nothing we can do for him now. The rest of the team doesn't even remember him."

That makes Bastian glance sharply at Henry. "What?"

"Some protocol Major Valentine used on them. They forgot. They seem fine otherwise." He hesitates. "This room—what do they do here, exactly?"

"Experimental recovery. Why?"

"It seems…familiar, somehow. And I overheard the major talking about recent experiments—"

"Captain, have you…been eavesdropping?"

Henry shakes his head. "Sort of. The jammer picked it up. Never mind; we'll figure it out later."

Once he's sure Bastian isn't going to fall over without support, Henry gets up and looks around for Bastian's clothes. Nothing doing. He does find a robe in the drawer next to the bed, which would be better than wandering around in just a hospital gown, at least.

"No gloves," Henry says, helping Bastian put on the robe. "Sorry."

"It's fine," Bastian mumbles, focusing on getting his hands through the arm holes.

"Okay," Henry says once it's done. "Ready to try standing?"

Bastian nods grimly. His dubious expression turns to pain as he stands, leaning heavily on Henry. They stand there for a moment, Bastian's shallow breathing the only noise in the room now that the machine is turned off. Henry can feel Bastian's heart beating quickly—too quickly—from where Henry has a hand on his chest.

"All right?" Henry asks.

Bastian nods.

"Walking?"

Bastian nods again, his grip on Henry's arm tightening almost imperceptibly.

He's extremely wobbly for the first few steps, but the next few after that go a little better, and the next ones better than that, until they're walking fairly normally, if slowly. Not going to win any races, but they'll do all right, Henry thinks.

They exit the room slowly and carefully. There's time to make it back to the stairwell before the jammer timer runs out. Then they'll have to book it to the vehicle loading dock and get Bastian out of here. The clearing is probably his best bet for now—it's familiar ground, and his friend is probably still there, unless she's moved on—but it'll take several days' travel. Of course, once the major realizes what's happening, they'll have to find somewhere else to go.

It's a long shot. A *really* long shot. But Henry can't leave him here, *won't* leave him here, and if that means there are consequences…well. He has to do it anyway.

"No."

Startled, Henry glances over at Bastian. "What?"

"Whatever you're thinking…no. We have to…go somewhere first."

"Where?"

"The library."

Chapter 21

WALKING AND ARGUING at the same time requires more focus than Bastian really wants to spend right now, but Henry's not giving him a choice.

"Bastian, this is stupid. You can barely move."

"Won't…get another chance. We have to—"

"What's so important there? Do you even know where it is?"

"Level 20."

Henry pauses. "Big, open area? Storage must mean books, then."

"How do you know about it?"

"Kent found it in one of his searches. How do *you* know about it?"

"John Doe…mentioned it. Said it had…information. On the asset program. Maybe about…him."

"When were you talking to John Doe?"

Shit. "No time for…that. Later."

Henry checks the jammer, looks around, and sighs. "Well, we can't take the elevator."

"Insightful observation."

"You really think you can manage a flight of stairs right now?"

Bastian doesn't, of course. He feels like he's going to collapse any minute, even with Henry holding him up. He's coming back to himself a little more as they move around, but he's weak and stupid, which he *hates*, especially since Henry knows it.

Then there's the other distraction.

He wasn't sure at first, thought it was just leftover grogginess from being drugged and drained and having a needle in his arm (no other samples or tests this time—small favors). But it's getting stronger the more he wakes up. And it makes no sense.

He can feel Henry.

The worry-anxiety-protective is coming from far off, like he's picking it up through a fog, but he definitely feels it. And the shifts in emotion as well.

He shouldn't be able to. Not unless Henry's somehow lowered his negation field far enough. Or…something. Bastian's not entirely sure how negation works.

Another reason to go to the library.

(John Doe could do it, could feel through Henry's power. Did Wright do something similar to Bastian, then? Was it more than just an enormous blood draw?)

"Bastian?"

They're at the stairwell. Henry uses some sort of rectangular thing to unlock the door, then shoulders it open and helps Bastian through. Once inside, he moves them to a camera-free angle and shuts the jammer off to let it charge back to full. As they're waiting, they look down the flight of stairs, each step only slightly visible in the dim light.

Henry shakes his head. "Unless you can fly, I don't think this is a good idea." He turns to Bastian with a slight smile. "You can't fly, can you? Or, I don't know, hover? Float?"

Bastian's mouth twitches. "No."

"But you definitely want to do this?"

"Yes. While we…still can." Because if either of them is ever on this level again, it'll only be if they're hooked up to one of those machines. Henry would probably go to a room Bastian doesn't even know about. Where Bastian would never see him again.

"All right." Henry sets his shoulders. "I'll carry you."

"That's—I don't—" He hates that he can feel his face flush, though it's probably a good sign, considering the blood loss.

Henry smiles. "I'm stronger than I look. And you're practical skeletal right now. Seriously, I'm buying you dinner when this is all over." He blinks. "Uh. I mean—"

Bastian doesn't intend to say it, but: "Deal."

Henry's startled-embarrassed-pleased nearly bowls Bastian over. The grin doesn't help, either. (The last thing Bastian needs is something else that could stop his heart.) "Yeah?"

Bastian realizes he's grinning back. Because he's an idiot. "Definitely."

They smile at each other for longer than is safe before Henry clears his throat and positions them closer to the first stair. They're steep, but it's only one flight.

"Okay." Henry loosens his grip on Bastian for a moment to shift his weight. "Put your arms around my neck."

Bastian is still dubious about this—less about Henry's strength and more about getting around the angles of the staircase in low light while carrying someone. And staying out of the view of the (admittedly poorly positioned) security cameras. And of course there's the part where Bastian might pass out, which would make things more difficult. But Henry's right: there's no way he's going to make those stairs by himself in his current state.

So Bastian swallows his objections, puts his arms around Henry's neck, and clings to him as he's quite literally swept off his feet.

Henry's struggling a bit—no powers required to feel the slight shakiness in his limbs as he starts walking down the stairs—but he's managing far better than Bastian would have expected. The movement does make Bastian start to feel woozy, and he concentrates on not throwing up. Sheer will seems to work pretty well.

"You all right?" Henry asks sometime later. Bastian realizes they've reached the bottom of the stairs, and Henry has put him down. And is still letting Bastian hold onto him in an arrangement that's not quite a hug.

Bastian immediately backs away as much as he can, given that he needs Henry's help to stand. "Yes. Fine. Let's go."

Henry takes out the jammer and flips the switch. "Half an hour," he says. "Hope that's enough. I don't really see how we're going to get you stuffed under a bed or in a bookshelf if it isn't." He opens the door and starts moving them purposefully.

"You…know where it is?" Bastian asks.

"Sort of. Kent found the general area."

They make their way to the south side of the floor. Bastian gets a little more sure-footed as they go, but he's still choking down frustration and embarrassment at being so weak and slow.

He also notices that if he doesn't focus on reaching out, he can stay comfortably in Henry's normal nothing-nothing-nothing field. Advantages: calming, soothing, makes moving easier. Disadvantages: inclination to lean into Henry more than is necessary.

Bastian forces himself not to do it. Or think about it.

After ten minutes or so, they come to an intersection. "I think that's as far as Kent's instructions can go," Henry says. "What now?"

Bastian takes a breath, straightens up a bit, and feels out.

It hurts, which startles him, but he closes his eyes and ignores it. Pushes harder.

Is it getting past Henry's negation that makes this so hard? Or just that Bastian's weaker right now? Or both? Either way, his head and stomach immediately start protesting. He can almost feel it….

(This shouldn't work at all, it's too much like last time, when his power started to change and there were headaches and nausea and stomachaches but Valentine didn't care because all that mattered was the objective—)

"Bastian—"

There. Bored-calm-tired coming from a room a few doors down. He sags slightly as he pulls back. "It's that one. The one with the…double doors."

"You're bleeding."

Henry's concern-worry-fear is blinding—enough that Bastian belatedly tries to shore up his shield a bit (mixed results; hard to focus on multiple energetic tasks when your energy is already low). Past the pounding in his head, he realizes his nose is bleeding.

"It's…nothing. Let's go."

Henry looks at him for a moment, obviously not buying it but also not wanting to waste time. He pulls a handkerchief out of his pocket (Standard officer issue or just Henry's need to be helpful in any situation?) and hands it to Bastian. Then he guides them to the door.

The frosted glass makes it impossible to tell what's inside, and of course nothing's labeled. But Bastian can still feel the bored-calm-tired coming from inside, so he knows this is the place.

Carefully and quietly, Henry opens the door.

The room is huge. High arched ceilings. Shelves made of dark mahogany. Spiral staircases leading up to an open second level. Perfectly aligned desks with elegant lamps running through the central area. The lighting is a bit dim, but it's still easy to see everything—much better than anywhere else they've seen on this floor. Everything is visible.

Including the books. What looks like thousands of them.

Henry and Bastian stare in silence. Whereas everything else in the compound is gray, uniform, and efficient, the library is comfortable, a bit dusty, and graceful without being too ostentatious. It belongs in a well-endowed university, not in a concrete prison deep underground.

"Oh!" The bored-tired-calm is now laced through with startled-excited-concerned. Bastian's feeling it through a fog, but he's definitely feeling it, despite Henry's proximity.

"You're not supposed to be here!" adds the middle-aged woman hurriedly approaching them.

"Private library, is it?" Bastian says as he checks that his nosebleed is winding down. "Do we…need to pay dues?"

The woman gets a good look at Bastian, and the concern shifts to the forefront of her emotions. "You look done in," she says. "I have tea. Would you like tea?"

She moves off to a corner of the library without waiting for a response.

Henry and Bastian look at each other. Henry shrugs, and they start off after her.

The corner she leads them to is very cozy, sectioned off by a few shelves, all of which are full to the brim with books of all shapes, sizes, and colors. There are also several comfortable-looking chairs and a small table with a teapot, a few mugs, and a carafe of hot water.

"Good," says the woman. "I couldn't remember if it was here or not." She pours some tea into one of the mugs, then turns to them again. "You should probably sit down."

Bastian's not looking forward to that, but being seated does sound good. At least Henry's patient and gentle about it. He walks Bastian over to one of the chairs and helps him lower himself down into it extremely (embarrassingly) slowly. Bastian gets a bit dizzy part way through, but he makes it. He's more gratified than he'd like to admit when Henry pulls another chair closer and sits down next to him.

The woman nods, then turns back to the tea table. "Oh! I've already got one in my hand." She gives it to Bastian. Then she pours another one and hands it to Henry. Without bothering to get herself any tea, she sits down across from them.

"So! What brings you to the library?"

Henry opens his mouth, but Bastian cuts him off. "We need information."

The woman smiles. "You've come to the right place." Then her shoulders slump. "Only you're really not supposed to be here, so I'm not sure I should be helping you. It might upset the major."

"We wouldn't want that," Bastian mutters.

"What he means," Henry says quickly, "is that we'd be very grateful for your help. What's your name?"

"I didn't say? How rude! I'm Anna. I think." She frowns. "Yes. Anna. That's right."

Bastian clears his throat. "Since we're pressed for time, maybe we could skip the—"

"Excuse us a moment, Anna." Henry turns to Bastian. "You might want to think of a less combative way of asking for whatever it is we're looking for," he says in a low voice. "We don't want to spook her."

"We don't have time for…less combative." It's better, but it still hurts to talk. Speaking of things they don't have time for. "Tell her we need to see… the database. She won't show us the restricted stuff, but…get her password. We can hack it later."

"Why do we need—?"

"Asset program information. And…John Doe has access. We need to know what he knows. And what he…doesn't. If we can reach it."

Henry frowns. "You still haven't told me how or when you talked to him."

"Later. Ask her."

Looking up and giving Anna a smile, Henry asks, "Could I have you show me the library database? I'd like to see what you have here."

"Certainly!" She jumps to her feet. "Well. I can't show you the restricted section, of course…."

"Of course," Henry says, obviously trying to ignore Bastian's told-you-so eyebrows.

Bastian steels himself to stand as well, but Henry reaches out and puts a hand on his chest. "Don't be an idiot. Stay there and let me do this."

Bastian starts to protest, but Henry sets down his mug and slips around the corner and out of sight with Anna. It makes sense, Bastian supposes; he'd only slow things down. Still. He hates waiting.

He scoots himself further into the chair and tips his head back. The dizziness and weakness aren't so bad while he's sitting down and not moving much, but it's still embarrassing to be so useless.

He sits as quietly and patiently as he can for about a minute. Then something catches his eye.

On one of the low shelves to his left, there's a small flash of something. He turns with only a little difficulty and scans the spines for the glint he saw—gold leaf, there, near the bottom. He'll have to get out of the chair if he wants a better look—and he'll have to do it quickly if he doesn't want to deal with irritating flustering when the others get back and find him up and about.

He sets down his mug, grimaces, and slides forward until he's on his knees on the floor. Bending down further than that sends a wave of nausea through him, and he has to stop moving for a few seconds before he can continue.

It's worth it. The little book, dark green with the gold leaf, is titled *On Negation in Subjects*. It looks ancient, and it doesn't match any of the books on either side of it. Misshelved, then. Anna would probably have a conniption.

He hears footsteps coming closer, so there's only one thing to do: he grabs the book, tucks it into the inside of his robe, and shoves himself back into the chair, biting back a pained gasp.

Anna returns to the nook, and Bastian frowns before she even says anything (confused-surprised-wary)—

"What are you doing here?" she demands, a hand over her heart like she's been startled nearly to death. "You're supposed to wait to be greeted at the entrance." She peers at him, and her look becomes less severe. "You look very ill, young man. Would you like some tea?"

Bastian sticks to frowning, trying to understand his read on her, until it dulls with Henry's approach.

"Oh! There are two of you!" Anna looks back and forth at them. "I suppose—I can help you both, if you like. But you really shouldn't be here."

Henry and Bastian exchange glances. "Anna," Henry says, "we were just looking at the database together. Remember?"

"I think I'd remember if I—" She stops, then sighs. "No, I wouldn't."

"You...forgot?" Henry is dubious (dubious-concerned-skeptical).

Forgetting.

Bastian thinks of Snyder in the jail cell, ranting about someone trying to make him forget—making all the people Bastian interrogated forget what happened to them. Henry saying Valentine used some sort of protocol on his team to make them forget Johnson.

"You're an asset," Bastian says.

They both look at him—Henry with surprise, Anna with resignation.

"I don't remember, but...yes, I think so." Anna sits down in one of the nearby chairs and taps her head a bit more forcefully than seems wise. "Mostly it happens to me—I forget things, then I remember, then I forget again. I don't know why. But the major said it was useful, so she put me in charge of the library."

"Is it...just something you do to yourself?" Henry asks warily. "Or can you...?"

She looks up at him, then over at Bastian. "I'm supposed to make anyone who comes in here forget. So they can't find it again. Sometimes I make other people forget, too. There's a reason for it, but I don't remember." She stands back up and faces them. "I'm sorry."

Henry holds out a hand. "Don't—"

She closes her eyes. Bastian expects to be able to feel her effort and focus as she uses her power, but everything's gone blank. He can't feel anything at all. Which means—

She frowns and makes as if to try again. Nothing.

She opens her eyes and glares at them. "I'm just trying to do my job! Whatever that is! Why are you stopping me?"

Bastian looks at Henry, who still has his hand out and is standing between Bastian and Anna, looking a bit startled but determined.

That answers the question of whether he can use his power consciously, then.

"You made them forget," he says (anger-hurt-frustration coming vaguely through now, so he's already backed off whatever he was just doing, whether he knows it or not). "My team. The protocol the major talked about—is that how it works? Something happens, and she has you just...make people forget?"

Anna shakes her head. "I think so? I don't know. What were we talking about again?"

"How does that help?" Henry continues, his voice rising. "What's the point of making people forget their teammates or—or anything? How could that possibly—?"

"I don't know!" Anna cries. "Or I don't remember. I just do what the major says! I do my job! I think it—maybe it's because some things are just better not knowing."

Henry's fury-remorse-self-loathing is so intense, it feels like a punch to the gut. Bastian can't breathe for a moment. He tries not to think about how it would feel without the fog of Henry's power.

"No," Henry says at last, his voice cold. "It's never better not knowing." He turns to Bastian. "We should go."

Anna doesn't follow them as Henry guides Bastian back toward the library entrance.

Bastian hesitates to risk the consequences of breaking the stony silence, but—"How much time on the jammer?"

"Shit." Henry grabs it from his jacket pocket. Even at this angle, Bastian can tell it's at zero.

Bastian feels the determined-focused-irritated a moment before he hears the incoming footsteps. Pushes a bit further past Henry's barrier just to make sure. Feels the nosebleed start again. There. Great.

"Did you get the password for the database?"

"Yes, but—"

"Okay. Take this." Bastian shoves the book he took at Henry. "And do a good job of hiding it."

"What—?"

"*Do it.* Quickly."

Henry stows it away, and then his head shoots up—he's obviously heard the footsteps as well now. His arm tightens around Bastian's waist, and he opens his mouth to say something, but of course it's too late.

The doors of the library slam open.

"Hello, gentlemen," says Major Valentine. She's flanked by a large contingent of black coats. "I believe it's time we had a word."

Chapter 22

HENRY IS TOO exhausted to be angry at this point. All he can think about is having to watch—again—as Bastian is taken from him.

Bastian doesn't even look at him as the black coats roughly cart him off. While Henry just stands there.

Henry was able to stuff the jammer into a pocket fast enough that they didn't find it, but only just. He's got the book Bastian gave him in there as well. It doesn't set off any alarms on their way out—Anna's security method of just making everyone forget before they leave must be efficient enough that they don't bother with RFID on the books themselves.

He has no idea why Bastian gave the book to him, since he hasn't had a chance to look at it beyond catching a flash of gold. But it must be important if Bastian went to all the trouble.

The major takes Henry back to her office in complete silence, apparently ignoring his quiet seething.

"Explain," she says as soon as they've walked in, and she's closed the door behind them.

"Where are they taking Bastian?"

The major smiles thinly. "Not what I asked, Captain. What were you doing on Level 20? You know perfectly well you're not authorized to be there. Explain."

Henry takes a breath to steady himself. "You assigned me to look after Bastian and to help with the investigation. He was missing for an extended period of time, so I went to find him."

"I see. And it didn't occur to you to ask me about his status before breaking compound rules?"

"I—"

"Or to simply trust that your superior officer had the situation under control?"

"That—"

"Or perhaps to focus on following orders, which, if I recall correctly, is your job?"

There's no appropriate response to that, so Henry keeps his mouth shut.

Major Valentine sighs. "Captain. Do you ever wonder why we do things the way we do? We don't keep information classified to irritate or frighten people. It's not some big conspiracy. We do it because it's necessary—vital, even—for keeping both staff and assets safe. Any one person with too much knowledge could be compromised during a mission. We're only able to continue our work if the compound remains secure. But you learned all of this in training."

She seems to be waiting for an answer, so he gives her the appropriate one. "Yes, ma'am."

"Whatever Sebastian might have told you, you must understand: he's very troubled. If he's telling you stories about diabolical experiments or assets with unusual powers, it's only because—"

"We saw one. An asset with the ability to make people forget. You used her power on my team, didn't you?"

Major Valentine raises her eyebrows. "Is that what you think?"

"Based on what Anna said—"

"Anna spends days on end alone in that library, cataloging and sorting through massive amounts of data. It's not surprising that she'd try to appear special in front of the first people she's interacted with in quite some time." The major smiles. "Did she use her...power on you?"

"No, but that's because—" Henry barely manages to stop himself.

He recognizes the look on the major's face. It's the one she made before, when they were discussing the serum and how he ought to use more of it. The one that makes it seem like she's waiting for him to slip up, to admit that he knows what he is.

"As for experiments," Henry continues, "Bastian was nearly catatonic when I found him. Dr. Wright's latest experiment drained him of enough blood to almost kill him."

"Forgive me, Captain, but you aren't a doctor. Your medical skills are limited to first aid in the field. The intricacies of more complicated medicine—"

"I can read a chart well enough to recognize extreme blood loss when I see it."

Major Valentine sighs. "Dr. Wright can be...overly enthusiastic. With a murderer on the loose who has powers similar to Sebastian's, you can see why we're more eager than ever to understand."

"You can't understand if he's dead." He realizes his hands are clasped too tightly behind his back. "Ma'am."

"I assure you, the doctor is fully aware of the parameters of his duties." She pauses. "Are you aware of the parameters of *your* duties, Captain?"

He forces his face into something neutral. "Yes, ma'am."

"Good. Then continue with the investigation. After that mission is successfully completed, we can discuss your future here at the compound."

Well, that's not worrisome. "Yes, ma'am."

"You're dismissed."

He doesn't realize how tense his shoulders are until he's out in the hall making his way to his room. He's tired, worried, angry, and helpless—all his favorite things. Maybe Bastian was right about the advantages of not having feelings.

How does Bastian do it, then? He must have had hundreds, if not thousands, of conversations like that with the major. How has he not given up? He's still sharp, he's still fighting, even though they've been slowly killing him for years. He's not afraid to ask questions and demand the answers Henry's realizing he should have been going after his entire career.

(And when he's not busy being an asshole, he's funny and kinder than he thinks he is, and when he laughs, it's—)

Henry shakes his head. Stupid, what he said on the staircase. You can get away with that sort of thing in training, but once you're a commanding officer, you have to think of everyone who's your responsibility, not just one person. What you want doesn't matter anymore.

He briefly puts a hand on his chest where the book is hidden in the inside pocket of his jacket. Answers are what matter right now. And since he's not going to get those from the major, he'll have to find another way.

***

It's not completely unusual for an officer to be alone outside on the grounds, even at 0600. To find an officer alone outside on the grounds reading is a little bit stranger. To find him doing all that behind a tool shed borders on questionable.

It wouldn't be Henry's first choice for a place to read, but security is lax here compared to the rest of the compound, and he doesn't want to risk trying to make the jammer work for extended periods of time, especially when he's already under quite a bit of scrutiny.

All he can do at the moment is figure out this book Bastian gave him.

With a title like *On Negation in Subjects*, it's clear why Bastian though it would be of interest to him. There's no author listed, and the binding looks amateur, which leads Henry to think it's more of a collection of research hastily stuffed into book format rather than a published scholarly treatise. Someone must have cared about it a lot, though, to give it such a nice cover.

Henry wonders if every asset in the program gets something like this—a guide to who they are and what they can do. Or do they just inherently know how everything works? Bastian said he couldn't remember a time when he didn't have his power, but Henry's gone for years without knowing he's…whatever he is. Is one more normal than the other?

Just one more thing he doesn't know and never bothered to ask.

He grimaces and turns to the forward.

The following represents a collection of theories based on anecdotal evidence and observations of the negation ability. While there are indications that true negators have existed in the past, an official case has never been documented.

Never? Henry blinks and flips ahead.

A negator's power appears to exist solely in reaction to other powers, lending credence to the theory that a negator may manifest without knowledge of it. The minimal amount of written and colloquial evidence available suggests that, at least initially, a negator's power only works intermittently and at various levels of strength: for example, dimming rather than negating powers entirely or else providing complete negation for only short periods of time. After a negator is fully awakened, however, no other powered individual can act in the presence of their negation field.

Henry follows a footnote on that last bit. Reading it, he suddenly feels his stomach twist.

One exception to this appears to be individuals whose powers have been enhanced via artificial means. Augmented rare power types, such as memors or empaths, may be able to break through a negator's field, though they do so at a physical cost. Several stories describe such an occurrence, each ultimately resulting in extreme injury to the powered individual attempting to work through the negation.

That explains the nosebleeds on Levels 19 and 20. Bastian was trying to use his power through Henry's negation field and hurt himself in the process.

Henry swallows and flips ahead again. He wants to spend more time on this, but he can't risk being caught with it. He'll need to read in short bursts, and right now, he just wants an overview.

One set of recovered notes suggests that negation resembles typical shielding. Whereas an energetic shield protects the one manifesting it from surrounding energies, a negator's "shield" blocks all other powers within a certain area.

Okay, that seems like a good place to start. Henry understands the basic concept of shielding, though he's never needed to use it much beyond training. In the field, he's always had the serum. And in the compound, he never directly encountered an asset until Bastian. Theoretically, though, he should still remember how to do it.

He closes the book, puts it back into his jacket pocket, and takes a few deep breaths. He won't know if he's actually negating, of course, since there aren't any assets around. But maybe he can visualize or whatever and get an idea of how this is supposed to work.

He lets his eyes fall shut and starts by…feeling a bit awkward, really. Then he sternly tells himself to focus anyway. Right. Senses first. Smell of the damp wood and stone that make up the shed he's sitting against. The feel of the dew on the grass next to his hands. Bit of a smoky taste coming through his nose and onto his tongue from the vehicle maintenance area—a car was being worked on recently.

In training, they say to see the energy around you and follow it to the very edge of whatever makes up "you." Imagine the energy there as a barrier: one that lets some things in or one that doesn't let anything through. Thick or thin, porous or solid. Extending all around you.

He tries to envision a sort of mesh bubble around him. He can pull it closed and block everything out or loosen it and allow some things in. It's deceptively thin and much stronger than it looks. Once he's got that in mind, he considers whether or not it should expand and contract. Maybe it could protect other people if it were wide enough—or cover just him if he could get it small enough….

He sits there with his eyes squeezed shut for he doesn't know how long before sighing and opening them again. It's pointless; there's no way to tell if it's even working, and he just feels silly.

And none of this is doing anything to help Bastian.

"Captain?"

Henry nearly jumps out of his skin at the sound of the voice. He stumbles to his feet and turns to find Officer Michaels standing placidly just around the corner of the shed.

He clears his throat. "Good morning, Michaels."

"Good morning, sir. I've been sent to tell you we have another mission."

"The investigation?"

"That's correct. The police found another body."

Dammit. "Let's go, then."

"Mr. Lucas will meet us at the vehicle loading dock in five minutes," Michaels says.

Henry, who had started walking in that direction, stops and turns back to her. "Bastian's well enough to come?"

"Of course." Michaels looks confused. "Has he been ill?"

"I—no, I suppose not. Let's go."

"Very good, sir."

He won't think about what it could mean that Bastian recovered so quickly. He also won't think about his relief or the way he has to stop himself from walking too quickly. Murder, he reminds himself. Not something to be happy about.

(He'd be lying if he didn't admit he's a little happy anyway.)

The driver already has the vehicle running and ready to go when they get there. Bastian is leaning against one of the side doors, arms crossed, looking the other way. No hospital gown.

"Another senator," he says when he sees them. He straightens up and opens the car door. "Happened earlier this morning." His eyes meet Henry's, then quickly skitter away.

"Details are still forthcoming," Michaels explains as she loads the machine into the back, "but it looks like another suicide. Or a murder that appears to be a suicide."

"Which senator?" Henry asks.

"Senator Haldis."

Henry freezes. "What?"

"Try listening," Bastian says sharply, getting into the car. "We don't have all day."

Henry thinks of the conversation he overheard. That level of animosity between the major and the senator, and now Haldis is dead? It's circumstantial, but....

But what? Does he really think Major Valentine would order senators killed? And even pretending for a moment that she would, why order her officers to investigate? Sure, the request came from the Council, but she could've found a way to pass it on, couldn't she? Or is this all part of hiding her tracks?

Then there's the implied idea of bringing Bastian back to the compound to "fight fire with fire." Does the major want Bastian to challenge John Doe? Is John Doe the one Senator Haldis said she'd lost control of?

"Captain?" Michaels is on the other side of the vehicle, about to get in.

"Right. Sorry."

It still feels weird not to be driving like he always does on retrievals. Their driver is efficient and silent, though, getting them to the city and onto Hall grounds in record time.

A harried policewoman meets them in the rotunda after they get past security. "You from the compound?" When they admit it, she continues, "Make sure to check with the CSIs once you've been to the scene. There was a message for you on the body."

"A message?" Bastian frowns.

The policewoman shrugs. "That's all I know. You'll have to ask upstairs. Fourth floor."

The day's sessions haven't started yet, so the whole area is only sparsely populated by aides and a few early risers (Haldis said he was one of those, Henry remembers). Their footsteps echo in the quiet all the way to the elevator.

"Are you all right?" Henry asks Bastian in a low voice as they wait for it.

"Fine."

"Listen, there's something I need to—"

"No."

Henry blinks at him. Bastian is studiously ignoring everything except the changing numbers as the elevator gets closer.

"Why are you—?"

"I said no."

The elevator arrives. They get on and ride up in silence to the fourth floor.

A police detective is waiting for them. "Men's restroom, third stall," he says, sounding tired. "They haven't moved him yet, but they'll want to get him to the morgue soon, so hurry up."

"Thank you," Henry says. The guy looks like he could use some common courtesy at this point. And a nap.

The detective smiles wanly at them and gets on the elevator they just vacated.

The restroom is cordoned off with police tape, but there aren't really enough people around to merit the caution. Another detective is talking with a CSI when they get there.

"Compound?" she says. Henry shows her his ID, and apparently, that's enough. She nods toward the restroom. "Go on in. You probably won't want to stay long, though. You guys do suicides now?"

"Something like that," Henry tells her.

Bastian goes through the door without further preamble, and Michaels follows. With them in front, Henry doesn't immediately see what's going on. When he does, he thinks maybe it would've been better if he hadn't.

Haldis obviously slit his wrists in the sink, then dragged himself over to the stall till it was over. Whatever he used to do it isn't here anymore—the police probably have it. Looking at the mess, though, it's hard to see it as anything other than a suicide. Odd venue, given how public it is, but what happened here is pretty obvious. Except Haldis didn't show any signs of suicidal ideation when Henry talked to him or when he was talking to the major.

But of course there's John Doe.

Henry expects that Bastian, given his prickly mood, will get right to the read. Instead, he pauses for a long time, looking at Haldis's body.

"Bastian?" Henry says quietly. (Don't think about the scars on Bastian's wrists.)

Bastian stares a moment longer, then shakes himself, goes over to the sink, and reaches out a gloved hand to touch it.

Henry clears his throat. "Maybe I should go talk to that detective, see if—"

"Not necessary," Bastian says, closing his eyes.

Henry thinks of the book. Of Bastian's nosebleeds. "She might have something useful to—"

"Stay put and shut up." Bastian opens his eyes and looks at Henry, a strange expression on his face that Henry finds familiar but can't read.

"Please," Bastian adds, barely audible.

Henry remembers. When he first brought Bastian back and went to pick him up from Dr. Wright. The moment Bastian saw Wright, there was that expression on his face, quickly hidden: fear.

Henry nods and stays put.

It doesn't look like much, watching someone use their power. Bastian is just standing there, bent over the sink slightly, hands on either side of it, eyes closed. After a while, he tightens his grip and scrunches up his face a bit, like he's trying to concentrate harder. Trying to work through Henry's barrier?

Well. Here's an opportunity to try out what the book said. Not like Michaels or anyone else will know. And if he can keep Bastian from hurting himself, it's worth it.

Henry doesn't close his own eyes—might be too obvious. He does try to visualize the shield like he was doing earlier this morning. Mesh bubble. Strong but thin. Feel out to where it's creating a wide barrier and try to bring it in a little....

Bastian looks up sharply and starts to say something but cuts himself off before he can make a noise. He's breathing a little heavily but seems to be fine otherwise. No nosebleed.

"Michaels," he says, voice slightly shaky. "Let's record outside. I'm guessing getting blood on the machine would be considered unhygienic."

"A good guess, sir."

Henry follows them out. Rather than waiting for the recording, though, he goes to talk to the detective about the message the policewoman mentioned.

He gets punted around between four people before finding the CSI who has the note (good to know these guys aren't overly burdened with efficiency). The man hands it over, sternly tells Henry they'll need it returned as soon as possible, and then goes back to ignoring him.

When he gets back to Bastian and Michaels, they're finishing up. The machine is whirring quietly, and Bastian is ripping electrodes off his skin with more force than is absolutely necessary. He notices Henry approaching and grabs his arm. "We need to talk."

"Oh, *now* we need to talk?"

"Not here."

"We have evidence to—"

"In a minute."

Henry looks at him, then over at Michaels. "Bastian needs a quick break before we review this." He hands her the evidence bag and ignores Bastian's withering glare at the implication that he needs a rest. "We're going to go grab coffee at the cart in the atrium. Can we bring you anything?"

"Triple shot macchiato with extra foam and four sugars." She looks up from the machine after a moment. "Yes?"

"You…don't seem like a triple shot macchiato kind of person," Henry says.

"Maintaining a constant lackadaisical air can be tiring, Captain."

(Is she…smiling?) "Um. Right. Well. We'll be back in a little bit."

When they get to the atrium, Henry starts for the coffee cart, but Bastian pulls him around to a side hall.

"What the hell were you thinking?" he demands, keeping his voice low.

Henry narrows his eyes. "Is this the part where you tell me what's been going on with you all morning? Or is it the part where you berate me incoherently, and I'm just supposed to stand here and take it?"

"We don't have time for this."

"No kidding. Start talking."

"I can't."

"Bastian—"

"Look, it's more dangerous now. You can't just start using your power on purpose. I told you, didn't I? What would happen if she figured out that you know?"

"Then why did you give me that book? Was I supposed to just use it as a doorstop?"

"I—" Bastian rubs his eyes. "It's not that you shouldn't read it. Or use it. But I didn't know when I gave it to you that…."

The pause goes on long enough to be a proper silence. And they really *don't* have time for this. "If you're not going to tell me what's going on, there's no reason for us to stand around here," Henry says, more than a little irritated. "And I owe Michaels that coffee."

"Wait." Bastian touches his arm, and as Henry turns around, he thinks he sees Bastian flinch. (Is Bastian reading him? Is there something messed up about the negation field, since Henry was just manipulating it?)

"She knows," Bastian says. "Or thinks she knows. Maybe it was what happened with Anna, or some other little thing, but she definitely—" He straightens his hunched shoulders and looks at Henry. "You're already stronger. You can consciously manipulate the negation field. It's only a matter of time before she sees it in action, and then she'll—"

"What?"

Bastian shakes his head helplessly. "I don't know. She'll do more than just stick you in the asset program, though, that's for sure. All it takes is, say, one concentrated use at a crime scene, and—"

"Hey, I was helping—"

"Stop helping!" Bastian's voice is unnaturally loud in the hallway. "Helping is going to get you killed. Or worse."

"Why are you being so—?"

"Why do you think you were ordered to bring me back to the compound?"

Henry blinks at him, thrown by the apparent change in topic.

"Valentine must have known where I was for most, maybe all, of the year I was gone," Bastian continues. "Why wait until just then to have someone bring me back?"

Fighting fire with fire. "She wanted to pit you against John Doe. Use your power against his."

"Because she lost control of him. Without control, he's worthless. Without control, any asset is worthless. Whether killing the senators was her idea or his, in the end, whatever experiment he was a part of didn't go as planned. So she needs to get rid of him."

Bastian smiles humorlessly. "She lost control of me, too. So why not make the most of the opportunity and have us duke it out? If one of us survives, she can arrange for that one to have an accident. Or maybe we'll take care of her problem ourselves."

"And you think, what, if I learn to control my power, she'll have someone take me out, too?"

"I don't think. I know. She told me."

Henry stares at him. "What?"

Bastian crosses his arms over his chest and turns away. "While they were… fixing me. She said it was my fault you broke so many rules to get to Level 20, so anything that happens next is my fault, too. She said she's had some conversations with you that were 'troubling.' She also assumed since we got into the library, we got hold of information we shouldn't have. So if anything changes, she'll notice. And then she'll have to act."

"It's not," Henry says. "Your fault, I mean. I made a choice. I don't regret it. Especially not after seeing what they did to Johnson and finding you hooked up to that—" He clears his throat. "I don't regret it."

"Maybe you should."

They lock gazes then, and something funny happens in Henry's stomach.

(He can't help but think of the awkward stairwell conversation again and wonder if Bastian remembers it, too. If that was an actual thing or just something you say when you're about to carry an injured person down a staircase and definitely not spend any time thinking about his arms around your neck or his face pressed into your shoulder or the fierce something that wells up in your chest when you think about what they did to him and how you'll never let anyone hurt him again with the possible exception of an occasional smack upside the head when he's being an idiot who thinks he can just not tell you things and order you around—)

"It's not that I'm not grateful," Bastian says awkwardly. "I just—I don't want you to—"

He sighs, then goes cold again. "Never mind. Read the book, do your tricks, whatever. If she finds out, it's on you. I just thought you should know the potential consequences of your incessant need to be helpful all the time."

Henry can't decide whether he's confused or stung or both. "I'm not going to stop figuring out how to use my power," he says. "Especially if I can use it to help people. You might as well give up trying to talk me out of it."

"You know you don't actually have to always be Doing the Right Thing and Caring About Everyone and Helping All the Small and Innocent and Needy—"

"Oh, for—it's not *about* that! Can you maybe take two seconds to consider the possibility that even though you're a pain in the ass sometimes, someone might actually care about you?"

That shuts him up instantly.

When it becomes apparent that Bastian isn't going to think of anything else to say, Henry nods once. "I'm getting coffee for Michaels. Then we're going to go see about that message."

He walks toward the atrium and doesn't look back.

Chapter 23

BASTIAN HOLDS THE evidence bag in his hands. Inside is a single piece of white paper about the size of a notepad. It has the Hall logo and header on it—the sort of thing you might find on any senator's desk. This one, unsurprisingly, also has Senator Haldis's name on it.

"We found it next to the body," the CSI is saying. "Odd sort of suicide note, but it's all there was." The CSI shakes his head. "I know you people think it was a murder, but all the evidence...."

"You think the senator wrote it, then?" Michaels asks.

The CSI shrugs. "It matches the handwriting we found on various documents in his office. We'll have to conduct a more thorough handwriting analysis to make sure it wasn't forged, but that seems to be the case."

Bastian turns it over and looks at the writing:

Have fun being a scapegoat.

"Any idea what it means?" asks the CSI.

Bastian ignores him and tries to focus. There's a lot of emotional residue around, so it takes him a few moments to really hone in.

And then that focus is shattered by the sound of approaching footsteps.

"Anything?" Henry asks, giving Michaels her coffee, which she starts drinking at an alarming rate.

Bastian hands the note over without looking at Henry. "That'll be all for now," he tells the CSI.

"Hey, you can't just—"

"We'll get it back to you before we go, don't worry," Henry says.

"Just like I've already told everyone," he adds under his breath as the CSI walks away. "Do they think we've never been to a crime scene or something?"

This from a retrieval expert who'd never worked a case before this one. Bastian almost smirks before he remembers he doesn't have time to think Henry's funny.

"Mean anything to you?" Out of the corner of his eye, Bastian can see Henry flipping the note over and frowning.

"Not yet." Bastian holds out a hand, and Henry passes it back to him.

Bastian doesn't bother to get more distance between himself and Henry's negation field this time, since Henry's made it clear that he's going to be an idiot. Instead, Bastian just refocuses, takes a deep breath, and closes his eyes.

It's harder with Henry around, though not as hard as it should be—good to know he's going to completely ignore what Bastian just told him. But even with less of Henry's negation, it takes awhile to get anything. One layer is the dull gray of Senator Haldis's emotions being manipulated as he wrote it. Underneath that...something else.

Bastian presses his lips together in irritation. The police are still milling around, though there seem to be fewer of them now (bored-sleepy-listless). Michaels is more subdued but close enough to be felt fairly easily (curious-focused-determined). And Henry—

Bastian strengthens his shield as much as he possibly can, given his divided attention. He doesn't want to be able to feel Henry right now, even through the fog of negation.

(He does feel him, though. A little bit. Because he always feels everyone despite the different shield configurations he's tried over the years—until Henry, of course. But whatever Wright did to him this time has made him stronger, which means everything is more intense now. So when he brushes against Henry's concerned-thoughtful-awkward, he can't *not* feel it, but he can sure as hell shift away from it because dammit, there's a job to do, and thinking about anything else, like a stupid argument, is just—)

Before Henry or Michaels have the chance to protest, Bastian opens the evidence bag, takes out the note, and holds it in his left hand. He uses his teeth to pull off his right glove and sticks it in his pocket. Then he rests that hand, palm down, on the note.

It's vague at first, whatever other emotions happened around this thing. But he can feel more than just the gray now; it's familiar, the smugness, the knowledge that *he could have decided not to do this one—he's powerful enough now—but he doesn't mind following orders when it means he gets to take care of an arrogant know-it-all who didn't think he could do it...just goes to show, no one is immune to him...and he even got the bonus of knowing it made her scared, she knows she's not pulling the strings anymore, that she can ask, but he can choose not to, and what is she going to do about it? That's why she thinks he has to go, why she's going to pit them against each other; because someone has to go down for this before she gets connected to it, and killing Haldis only helps temporarily...so maybe he'll just leave a little message....*

Bastian blinks and looks down at the actual text of the note again: *Enjoy being a scapegoat.*

"It's for me," he says.

He can practically feel Henry's frown boring into the back of his head. "What does it mean, then?"

"Trouble."

"Excuse me!" someone calls from down the hall. "What are you doing here?"

A smartly dressed woman, flanked by two security guards, walks briskly toward them.

"This is a crime scene, ma'am," says one of the policemen. "We need you to—"

"Not you." The woman nods to Bastian, Henry, and Michaels. "Who are these people? Have they been properly cleared?"

Henry steps forward. "We spoke with security before we came up. I'm Captain Mortimer, and these are my associates. We're investigating alongside the police force. Can I ask who you are?"

"Senator Nunez. I'll need to see some identification. Immediately."

Henry hands her his ID, which doesn't seem to impress her much (disdainful-irritated-determined).

"From the compound," she says. "Of course you are. Senator Haldis's little side project. I suspect you're here to see what you can cover up."

She hands the ID back. "I'm not a fan of shadowy organizations that think they're above the law, Captain. Particularly when there's been a string of suspicious suicides directly related to Hall officials. You say you've been investigating these incidents?"

"Yes, that's right."

"And you're receiving your information from where, exactly?"

"Our superior officer, Major Valentine, received a request from the Compound Council to have us assist the police with this case."

"The Compound Council has no jurisdiction here. You have no sponsoring senator?"

Henry hesitates. "Senator Haldis was—"

Nunez smiles thinly. "If your only connection to the Hall was Haldis, I think you'll understand why I'm asking security to confiscate your weapons and detain you."

"Ma'am?"

"What happened to Senator Haldis was unfortunate, but it doesn't change the fact that he had recently come under investigation, along with several other senators, regarding illegal activities." She glares around at them. "Five members of our community are now dead, and the only connection appears to be you compound operatives. You see why we're forced to take action to get to the bottom of this."

She nods to the security guards. "Gentlemen?"

Henry flicks a glance at Bastian, who shakes his head slightly. (Is this something Valentine set in motion? Is this what John Doe meant with that note?)

"Of course we'll cooperate," Henry says. "But it would be helpful to be able to discuss things with—"

"Oh, don't worry about getting a chance to agree on your story. Major Valentine is on her way."

***

The Hall doesn't have a deep, dark dungeon to throw them into, so they're stuck with being locked in an aides' meeting room until Valentine comes for them. It's probably indicative of how much the senators' aides are valued that the room is small, cramped, and only has a whiteboard, a beat-up table, and a few chairs in it. Since Henry's and Michaels's weapons and phones have been taken—and Bastian's never been allowed either—there's no way to know what time it is. Or any way to shoot someone out of boredom.

Bastian sighs and flops into a chair, pushing it back so he can rest his feet on the table. "Cheer up, Michaels; I'm sure they'll put the machine back together again after they finish searching it for anything devious."

Michaels sits down across from him. She's actually nervous about it, he realizes: nervous-worried-concerned. "As you know, Mr. Lucas, there are very few of those machines in existence, and their construction is an arduous process that most engineers wouldn't attempt. The major will be displeased if we lose possession of one."

"I'm sure we can just rob another compound if we need to. Their machines would be pretty dusty, since it's been several hundred years since they've had to use them, but—"

"They won't do anything to the machine, Michaels," Henry says over him. "The major will be here soon to sort this all out."

Bastian snorts. "Is that what you think? After all this time?"

"Major Valentine values the autonomy she has at the compound," Henry says, sitting down next to Michaels. "So she'll want to keep on everyone's good side to maintain it. But she's also not going to let the senators take away her tech or hold her operatives indefinitely. There's compromise, and then there's showing too much weakness in front of the enemy."

It's solid logic, actually. "You think the senators are the enemy?"

"There's got to be some sort of connection between the senators who are under investigation." He pauses, then looks at Bastian. "Do you have any idea where John Doe went after he…did whatever he did to Senator Haldis?"

Bastian shakes his head. "The read dissipated after I got everything out of the note, and we didn't have time to record to see if there's anything else in the background. All I can say is it's definitely him. And Valentine had something to do with it."

Michaels looks up sharply. "You think the major—?"

"Someone ordered him to kill Senator Haldis, and all signs point to Valentine. At the very least, she knew what he was doing. Her connection to this one was the strongest out of all the murders we've looked into."

He rocks a bit in his chair. "I got the sense that Stacey Cambridge was his idea, but the others were assignments. This one was, too, but it wasn't as well planned as the others. It was desperate. Short notice. It put John Doe in a more powerful position—he could have said no, but he didn't. He wanted to do this one. He took pride in that, in turning the tables on her."

"And you know for sure he was thinking of the major?"

"I mean, he didn't think her name or anything, but he obviously knew her when we ran into him in the city. And he said then that he was following orders. So it has to be Valentine who's ordering him to kill the senators. What I can't figure out is why this one was more important than the others."

"You're suggesting that Major Valentine is behind this?" Michaels says, still struggling with the concept (shocked-lost-confused). "She would never do something like that."

"She would do something *exactly* like that if she felt threatened," Bastian says grimly. "I don't get what would push her this far, though. Something about John Doe and me, I think. The experiments. They didn't go according to plan, so…."

Henry coughs. "I may know something about that. And the senators under investigation. The, uh, piece of tech I was testing for one of the hackers picked up the major talking to Senator Haldis."

"That's right, you mentioned." Bastian was a bit busy at the time being weak and useless from blood loss. Amazing he can even remember this now.

(He remembers other things from that day, too, but—) "What did they say?"

"It sounded like there was a committee she had to report to. And Haldis wasn't impressed. He was concerned she wasn't on top of things, that something had gotten out of hand. She told him it was fine, but it didn't sound like he believed her. He mentioned some sort of fail-safe if things didn't work out."

"That must be it. This committee wanted her to do something, and she couldn't pull it off—or they just didn't like how she was doing it. Haldis was in charge of delivering the ultimatum, and she responded with this."

"With all due respect," Michaels says, "don't you think this is overreaching? We don't have any proof."

"Not traditional proof, no," Bastian agrees. "We have the reads that put John Doe at the scenes, though it'd be more damning if we could corroborate with an official read on him. We've got Henry's eavesdropping, though of course that won't hold up unless there's a recording of the conversation somewhere."

The very idea fills him with disgust, but…."What I really need to do is read Valentine."

Henry raises his eyebrows. "Is that even possible? I mean, without her agreeing?"

"Falls pretty squarely into the not-even-if-hell-freezes-over bucket. I can read her a little when she's in the room, but her shield is really good, so it's not like I can—"

He cuts himself off, just catching the muddle of emotions closing in (angry-smug-determined-loyal-frustrated-worried) before the door slams open. Valentine, several black coats, a Hall security guard, and Senator Nunez file into the room. Henry and Michaels stand. Bastian doesn't bother.

"Are you all right?" Valentine asks them (sounds concerned but doesn't feel it—game face on, then).

"Yes, Major," Michaels says. "We apologize for the inconvenience."

"Not your fault, Michaels."

"If the niceties are out of the way, can we please proceed with the issue at hand?" Senator Nunez narrows her eyes at them all (disdain-anger-fear). "Major, I believe you have some explaining to do."

"As do you, Senator." Valentine turns toward her. "Why have you locked up my officers? They have full permission to be on Hall grounds and to assist with the investigation."

Bastian notes she says "officers," which doesn't include him.

"That permission was given by Senator Haldis, who is now dead, along with four others. I suggest that if your compound wants to interfere with city business from here on out, you get your permissions from a higher authority."

"That won't be an issue. This isn't city business anymore." Valentine nods at the black coats with her. "Please take the suspect into custody."

It would be nice, Bastian thinks as the black coats move toward him, if he could be surprised by anything she says or does anymore. "Enjoy being a scapegoat," he mutters to himself.

"Hold on—" Henry says at the same time Senator Nunez says, "What are you—?"

"The issue will be dealt with back at the compound, after which we will file the appropriate reports with the city police," Valentine says over both of them. "My officers have been put in danger and need to be debriefed. And the suspect needs to be interrogated."

Bastian laughs.

When everyone stops and stares at him, he says, "It's irony, get it, because I used to…never mind." He lets the black coats take his arms and haul him to his feet.

"I trust I'll be kept apprised of developments," Senator Nunez says stiffly.

"Of course." Valentine waves a hand at the black coats. "Let's move. We have work to do."

Her favorite phrase. It makes Bastian want to laugh again, but then he catches Henry's eye accidentally (concern-anger-helplessness immediately blocked by one of his negation fields), and suddenly all Bastian can do is clench his jaw and follow the others out.

Chapter 24

"I'VE BEEN REVIEWING the case data, and I'm glad I was able to reach you in time," Major Valentine says once they're back in her office at the compound. "There are concerns about these murders, given the way they occurred."

"Excuse me, ma'am, but—you really think Bastian is involved?" Henry says incredulously.

"I'm afraid it's very possible. The existence of a second empath is extremely unlikely. Our retrieval data would have turned up such a potential. And the reads taken at the crime scenes have been…inconclusive. Particularly the more recent ones. The recordings also show some unusual interference that could easily have been intentional on Sebastian's part, possibly to hide evidence."

Or it could have been interference from a negator trying to figure out his power, Henry thinks guiltily. "Michaels?"

She looks uncomfortable. "It's true that some of the reads are less precise than what I've usually seen from Mr. Lucas. And some appear to have been tampered with."

Henry turns to her. "What? Why didn't you say?"

"I only got the rendering results back just now. The basic reads are still there, but nothing is as clear as it should be."

"How is that even possible?"

"There are a variety of ways," Michaels admits. "Mr. Lucas himself could have actively interfered during the recording, or the rendered files could have been manipulated."

Henry shakes his head. "But how would Bastian have been able to get out of the compound to kill the senators? And the first two happened before he got here. Why would he have risked being found?"

The major sighs. "The earlier murders will need to be investigated more thoroughly—something you were assigned to do, as I recall. As for the later ones, I believe you're aware of Prison Officer Templeton's…sympathy for Sebastian. There has already been an incident in which he was able to convince her to help him circumvent security. It's hardly outside the realm of possibility that there are others within the compound who would be willing to get him where he needed to go."

"Why kill them, though? What could he possibly gain from that?"

"I intend to personally interrogate Sebastian to find answers to our remaining questions and to understand his motives. In the meantime, I trust you two will keep clear. If I require your assistance, I'll let you know. Officer Michaels, you may go."

"Yes, ma'am."

As soon as Michaels closes the door, Major Valentine hits Henry with a very serious look. "I appreciate your service on this case, Captain. Though I think you'll agree your performance hasn't always been ideal, in the end, I believe you've done some good."

"Thank you, ma'am," he says. Because there's nothing else to say to that.

"I do have another request for you."

She comes around to the other side of the desk where Henry's standing and hands him his gun. "I need you to do what must be done to protect the compound."

He stares at his weapon. "I don't—"

"Sebastian may still be equipped to avoid surveillance. Or he could…find a way of doing so again, if he can't at present."

She must know about the jammers. Or suspect.

"It seems logical to assume that if he did have free rein, he'd try to escape again to avoid the consequences of his actions," Major Valentine continues. "If that's the case, whoever tried to stop him would need to be ready to fulfill their duty."

"You think he'd…?"

"I hope not." She smiles sadly. "But it's my job to be prepared for all possible contingencies. It's the job of any officer, as I'm sure you know."

Henry swallows. "Understood." He takes his gun and returns it to his belt.

"And Captain? One last thing."

Twenty-two years ago

"TELL ME WHAT it's like."

Bastian keeps his body as still as he can, but his eyes scan the room warily. A mirror covering one wall, a clock on another, a little box near the ceiling on the third, and the door, steel gray and now closed. Like he's been arrested.

Major Valentine must have caught the look on his face because she sets aside the tablet she was looking at and smiles. "Don't be afraid, Sebastian. I just need to find out how we can best help you here."

The way she talks is sort of fussy, but he likes that she speaks to him like he's a grown-up. Like what he has to say matters.

Like he's not some overly sensitive freak.

"What it's like," he repeats.

She nods, lacing her fingers together. "When you use your power. What happens?"

He thinks of hiding in the alley where she found him, dirty and too full of everything, and shudders. But it's not always like that. He tries to think of a good way to explain.

"One time Mom and Dad took me to the ocean. It was when things weren't so… anyway, Mom had a whole plan for what we were going to do and when, but all I wanted to do was sit by the water. They had to drag me back to the hotel every night, or I would've stayed there. I liked the way the waves went in and out, the sound they made, like breathing. Sometimes these quick, little things, and sometimes these bigger, louder things. But always something. Back and forth. If you're not paying attention, it all blends together. But if you do pay attention, you can pick out each wave and figure out right when it's going to hit the sand."

"*Waves,*" *says the major. She looks sort of bored by his explanation, but she's nodding. "And when you were in the alley? Still waves?"*

"*Not…exactly. It's…when there're too many people, it's like—a really big wave. Or a—what's it called—?"*

"*Tsunami.*" *She seems lost in thought for a moment, then turns back to him and smiles a little. "You said you like the ocean, though. Does that mean you like your power?"*

"*No.*" *It comes out before he's even had a chance to think about it. "It's* awful. *Everyone is hurting and angry and sad and happy* all the time *and* all at once, *and it's—sometimes it would wake me up at night, and Dad would yell and Mom would tell me to go back to sleep and that would start it all over again and I couldn't shut it out and—"*

"*Sebastian.*" *She puts her hands on top of his (jolt of something, but it fades, and there's just calm). She gently pulls his hands away from where they're holding his head. "Open your eyes."*

He does. She's smiling again.

"*You'll learn how to control your power here, like I promised. That means separating out these feelings and learning how to shield yourself from them. There's absolutely no reason why you shouldn't be pleased with what you can do. It's remarkable, and you'll be able to do amazing things once you've learned how to use it."*

He wants her to stop touching him, wishes he had some sort of barrier on his hands between his skin and hers. But he doesn't say anything about it.

She sees the look on his face and laughs. "I know you don't believe me, but it's true, I promise. There's something I'll need from you, though."

He narrows his eyes. "What?"

"*Honesty. Answers to some questions. The compound was created to understand and help people with powers like yours, and we can't do that if we don't ask you questions and find out more about what you can do." She lets go of his hands and sits back in her chair. "What do you think? Can you do that for me? Answer some more questions? Help me and my team understand?"*

"*Questions? Like about how it feels?"*

"*Exactly.*"

A part of him doesn't want to do it. But what other choice does he have? The major wants to help. And it has to be better than hiding in the alley and everything that came before it.

He nods slowly. "All right."

"*Excellent.*" *She nods to the glass, and there's a knock at the door. After a moment, it opens to reveal a man in a lab coat, carrying a tablet and smiling in a way that isn't entirely pleasant.*

"*Sebastian,*" *says Major Valentine, "this is Dr. Wright. The two of you are going to get to know each other very well."*

Chapter 25

"SEBASTIAN."

He's confused for a moment, blinking repeatedly until the room comes back into focus. Until *she* comes into focus.

"There we are." Valentine smiles at him. "How are you feeling?"

It's a non-question, so he doesn't answer. Instead, he focuses on clearing his head and trying to remember what happened. The black coats were taking him out of the aides' room at the Hall, and then…? Henry and Michaels were gone, and there was a small, sharp pain in his arm, and—

"Drugging me? Really?" He realizes his hands are shackled together, but at least she let him keep his gloves. He's sitting on a chair in front of a table in a room with a mirror on one wall, a PA system up toward the ceiling, and a steel gray door.

She wasn't kidding about the interrogation, then.

Sitting across from him, a tablet next to her, Valentine continues to smile. "Fond memories?"

"Not particularly. Are you actually going to interrogate me?"

"No. The hackers can manipulate earlier voice recordings to produce the appropriate confession. This is just for show."

He raises his eyebrows. "You're really going to do this. He was right."

"I would have preferred to have you take care of this unfortunate situation."

"Your failed experiment, you mean."

"Experimentation by its nature includes successes and failures. We can learn from both. Unfortunately, Senator Haldis's committee was having trouble seeing that."

Bastian is suddenly confused. He assumed the drug she used on him was the same one Henry used to bring him in, which means he should be starting to get his power back by now. But instead, there's a dull *nothing* buzzing around in his head, giving him a headache and a sense of…hollowness. Of lacking. It makes his skin crawl.

"Ah, it works, then," Valentine says, watching him closely. "Dr. Wright wasn't sure it would."

"What did you do to me?" Bastian asks around gritted teeth.

"It's an improved version of the serum we use to negate assets. Dr. Wright thought it would be best to test it out on a more powerful asset to determine its efficacy, and given your recent changes, you seemed like a good candidate."

Changes. Not augmentation. He's not sure what to think of that. "Good to know you're still experimenting on people without their consent." He pauses. "Negation. Of course. Have you been stealing Henry's blood this whole time? Or just since he manifested?"

Valentine leans back in her chair. "I'm glad you brought the captain up, actually. I suspect he knows quite a bit more than he should at this point. You realize this makes my job more difficult."

"Good."

She smiles thinly. "Up till now, we've gotten complete cooperation from him. Now that he's…aware, I suspect it will be more difficult. We may have to institute more extreme measures."

"Wait. Cooperation? He's been *letting* you do this to him?" Bastian tries to swallow the anger, but he can feel it bubbling to the surface. (Stupid, calm down, it won't help, it's just one more thing she can use—)

"The captain is unaware of his contributions at the moment. Dr. Wright takes samples periodically. As you can imagine, there isn't a particularly effective serum that can be used on a negator, but when the captain's power was dormant—or only recently manifested—it was easier to keep him pliant. And forgetful."

She actually looks sad, but he doesn't need his power to know it's not real. "Unfortunately, now that he's getting stronger, our previous methods won't be as effective. Unless…."

Here it is. "Unless what?"

She slides over the tablet. "A signed confession for the murders. That, combined with the digital audio reconstruction, should seal things up nicely. No need for Captain Mortimer to experience any undue hardships."

"You're *blackmailing* me?"

"Absolutely not. I'm offering you a deal, Sebastian. Help me with one last mission—closing this case—and your friend will be safe. If you make your decision quickly, I'll even minimize the damage you've caused for Prison Officer

Templeton and the hacker. They've suffered enough because of you, don't you think?"

"And what about your other little problem? Even if I take the fall, he's still out there."

"Measures will be taken to ensure that individual is not a threat."

Bastian glances down at the file on the tablet. "And if I don't agree to this?"

Valentine shrugs. "There are consequences for one's actions, including consequences that affect others. You've made a surprising number of connections here in the compound, Sebastian. I've let them remain because I thought it was good for you, but now I suspect they're just one more way for you to avoid accepting responsibility. If you don't take this deal, you may find that the resulting unpleasantness affects more than just you."

The drug is starting to wear off at last, and he can feel the cloying emptiness coming off her, giving him a headache. At the same time, there's something building up in him, burning his chest and throat. He knows he should just take the deal if he wants to save Henry and the others—it's the sort of stupidly heroic thing Henry would do, anyway—but Bastian's not heroic.

He's angry.

"No."

Valentine sighs. "I thought you might say that." She stands and gestures toward the mirror. "I'm very disappointed in you, Sebastian."

"No."

"Yes, I heard you."

"I don't think you did."

She raises her eyebrows at him. "I assure you, I—"

"You don't get to be disappointed," he snaps, getting to his feet. "You don't get to hurt people because of something I didn't do. You don't get to belittle Catherine or threatened Kent. And you sure as hell are never touching Henry again."

"Sebastian, please. This is hardly—"

"*No.*"

He doesn't mean to do it, but it just sort of happens: all the anger rises in his chest and explodes out of him in a huge wave of rage.

The excruciating pain comes next.

He's peripherally aware that Valentine has stumbled back, eyes wide. The officer who opened the door at her summons is doing the same, holding his stomach and grimacing.

Bastian's entire body is on fire with pain, he thinks he's going to be sick, his hands are still shackled, and he can barely walk straight.

So it seems like a great time to stagger out of the room as fast as he can.

The compound will be on alert soon, Bastian thinks grimly. He knows a few hiding places here and there, but without a jammer, they won't offer much safety. He needs Kent.

(It's like last time, only getting to Level 1 was harder then, what with all the bleeding. Now he can feel his strength slowly coming back, and his power is returning to normal after that whatever-it-was, the pain and nausea fading. If he can find a place to hide for a few minutes, maybe he can—)

Hello? Can you hear me?

"Ow! Laurel, now's not a good—"

You said that last time, but it's important. And—wait, why is it so hard to connect? (fear-concern-worry) *Are you okay?*

"Sort of. Listen, I'm in a hurry, so—"

He's here.

Bastian goes cold. "At the clearing? Laurel, you need to get out of there. Now."

No, not the clearing. Here. Your compound.

"You're *here*?"

I followed him. (nervous-proud-pleased) *I wanted to know who he is and what he's doing. He hasn't seen me, I don't think.*

"Laurel, he's an empath, he can feel—"

A group of black coats is coming down the hall toward him. Leisurely, so no alarm raised yet. Bastian's not taking chances, though. He ducks around a corner.

"That was incredibly stupid," he hisses at Laurel. "Even assuming you somehow managed to evade his power, if he sees you—"

I stayed really far back! Anyway, if he gets cheeky, I'll tie him up in vines and choke him to death. Or something. I had to come, you know. The trees are worried about him. You're worried about him.

"Understatement."

Right, so go get Henry, and let's take this guy out.

He almost wants to laugh. "Bit bloodthirsty, are we?"

He killed people. He upsets you. I want him gone, so let's do it.

"It's not that simple."

Why?

"I'm sort of…busy escaping right now."

(gleeful-worried-satisfied) *Oh! Took you long enough! I'll help.*

"No, Laurel—the whole compound is going to be on alert any minute. You should—"

Remember the part where you're not the boss of me? There's a pause. *Oh. That's not good.*

"What?"

A conifer just told me he's on the move. I'm going to figure out which direction.

"Laurel—"

I'll check in again to see when you're out. I know where we can go. But we'll need Henry. I think. He's a what's-it-called, negator, right?

"How do you—?"

You think about the nothing feeling pretty loudly. And you connect it to him. You should tell him, by the way.

"What, that he's a negator? He already knows."

No. The other thing.

"I don't know what you're—"

Yes, you do.

Bastian swallows. "That's—"

Well. Maybe not in the middle of escaping. Be careful. I'll see you soon.

"Laurel—"

But she's gone.

***

He gives himself a bloody nose and a throbbing headache convincing a passing black coat she feels like dropping her cuff keys and wandering off. Probably should have found one who carries a handkerchief like Henry, but time's too short. At least the compound cuff keys are universal, so it doesn't take too long for Bastian to free his hands.

He takes the stairs down to Level 4. It feels counterintuitive to go further away from the compound exit, but he's not going to make it without a jammer. He could go all the way down to his cell on Level 15 and get the one Kent already gave him, but that would require a lot more effort to avoid detection.

At least Bastian doesn't end up having to go so far as the main hacker ops area. He runs into Kent in the hall. Kent starts, takes one look at Bastian's face, and jerks his head toward the secure corridor.

As soon as they're in the unmonitored part of the hall, Kent starts flapping his arms. "What the hell, Lucas? Between you and your captain, I'm gonna be—"

Bastian cuts him off. "I need another jammer."

"Of course you do." Kent shakes his head. "Never mind that it's my career on the line."

"It won't be. John Doe is close. I need to get out of here and find him. Once I do, this all goes away. Valentine won't be able to threaten you anymore."

"You're seriously trying to say you're doing this for me or something?"

"Yes! For you and Catherine and Henry and Michaels and this whole stupid place. If he keeps killing people, Valentine will keep finding scapegoats to cover it up. So I need to stop him. Now."

Kent looks at him for a long moment (surprise-interest-calculating). "All right. But first, you're gonna do something for me."

"Now really isn't the—"

"You owe me, Lucas."

Bastian sighs. "Okay. What?"

"I'm going to go in there and get your jammer. You're going to read Sybil when I talk to her. Find out if she, um—"

Bastian pinches the bridge of his nose. "Fine. Go."

Kent's surprisingly quick about it. He does linger talking to Sybil, but it's not too bad. Bastian hopes he's upgraded the camera jammers in the hall, though.

Kent comes back out and stuffs the device into Bastian's hand. "Well?"

"Ask her out. You'll be fine." He turns to go.

"Hey, Lucas."

Bastian turns back to find Kent scratching his head awkwardly. "Don't get killed," he says. "You do that, I have to watch it on the monitors, and that kind of thing puts me off my lunch."

Bastian half smiles. "I'll do my best. And thanks for this. And…before."

"Yeah. Now get out of here."

***

The alarms start going off as soon as he reaches Level 1.

Figures that he'd be on the most populated floor when it happens. The jammer will keep the cameras from getting him, but if he's not careful, he could smack into an officer or a black coat turning the corner.

Bastian tries to focus on separating out individual emotions so he can know when people are close enough that he needs to avoid them. The trouble with focusing on one thing like that, though, is that it's hard to focus on anything else. Which is why he only has about a second of warning before he literally runs into someone he knows.

Henry immediately grabs Bastian's arm—too hard, and he's got an aggressively solid negation field going on, so Bastian can't feel anything from him.

"Captain?" A female officer is standing behind Henry.

"Check on the others, Smith. I'll take care of this."

There's too much negation for Bastian to be able to read her, but her dubious facial expression pretty much sums it up. She nods and hurries off anyway.

"Are you all right?" Henry asks, his voice low.

"Yeah, fine. I—"

"Good." Henry takes a breath. "I'm going to need you to come with me."

"Uh, in case you hadn't noticed, I'm a little busy."

"Escaping. I know. I can't let you do that."

Bastian stares at him. "Are you serious?"

Henry clenches his jaw, then uses his free hand to draw his gun and point it at Bastian's chest. "Yes."

It's ludicrous enough that Bastian's still waiting for the punch line. Except Henry looks absolutely prepared to shoot him.

Valentine must have said something to him. This can't have been his assignment all along, right? To buddy up to the escapee and make sure he's complacent enough that he doesn't want to escape a second time? And if he does, to take care of it?

There are options. Bastian's more powerful now. He could probably break entirely through Henry's negation, even at its current level. Of course, it'd hurt like hell, but all he would need after that would be to manipulate Henry enough to get him to put the gun away, and then….

There's no way Bastian can do it.

(Pathetic, that it's come to this, that his stupid feelings are going to get him killed because he can't just—)

Bastian reaches slowly into his pocket and pulls out just enough of the jammer that Henry can see it. "I recharged it before I got to Level 1," Bastian says. "We have fifteen minutes left for you to tell me what the hell is going on."

Henry stays still for another few seconds, then lets go of Bastian's arm and lowers his gun. "My team," he says very quietly. "She said if I didn't keep you from escaping, she'd…well, she wasn't specific. I suppose vague threats are more terrifying. But I got the impression we were talking about more than just demotions and transfers."

"She's cornered. She's looking for weaknesses to exploit so she can try to salvage the situation. Your team is yours, obviously."

"Thanks. Very reassuring."

Bastian shakes his head. "Henry, I have to go. John Doe is outside somewhere. Near the compound. If I can catch him and neutralize him—"

"Are you out of your mind? He's killed five people—that we know of. You've flat-out said he's stronger than you. How can you think some sort of showdown is going to—?"

"What's your solution, then? Just let Valentine get away with it? Or maybe you want me to surrender myself and get charged with everything John Doe's done just so everyone stays 'safe'?"

He glares at Henry. "Keeping Valentine in power, keeping this project of hers going, it's only going to get more people killed. Catching John Doe is the way to end it, and no one's more suited to that than I am. We're enough alike—"

"You're *alike*?" Henry says with startling vehemence. "When was the last time you killed someone?"

"A little over a year ago. Sort of."

Henry falters at that. "What?"

"I don't have time to talk about this." Bastian checks the jammer, then turns back to Henry, forcing himself to meet his gaze. "Look, I don't want to get you or your team in trouble, but I can't stay here. If that means you have to shoot me, then get on with trying so I can stop you."

Henry starts to raise his gun again, an expression on his face that Bastian can't read. Or feel.

Then he stops. "I can't."

(Come with me, Bastian wants to say. I don't want to do this alone. I don't want you to think I went around killing people like John Doe. I need to explain, and if explaining means you don't want to do what we talked about in the stairwell anymore, that's fine, I just—)

"Don't worry, Captain," says a voice. "I can do it for you."

Bastian and Henry whip around to find Officer Michaels standing behind them, her gun drawn. "Please step out of the way, Captain," she says.

Bastian sighs. "Okay, can people stop pointing guns at other people? Michaels, don't be an idiot. I need to—"

"I'm afraid that's not going to happen, sir. I have my orders."

"And what are those? To kill me?"

"To prevent you from escaping."

"Valentine doubled up, did she? You two should've coordinated."

Michaels hasn't lowered her gun, and her expression seems to be flickering between several emotions—none of which he can feel, thanks to Henry's current level of negation. A muffled voice comes from her headset, and she tips her head to respond. "Yes, I've found him. The teams can move back and focus on securing the compound exits."

She looks back at Bastian and Henry, face carefully placid. "The major didn't want the captain to be aware of my coinciding orders," she says. "I was only supposed to act if he seemed…disinclined to do his duty."

Henry, at least, has let his gun drop to his side. But he's tense enough that Bastian's not sure he wouldn't still shoot someone if the opportunity presented itself. "Michaels—"

"Excuse me, sir, but I'm going to need you to comply immediately. The major requested that Mr. Lucas be brought to her as soon as he was found." She hesitates, then adds, "I admit this particular assignment doesn't appeal to me. But I have my duty."

Out of the corner of his eye, Bastian sees Henry tighten his grip on his gun.

"Don't," Bastian says quietly, steeling himself to push through Henry's negation field. (Doesn't want to do this to her. Hates that he has to. No choice.)

"Captain. I won't ask again."

"Fine."

Henry's gun is raised again and pointed at her. Steady and calm, though his negation field is weakening as he puts all his focus somewhere else, so Bastian can feel the foggy hurt-frustrated-tense—and the healthy side dose of self-loathing.

"Seriously. Stop with the guns," Bastian says, his voice sharp.

Why is Henry doing this? It'll be the end of his career, if not his life. There's no reason he can't just let Bastian deal with it. Bastian's the troublemaker, anyway; he's the one everyone expects to do things he shouldn't be doing. He escaped once, and he can do it again. He doesn't want his actions here to cause problems for Henry. Or Michaels.

But it's too late for that. And he shouldn't care anyway.

He hears a tiny sigh from Michaels. "I'm very sorry, sir," she says, and pulls the trigger.

Bastian hears the shot go off at the same time he shoves Henry to the ground. He also hears something from Michaels's direction—a sort of shuffling and a thud, and then voices.

"Is she down? It looks like she's down. Ugh, I am so not cut out for this."

"She'll be fine," says someone else. "Get her gun. We don't want any more accidents."

"Shooting me is an accident?" Henry mutters, shifting under Bastian's weight. Bastian feels a hand on his shoulder. "Hey. It's okay now."

"You've been shot. It's not okay." (What a stupid thing to say.)

He sits up, and Henry does as well, wincing. Now Bastian can see that Michaels got him in the leg.

"She missed the femoral artery," Henry says, seeing the expression on Bastian's face. "It hurts"—he sucks in a sharp breath—"but it's not going to kill me. Where's my gun?"

Bastian ignores him, distracted by Catherine tying up Michaels's hands with a zip tie and Kent gathering up weapons. Kent notices Henry's gunshot wound and goes pale. "Uh, Templeton, I think you better take a look at this."

Leaving Michaels passed out and propped against a wall, Catherine comes over and kneels next to Henry. "You should go to medical, but for now…." She takes off her jacket, rips part of the sleeve, and wraps Henry's leg. "This is a bit exciting, isn't it?" she says cheerfully. "Well. I suppose getting shot isn't really—"

"Can someone please explain what the hell just happened?" Bastian demands.

Footsteps head toward them, probably alerted by the gunshot. Finished seeing to Henry's wound, Catherine gets to her feet and yells down the hall, "He escaped toward the north exit. Go on, and I'll tell the others when they come by. Hurry!"

Once the group of black coats is past, Bastian glares at everyone and opens his mouth to begin the appropriate tirade, but Kent interrupts. "Lucas, before you start yelling at us, there are things we need to tell you. Like your John Doe is just outside the compound."

"I know."

That stops Kent in his tracks. "Wait, what? How?"

"Doesn't matter. You were explaining why you're both colossal idiots."

Kent frowns at him. "I saw your guy on the outside monitors—finally a hit on that image, right, Captain?—and then I saw him disappear. I thought maybe the info ought to accidentally miss proper channels and go to you personally."

"I was using a jammer," Bastian says. "How did you find us?"

Kent grins and takes a device out of his pocket—a bit like a jammer, but more compact. "Meet Jammer 2.0, Jammer Squared, Son of Jammer—"

"Kent."

He sighs. "It jams the jammer. Makes it possible to track someone who's jamming. It's just a prototype, but now seemed like as good a time as any to test it out.

"So when the alarms went off, I found Prison Officer Templeton right away," Kent continues in a rush, "since she knows how to find escaped prisoners. And here we are. Now you'd better go before the rest of the black coats catch up."

"I can't," Henry says. "My team—"

"Captain, if you don't bring in this murderer, he'll go on killing people, right?" Catherine gives him a comforting look. "That will be bad for everyone. You should let us look after your team for now. We can't promise anything, but we'll do our best."

Henry gets to his feet slowly, grabbing onto Bastian's hand for leverage. He hesitates, then says, "Templeton was right before; I should really get to medical. I'll just slow you down."

Fun being on the other side of that argument now. "Laurel's out there. She's good with healing," Bastian points out. Then he sighs. "But you're right, you should probably—"

"Good, it's settled," Catherine says. "You should get going. We'll make sure Michaels is all right."

"Take the south corridor to the back exit," Kent tells them, handing Henry back his gun. "It should be the least populated right now. Oh, and one more thing: I was playing with that level 3 data access, and I found out John Doe has been combing the database for information on asset experiments and early asset programs, among other things. Based on the case data you guys had me go through, I think he's trying to figure out where he came from."

"That makes sense," Bastian says. "He said he had people helping him to get data."

Kent pales considerably. "He's got someone on the inside? Who?"

"It's complicated. If you catch any other hackers looking into anything similar, make them stop right away."

"Yeah, sure. You want me to point a gun at them? Or just ask real nice?"

Catherine rolls her eyes. "All right, children, that's enough. Bastian and Henry need to get going. Shoo, you two."

Bastian clears his throat. "Don't, um. I mean. You know."

"We'll be careful." Catherine smiles at him. "You should be, too. Now go."

Bastian takes Henry's arm and helps him down the hall.

Chapter 26

IT'S POURING RAIN outside. It would be.

They have to hide here and there from officers securing the grounds, but the rain is limiting everyone's vision. Hopefully the cameras', too, since by Henry's count they're well out of time on the jammer, and there hasn't been anywhere to stay long enough to safely recharge.

His leg has become a dull throb of pain he can mostly ignore except when they crouch behind something. Every time Henry winces, he sees Bastian do it, too. Sympathy? Or empathy?

It must be the latter because Henry's pretty sure he's let his negation field mostly fade out. Too hard to focus on keeping it going *and* on not thinking about the pain *and* on not thinking about anything else. Like his team. Whom he's just abandoned.

"You don't have to do this," Bastian tells him, peering around the storage boxes they're currently using as cover. "If you go back, at least medical can take care of your leg. And you won't be in much trouble, especially if you say I coerced you into coming out here or something."

Henry laughs. "Okay, first of all, the idea that you could coerce me into doing anything I don't want to do is ridiculous."

He suddenly stops being able to see anything remotely amusing about this. "Anyway, I just directly disobeyed a pretty serious order back there. Getting in trouble is the least of my worries."

(It's a betrayal, that he's left his team to deal with whatever Major Valentine throws at them. The entire point of being a commanding officer, the vow he took, is to protect his team. This is his fault; he should be the one to deal with—)

"*Bastian*!"

Something launches itself at Bastian with such force that he nearly loses his footing—and briefly loses hold of Henry. Henry staggers back, trying to ignore the jolt of pain in his leg as he lands awkwardly on it. His gun is in his hand before he realizes what's going on.

"Quiet!" Bastian hisses at the girl hugging him. He's almost-sort-of hugging her back, Henry notes with amusement.

"Right, sorry." She turns to Henry, and he confirms that she's the girl from the clearing. "Oh, Captain! You're hurt! Do you want me to—?"

"Yes, but not here." Bastian looks around, obviously trying to determine if the area is clear enough for them to move. "Where is he, Laurel?"

"Bastian Lucas," she says sternly, "we're in the middle of a torrential downpour, your Henry is hurt, and you want to go after a murderer?"

"More people than Henry will be hurt if I don't find him," Bastian retorts, skipping over her use of possessive pronouns.

They glare at each other like little kids having an argument, their wet hair plastered to their faces.

Then Laurel clears her throat. "Doesn't matter, anyway. He's gone."

"You *lost* him?"

"Conifers don't have much of a range, as you well know! And it's raining, so the trees are busy right now."

"Laurel—"

"We'll find him again, okay? The trees will help when they're done drinking. But we need to get to safety first."

Bastian swats at the raindrops that are falling from his hair onto his nose. "Fine. Where?"

"The clearing. Obviously."

"That's the first place Valentine will look!"

"Yeah, but she doesn't know what's there. Still there." Laurel beams. "And you brought Henry, so we'll be extra safe, at least for a little while."

Henry raises his eyebrows. "I appreciate the vote of confidence, but I don't see how—"

"Enough talking, more walking." She gives Henry a sympathetic look. "Sorry."

"It's all right."

They don't run into any more security. By now, everyone in the compound is busy checking inside, generally the first line of defense, since most would-be escapees never make it outside. There are still a few officers and black coats milling around the loading dock, but they seem mostly concerned with doing their rounds as quickly as possible and getting back inside. Once the compound itself is secure, they'll send a scouting team out further into the forest and the rest of the surrounding area. Henry estimates they have a window of a few hours before they're in trouble.

Right on the edge of the forest, Laurel stops and frowns. "Henry, I need you to go—"

"He doesn't have to." Bastian turns to Henry, whom he's been helping to walk. "You need to focus on pulling in your negation field so Laurel can use her power."

"Bastian, you can't ask him to do that while he's hurt!" Laurel protests. "Wait, he can do that? Really?"

"Sort of," Henry tells her. "I'm getting a little better at controlling it, anyway." He's already trying to envision it like he has before, figure out how to recreate the way he shrank it down at the crime scene. The book said it would become second nature, but for now, it seems to be a combination of extreme focus and completely random flailing, much to his irritation. It also gives him a bit of a headache, but at least that gets his mind off his leg. A little.

Laurel's fingers are twitching, and after a moment, she nods. "Okay, good. I can make this work. Let's get far enough in that we're safe, and I'll look at Henry's leg."

They start to walk again, and Henry discovers the delightful challenge of moving, being in pain, and keeping the negation in check all at the same time. It also helps that he's sweating and starting to feel a bit dizzy. And then there's the distracting way the forest path behind them is closing up with brush and foliage, masking their trail.

"So…you can manipulate plants," Henry says to Laurel.

Laurel frowns. "I don't *manipulate* them. I ask very nicely. I'm a very nice person."

Bastian snorts, which makes Laurel turn and regard him sternly. "Look, you. Behave, or I'll have the trees shift their leaves and let all the rain fall on your head."

"Better listen to her," Henry advises. "I'm not sure the drowned rat look is really doing much for you."

"Pot-kettle-black," Bastian mutters. Henry half expects him to stick out his tongue for good measure.

"See?" Laurel grins. "Running for our lives can be fun!"

"Can we maybe do this *after* we get somewhere safe, and you make sure Henry doesn't bleed out?"

"Yes. Right."

Henry suddenly feels self-conscious—on top of everything else. (Seriously, why is the ground spinning?) "It's not that bad," he tells them. "We don't have to—"

"Oh, well, if it's not that bad...." Bastian abruptly stops supporting his weight, and Henry begins to stumble.

"Bastian!" Laurel cries.

He's holding Henry again a split second before she finishes saying his name. "Don't be a hero," he says quietly.

Something about the concern in his voice—he's not even trying to hide it—makes Henry's chest feel tight. He nods.

Laurel leads them further into the forest, the path continuing to close behind then. It's a different route from the one Henry and his team took what seems like a lifetime ago to bring Bastian in. This one is wild with huge trees on either side and small plants underfoot, most of which he doesn't recognize. He wonders if it was always like this or if Laurel talked the plants into redecorating.

The rain lets up as it moves into afternoon, but by now, Henry's soaked enough that it doesn't help much. He's also started to shiver, which he vaguely thinks is probably a bad thing. Potentially an infection to go along with the feverish heat in his cheeks and at his temples. He can't wait to sit down and sleep for a week. Or forever.

"Here. I recognize that log." Bastian stops. "Laurel?"

"On it."

She does another sort of movement with her fingers, and the brush and trees in the area somehow...move back. There's now a little opening of sky and grass, like a small campsite, with Bastian's log at the center.

While Bastian helps Henry over, Laurel hurries to the log and pulls a duffel bag out of the hollow. She opens it, takes out a blanket, and throws it at Bastian, who barely catches it with his free hand. She also removes a small bottle.

"I need to get things," she says. "Make him lie down, and give him some of this. It'll help with the pain."

Laurel hands Bastian the bottle, which he, in turn, hands to Henry. After that, there's a bit of hustle and bustle while Henry sits on the log, a bit bemused and feeling more than a little wretched.

"Hey. You're supposed to drink some of that."

Henry blinks at Bastian, then shakes his head (bad idea; now the dizziness is worse). He fumbles with the cork until Bastian—surprisingly without rude commentary—takes the bottle from him, opens it, and watches while he drinks some of it. It's not disgusting, exactly, but it's floral in all the wrong ways.

"You're sure Laurel's not trying to poison me?" Henry asks, handing the bottle back.

Bastian smiles and sets it aside. "Probably not. You need to lie down now."

Bastian gets him settled on the blanket, at which point Henry firmly decides he's done moving for the rest of his life. The pain is blurring with the wet and cold, and he's having trouble concentrating on Bastian's and Laurel's voices.

"Can't you hurry it up?"

"I'm doing the best I can. Now hush." Laurel's voice near his ear: "Henry, I need to take the bullet out. The plants are going to help, but it's probably going to hurt a bit anyway."

"S'fine," Henry mumbles.

"We should have done this earlier. Now he's—"

"It wasn't safe, and you know it. The plants will take care of the fever, too. Now stop worrying."

"I'm not—"

"You are. *Quiet.* Let us work."

He hears something tear (good thing he doesn't care about these pants). Then a breath, and something sharp digs into his thigh. He tries to be stoic about it by clamping his mouth shut, but a noise slips out anyway. He immediately feels Bastian grab his hand, and he clings to it harder than he meant to.

Then he's drifting a bit, but he thinks Laurel gets the bullet, dresses the wound, and wraps it. Someone puts another blanket over him (surprisingly not sopping wet, though it's a little damp). He probably shouldn't sleep, even though he wants to…they really shouldn't stay here too long…but his eyes don't care and are closing anyway.

The voices keep going, quieter now.

"He needs dry clothes, otherwise the infection—"

"The plants will take care of it for the time being. They promised."

"That's not actually how medicine works, you know."

"Excuse me, who's the plantspeaker here? Oh, right. Me. If you want to talk about feelings, since you're the expert on those—"

"Absolutely not."

"You know, it might be better if you just—"

"No."

"Okay, but it's pretty obvious."

"Can you just focus on making sure he's—?"

"Bastian. He'll be fine. Really. Let him sleep."

The voices stop then, and Henry drifts off.

***

He wakes, disoriented, sometime after it's started to get dark. The makeshift clearing is quiet and shadowy, and all he can think of for a moment is how indefensible it is.

Henry keeps waiting for the pain to hit, but it doesn't. He's cold and damp, but otherwise…nothing. Sitting up (carefully) doesn't seem to bother him, and when he touches his leg (gingerly), there's still nothing.

"Must've been some plants," he says.

Bastian, sitting on the log next to him, looks over at the sound of Henry's voice. Henry's pretty sure that's the worst I'm-not-emotionally-invested-in-this-situation look he's ever seen. "Better?"

"Much." Henry cranes his neck. "Where's Laurel?"

"Talking to the trees. Asking if they've seen John Doe." When Henry raises his eyebrows at him, Bastian raises his back. "What? You've dealt with how many potentials, and *this* is what's weird to you?"

"Sort of? I mean, I've never heard of a—what did she say she was? A plant-speaker? That's not exactly common, is it?"

"Not common, no. But not rare. I remember one in the compound when I was growing up. Keeping a plantspeaker underground was one of Valentine's more thoughtful moves."

He doesn't say what happened to that plantspeaker, Henry notes.

Against his will, Henry finds himself distracted by the mention of Major Valentine. (He broke his word, couldn't complete his assignment, and now the major is probably making good on her threat, whatever that actually was, but it means his team is likely suffering, and—)

"Hey." Bastian is frowning at him. "They'll be fine."

Henry rubs his eyes. "First of all, you're lying. Second of all…." He stops. "Second of all, you're reading me, and I'm not doing anything with my power. How are you—?"

"The trees have spoken!" Laurel joins them with a grin, sitting down on the ground across from Henry. When neither Henry nor Bastian looks particularly impressed, she shrugs. "What? It's fun to say. Stop being grumpy. I actually do have news: The trees say they saw your John Doe."

"Where?" Bastian demands.

"Hang on," Laurel says. "You can't just go running off—"

"I need to find him."

Henry frowns. "Don't act like you're going after him alone. I came with you for a reason, which is mostly to keep you from being stupid about this, so—"

"I don't need a babysitter; I need to—"

"Will you both just *hush*?"

Henry and Bastian both snap their mouths shut and look at Laurel. It's probably a good thing the light is fading, Henry thinks, because he's pretty sure neither of their looks are particularly polite.

"The trees lost sight of him not too long ago," Laurel says. "And—seriously, shush, Bastian!—they said they think he's headed for the clearing. So we need to go there, too."

"Laurel, we can't—"

"Yes, we can. In fact, we want to get there before John Doe does so we can set up fortifications and stuff." She smiles at Henry. "Right, Henry?"

"Uh. Can we?"

"Well, *you* can. And I can help."

Henry wants to ask what the hell she's talking about, but Bastian apparently has more to say. "Why would we want to let him get to the clearing? I thought you said there was something there that you wanted to protect. You really want him to find it?"

"No," Laurel says. "Like I said, that's why we need to get there first. And then we capture him and bring him to justice!" She frowns at their dubious expressions. "That's what you do with criminals, right? You bring them to justice."

"Except justice in this case is Valentine, since she's in charge of the compound," Bastian says. "And since she made him, she's not likely to care if he's running amok in the forest. Better that than potentially refusing to kill senators she's told him to kill and making her look bad."

"We could contact the Compound Council," Henry suggests. "They're the ones who wanted us to investigate to begin with, and they're supposed to deal with situations like this where the highest-ranking officer can't be trusted anymore. If we tell them what the major has been up to and bring them John Doe—and your reads from the crime scenes—that'll have to count for something."

"And how were you thinking we'd transport John Doe across the country to Council HQ?" Bastian asks. "Just tie him up and walk him over there? Or maybe invite the Council here based on the word of a seemingly disgraced captain and a murder suspect?"

Decent questions. They don't have the supplies, and with only three of them, they don't have the manpower, either. Unless....

"We take the compound."

Bastian stares at him. "You want to *mutiny*?"

"We're not on a ship, so it isn't mutiny. It's—"

"—something that would definitely ruin your career, not to mention getting you killed if it doesn't work."

"First things first," Laurel says briskly. "We need to get to the clearing. Like I mentioned at least three times." She gets to her feet and brushes damp dirt off her pants. "Bastian, you take the bag. Henry shouldn't have to carry anything right now."

"I'm really fine," Henry protests.

"Nah, it's more fun to make Bastian do it. Besides, they're his supplies."

Henry turns to him. "I did wonder where they came from."

"I made caches all over the forest. Before. In case I had to run again."

Henry feels a twinge of guilt. Bastian could've run if he'd known Henry was coming to take him back to the compound. But because of Henry's power…. "Where did you get the supplies?"

"Plenty of compound officers coming through the forest during the year. Sometimes they were…inclined to leave things behind."

Now Henry has unpleasant mental images of Bastian injuring himself to manipulate compound staff. Just to stay alive.

"Come on!" Laurel calls. "I need to close the opening here. Bastian?"

Bastian pauses with the bag slung over his shoulder. "I don't feel anything," he says, not giving Henry time to adjust his negation field. Despite that, Bastian doesn't look like he had any trouble at all.

As soon as they're back in the thick of the forest, Laurel asks Henry to contract the field more firmly. He tries to concentrate, but it takes him an embarrassing amount of time and effort to feel it move at all, especially with Bastian and Laurel staring at him impatiently. So much for being inherently amazing at this.

When he's finally managed it, Laurel waves her fingers, and the trees and brush close in. After a moment, it's impossible to tell that there was ever an opening here.

They walk for most of the night. It's less than comfortable in damp clothing, tripping over roots here and there, but Henry's just glad to be able to walk, frankly. The path, which ought to be more treacherous in the dark, is remarkably clear. It occurs to him that Laurel is probably having the greenery get out of their way.

By the time the light shifts enough to indicate dawn, they're all exhausted. Henry's prepared to press on regardless—they still have a full day's walk ahead of them, and the compound scouts must be out and about by now—but Laurel is yawning, and Bastian nearly falls flat on his face a few times.

"Laurel, can you do that thing again?" Henry asks. "Make us a place to rest for a bit?"

"Not when I'm so tired," she says, yawning again. "Takes too much negotiation to get that many living trees to move. But I can do this."

She makes another hand gesture, slightly bigger this time, and a collection of old branches, brush, and downed trees twists and turns itself into a squat, dome-shaped structure, a bit like a lean-to.

"Hope there are silk sheets in there," Bastian mutters, following Laurel toward it.

"This thing will be noticeable from the path," Henry says, looking over his shoulder. "What if the scouts have been going full tilt and manage to catch up?"

Laurel waves him closer, then points. He turns and watches the surrounding plants cover their tracks and hide their shelter from view. The trees stay still, he notices.

"Good?" Laurel asks sleepily. She crawls inside the shelter.

"Um. Yeah. Good."

Henry watches Bastian crawl in as well, then sticks his head inside. "We should really set watch, don't you think?"

"Don't be stupid; the plants will tell me if there's any trouble. Now come and get some sleep."

The inside is surprisingly spacious—enough room for three people without having to be on top of each other. No silk sheets, but Bastian gets out blankets and passes them around. Laurel immediately curls up on one side. Bastian takes a side where he can have his back to the structure and face the opening—a protective stance so he can see who's coming, Henry thinks, trying not to consider why Bastian would want to do that.

"Fire's probably not a good idea in here," Bastian says, covering himself with a blanket. "There'll be dry clothes and more supplies closer to the clearing."

"I dunno, I was getting used to being cold and wet all the time," Henry tells him.

Bastian smiles slightly, but it fades. "You're all right? Your leg?"

"Yeah. Laurel's pretty good."

"Yes, I am," Laurel mumbles from the other side of the structure.

Henry huffs out a small laugh and doesn't miss that the corner of Bastian's mouth twitches.

"So. Good night. Or morning. Whatever." Henry lies down between Bastian and Laurel and wraps himself up in the blanket.

Bastian makes a noise and closes his eyes.

Henry watches him for a moment and definitely doesn't think, yet again, about waking up in the hotel and feeling Bastian against his back. He listens to the forest noise for awhile before finally falling asleep.

***

Henry's not sure what wakes him at first. Beyond the wind and the bird song, there isn't much noise.

Except.

He's managed to end up closer to Bastian than he meant to—must've rolled over in his sleep (thanks so much, subconscious). Maybe it's just as well, though, because Henry realizes what woke him: Bastian is muttering something, his face contorted, starting to shift around but obviously trying not to. Nightmare?

Henry sits up. He vividly remembers an overnight mission where Johnson had a nightmare (pang of regret at the thought of Johnson—never mind, can't do anything about it now). When Henry tried to check on him, Johnson head-butted him in the nose. The rest of the team thought it was hilarious, of course, and Johnson was extremely apologetic afterward. But Henry learned his lesson about waking someone up suddenly.

Bastian's started thrashing, and there's sweat at his temples. The mumbling is still incoherent, but it's faster and more desperate. Henry can't sit still anymore. Headbutt be damned.

"Bastian?" He tries to keep his voice down to avoid waking Laurel. "Hey. Wake up."

Bastian makes another unhappy noise.

Henry's chest is uncomfortably tight. He reaches out and touches Bastian's arm. Starts to say his name again.

Bastian gasps and sits up suddenly. He turns to Henry, eyes wild, chest heaving. He looks terrified.

Henry swallows around a dry throat. "Ba—"

He doesn't get another syllable out. Bastian is suddenly clinging to him, hard, burying his face against Henry's chest. After a split second of being startled, Henry ignores the wet and cold and hugs Bastian to him, silently stroking his hair.

Henry has a series of stupid thoughts at this point: wanting to fight whatever's upset Bastian; enjoying holding him and immediately feeling guilty about that (because how you can enjoy someone's suffering?); and a bigger, even more stupid thought: that it's ridiculous to keep pretending he can avoid this, that the mission still comes first, that his priorities are still in line with his training and not with the idiot in his arms.

At some point, Henry realizes Bastian's grip on him is loosening. He's alarmed until he realizes it's because Bastian's falling asleep again.

In the end, Henry finds himself leaning against the wall with Bastian half in his lap (potentially awkward), Henry holding him to his chest. Any moment now, Henry's going to stop running his fingers through Bastian's hair (that's supposed to be soothing, right?).

"I've never seen him do that," Laurel says quietly from the other side of the shelter.

Henry nearly jumps out of his skin but manages to stall the movement before it can wake Bastian.

"I'm surprised he even came in here, frankly," Laurel continues, sitting up. "He hates sleeping in front of other people. Used to make me put together two shelters in the clearing so he could have one to himself. Totally rude." She pauses. "I think he was scared after what happened."

Henry looks down at him. "What happened?"

"I'm not sure. He never said. I think it was an experiment that went wrong. He was dying when I found him."

"But you healed him."

"The plants and I stopped the bleeding, yeah. He got better. But he wouldn't talk about it."

Bastian shifts slightly in Henry's arms but doesn't wake up.

"I didn't like it when you took him away," Laurel says, an edge in her voice. "I knew you'd take him back there, back to where they hurt him."

"I didn't know," Henry says awkwardly. It sounds pathetic because it is.

She softens. "I know you didn't. They don't tell you stuff like that. It's easier if you don't know. But you found out in the end, didn't you? Otherwise you wouldn't be here."

"I…yes. I think this is where I'm supposed to be." Crushing guilt about his team aside.

"Good." Laurel nods. "So this is the part where I tell you Bastian is my friend, and if you break his heart, I'll string you up in vines and set loads of wasps on you."

"That's not—wait, did you say wasps?"

"You can probably get another hour of sleep before we have to move."

"Hang on—Laurel—"

She doesn't say anything else. He can hear her lie back down, her breathing evening out.

Henry sighs and leans his head back against the wall. He knows he won't be getting any more sleep, but having Bastian breathing steadily against his chest is a decent trade-off.

Chapter 27

BASTIAN GETS THE idea from Valentine. Which means it's a horrible idea, and he's not sure why he does it.

(Yes, he is. It's because he's beginning to give a damn about other people, which might be the stupidest thing he's ever done.)

It starts as soon as they get into the forest. Laurel said the trees lost sight of John Doe, but Bastian keeps a steady watch anyway, not just with his eyes but also feeling out. Doing it constantly while helping Henry and working through the varying levels of his negation means Bastian's almost immediately exhausted, and it only gets worse throughout the day.

He keeps it up anyway, sifting through pinpricks of bird minds (sing-mate-fight, the usual tinny buzz he gets from animals, harder to read than humans) and other things shuffling through the underbrush.

There's nothing, though. He's not sure if that's because he's having to read through Henry's barrier or because there really isn't anything.

When they stop the first time so Laurel can treat Henry's wound, Bastian reaches out harder. Enough that his nose starts bleeding and his head starts throbbing. Still nothing.

Except he can feel some of Henry's pain through the negation fog, and it twists Bastian's stomach up in knots. Because Henry was stupid enough to go against his orders and get shot. Because of Bastian. He's in pain now, and it's Bastian's fault.

It's not until they settle in Laurel's makeshift shelter that something changes.

He's drifting off to sleep when he feels it: something brushing up against his mind. Or barging in, really.

Well, hello there. Are you enjoying your little forest vacation?

"Where are you?" The others are asleep, so Bastian keeps his voice low.

Close. Maybe you should start to get worried.

"Maybe you should hurry up."

(surprise-interest-amusement) *You want me to come kill you and your friends sooner rather than later?*

"I have a deal for you."

Really.

"You're headed for the clearing, right? We'll talk there."

Well, this is an intriguing development. You sure you don't want to give me a hint? There's a pause, then something like laughter. *You haven't told them, have you? That you're trying to find me. That you have something up your sleeve. A pretty stinky sleeve by now, I bet. You were never much of an outdoorsman, were you?*

"Stop wasting time."

Speaking of trying to find me, your plant girl is really bad at being stealthy. I don't know why she even bothered to follow me to the compound. Did she forget how empaths work? But I left her alone for now. More fun this way. Does make me question your choice of friends, though. Are you sure it's worth it to keep them out of this? That's awfully heroic of you.

"It's not. I'm just tired of dealing with you. I'm tired of this investigation. I don't need them to end you and move on to better things."

What, like hiding in the forest? You think she's going to let you do that?

Lying on the hard floor of the shelter, Bastian opens his eyes and watches Laurel and Henry sleep. "No," he says quietly. "I don't think she will."

The laughter feeling again. *So you're going to do what she wants you to. Just like you always do.*

"She literally made you to follow orders. I don't think you have any room to judge here."

I've broken free. You haven't, even if you like to pretend you did.

"Murdering all those senators because she wanted to keep them from messing up her plans? That's breaking free?"

I killed them because I wanted to. Because I was growing my power. And Haldis, well, he was just fun. He never liked the project. He thought there'd be no way to contain me. He was right.

Oh, I never asked—did you like my videos? Manipulating all those techs to erase me from the security tapes was a pretty big feat. That one was all me, incidentally; Valentine was never good at those kinds of details. Almost like she didn't care if I got caught. After she lost control of me, that is.

"Good for you. Now get out of my head and go to the clearing."

Interesting, John Doe says after a moment. *I think I know what's going on here. Would you like to know what's going on here?*

"Not particularly."

I think you're afraid.

Bastian snorts (and doesn't think about how Henry said the same thing). "What gives you that idea?"

Because you care about these people, and you don't want them to get hurt. Really pathetic, by the way. Caring about people makes you weak. It's something she can use against you. You know that.

"Okay, we're done. Focus on catching up to us."

Oh, I'll catch up, don't worry. But first, I think you should see why you're going to lose.

"Not interested."

No, really. Let me show you.

He's getting used to being able to feel emotions through this kind of connection, so at first he doesn't realize what's happening. Then he feels this one get bigger and louder, faster and faster, curling around his lungs and sticking in his throat. It's not John Doe's emotion; not exactly. He's…projecting it. Sort of like Bastian projected his anger in the interrogation room. Except now Bastian's on the receiving end.

Fear.

He bolsters his shield immediately, but it doesn't matter. The fear gets stronger and stronger, and he can't break the connection. He feels himself start to panic, airway getting cut off, sweat breaking out on his face, his concentration shot to hell. (It's disgusting and overwhelming and everything he hates about emotions and he wants it to *stop*—)

Wright has no idea what he did to me, John Doe says. *I can do things no empath has ever done.*

Not true, Bastian thinks, but it's swallowed up by the fear.

That's why I'm going to kill you. Maybe your plant girl and your captain, too. Because I want Valentine to know what a mistake she made with me. I want her to regret it. I want you to regret it, too. That you ever thought you were stronger than me.

See you soon.

He expects it to go away as soon as John Doe breaks the connection, but it gets worse instead.

(He remembers the alley, hiding and holding his head and waiting for his power to kill him, until Valentine found him and brought him back to the compound, and after a while, he didn't wake up hyperventilating anymore, learned how to shield and protect himself, and if Valentine wanted something in return for saving him, that was only right because she made it better, there was nothing he could do or say that would ever make up for that, and she knew that and used it against him and—)

He hears his name from a million miles away. "Hey. Wake up." A tentative hand on his shoulder.

Bastian jolts out of his stupor, sitting up and trying (and failing) to breathe. He's vaguely aware of Henry next to him, that concerned/frowny look on his face.

(Don't do something stupid don't do something stupid don't do something—)

He does something stupid.

To be fair, he doesn't mean to do it. But Henry's right there with his soothing nothing-nothing-nothing subconsciously at maximum, and Bastian is too weak to care anymore. He throws himself at Henry, clinging to him.

The fear goes away instantly (negation has its advantages), though it's so abrupt that Bastian gets something like empath whiplash. Doesn't matter. Henry is warm and calm and…putting his arms around Bastian and pulling him close enough that Bastian can hear his heartbeat. (Quicker than normal, probably startled, don't read anything into it, bet he has terrified people throwing themselves at him all the time—wait, that's really stupid—never mind, Bastian can breathe again, that's good, breathing is important, right?)

Henry doesn't say anything, just holds him and strokes his hair (don't think about how good that feels). Bastian's breathing slows. He leans into the nothing, leans into Henry, and gradually falls asleep. He doesn't wake up until an hour later when Laurel says it's time to go.

***

Bastian can feel the scouts as he, Henry, and Laurel walk, but they're far enough away that they're not likely to be a problem. The forest here is too thick for vehicles—Henry and his team must have come a different way when they first came to the clearing—and that means the scouting party is on foot. Of course, they should be much farther behind than they are, so they must have a tracker asset with them. If Bastian, Henry, and Laurel aren't careful, the scouts could catch up before they get to the clearing.

Bastian expects Henry to ask about what happened in the lean-to, but he's remarkably quiet as they trudge along. Probably because he's busy trying to walk and read the negation book at the same time. Bastian thinks it's a recipe for disaster, or at least a tree to the face, but so far, so good.

Laurel doesn't say anything, either, even though she must have heard something.

The sound of water starts around midday. It drowns out the complaints of Bastian's stomach, which would like to know when they're going to get some real food. The water's good, though, because it means they're close to another one of Bastian's caches.

"Supplies," he says when they reach the creek. It's the first time any of them has spoken in hours. "I'll get them, and then we can move on."

Laurel sighs and plops down next to the water. She takes off her battered shoes and socks and plunges her feet into the cold water. "We are definitely staying here for a little bit."

Bastian frowns. "We can't. The scouts are—"

"—far enough away for now." Laurel looks up at him. "Get the supplies, and let's rest. Just for a while. You had a rough night. Or morning, I guess."

Bastian flushes and turns away. He tromps through the brush to the hole at the bottom of a particular oak. The bag isn't in great shape, but it has a few more things than the last one: clothes and energy bars, for starters. He remembers indiscriminately gathering up the clothing from a group of passing officers while they were asleep, so he has no idea if any of it will fit. But at least it's dry.

He drops the bag in Laurel's lap and follows suit with the feet-in-the-creek thing. Henry puts the book away and does it as well. The three of them sit there for a while as Laurel rummages through the bag.

"All right, first things first. Wash in the creek, clean clothes. We'll get to the clearing tonight, but I don't want anyone getting sick before then, especially since *someone* was already rude enough to get a fever on this trip." She glares at Henry, who holds up his hands in defeat and almost smiles.

"Then food," Laurel continues, tossing each of them an energy bar. "They're disgusting, but they'll keep you going for the rest of our walk. And I suppose we'll have to bury anything we don't take with us. Just to be safe."

She nods once, gets to her feet, and starts to unbutton her shirt.

Henry jumps up, grabs some clothes from the bag, and backs off downstream. "I'll just, uh, be back in a minute."

Laurel pauses, then grins at Bastian, who rolls his eyes. "You've probably scarred him for life," Bastian tells her.

"I think it's very chivalrous," Laurel says, obviously on the verge of laughing. "Anyway, I'm pretty sure *I'm* not the one he wants to see undressing."

Bastian studiously ignores her, takes another set of clothes, and heads in the opposite direction.

All the little cuts and bruises he's managed to collect sting in the water. Even so, washing off does somehow make everything a little better. The new clothes are slightly too big, but he was right about the importance of being dry versus being fashionable.

Even though he still doesn't think they should linger here, he ignores his own advice for a few moments, taking off his gloves and letting the creek water flow over his fingers. The rocks at the shallow bottom are cold and smoothed into roundness. He closes his eyes and listens to the gurgling, feels the small, steady emotions of the squirrels and birds, the dim echo of hundreds of years of it.

"It's beautiful."

Bastian starts even though he knows who it is. "Pick one," he says irritably. "Negate or don't."

He dries his hands on his pants, puts his gloves back on, and turns around. And has to bite his lip to keep from laughing.

"Shut up," Henry says, looking a bit embarrassed. He's had to roll up the pant legs quite a bit—not because he's particularly short, but because the officer who owned them was obviously a lot taller. The shirt works okay, though, and he's kept his jacket.

"I can't," Henry continues. "Pick one, I mean. Not really. If I'm not thinking about it, the negation just sort of…does its own thing. The book says it'll get easier, but I need practice."

He looks at Bastian, who narrows his eyes. "What do you mean, 'practice'?"

"Tell me what you meant before. About having killed someone."

Bastian clamps his mouth shut.

"It was your power, wasn't it?" Henry continues. "Like what John Doe does. Convince people to—"

"No. And what does this have to do with anything?"

"Answer the question, Bastian. What happened?"

What's Henry going to do, lock him up? Shoot him? It doesn't matter. He would've liked Henry to think he's—ugh—a good person. But he isn't, and if Henry knows that, so what? Bastian already has a plan to take care of all of this. Henry's opinion of him isn't part of that plan, so it doesn't matter. What Valentine had him doing doesn't matter. Not anymore.

"I was an interrogator. Sort of like what you saw on the case, only the police brought us suspects, and I did reads on them at the compound and at the scene to compare emotional signatures. We usually didn't get the cases until the police had exhausted every other means of getting a confession.

"They…didn't always want to confess. The suspects, I mean. I didn't realize what was happening at first, but the people I read started to give in really quickly. They'd get quiet. Docile. Their emotions just went gray. Valentine didn't tell me, and I didn't ask, but I learned later that I was destroying their minds. Like John Doe tried to do to you in the city."

He's definitely not looking at Henry now. "I found one of them when I was in Catherine's jail block. He was completely insane. I think he died not long after.

"So that's what I meant." Bastian forces himself to look Henry in the eye. "I'm just like him. I've killed people, too. Probably more than he has. Snyder was the only one I actually saw, but Valentine sure as hell didn't send them all to the authorities like she said she did. Not the ones who were that far gone. They probably died somewhere in the compound, and no one will ever know."

Everything goes quiet. Even the forest seems to settle for a moment.

Then Henry nods. "Okay. That thing that you did back then? I need you to do it to me."

Bastian stares at him. "*What?*"

"Practice. I need to know how to—"

"No."

"Bastian—"

"*No.* Were you listening to anything I just said? Especially the part where I told you I killed people doing that?"

"You really think when we run into John Doe again, he's going to take it easy on us? I have to know how to defend myself, Bastian. Better yet, how to defend anyone who gets caught in the cross fire."

That's not going to be an issue, assuming Bastian's plan works, but—"You're being ridiculous. Dying doesn't help anything."

"Why are you so convinced you'll kill me? Was it something I said?"

"Don't."

"This isn't just a whim, you know. I don't understand why you think you're going to—"

"Because I'm stronger, okay? Wright must've done something to me before you found me on Level 19, and now I can break through your negation field, and my range is broader, and I can feel more, and I just—I don't want to hurt you!"

He immediately wants to take it back…but also doesn't. Because it's true, dammit. He's hurt too many people. He can't stand the idea of hurting anyone else. Especially someone he—

"I know," Henry says quietly. "But we don't have time to dither about this. You have your power, and Laurel has hers. I need to have something, too. Even if all I can do is protect you, I need to be able to do that to the best of my ability. And the book only goes so far."

Something in his eyes keeps Bastian from being able to look away.

"We don't have time," Henry says again.

Bastian swallows. "Okay. With the understanding that this is an incredibly dangerous and stupid idea, and you're no good to me if your brain is completely addled, so do us a favor and don't let that happen."

"Honestly, how long does it take you two to—?" Laurel appears and stops several paces away, frowning. "Someone just had a bad idea, didn't they?"

Bastian points to Henry.

"Wow, really? I totally thought it would be you."

"Thanks."

"Laurel, we need to practice something," Henry says. "We'll be ready to go after."

"Oh, well, if you need to 'practice'—"

"It won't take long," Bastian says loudly. "Can you just watch for those scouts?"

Laurel crosses her arms over her chest. "I think you'd better tell me what this is about."

"John Doe. He's going to catch up eventually. We need to be prepared." Henry pauses. "*I* need to be prepared. Bastian's going to help."

Laurel looks at Henry, then at Bastian. "You're right. That's a really stupid idea."

"I'm pretty sure Henry has a death wish," Bastian agrees.

"Look, it's not like I've been sitting on my thumbs since I realized I have this power. But reading a book and flailing around isn't going to help us if John Doe goes after me again. Or any of us."

Laurel looks alarmed. "He's gone after you before?"

"Before we knew what Henry can do." Bastian glares at Henry. "Broke through in seconds and tried to kill him."

"You already agreed to help, Bastian. So shut up, and let's get started."

He walks a short distance away.

Laurel comes over to Bastian's side. "What do you want me to do?"

"I told you."

"Uh huh. What else?"

"Laurel—"

"I'm not letting you idiots do this on your own. What can I do?"

Bastian sighs. "Just…keep an eye on things. Get away if we lose focus, and our powers start to affect you." He hesitates, then adds, "Do whatever you have to do to stop me if I don't stop on my own."

Her eyes go wide, but she nods. "I'm sure he'll be fine. He's pretty good at controlling it already."

"It's not him I'm worried about."

"Bastian—"

"Ready when you are!" Henry calls.

Bastian closes his eyes and feels out.

It's a test for him, too, he supposes. He knows he's stronger—he wouldn't be able to feel Henry otherwise—but he has no idea what else, if anything, is different.

Increased range, to start. He picks up the chittering and emotions of the birds like he has been; the concern-curiosity-determination of Laurel next to him; and the scouts—not a danger yet, but close enough, particularly with a tracker in their midst.

This isn't what he said he'd do, though.

He finds Henry's shield almost immediately. He's come up with a configuration that incorporates the negation field and makes it stronger—something the book mentioned? All Bastian can feel is his usual nothing-nothing-nothing, more fortified than usual.

They already know Henry can expand and contract the negation field even if he can't always do it without significant effort and focus. He's got the basics down, more or less.

But nothing about John Doe is basic.

Bastian keeps his eyes closed, less because he needs to and more because he can't look at Henry while he does this. Very gently, he sets about dismantling Henry's shield.

It's too easy.

He can't bring himself to do more than convince Henry he feels like sitting down before backing out of his mind and fighting against the queasy feeling in his stomach.

Henry blinks and takes a moment to realize he's on the ground. Then he's back on his feet, taking a deep breath and nodding to Bastian. "Again."

(Bastian sees Snyder in the cell, laughing hysterically, his mind destroyed—Valentine saying she never told Bastian what he did because he never cared, the work was more important than the people he killed, who died slowly and in agony as their minds rotted away—she was right, he never cared, he *shouldn't* care, he'd have no trouble doing this if he didn't—)

They go again. And again. Henry's negation gets stronger, but it never takes Bastian long to break through. Bastian doesn't push hard; just enough to dull Henry's emotions and get him to do little things: take a few steps, turn around, raise his hand.

"Is that all you got?" Henry calls, sounding a little out of breath as he gets to his feet again. "John Doe isn't going to play nice, Bastian. Stop holding back."

Bastian wonders if maybe that's the way to go: beat Henry so thoroughly that they can be done with this. Maybe then Bastian won't even have to argue with him about staying out of a potential fight with John Doe; he'll just admit it's a bad idea. (Fat chance.)

It's not going to be an issue if Bastian has his way. Except John Doe could easily attack even if he does take the deal. From what Bastian's seen, Henry would do okay protecting himself and Laurel against the usual sort of asset attack. It's the *un*usual sort of attack—the kind John Doe favors—that might be an issue. And Bastian doesn't want a repeat of the alley.

So. Time to finish this. Prove to Henry that being on the front lines isn't happening.

He closes his eyes again and *pushes*—

—and actually staggers back when he hits a brick wall of a shield.

Good sign, that Henry can defend against a stronger onslaught. But he can't do it consistently. And not with any finesse. It won't be difficult to....

It *is* difficult, actually.

Bastian blinks open his eyes. Henry's just standing there, his eyes still closed, hands curled into fists at his side. If he's struggling at all, it isn't evident from this distance. He just looks like he's concentrating intently.

Promising. But that's not the worst that could come at him.

Watching him this time, Bastian feels out, gently touching the barrier but not actively trying to push through. Henry frowns but doesn't move, and his shield stays in place. The usual nothing-nothing-nothing of the negation is still there, but with more of an edge to it. Still not enough strength to stop Bastian from being able to use his own power.

He doesn't push aggressively this time; he does it more subtly, like John Doe did in the alley, so it's not even perceptible. Not like a full frontal assault. He doesn't try to affect Henry's mind at first, either; just feels out to touch it, to get a sense of his emotions.

At first, it seems like it's working. He's almost through before the barrier clamps down on him, cutting off his breath for a moment.

Okay, subtlety isn't going to work. One more thing, then.

Without giving Henry time to recover, he uses all his power to *push* against the negation field.

His stomach immediately protests, and he can feel his nose start to bleed, but he doesn't stop. Whatever John Doe can do will be worse than this, and while Henry's shield is holding (wobbling, but holding), there's no telling how long he can do it. Bastian is vaguely aware of Laurel saying something from far off, but all he can think of now is the *push*, which comes with all his anger and fear and frustration about this whole thing.

(And it's like it was then, when the suspect wouldn't confess, they couldn't get enough data to make the conviction, and Valentine said by any means necessary, and he'd done whatever she—)

Laurel's voice is louder now, but he still can't make out the words. He knows something's not right, but all he can do is focus because he's almost through, and that means—

When it comes, it's not at all what he was expecting. It's not like running into a wall; it's more like running into something that goes soft all around him, holding him steady, preventing his power from working but also giving him a sense of safety and comfort. It's Henry's brand of nothing, but more intense than Bastian's ever felt it. It's calm and peaceful and—

Bastian gasps and drops to his knees, closing his eyes against the dizziness. Laurel immediately crouches next to him, obviously wanting to touch him but holding off, knowing it would be too intense for him right now. "Are you all right?"

Bastian forces himself to nod and try to remember how to breathe.

"Hey." Henry waits until Bastian opens his eyes and looks up at him. There's a sheen of sweat on Henry's face, but otherwise, he looks fine. "You're bleeding."

Bastian swipes at his nose. "What did you do?"

"I'm not sure, exactly." Henry shrugs, embarrassed. "You got through so many times, I just thought I'd try...letting you. A little bit, anyway."

Bastian considers this, then nods. He ignores the hand Henry offers him and gets to his feet on his own. "Happy?"

"Bastian—"

"Let's never do that again." He turns to Laurel. "We should bury the leftovers and go."

Then he walks away, trying not to stumble.

Chapter 28

THE SCOUTS CATCH up early that evening.

"How the hell—?" Henry asks helpfully when Laurel tells them.

Laurel shakes her head. "I don't know. They shouldn't be able to. The trees have been trying hard to help us, too. They felt really bad when they told me." She sounds disappointed, which makes Henry wonder how exactly a tree apologizes.

"They have a tracker asset," Bastian says.

Henry and Laurel stare at him. "And you were going to tell us this when, exactly?" Henry demands.

Bastian shrugs. "Would it have helped? A tracker can find anyone. There's nothing we could have done."

"You can't just keep information from us, Bastian! We need to work together to—"

"This isn't one of your missions. You're not in command. You don't get to know everything all the time—"

"Stop fighting, you're scaring the saplings!" Laurel glares back and forth between them. "If anyone's in command here, it's me, so we do what I say. Get up into that tree for now. The forest will look after us while the scouts pass. Then we need to go around the back way to the clearing so we can get there before they do."

Seeing that Henry and Bastian haven't moved, she shoves them toward a beech. "Go!"

The trunk doesn't separate into branches until a fair way up, so it takes a bit of shimmying to get there. Henry looks up into the canopy of green above him and thinks there's room to climb a bit higher and hide in the foliage while still getting a decent view of the forces coming after them.

Laurel climbs around Henry easily and follows a branch off to the right. "Stop dawdling!" she hisses.

Henry has already started to climb further up when he happens to look down and see Bastian still on the ground, eyeing the trunk.

"Come on," Henry says.

"I'm not—this isn't—" Bastian clamps his mouth shut and fiddles with the strap of the duffel he's carrying with their consolidated supplies.

Henry sighs. "What, you never climbed a tree as a kid?"

"No. I was busy being trained how to kill people by destroying their minds."

Oh. "So you lived in a forest for a year, but it never came up?"

"I lived in a clearing for a year. And no." Bastian flushes and looks away. "Can you just—help me up, will you? Please."

Henry does, feeling a little bad about giving Bastian a hard time. After the first bit of awkward scrabbling, Bastian takes off his gloves and stuffs them in his pockets. His bare hands grip better, and once he's gone up a little way, he's able to follow Henry to a higher, more hidden branch without too much trouble.

He does lose his balance once when the bag slips, and Henry grabs him around the waist to keep him from falling. He lets go as soon as Bastian's steadier and definitely doesn't think about holding him after the nightmare.

They eventually get themselves situated on branches not far below Laurel's, then wait for the scouts to close in.

"The beech says fifteen minutes," Laurel tells them.

"Why don't I just negate the tracker?" Henry suggests. "Then we don't have to go through all of this."

Bastian shakes his head. "You're the only negator in existence. They'll notice something's wrong with their power, and it'll alert them that we're close."

Henry doesn't want to suggest it, especially after their little sparring match, but: "You could…convince the team that they don't want to keep following us."

"I could." Bastian's tense but doesn't seem angry, exactly. "I don't think I could keep it up for any length of time, though. I'm stronger, but that would be…a lot."

Henry thinks of Bastian's file. The list of negative reactions. "No, you're right," he agrees quickly.

The daylight starts to fade as they sit in the tree. Henry wonders just how they're supposed to find some back way into the clearing if they can't see. Maybe Laurel could strike up a conversation with a fern or something. Still doesn't sound like fun in the dark, particularly with the scouts nearby.

To avoid fidgeting, he starts thinking strategy.

He has his gun, but it's not exactly a long-range weapon, and there's no way he'd be able to disarm an entire team.

Some sort of attack from Laurel and her trees, then? That might work for a while, but a tracker asset could easily lead a team through whatever Laurel threw at them.

So. Waiting and hiding, it is. Hiding next to an extremely irritable empath who obviously thinks he still needs to be upset with Henry for the power face-off and would probably rather jump out of the tree and let himself be taken back to the compound than stay up here stuck next to Henry. Maybe the scout team would be pleased to listen to Bastian's prickly commentary and inability to admit he might not always be right.

Henry hears a faint noise. It takes him a moment to realize what it is. "When did you last eat something?"

Bastian shakes his head, watching the path. "Busy."

"Your stomach is going to tell them exactly where we are. Did you eat the energy bar Laurel gave you?"

"I put it back in the bag for now. Did I mention I'm busy? And don't be ridiculous."

"I'm not ridiculous; I'm prepared."

Rather than try to grab anything from the bag on Bastian's shoulder, Henry opts for taking the energy bar out of his jacket pocket and shoving it at Bastian. "Eat. We still have a lot to do tonight. And I'm guessing you don't want to be eating when the scouts get here."

Bastian eyes the energy bar like it's a personal affront, but he takes it. "Are you saying I'm a noisy eater?"

"I'm saying they're not going to be impressed by you dropping crumbs on their heads."

"Hmm. Better go with pine cones instead. Unless you've also got hot oil in your jacket."

"Bastian, we're in a beech tree. There aren't any pine cones."

"Is that a no on the hot oil, too?"

Henry looks over at him and sees that he has the energy bar halfway to his mouth and is about two seconds away from laughing. Henry tries very seriously to swat his arm, but that just makes Bastian do something that might be called giggling. Unfortunately, it's contagious.

"Shh!" says Laurel from somewhere above them.

"Would you like an energy bar, Laurel?" Henry asks politely.

"No, thank you. But it's very kind of you to ask. *Some* people haven't bothered."

Bastian frowns. "I can't get to any—"

"It's the thought that counts."

"That doesn't even make any sense," Bastian mutters. Catching sight of Henry smirking, he adds without much heat, "Shut up."

They sit in silence a few more minutes. Henry's pretty sure his foot's asleep—and possibly every other part of him. That must include his brain because he's not aware of having decided to say something. "This isn't exactly what I meant."

"Hmm?" Bastian's watching the path again, eyes half-closed. Probably using his power. Henry immediately tries to pull in his negation field.

"When I said I'd buy you dinner," Henry continues, struggling to keep focused on two things at once. "I didn't mean hide in a tree and hand you an energy bar while we wait for compound forces to come capture us."

(What the absolute hell?)

Bastian looks over at him, then quickly away. "I dunno, there's a certain ambiance to being incredibly uncomfortable and in perpetual danger. Food's not that great, though." He hesitates, then adds, "I thought you'd…forgotten about that."

"I thought *you* had." (He's an idiot. This is *not* the time. He should get out his gun immediately, and not for the scouts.)

"No. It's—I could've done without the being bled nearly to death thing, but that part was…good."

They look at each other, and Henry finally realizes it's a lost cause. "Bastian, I—"

"Double shh!" Laurel hisses, coming closer. "They're here."

The scouting party comes into view: thirty of them, walking mostly in a straight line, armed officers in front and behind. A teenage girl—probably the tracker asset—is at the head of the group, showing the others the way.

Henry divides his focus so he's got some on keeping his negation field small enough that they won't be noticed while still being able to observe what's going on. But he gets distracted when he realizes who's at the back of the line, talking to one of the officers.

"What the hell?" he says under his breath. "Major Valentine never comes with scouting parties."

"We should be flattered," Bastian says grimly.

"I will kick your heads if you don't shut up," Laurel whispers. She taps Henry's head with her foot.

They're too far up to hear everything, but some of the voices are loud enough that Henry can make out a conversation.

"It's vital that this mission end quickly and quietly," the major is saying to the officer. "Unfortunate that it's come to this, but we do have a murderer on the loose. We need to stop him before he hurts anyone else."

Henry wonders if she's talking about John Doe or Bastian.

"Understood, ma'am," says the officer.

Major Valentine puts a hand on the officer's shoulder. "You did the right thing, Michaels. It's important to immediately cut off anything resembling a mutiny before it can become a more significant problem."

Bastian raises his eyebrows at Henry. "I thought you said a mutiny was—"

"Shh!" This time both Henry and Laurel are in on it.

There's not much Henry can tell about Michaels from up here, but she seems stiff (well, stiffer than usual). She's not looking at the major, instead focusing on marching along with the others. He's not sure why she's in the field, since as far as he knows, she's only assigned to small errands for the major and working with the machine. Maybe Major Valentine is hoping Michaels will have some insight into finding them?

Henry supposes he should be upset with her—she did shoot him, after all—but she looks so miserable, he can't bring himself to be angry, really. She was just doing her job.

(Is that what he was like? What he *is* like? Don't ask questions, ignore your morals, and just do what you're told, no matter what it is? Does the major have something on Michaels to keep her in line? Or is it just loyalty?)

"Ma'am," says another officer, making his way toward the back. "It's coming on nightfall. Should we stop before it gets too dark?"

"Absolutely not. We have the means to keep going." She nods to the tracker girl.

"Excuse me, ma'am, but—"

"Keep moving. That's an order, Officer."

"Yes, ma'am."

Henry, Bastian, and Laurel watch them move on down the path.

"They'll be at the clearing in a few hours," Bastian says when they're gone. "There's no way we can beat them."

"Don't be silly. Of *course* we can beat them." Laurel grins, then adopts a dramatically forceful tone that echoes Major Valentine's. "Keep moving!"

They get down from the tree relatively unscathed. Bastian slips a few inches on the trunk and grunts, getting the strap of the bag wrapped around him awkwardly, but of course he won't let anyone help.

Laurel takes them west. There's no path here, just underbrush and trees beneath a slowly darkening sky. Henry's pretty sure they should be tripping over things and banging into low-hanging branches, but everything goes smoothly. Almost like the greenery is shifting out of their way and then shifting back again. Which of course it must be.

They walk for about an hour before the foliage thins out, and Henry can see a familiar ring of trees up ahead.

"Ta da!" Laurel waves a hand. "The clearing."

Bastian stops just before entering, resting his hand on a tree trunk. He's put his gloves back on, so Henry can't be sure, but it looks like he's gripping the wood pretty hard. Feelings about being back here?

Over Bastian's shoulder, Henry can see the area he remembers: an open patch of green grass, a bit too long; two lumps he now realizes are Laurel's shelters; near those, a small patch of dirt that looks a bit like a garden; and a small pool of water at the center.

Smith and the rest of his team stood behind these trees forever ago, waiting for Henry's order to shoot Bastian with the serum and take him back to the compound. Like he was just another potential.

"The clearing," Bastian says. "Great. Now what's to keep Valentine's minions from just walking right in?"

"That's the next part." Laurel hops into the clearing and waves Henry and Bastian over to her.

"The trees surrounding the clearing have root systems that're really close to each other," she explains. "So if we do something to one of them, it'll carry over to all of the others, creating a ring around the clearing."

"A ring of what?" Henry asks.

"Protection. Against assets. Or anyone, really."

"All right, that sounds good. So how do we do it?"

"Wait." Bastian frowns. "If you knew about something like this, why didn't you set it up before? Say, to keep compound officers from barging in?"

Laurel picks at a fingernail. "Obviously because I thought of it since then. And anyway, I wouldn't have been able to do it before."

"Why?"

"Um. Well. Because I would've needed something…special to do it."

"And what's that?" Bastian already sounds wary.

"Henry's blood."

"No," Bastian says immediately.

Since "no" is Bastian's default answer to everything, Henry ignores it. "Why would you need my blood?"

"You're a negator," Laurel says. "If I make a protective tincture with your blood and have the trees pass it around, it'll be better than just having some angry plants keep watch; it'll stop assets in their tracks. Which, y'know, is important, since it's a tracker. Get it? Tracks? Tracker? Ahem. If the trees pass it far enough, it'll keep the scouting team lost a bit longer, too. They might not even be able to make it to the clearing at all."

"No."

Henry makes a face at Bastian. "You realize this isn't your decision, right?"

"I don't need *all* of your blood," Laurel says hastily. "Just some of it. If you're willing." She looks over her shoulder toward the forest. "But you should probably decide soon because if we don't do this, we'll need to think of something else."

"Something else. This isn't happening."

"Bastian—"

"I won't let Laurel do what Valentine was doing to you!"

Henry's anger dissipates slightly. "What?"

Bastian turns away. "How did you think she was getting the serum you use to bring in assets?"

"I suppose…she could have had Dr. Wright synthesize—"

"From what? She had a negator in the compound for fifteen years. All she had to do was figure out a way to get your blood, and boom, more serum. Maybe that's why she didn't tell you about your power—if you knew, you wouldn't need the serum, and then you might question why the compound uses it and how they get it, and then…mutiny." He waves a hand. "Or whatever."

Henry thinks about Major Valentine's insistence that he use the serum. About how it would protect his team. About how he should trust that his superior officers know what they're talking about when it comes to safety during retrieval. The way she'd looked, like she was waiting for him to slip up.

"There *were* days when I lost time," he says slowly. "Like when we went to the Stacey Cambridge crime scene. I thought I overslept or something, but I couldn't remember a big chunk of that evening. And it's happened before."

And Level 19, the experimental recovery room, had looked awfully familiar. Had he been there before, recovering from whatever they did to him?

Bastian turns back. "Lost time. Like you forgot."

"Yeah." Henry frowns. "You think…Anna?"

"Either that or some sort of drug with her power."

"How could it work on me, though? Wouldn't I just negate it?"

"I don't know. Would you?"

The book did say negators can be slow to manifest, and they aren't always able to control their power right away. "That's…maybe I wouldn't. Maybe not if they knocked me out first."

Bastian looks over at Laurel. "So no, we're not going to use his blood."

"I didn't say that." Henry's glare puts a quick stop to Bastian's next protest.

"My choice," Henry continues. "That's what the major never gave me. But Laurel is." He nods to her. "Do it."

She smiles. "Thank you, Henry."

Clapping her hands together, she adds, "I need supplies. Oh, my poor garden! I hope it's been doing all right without me! Anyway, this won't take long. Don't move." She gives them a stern look, then hurries over to the patch of dirt near the shelters.

"You're right," Bastian says quietly after a moment.

"It happens sometimes."

"I mean…this." Bastian waves a hand, which doesn't do much to explain what "this" is. "It's not my decision, whether or not you give Laurel your blood. And I should trust her enough by now to know she'd never hurt anyone like that. She saved my life; she deserves the benefit of the doubt."

He's looking out across the clearing, avoiding Henry's eyes. "I don't mean to be an ass about it, I'm just…not good at this."

"What's that?"

"Caring about people."

Henry doesn't get a chance to respond (as if he'd even know what to say) before Laurel comes running back. In one hand, she has a bowl filled with some sort of green liquid; in the other, she has a large, very nasty-looking thorn.

"Let's do this. Quickly!" She sets the bowl on the ground and sits down, cross-legged. Then, to Henry: "Come here and give me your arm."

He sits across from her, then takes off his jacket, rolls up his shirt sleeve, and holds out his right arm. She grabs it, turns it so his wrist is facing up, and slices the thorn across his palm. It's so quick and fluid, he doesn't realize she's done it until he sees the blood well up and, a second later, feels the sting.

"Turn, please."

He rotates his hand and holds it over the bowl.

He's not sure how long he sits there bleeding, but it feels completely surreal—and, oddly, not too painful. Apparently, this is what his life has become, he thinks wryly: sitting on the ground in a clearing with an asset who can talk to plants, bleeding into dinnerware, while an empath hovers over his shoulder in poorly disguised agitation, and outside of their forest getaway, Henry's superior officer and a team of scouts are coming to lock them up for a very long time. And they'll probably throw away the key for good measure.

"Done!" Laurel moves the bowl, pulls a surprisingly clean rag out of her pocket, and wraps Henry's hand securely. Then she's on her feet and rushing over to the trees at the edge of the clearing.

"Do you need us to do anything?" Henry calls.

"Nope! Just go stand over there." She motions vaguely to the shelters.

Henry picks up the duffel Bastian was carrying, and the two of them walk in the indicated direction. They pass the pool, now reflecting early moonlight. It would be pretty under other circumstances, but Henry's suddenly distracted by a much brighter light.

The trees surrounding the clearing are starting to glow, one after the other, shining from the lowest part of their trunks all the way to their uppermost branches. One tree lights up, followed by the one next to it, and the one after that, until every tree immediately surrounding the clearing is alight. It keeps getting brighter and brighter. Henry squints, then has to close his eyes entirely when it reaches the point of beautiful-but-eyeball-scorching.

A second later, it goes dark all at once.

The trees are back to how they were before, only everything seems darker in contrast to the light.

"That's done!" says Laurel from his elbow. He nearly smacks her in the face when he starts, but she seems unperturbed. She's too busy being pleased with herself, he thinks. "We should be safe from the scouting party for a while now."

"Unless they get in," Bastian says. "What then?

"Wet blanket," Laurel mutters. "Do I have to do everything myself?"

"You did say it's *your* clearing."

Laurel huffs. "Luckily for you, I have this covered as well. You can thank me later."

"Thank you," Henry says immediately, grinning, mostly because he knows it'll annoy Bastian. (It does. Henry gets a solid glare for his efforts. Mission accomplished.)

"You're very welcome, Henry." Laurel sticks her tongue out at Bastian. "Move back, please. Both of you. And Henry, keep your negation field contained. I'm going to need everything I've got for this."

The first thing she does is wave her fingers at the brush that makes up the shelters. It dismantles itself and recedes back into the ground, leaving the area flat and open.

Now the gestures Laurel makes are quicker and more animated. She narrows her eyes at the ground, like she expects something to happen.

It happens.

The grass itself slowly shifts away, like someone rolling sheets of sod in opposite directions. At first glance in the low light, it looks like there's more dirt underneath. But—

"Metal," Bastian murmurs next to him.

As more and more of it gets revealed, Henry realizes it's a bunker of some sort. The metal has a weird tint to it, and when he gets closer and crouches down next to it, he can see it's been burned. Badly.

"Laurel, what is this?" Bastian asks.

"Someplace safe," she says, brushing her hair out of her eyes.

Laurel's power has revealed a small set of stairs leading down into the ground and ending at a metal door. She starts heading over to them but pauses before going down. There's a small patch of grass, like a little garden, next to the entrance. Henry can make out a circle of broken stones, which seems to be what she's looking at. He counts quickly: twenty.

No, not stones. Gravestones.

"Laurel." Bastian's voice is low.

"You get it now, right?" she says. "This is what I have to protect. Why I can't leave."

Henry stands and looks the structure over. It's odd that it's completely underground rather than having some above-ground components, but the sigil on the side of the building is unmistakable.

"This is a compound," he says.

Laurel nods.

"There's no record of a compound this close to ours. Was it decommissioned recently?"

"You might say that." Laurel looks at the burned door. "Things…happened here. Things people wanted to keep secret."

She shakes her head. "Anyway, no one knows it's still here. If I have the grass cover it up again, we'll be completely invisible from the outside, even if the scouting party gets through the barrier. Which they won't because it's an excellent barrier, thank you very much. But just in case."

She starts down the stairs, then turns when she realizes they aren't following her. "Well? If you're waiting for an invitation, here you go: You're invited! Now hurry up!"

"Laurel," Henry says carefully, "are you sure you want to stay in a place where something…unpleasant happened?"

Laurel smiles. "I like running water, don't you? I mean. Sometimes there's running water in here, when things work. And I've cleaned up a bit. But it's still…you know."

She stops, takes a breath, and puts her usual smile back into place. "Let's go."

She pushes at the door, which opens with a groan. Henry enters after her, Bastian bringing up the rear.

There's another set of stairs once they're inside, leading down to a long, scorched hallway. The doors on either side probably used to open on the usual kinds of compound rooms: storage, training, offices, barracks. Now, most of them are caved in and impenetrable. And everything is burned.

Henry hears a noise and turns to see Bastian stagger slightly. Henry grabs his shoulder. "Hey, what's—?"

"Nothing." Bastian shakes his hand off and walks around him to follow Laurel.

They turn a corner. More burned-out rooms interspersed with a few that look like they're still intact.

Then there's a wider area that used to have glass on either side so you could see inside the rooms. Said glass is shattered and littering the ground now, with paint peeling off the walls nearby. Inside the rooms, everything is rubble, but Henry's spent too much time in similar places not to recognize what this once was: training facilities.

Laurel hasn't stopped marching down the hall. Henry's about to follow her when he realizes Bastian is just standing there, clutching the frame where the glass was.

"I need you to negate. Now." His voice is low—maybe to keep Laurel from hearing? He also sounds like he's in pain.

Henry immediately focuses on spreading his negation field as quickly and as strongly as he can. He can feel its awkward, amateur shape, but he can also tell it's working because after a moment, Bastian relaxes slightly.

"Thank you," he says, removing his hands from the frame. It's so quiet, Henry's not sure he actually said anything.

"Maybe this isn't a good idea," Henry says. "We can go back outside if you—"

"Don't coddle me," Bastian snaps. Then he rubs his eyes. "Sorry, I—there's a lot of emotion in here. But I don't want her to worry about it. If this emotional residue is from what I think it is, and if any of it's hers, it took a lot of guts to even show us this place. She doesn't need to deal with anything else right now."

Henry smiles. "I think you're pretty okay at it, whatever you say."

"What?"

"Caring about people."

Bastian rolls his eyes and goes after Laurel.

One more turn, and they're in another area familiar to Henry: officers' quarters. These seem to have survived a little better. Still a few doors in bad shape, but more of them are just closed. They run to the end of the hall, where there's an elevator (definitely not in working order, given the degree to which it's caved in) and what looks like a door to a stairwell.

Laurel stops and turns to them. "These are the nicer rooms, the ones I was sort of able to fix up again. Some of them still have plumbing and working lights and stuff, thanks to the generators. They ought to be all right for to-night, anyway. Go ahead and take your pick. Tomorrow, we can figure out what to do next."

Henry considers arguing again about setting a watch, but he's pretty sure he already knows how Laurel will respond. Guess it should be left up to the green-ery, then. And they did put up that barrier. (His hand doesn't even hurt any-more, he realizes. Laurel could make bank with these fast-acting cures of hers.)

"Laurel." Bastian scratches his head awkwardly. "Um. Thanks. For showing us this place. And for getting us through the forest."

"And for saving your life like a million times? And being the coolest and best friend you've ever had?" She grins. "No offense, Henry."

"None taken."

Bastian makes a face. "Forget I said anything."

"Nope!" She kisses his cheek and says something into his ear that makes him flush.

"Good night!" she adds, letting herself into one of the rooms and closing the door.

Henry opens the door closest to him. Seems promising—the light turns on when he flips the switch. "I'll take this one, then. Night."

"Good night." Bastian walks over to the one across the hall and shuts the door.

Henry takes a last look at the dimly lit, burned-out hallway around him, then goes into the room and closes his door as well.

Chapter 29

BASTIAN FINDS OUT very quickly that the lights work (sort of; they flicker now and then, and everything's still dim) but the water doesn't (at all). Frankly, he's surprised this entire place hasn't collapsed, so maybe he should just be glad for what he's got.

There's not much by way of furniture in the room: a bed that dips precariously toward the floor, a dresser with half the drawers missing, a small desk, and a chair. None of these looks like it could survive actual use—he certainly won't be sitting on that chair—but overall, it's still better than a jail cell.

Or it would be if it weren't in the middle of a compound with the strongest emotional echoes he's ever felt.

Sighing, he sits down tentatively on the bed and is relieved when it doesn't immediately cave in. It's not as bad in here, he thinks. But he can still feel the emotions seeping in from the hall: mostly a cacophony of fear-anger-hate, enough to choke him, even with his strongest shield.

He wants to ask Laurel what happened—and doesn't. He wants to ask why she never told him about this place, how she could have spent the better part of a year using her power to hide it from him. He was only busy nearly dying for a few days; after that, all the time he was here, it just…never came up. All this pain and suffering, and for him, it didn't exist.

But it did for her.

Bastian sighs again, gets to his feet, and goes back into the bathroom to have a stern word with the sink. He even takes off his gloves so he can grip better (bored-tired-lonely from whoever last stayed here, muted compared to the mess in the hall). The sink still refuses to be swayed, though. He's pretty much given up when a particular smack to a pipe makes a gurgling noise. Murky brown water sprays out, prompting him to make what is absolutely not an undignified yelp.

He shuts the tap off quickly and looks down at his shirt. Definitely a lost cause. There aren't any towels, of course, so he settles for grumbling as he ditches the shirt, using it to get the grossness off his face. Then he goes searching for another one in the supply bag.

There's a quiet knock at the door. "Bastian? About the negation—you didn't say if you still need me to—damn, sorry, these doors are more damaged than they—holy shit."

Bastian freezes. Henry still has his negation field up, so Bastian can't be certain, but he's pretty sure the reaction is less about Bastian's stunning physique and more about the huge network of scars covering his back. Which is facing the door. Which Henry must have accidentally opened.

(He doesn't think about the scars much anymore, but he remembers how he got each one, the samples and the burns and the experiments gauging an empath's reaction to pain. He'll always have a convenient reminder of how little Wright cares about the assets Valentine lets him play with.)

"I saw part of your file back at the compound," Henry says carefully after an awkward silence. "It said Dr. Wright took a lot of blood and samples over the years. Are those from…?"

"Yes."

Bastian forces himself to turn around. Henry is standing in the doorway. Bastian can't decide if he's glad the negation field is still up or if he'd rather it were down so he could read Henry better.

(He could push through the field, of course. But he can't bring himself to do it. Maybe he really doesn't want to know.)

Henry clenches his jaw, then lets it go. "Can I come in?"

Bastian nods once, not trusting himself to speak.

Henry closes the door behind him. He comes over to Bastian, gently takes his hands, and turns them over so the scars on Bastian's wrists are facing up. "And these? Are they from the experiments, too?"

It was years ago, it shouldn't matter, but Bastian still can't get the words out.

Henry suddenly looks embarrassed and drops Bastian's hands. "Sorry, it's none of my business. I shouldn't—"

"It was…bad for a while," Bastian hears himself say. "I thought—Valentine promised things. Said she'd help me figure out my power and what to do with it. But there was a price for her help."

"Dr. Wright."

Bastian nods. "It—I mean, they do tests on all the assets, but I was the only empath, so it was different for me. And then there were blood draws like what you saw on Level 19. To have something to study."

"Lots of something to study," Henry says grimly.

"I tried to fight it for a while, but it was obvious that that wasn't going to work. So I…tried something else. But that didn't work, either."

The room goes silent. Bastian can't look at anything other than the floor. (This is weak and stupid and pointless—why did he even say anything?)

"That's why you were so uncomfortable at Senator Haldis's crime scene," Henry says quietly. "It looked too much like what you…."

"It doesn't—it was a long time ago. It doesn't matter."

"It matters to me." Henry gives him a small smile. "I'm glad it didn't work."

Bastian looks up, startled. He and Henry lock gazes, and Bastian thinks vaguely that he's probably supposed to be breathing or blinking or something, but he can't remember how.

(He doesn't understand why Henry is looking at him like that, like having Bastian around matters, like he's thinking about the dinner comment again, like he doesn't care that Bastian's prickly and awkward and doesn't know how to do this and really ought to let this whatever-it-is go.)

(He can't let it go.)

Bastian leans forward and kisses him.

Henry doesn't even hesitate to pull him closer and kiss him back, one hand moving to his hair like last night after the nightmare, only it's nothing like that because instead of being calming, it makes Bastian's heart beat faster, but in a good way, he thinks, and then suddenly his mouth is open and Henry's is, too, and he feels Henry's tongue against his, and it would be amazing except—

Bastian flinches and pulls away.

He still has his eyes squeezed shut, but he can hear Henry's attempts to get hold of his breathing. "All right?" he asks. There's a hesitation in his voice that makes Bastian anxious.

"Yes," Bastian says quickly. "I—the negation field was down, and—"

"Oh." Bastian opens his eyes to find Henry flushing. "Sorry, I got…distracted. If you want, I can—"

"No, I—I want to feel this. Feel you. It's just…a lot."

He *can* feel it, loud enough now that the racket in the hall is dimmed—mostly concerned-embarrassed-*want*, that last so strong, Bastian thinks he might have to sit down, only that would mean he'd have to move away from Henry, which is out of the question.

"Yeah, well." Henry smiles and touches Bastian's cheek. "I have a lot of feelings where you're concerned."

Bastian lets out a shaky laugh and covers Henry's hand with his own. "I know. You—"

He goes still abruptly.

(He knows this one, should know this one, he's felt it from some of the people he's interrogated, felt it from the occasional compound officer, felt it in city crowds when he was able to pick it out. But it's not common, certainly not something he's ever felt himself, except…except of course he has, because of this ridiculous man in front of him who's stupidly kind and brave and unflappable and all right, extremely nice to look at, and Bastian should have realized it sooner, realized how much trouble it's going to cause, has *already* caused, but it doesn't matter right now because—)

"You—"

Henry looks uncomfortable (worried-awkward-hopeful). "Bastian—"

"You love me."

Henry smiles awkwardly. "Yeah. I mean, I was going to tell you rather than just have you read it, but—"

"Tell me."

The smile turns both fond and exasperated. "I love you."

"Good." Bastian leans his forehead against Henry's. "I love you, too."

Henry pulls away far enough to grin, then kisses Bastian's nose, cheek, ear, and chin.

Bastian rolls his eyes. "I think you're forgetting something."

"Am I?" Henry asks innocently. "Can't think of what."

Bastian puts a hand on his neck and pulls him close enough to kiss his mouth.

As he backs them up, still kissing, toward the bed, Bastian is vaguely aware that Henry's restored a bit of the negation field—nothing Bastian can't feel through, but enough to keep him from getting overwhelmed again. It's not like the usual one; it's more like what Henry used when they were sparring, strong but enveloping him in something warm and calm.

This can be another sort of test, Bastian thinks dimly as he pulls Henry down onto the bed. Very important and scientific. See if he can still negate while—

The bed shifts further toward the floor with an ominous creak.

"That's…probably not good," Henry says against Bastian's mouth.

"Pretty sure Laurel will kill us if we ruin the furniture," Bastian agrees. "Let me up."

Henry makes a disgruntled noise, then moves to let him get off the bed. Bastian rummages around in the dresser and, to his surprise, finds some extra sheets. He arranges them in a sort of nest on the floor. Then he kicks off his shoes and socks and just sort of…stands there.

Henry brings over the sheets that were on the bed, adds them to the pile, then turns back to Bastian. "So, where were we?"

"You were taking me to bed." Bastian pauses. "Or to giant-pile-of-questionable-sheets-on-the-floor, actually."

"First one sounds a bit more romantic." Henry kisses his neck.

Bastian inhales sharply and grabs onto Henry's arm, which makes Henry smirk against his skin and spend some more time there.

The sheets are looking pretty inviting at this point, mostly because Bastian's not sure his legs are going to keep holding him up much longer. "Henry, can we—?"

Henry casts a glance down, then back up at him. "Yeah, I—yes. Absolutely." He cups Bastian's face and kisses him, hard.

At some point Bastian manages to get rid of their clothes with shaking hands (deflect by snickering at Henry's many-times-rolled-up pants, which just earns him a swat with said pants). Then they lie down in the nest of sheets—not as comfortable as a bed, but Bastian's got other things on his mind right now.

It's more overwhelming like this, with Henry looking down intently at him, already starting to move against him slightly, the want-need-love so intense, it's doing something funny to Bastian's chest, not to mention other parts of him. There's really only one recourse for that kind of thing: He grabs Henry's ass and rocks against him.

"Sh—Bastian—"

"Use your—ah—words—" (Ludicrous statement, since he can barely speak himself.)

Henry grins. "How about I—use something else?"

"Could you be any more ridic—?"

When Henry's hand closes around him, Bastian makes an extremely embarrassing noise he is never going to admit to.

On one level, it's terrifying, knowing he has no control over what his body is doing (thrusting into Henry's hand as it strokes him, mostly); on another level, it feels incredible.

(Henry's projecting mostly the *want* part now, but the *love* is there, too, and it's almost too much despite the negation field, except it doesn't matter because for the first time in his life Bastian actually wants to feel it, wants to have that connection, and even if part of him is still screaming that it's stupid and weak, he can mostly ignore it because all he cares about right now is Henry touching him, and speaking of—)

Henry curses very creatively when Bastian manages to get his own hand in the right place to mimic what Henry's doing. Seems to work pretty well, based on the noises Henry's making.

That's about it for coherent thought. Henry's hand on him speeds up and goes just hard enough that Bastian is coming before he even realizes it's happening. He feels Henry thrust into his hand a few more times before groaning and coming as well.

Which is…awkward.

He hears rather than sees Henry collapse next to him. Their shattered breathing is the only sound in the room. Bastian weighs the merits of dying of embarrassment versus finding an acceptable reason to be touching Henry again.

"Bastian?" Henry's voice sounds too loud in the quiet.

Hell with it, he can do both. Bastian turns, pulls Henry's face toward him, and kisses him desperately until they both run out of breath. "Sorry," Bastian mumbles. "I just—I could feel it when you—"

Henry blinks. Then he laughs. "Well, that's going to be…interesting."

Going to be. Like this is something that will happen again.

(It won't. Not after Bastian's done what he needs to do tonight. But it means something, Henry saying that.)

"Does your water work?" Henry's gotten up and found the bathroom.

"Sort of. It may attack you."

There's the sound of running water, and then Henry comes back with his shirt in hand, now damp.

"I won." He's already cleaned himself up a bit, and he doesn't seem to mind that Bastian just lies there like a lump while Henry uses the shirt to clean him off, too.

Maybe he won't be able to find another shirt, Bastian thinks. He'll be forced to walk around shirtless indefinitely. That would be very unfortunate.

"Hey." Henry pauses with the shirt on Bastian's chest. "Are you all right?"

"No."

Henry suddenly exudes a burst of cautious-worried-careful through the negation fog. "What—?"

"You're too far away, and you're not kissing me."

Henry, who's literally sitting next to Bastian, rolls his eyes and sets the shirt aside. Then he leans over, brushes a hand through Bastian's hair, and kisses him. The exasperation-amused-love is enough to make Bastian want to—

—have a horrible thought.

He must have made a noise or stiffened because Henry pulls back immediately. "Okay, that's obviously not what's bothering you."

Bastian sits up, rubs his eyes, and tries to ignore the hollowness in his chest. "You need to go."

Henry stares at him. "What?"

"You heard me."

"Why would I—?" Henry takes a breath. "You're doing that thing where you know something or think you know something but you're not telling me. I'm not taking orders without knowing why, Bastian. Not anymore."

"Why not? That's what you've done your entire life. Why stop now?"

He doesn't have to use his power to feel the emotion behind Henry's stung look.

(What the hell is he doing? Why is he saying these things? It doesn't change anything, it's not Henry's fault—)

"Bastian. Tell me why you want me to go."

"How do I know if this is even…?" He ignores Henry's confused look. "This—I don't do this. I've never wanted any of this. But with you, I do. A lot. So how do I know I didn't make you…?"

Henry frowns. "You think, what, you made me fall in love with you? Made me want to barge in here like an idiot? Made me want to—?"

"Yes."

"You know I can negate powers, right? Including yours?"

"Not all the time. Not always with accuracy. I could have—"

"But you wouldn't."

"Not on purpose, no. But I told you, Wright did something to me. Made me more powerful. I could've…made you feel things you don't feel. Do things you wouldn't normally do. It's not like I haven't done it before. To other people, I mean."

Henry goes silent for a moment, then says, "You really think you'd do that."

"I…don't know."

Henry leans forward and cups Bastian's face. "You're one of the strongest people I know," he says. "All the things you've been through, and you've come out of it—"

"—an asshole?"

Henry snorts. "I was going to say 'resilient,' but that works, too. My point is, you're not the kind of person who would knowingly hurt or manipulate someone you care about. Not like that."

Good thing lying to people you care about isn't on that list.

"You're a better person than you think you are," Henry continues. "No, shut up, it's true. And what happened here—how I feel about you—that's not just something you're projecting onto me, all right? Besides, you said you wouldn't be able to keep up that level of power for extended periods of time, and I, uh, may have felt this way for…a while."

I could have this, Bastian suddenly realizes. At least for now. "How long?"

Henry's embarrassed-amused-love makes Bastian's chest feel tight. "I mean, I don't know when it started, exactly, but it's been…a long while now, and—"

Bastian sucks in a breath, then pulls him closer and kisses him.

"I'm sorry," he says after a not-nearly-long-enough moment of this. "What I said about you taking orders. It's not—it's conditioning. It's what Valentine does. You feel like you have to do what she says because if you don't…."

Henry is quiet, stroking Bastian's cheek but obviously miles away. "You know I followed orders to protect my team," he says eventually. "And yeah, I'm worried about what the major will have done to them by now. But you were right: following her orders blindly all these years has had consequences, too. I can't just not question what's going on at the compound, especially knowing what I know now. What they did to Johnson. What they might be doing to the other assets." He swallows. "What they did to you."

There's a controlled fury-frustration-loathing in his voice that startles Bastian. Especially since Henry is directing some of that loathing at himself.

"It wasn't your fault," Bastian says. "What happened to Johnson."

"I could have gone to Level 19 sooner. Then maybe I could have—"

"—gotten caught sooner? Gotten stuck down there yourself so Wright could do whatever he wanted to you? Never found the library and the book on negation so you could start figuring out your power?"

Henry smiles a bit wanly. "Well, when you put it that way…."

"You don't have to save everyone," Bastian says. "I know you like to try—which is incredibly irritating, by the way—but you don't have to. And you definitely don't have to feel bad when it doesn't work. Valentine wants you to so she can capitalize on your guilt, but you don't have to let her."

Henry looks at him silently for a moment. "You know, for someone who's decided not to have emotions, you're pretty all right at looking after other people's."

Bastian rolls his eyes, suddenly self-conscious. "I'm shit at it, and you know it. I always say the wrong thing, and I just—"

Henry doesn't give him a chance to explain what he just because apparently Henry's more interested in kissing Bastian senseless.

"Sleep," Henry says against his mouth eventually.

"This is better."

"True. But we—mmm—have a lot to do tomorrow. Fending off compound officers and capturing a murderer."

(Better not to disabuse him of the notion that he'll have anything to do with that.)

Henry pulls away slightly, kissing Bastian's forehead before climbing over him and rearranging the sheets into something they can sleep on. Bastian suspects it would be less pathetic to just lie next to Henry like a normal person, but instead, he curls up against Henry's chest. He can't stop himself from trying it out again: "I love you."

Henry's arm tightens around him. "I love you, too."

The room goes quiet, and Bastian's just starting to fall asleep when he hears Henry's voice again, softer this time. "Bastian?"

Bastian makes a noise that sounds a bit like, "Mphlm."

"Before, when you said you didn't do this. Does that mean you haven't done…any of it?"

So much for slipping that by. Better just get it over with. "No, I hadn't done that before, and yes, I wanted to with you, and I hope it wasn't too boring for you because I'd really like to do it again soon, preferably not in a burned-out, decommissioned compound with lots of people getting ready to kill or incarcerate us."

Henry's chest is moving; he's laughing silently, Bastian realizes. Rude.

"It wasn't," Henry says. "Too boring. At all."

He kisses Bastian's forehead and then his mouth. "I suppose we'd better stop a murderer first, but then I am definitely buying you dinner," he adds, voice low in Bastian's ear. "We can negotiate what happens afterward, but I'm voting for something not too boring."

Bastian clears his throat. "You realize saying stuff like that isn't really—uh— conducive to sleeping, right?"

"I think you'll manage," Henry says, eyes closed even though he's smirking. "Now stop making faces at me and get some sleep."

"You're not even looking at my face."

"I'm always looking at your face. It's a good face." Henry opens his eyes long enough to kiss Bastian's nose, then closes them again. "Go to sleep."

Bastian grumbles but curls up against Henry's chest again. He doesn't really expect to sleep, but the sound of Henry's breathing as it evens out encourages him to drift off.

***

Sometime later, Bastian wakes, confused about the calm nothing-nothing-nothing coming from the warm body next to him. Then he remembers and can't stop the stupid smile that breaks over his face. (At least it's dark enough that no one will see.) He lets himself lie there for a moment, resting his head on Henry's chest.

Then he realizes what woke him.

Through the fog of Henry's negation and the emotional residue coming from the hall, Bastian can feel the edges of a familiar sad-thoughtful-lonely that he recognizes as Laurel. It's moving past the room and toward the compound entrance.

He wouldn't begrudge Laurel a nighttime stroll by herself except that there's something else out there on the other side of the barrier (his range has massively increased, he realizes). With Henry negating full blast in his sleep, Bastian has to push hard to feel it, but the nosebleed and accompanying headache are worth it because now he can confirm the smug-amused-confident.

John Doe. Of course.

Bastian wipes his nose and carefully shifts away toward the edge of the sheets. Which ends up being difficult when Henry's arm tightens around him.

"Bastian?" His voice is remarkably focused for the amount of sleep they didn't get.

"Laurel's up. I'm going to go check on her." Bastian leans back in and kisses Henry's forehead. "Go back to sleep."

Eyes still closed, Henry squeezes him once in an almost-hug, then loosens his grip and goes still except for his chest rising and falling. Bastian watches for a moment, wanting to lie back down next to him. Instead, he rolls away and goes hunting for clothing.

There are a few odds and ends left in the supply duffel, including a shirt that completely hangs off him (Henry will see it as justice for all the pants comments). Definitely not perfect, but the ensemble should keep him from freezing to death in the cool night air.

He puts his gloves on last, then goes to find Laurel.

It's not hard. Once he gets past the entrance—she obviously had the greenery move aside so she could get out—he sees her sitting next to the pool, hugging her knees to her chest, rocking back and forth a bit. She turns toward him as he approaches and smiles. It's a small smile, not at all like her usual ones.

He sits down cross-legged next to her and doesn't say anything. He can still feel John Doe, stronger now, but that can wait. This is more important.

"So," Laurel says.

He stays silent.

"*So*," Laurel says again, elbowing him in the arm and smirking.

Never mind. This isn't more important. Maybe John Doe would be willing to kill him right now.

"So what?"

"How's Henry?"

"Fine. Sleeping."

"Okay, but when I say 'how,' I mean—"

"Something I am never going to talk to you about."

Laurel laughs and claps her hands. "I knew it! I told you if you made a move tonight, he'd—"

"Tell me about this place. What happened here?"

Laurel instantly goes quiet.

(He shouldn't have said it. Probably a good friend would wait till she's ready to talk about it, not use it as a diversion from—)

"A lot of things happened here," Laurel says. "Good things, but mostly bad things." She looks at Bastian, and her eyes suddenly go wide. "*Oh*! I didn't even think—you must have felt all that—I'm so sorry—"

Bastian shakes his head. "Don't. This isn't about me. I just want to understand and…do whatever you need me to."

She seems surprised for a moment (surprised-confused-thankful). Then she looks out over the water.

"This was a functioning compound once. There were assets and a program and everything. Experiments, too. At first, they were pretty noninvasive; just recording vitals, drawing blood and testing it, documenting a few power demonstrations. But then things changed."

Bastian shakes his head. "A hidden compound? Why bother with a regular one so close?"

"The experiments. If it's secret, the Compound Council doesn't know about it. That means no rules."

Bastian wants to say something, but there's absolutely nothing he can say that will make what he suspects is coming any better.

"The experiments got worse," Laurel says quietly. "They brought in more doctors, did more tests. Strapped us to tables, and—" She shudders. "I told you about the splicing? About the empath link? Stuff like that. They wanted to see what would happen if they mixed and matched our powers."

"Wait. If they taught you to use an empath link…does that mean there's another empath?"

"No." Laurel looks at him. "It means they used your blood and…injected it into other assets."

Bastian feels sick. "Why would they—? There was a connection, wasn't there? Between the compounds."

"Yes. A big connection."

It's obvious, but he almost can't say it. "Valentine."

Laurel nods. "And Dr. Wright."

"So you knew when I came here. Who I was."

"Not at first, but yes. And I recognized Dr. Wright's…handiwork." There's a coldness in her voice he's never heard before.

"What the hell were they trying to do?" Bastian demands, nearly choking on it.

"I think…I think they were trying to make another empath.

"I don't think it worked," she continues quickly, seeing the look on his face. "Something happened first that…."

She has to stop and take a breath before she can go on. "There were twenty-one of us, including me. James was a firestarter. They experimented a lot on him, and then—well. You can guess what happened."

"He lost control of his power."

Laurel nods. "There was a huge explosion. It practically destroyed the whole compound, all the research, everything. It…everyone died. All the assets, all the staff, all the officers. Dr. Wright and Major Valentine weren't there when it happened, so they didn't see…."

"But you made it."

"The plants felt the heat coming and warned me. They helped me get out, but just barely. I was burned all over and totally would've died if it weren't for them."

She swallows. "Major Valentine just wrote it off as a financial loss, I'm sure. I saw them move all the research they could recover to your compound before they just stopped coming. I hid, and they assumed everyone was dead, based on the destruction."

"You said you fixed the place up. Furniture. Generators."

Laurel flushes. "Yeah. It's stupid, but I kept as much of it in working order as I could. Sometimes I can go down there and just…pretend they're still here."

"I didn't know," Bastian says after a long pause. "This was here the whole time, and I—"

"I didn't want you to know. I hid it under all the plants and animals so you couldn't feel it through all their emotions. I thought you had enough to deal with, and…I wasn't ready to share it, I guess."

They look at the water for a bit, neither of them saying anything.

At length, Bastian clears his throat. "Thank you. For telling me. You can tell me this kind of stuff, you know. I mean, I hope it's not all horrible like this, but—uh—you're my friend, and—"

He stops and looks at her. Laurel's eyes have gone, for lack of a better word, starry. "What?" he asks warily.

"You called me your friend!"

"Because…you are?"

"You've never done that before!"

"Well, obviously I'm never going to do it again."

She hugs his arm. "Whatever, you can't take it back now! It's official!"

He rolls his eyes but doesn't try to dislodge her. Or think about her remarkable ability to be so bright despite what she's been through.

(He thinks maybe he finally understands Henry's need to protect everyone all the time. Bastian's pretty sure if someone tried to hurt Laurel, he'd rip their head off. And speaking of hurting people—)

"Laurel. You said they tried to use my blood to make another empath, right? So if they couldn't pull it off here…."

She sighs. "Yeah. After they moved the experiments to your compound, they must have used your blood to make John Doe. And it didn't go well."

Chapter 30

HENRY TRIES TO go back to sleep after Bastian leaves, but he only manages fits and starts, finally giving up. It just isn't the same without Bastian curled up against him, without feeling a steady heartbeat and warmth all around him, and he should probably be worried about the distraction, but honestly, he couldn't care less at this point.

Henry shakes his head and reaches for his clothes. He finds another shirt in the duffel—last one, so hopefully there won't be any more costume changes—and puts his jacket on over it.

He wants to go join Bastian and Laurel, but he hesitates. Somehow, he doesn't think he should be part of the conversation they're probably having. Not until Laurel wants to share what happened here with him, too.

He's also itching to go patrol the perimeter, never mind what Laurel said about plant sentries. Major Valentine and her scouts have to be close by now, so it's only a matter of time before they figure out the barrier and break through. If he's careful, he might be able to determine which direction they're coming from, at least.

Henry's about to open the door and head out into the hall when he's startled by a sudden tinny groan behind him. He turns on his heel and scans the room quickly before he realizes it must've come from the bathroom pipes. There's another noise, and it sounds…odd. Like the pipe isn't just protesting for the sake of being obnoxious; it's also scratching against something.

Frowning, Henry goes into the bathroom and considers the sink. It looks exactly like it did earlier: crack down the middle, faucet rusted, the whole thing tilted a bit to the side. He looks underneath, and that's when he sees a series of chipped tiles just where the pipe goes into the wall. The pipe scratches against them periodically as it shifts, which makes the groaning/screeching noise.

He'd leave it at the vagrancies of semi-destroyed plumbing, but something stops him from getting back to his feet: a flash coming from behind the cracked tiles.

Henry scoots forward and pokes at the wall. A few of the tiles fall to the ground and shatter, revealing a small cubbyhole with a little metal box inside.

He gingerly pulls it out. Not locked and a little worse for wear, but still in good condition, all things considered. It must've belonged to the officer who lived here—and it must be something they didn't want anyone else to see, if they went to all the trouble of hiding it.

The box is just big enough to fit a few sheets of paper, and that's precisely what Henry finds in it. Or rather, several pieces of paper rolled up tightly. The airtight metal kept them mostly intact, despite the fire. Henry sets the box down on the floor, takes the papers out, and unrolls them.

Tiny, cramped handwriting covers every available inch. It's hard to read, but after Henry squints at it a bit, he can make out a few of the phrases. Some basic personal diary stuff, and then:

> *Suspect the memor is helping them remember the experiments or whatever it is they do down there. Heard talk about hiding bits of something all over the compound, but of course they shut up when I'm around.…Benton found a slip of paper in the cafeteria wall yesterday. Reported to me but not to the major or the doctor. Everyone's a bit afraid of them, I think.…When they're done with the firestarter, I'll tell them.…Donovan found another one under the tiles in the cafeteria. Code? Need to decipher.…*

Helping people remember.…Henry's seen a few memors on retrieval missions. They're always desperate to be taken back to the compound as soon as they're told what it is. Probably hoping the compound can help them deal with being able to remember everything (and everyone else's everything).

If the assets were trying to remember the experiments and writing things down in code, they must have been building a case against whoever was doing it to them. Maybe Laurel will know. In the meantime, the best way to figure out more about what was going on here is to find the experimentation rooms and do a little digging.

He rolls the papers back up and puts them into the inside pocket of his jacket. After rummaging around in the duffel, he finds a flashlight. The experimentation rooms, if they're still accessible, are likely to be pretty far down.

He goes out into the hall and is heading for the stairs when he notices a plaque on the wall near where the caved-in elevator is gaping and open.

Henry backs up and goes to look: a directory. It seems unlikely that there were a lot of civilian guests here, this compound being well-hidden and all, so why a directory, when compounds generally don't have them? Visiting doctors, maybe? Or other personnel?

Unlike his compound, Henry notes, this one is remarkably small—only five levels. The fire's burned away most of the information, but one thing stands out: Experimentation Rooms, Level 5.

Henry looks at the plaque grimly, like he can glare it out of existence.

He checks the door leading to the lower levels and finds it opens, if reluctantly. The stairs are even more burned than Level 1, but it's passable. The lights aren't working, though, so he relies on the flashlight and hopes the batteries aren't going to give out anytime soon.

There's debris everywhere. Henry finds out about that when he stubs his toe on some and nearly falls down the stairs. Instead, he manages to grab hold of the railing and keep the flashlight in his hand at the same time, but it's a close call. Any vermin hanging out in the stairwell are treated to some startled, echoing cursing.

He doesn't bother with the middle floors, opting instead to go all the way down to Level 5. There's nothing in the stairwell there except a single door that won't budge. The handle breaks off in his hand, leaving a trail of soot on his skin. Pushing doesn't do much, either. He tries a few times and hears some screeching on the other side. Blocked.

Henry steps back and shines his flashlight around. Nothing inspiring for a few seconds, but then he sees some pieces of metal that might work as makeshift screwdrivers.

He grabs a few, sticks the flashlight in his mouth, and uses them to go after the door hinges. They're slightly melted, and of course bits of metal are no replacement for an actual screwdriver, so it's irritating, awkward work.

He eventually manages to get the hinges loosened. They still stick, their edges warped by the fire, but Henry claws determinedly at them until they come off and fall to the ground with a loud clanging noise.

He returns the flashlight to his hand, takes a deep breath, and shoves his shoulder against the weakened door.

There's a bit of give now, but it doesn't happen all at once. He grunts and pushes (and is probably going to end up with a huge bruise on his arm) before the door finally creaks open just enough for him to get through.

Déjà vu going through the hall—it looks a lot like Level 19, where he found Bastian. He tries not to think about it, instead focusing on looking around and seeing if any of the doors want to play nice. None of them do until he gets to the end of the hall, where everything is black and crumbly, and there's a lingering smell of something sickly sweet that Henry *really* doesn't want to think about.

He opens the door and decides he doesn't want to think about this, either.

The room is long and filled with cracked tiles that might have been white once. Counters line the side of the room, while the interior floor is covered with shattered lamps and several bent gurneys.

Henry swings his flashlight across one of the gurneys and catches his breath. The sheets are gone, of course, but the outline of a human body has been burned into the remaining metal.

It has to have been a firestarter, Henry thinks, feeling sick. Firestarters are notoriously uneven when it comes to controlling their power. A strong one who lost control could have easily burned down the entire compound.

Henry looks around in dismay. If there are more coded notes on this floor, they're probably not here in the epicenter of the blast. Still. Might as well look before moving onto the other rooms.

He sets his jaw and gets to it.

Time stops in the darkness of the experimentation room. Henry's flashlight only illuminates small sections at a time, but it's enough to get the gist of what happened here. The purpose of the broken, rusted instruments is obvious. The whole thing makes Henry's skin crawl. He's beyond glad Bastian isn't here, too; if the rest of the compound is bad in terms of emotional residue, Henry can't even begin to imagine what this room feels like.

He goes over the drawers and cabinets—even checks the walls for another cubbyhole like the one in Bastian's room—and comes up with nothing. Then he shines the flashlight back at the gurneys. Inspecting them more closely is the last thing he wants to do, but he's checked everywhere else, so it only makes sense.

Just as well he does. He runs his fingers underneath the gurney with the body-shaped burn marks and finds something stuffed between two metal sections: a folder. Pulling it out gingerly, Henry can see it was damaged in the fire, but most of the papers survived, thanks to their position between metal plates. Like someone stuffed the folder in there hurriedly so it wouldn't be noticed.

These are different from what he found in the room. Still notes, but they look more like they're based on experiments. There are numbers rather than subject names—twenty-one of them. Similar to what he saw in Bastian's digital file: age, date of entry into the program, power, amount of blood and samples taken, test results.

The last page looks like a partial list of experiments performed, mostly tests of the assets' powers. But other tests are related to something called a splicing program:

1+2: minimal results
1+5: 32% increase in response on third trial
1+6: instability noted and contained

Then it gets more disturbing.

1+3+(4 through 10 combination): 98% increase in instability; contained
1+3+(7 through 10 combination) + E sample: Untenable. Subject experiencing rapid cell degeneration, likely fatal within 48 hours. Put in request for new subject and recycle current experiment.

Henry looks at the information on subject 1: a young man labeled, of course, as a firestarter.

Rage chokes him. *Someone* thought it was a perfectly fine idea to experiment on these assets, combining them in some way, until one of them destroyed this compound and killed everyone in it.

That someone, he thinks, must have been Dr. Wright. Henry's never seen his handwriting, but the tone of the case introduction is familiar.

Twenty-one assets began in good health. A broad range of powers was selected for optimal number of opportunities. Initial splicing will commence between subjects, the most resilient of which will be further spliced with blood samples from subject AP367284.

Our objective is to create a successful system for the manufacture of assets with AP367284's abilities. Additionally, the successful splicing of assets could prove useful in expanding compound capabilities.

Updates to be provided monthly to both the committee and the overseeing officer.

No names. Convenient. But it's pretty damning circumstantial evidence for putting Wright away, at least for what happened here. The Compound Council would want to hear about illegal experiments.

Henry has to think about it for a moment, but he remembers that number, too: the ID Bastian gave the bridge guard when they went into the city for the first time. If Bastian's blood was involved, that gives more credence to the idea that Wright and whoever authorized him were trying to make another empath.

And they succeeded. Eventually.

He wonders about the memor. The firestarter who managed to get hold of this and hide it. The other assets who were apparently trying to collect this information. Is there more? Or were they killed before they could build a case?

Henry bundles the papers together and leaves the experimentation room.

The way back up is less treacherous, now that he knows where the pitfalls are, but he steps carefully, just in case. Toward the end, though, he's taking the steps two at a time, anxious to show Laurel and Bastian what he found and see if Laurel has any idea where other documentation may be hiding. If there is any.

When he gets outside, he sees Laurel sitting by the pool. She looks up as he approaches and grins at him. "Hello, Henry. Are you having a nice night? Anything…interesting happen?"

Even if he had the time, *that* isn't something he'd want to talk about, thank you very much.

"I need to show you something," he says. "Bastian, too. Where is he?"

She shrugs. "He said he was going for a walk and that he'd be back soon. You two know there's nothing wrong with actually sleeping at night, right? Or doing…other things." Her grin fades when she sees his face. "What is it?"

He's scanning the border of the clearing. "Bastian didn't say where he was going?"

"No." Laurel gets to her feet. "Why?"

He shouldn't assume, but…. "John Doe has to be here by now, right? And the major's team?"

"Well, the trees ought to have slowed them down a bit, but yeah, they're probably out there somewhere. You don't have to worry about that, though. Our barrier will keep them from getting in."

"But one of us could get out."

Laurel goes pale. "You think—?"

"I think we'd better find Bastian before he does something incredibly stupid."

Chapter 31

BASTIAN LEAVES LAUREL by the pool, telling her he needs a walk, which isn't exactly a lie. He just forgets to tell her that the walk will take him to the edge of the clearing and right up to the barrier.

He follows the smug-bored-amused to a particular maple. It's a little too dark to see clearly, but it's also close enough to dawn that it's not pitch black, which means he can at least make out John Doe's teeth gleaming in the low light like something out of a horror novel.

"Hello," John Doe says, stepping out from the shadows on the other side of the barrier. "Took you long enough. I was getting bored waiting."

"You've been waiting? I'm flattered."

"Don't be. I've also been sneaking a look at Valentine and her entourage. Your plant girl's flummoxed them for now, but it's only a matter of time."

"But you didn't have any trouble yourself, I take it."

"I did, actually." He brushes some leaves off his shoulder. "Did you tell your little friends about your nefarious plan?"

"Why would I do that?"

John Doe shakes his head. "I can't believe you're going with this selfless thing. That's what this deal of yours is all about, isn't it? Your life for theirs?"

"It's practical." Bastian crosses his arms over his chest. "Valentine is going to take one of us down for the murders, but it doesn't have to be you."

"Doesn't it? Go on."

"Here's the deal: I take the fall for what you did. In return, you leave Henry and Laurel alone."

John Doe sighs. "That's what I just said: selfless. Boring." He pauses. "You didn't say anything about not taking out Valentine. Or anyone else."

"I don't care about anyone else."

"That's not how being selfless works, you know. You're supposed to care about all the little people."

"I don't."

"Really?" John Doe raises his eyebrows. "I think we both know there are still people in the compound you care about. You're saying I can just do whatever I want to them?"

"You're missing the point here. If I take the fall, you don't have to. Plus, there's an added bonus: You get what you really want."

"Oh? What's that?"

Bastian smiles grimly. "You don't just want to get out of being blamed for the murders. You also want to be the only empath. The strongest."

"I *am* the strongest."

"Prove it."

John Doe looks at Bastian suspiciously. "You ran away the last time we faced off. Are you saying you want a rematch? Is that before or after you take the blame for the murders? Just so we're clear on the details."

"You didn't actually fight me last time; you just tried to kill Henry. And anyway, I'm stronger now."

Time to sell it. "We *could* just do an exchange," Bastian continues. "I play scapegoat, you leave my friends alone. But this is your chance to show off just how strong you are."

John Doe frowns. "They augmented you again? So what? I'm made of augmentation. Why would Wright poking you with a stick make a difference to me?"

"Because you didn't start out an empath, did you? There isn't another one. Valentine made you, like you said. But I've been an empath my entire life. Beating me means proving that you don't have to be born an empath to be the strongest. All you have to do is have the guts to use the power."

John Doe taps his chin thoughtfully and leans against the maple. "You've changed, haven't you? All those people whose minds you destroyed…you actually care about that now. All that time spent not having emotions, and now you've got plenty." He grins. "Especially for your captain. You know he'll drop you the minute he finds out what you did, right?"

No, he won't, Bastian wants to say. I already told him, and he didn't. Of course, when he finds out what I'm doing now…. "What's your answer?"

"It *is* tempting, I admit. Whether or not you survive it, I'll still win, which means you'll be my scapegoat—nice of you to read my note, by the way—and I'll come out on top. Hard to find a downside, really."

This is what was supposed to happen: take the fight directly to John Doe, plan on his hubris and conceit to get them into a fight Bastian can win. No room for Henry to be heroic or for Laurel to be helpful. Of course, if Bastian loses, there will be problems. But at least he can keep Henry and Laurel safe a little longer. "So?"

"What the hey, I accept. But if we're going to do this, we ought to do it outside your barrier, don't you think? Neutral ground. And your little friends can't impede us."

Confidence-amusement-glee. No indication that he's lying.

Bastian steps closer. Starts to raise his foot.

And jumps about a mile at the sound of a gunshot.

John Doe crumples to the ground, clutching his arm. As soon as Bastian regains his balance, he whips around to find Henry, gun in his right hand and, incongruously, a file folder in the other. Laurel is next to him, looking about as angry as Bastian's ever seen her.

"What the *hell?*" Henry snaps, his entire being radiating fury. Bastian has to go on body language for it, since he's got up the strongest negation field Bastian's seen yet. It feels like a punch to the stomach when Bastian reflexively feels out. (Should've realized they were coming, too focused on John Doe to pay attention to—)

"You were going to face him down alone?" Henry demands.

"Well, I certainly wasn't going to *shoot* him!" Bastian says, bristling. "I don't see how murdering a murderer will—"

"Not murdered!" groans John Doe, sitting up. "Just bleeding and in pain. A lot of pain, actually." He smiles at Laurel. "You're good with healing, right? Any chance you could—?"

"None." Laurel turns to Bastian, her eyes worried and angry and probably a lot of other things he can't feel right now. "Bastian, what were you thinking? How could you be so stupid?"

"Yes, I suppose trying to save your lives *is* pretty stupid. I'll make sure not to do it again."

Henry lowers his gun, eyes still on John Doe, like he's just looking for an excuse to shoot him some more. "I thought we were taking this bastard out together."

"What gave you that idea? I had this under control. You just—"

"You can't go wandering off into the forest with a murderer!" Laurel says. "The trees can only protect you so far."

"Yes, Bastian!" says John Doe. "Think of the trees!"

"Shut up!" Bastian, Laurel, and Henry all say together.

"Look, I had a plan," Bastian says in a low voice. "If you'd just let me—"

"How long?" Henry's looking at him in a way Bastian decides very quickly he doesn't like. "How long did you have a plan?"

"I suspect since we started having our little chats," John Doe says helpfully. Damn it.

"And when," says Henry through gritted teeth, "was that?"

Laurel stares at him. "You created an empath link with a murderer?"

"Of course not!" says John Doe. "He's not nearly advanced enough to do that. *I* created it. And then he invited me here. Very nice of him."

"You—" Henry takes a breath. "When were you going to tell us all this, Bastian? So we weren't blindsided and possibly put in danger while you risked your life and probably died, thanks to this lunatic?"

"Aw, I wouldn't kill him, Captain. Much."

Henry raises his gun again. "You have one arm and two legs left. Don't tempt me."

John Doe falls silent.

"So you're the only one who gets to protect people?" Bastian demands. "I didn't realize there were rules for this sort of thing. And what happened to choice?"

"You can't make a choice by yourself if it affects everyone and puts your life in danger. We went through all this so that we could deal with it together. I left my team behind because I thought you needed my help."

"Yeah, well. I don't."

Everything goes very quiet.

Henry puts his gun away. Still looking at John Doe, he hands the folder to Laurel. She takes it silently.

"Get up," he says to John Doe.

John Doe cringes slightly. "Well, you see, Captain, someone shot me, and—"

"Get. Up."

He winces as he does it, but he gets to his feet, still cradling his bleeding arm.

Henry crosses the barrier without hesitation and grabs the murderer's wrists, ignoring the indignant yelp of pain. "Laurel?"

She understands immediately and moves the fingers on her free hand. A collection of nearby brush twists itself into cords. Henry uses them to bind John Doe's hands securely.

"Dare I ask what happens next?" John Doe asks.

"We're going to the compound."

"*What?*" Bastian blurts out.

"He's a criminal. He needs to be tried for his crimes."

"And if you run into Valentine along the way? Or if you get to the compound, and there are orders to lock *you* up? And how is this different from what I was trying to—?"

"Because this is me, actually telling you my plan before executing it. And I'm not potentially putting you in danger—you're both safe here for now."

Bastian starts to take a step toward Henry, but Laurel gently holds him back until he remembers the barrier. "It's two days to the compound," Bastian says. "How will you—?"

"I'll talk to the trees," Laurel says. "Make sure they give you everything you need. You'll have to watch out for the major on your own, though. I can't teach you how to talk to plants, so they wouldn't be able to warn you."

"That's fine. Thank you." Henry nods to the folder. "And read those files. I think that's how we can fix all this, but it's going to take more searching from you two to get everything we need."

Laurel nods and hugs the folder to her chest.

Henry turns to John Doe. "Move."

"Henry." Bastian tries (unsuccessfully) to keep his voice level. "The last time you—he broke through your negation field, he—"

"I'm stronger now; I can keep the field up longer. It'll be fine." He turns back to John Doe. "I said *move.*"

(I love you I'm sorry I don't understand how this works why do you have to be such an idiot I just wanted to—)

"Bastian." Laurel touches his arm. "He's gone."

Bastian turns to her. "And you're okay with this?" he demands. "Henry just went off alone with a murderer like you told me not to, and Valentine and her cronies are probably lying in wait to bash his head in—"

"No, I think he's a complete moron. Almost as bad as you."

"Then why—?"

"Because he obviously had his mind set on it. Oh, and he has a *gun.* But there is something we can do. Something more important than going after him, at least right now."

"Yeah? What's that?"

Laurel waves the folder. "Figure out what this is. Find whatever it is Henry thinks we still need to find. *Then* we go after him, smack him upside the head, and take down all the bad guys."

Bastian looks out into the forest, then up at the lightening sky. He takes a steadying breath. "Okay. Let's do that."

"You know," Laurel says as they walk back to the pool, "you're still a moron yourself. No more secret life-threatening missions you don't tell your friends about."

He stays silent.

"*Bastian.*"

"Yes, all right, fine. Can we just focus on those files now?"

"Yup." She pauses. "And Henry, he's not really angry with you, you know. It's just—"

"Don't."

She squeezes his arm and doesn't say anything else about it.

Chapter 32

ONCE THEY'RE OUT of sight of the clearing, Henry stops and listens for signs of the major and her scouts. He can't make anything out, and he certainly doesn't see anything. He turns to John Doe, who's staring at him with wide, innocent eyes.

"Oh!" John Doe says after a moment. "You want me to see if I can feel them."

"Yes."

"Unfortunately, I'm tied up and in pain at the moment. I couldn't possibly—"

Making sure his gun is in easy reach, Henry kneels down and rips part of his pants (plenty of extra material, after all). He uses the cloth to wrap John Doe's arm—none too gently. Then he steps back. "Do it. And keep your voice down."

"You know I'm not your pathetic boyfriend, right? I don't do things just because people tell me to."

"You killed people on command for Major Valentine. I'd say that counts."

"Yes, about Valentine—maybe I should just yell for her."

Henry raises his gun.

John Doe looks unimpressed. "Are you really going to kill me, Captain? I thought we were in pursuit of justice."

"We are. But as I mentioned before, you still have another arm and two legs."

John Doe sizes him up, then says, "The polite thing for you to do would be to lower your negation field so I don't have to push through it. Not that I couldn't, but, as I'm sure you know, bad things happen when empaths push too hard."

Henry could refuse, make John Doe do it the hard way. But he's not sure it's wise. Too easy to give John Doe an idea of Henry's strength. And there's another option, anyway.

Normally, he'd weave his shield and the negation field together to make everything stronger, like the book suggested. Now, he lowers the negation field and strengthens his shield instead, hoping he's getting it right. "No more excuses. Are they nearby or not?"

John Doe gives him an appraising (surprised?) look. "You *are* stronger, Captain. Not strong enough to do any good, but I'm still impressed. So impressed, I won't even make an effort to read into how you're all aflutter with emotions right now."

He squints at nothing for a few moments, licking his lips. "They're on the other side of the clearing," he says at last. "Their tracker hasn't figured out we're over here yet, so we have some time as long as we don't make too much noise."

"Good." Henry throws the negation field back up quickly enough to make himself dizzy. "Let's go."

"Be gentle!" John Doe complains when Henry grabs his arm. "Was that what Bastian said when you—?" He stops, giving Henry a calculating look that turns into a grin. "What, really? Wow! I never thought he'd have the guts, frankly. Seems more like the pining-forever-out-of-sheer-idiocy type, don't you think?"

"I will shoot you in the head, murder case be damned, if you mention him again."

John Doe laughs and then falls silent.

Clenching his teeth, Henry leads them through the forest. John Doe doesn't try to speak again, though Henry occasionally feels a weird sort of tingling *push*, like he's tapping on the negation field to test it. Henry knows he's stronger now than he was in the alley, but despite what he told Bastian and Laurel, he's not sure he's strong enough to keep John Doe contained indefinitely. (Doesn't matter. No room for error.)

He's not expecting any of the temporary clearings Laurel made to still be around. But, true to her word, the trees do seem to be looking out for them, shifting slightly here and there to make their walk easier. They have no trouble finding logs when they need to sit down and rest, and a stream shows up later that morning so they can get some water.

Mostly, though, Henry keeps them moving. He wants to get to the compound as soon as possible, and he doesn't want to think while he's doing it.

(Doesn't want to think about whatever agreement Bastian had with John Doe, how long he'd been planning to betray them with some idiotic scheme to deal with this on his own, why he can't seem to understand that other people's input matters, that there are things you can do as a team that you can't do alone, and what would have happened if Henry hadn't gotten there in time—)

(Or Bastian's awkward attempts at kindness or his tragic inability to climb trees or the look on his face when Henry confirmed that dinner was going to be a thing or his laugh that starts in his eyes like he's trying to hide it only it spills out anyway or his hands and mouth on Henry's skin—)

"You know," says John Doe, "you really shouldn't let arguments fester. It's best to just talk things out, don't you think?"

Henry snaps his head up and raises his gun again.

"Whoa! Calm down, Captain! I'm just making conversation. We still have a long way to go. Were you going to march all the way back to the compound in complete silence?"

"Yes." Easier to focus on the negation field—if he can manage not to be distracted by his own thoughts. Not that he's going to tell John Doe that.

"That's too bad. I was thinking we could play a game."

Henry frowns at him. "What's the catch?"

"Who says there's a—? Okay, yes, there's a catch. But it's not a big one. I just want to get to know you, Captain. I'll answer one of your questions for every one of mine you answer."

This is a horrible idea. But there's always physical violence if it gets out of hand. And it *is* a long walk. And who knows; John Doe might let slip something that will help tie up the case.

"All right," Henry says warily.

"Perfect! I'll even let you go first."

Henry considers. "What's your name?"

This appears to flummox John Doe. "Really? That's your first question?"

"Yes and yes. And now I get two more."

John Doe throws back his head and laughs loudly—until Henry cuts him off by elbowing him in the side near his injured arm. "Ow! Right, sorry, avoiding detection. Anyway, well done. But I'm afraid I can't answer that one because I don't know."

"You don't know your own name?"

"I've been through hundreds of augmentations. I have no idea who or what I started out as, where I came from, any of that. I was trying to figure it out by searching the library database and exploring the forest for a secret compound I heard about, but nothing doing. No records, no notes, and obviously Dr. Wright didn't care much about memory retention."

Henry thinks of Bastian on Level 19, weak and hooked up to that machine. He thinks of the gurneys and the file he just saw about the assets at Laurel's compound. John Doe may be a murderer, but it's not like he didn't go through all of that, too.

Bursting into a rage in the middle of the forest with enemies nearby is probably a bad idea, but punching something—or someone—seems like the only way to get the sick feeling out of his stomach. He refrains, but just barely.

"Righteously angry looks good on you, Captain," John Doe says. "And on behalf of myself and all the other poor little assets who need a big, strong protector—"

"Ask your question. Unless you'd prefer I shoot you again."

John Doe smiles. "You sure you don't want to use your other freebie? You're down to one, by the way. Using it might help quell that anger."

"Fine. Which of the murders were ordered by Major Valentine?"

"Ah, here's the relevant stuff. All of them, more or less. Goldsmith, Anderson, and O'Connell were part of the greater plan. Or rather, they weren't, and that's what got them killed. They didn't want to go along with the committee, you see, and Valentine couldn't have that.

"Lovely Stacey was just a political aide in the wrong place at the wrong time. She'd been planning for months to get some juicy gossip to sell to the papers, and witnessing a suicide would've given her just what she needed. I took care of her before Valentine even told me to.

"Haldis was a last-minute thing. He'd been on Valentine's side all along, but then he got cold feet when they all realized they couldn't control me. So he had to go as well. It was my choice to make his so artistic, though."

"What committee was this, that you and Valentine were working with?"

"Nope, my turn!"

Henry clenches his teeth. "Go on."

"How long does he have to live?"

Henry manages to keep himself from losing a question by asking for clarification. Instead, he just frowns.

John Doe's eyes are dancing. "Oh, he hasn't told you! That's remarkably heroic. I did suspect he was developing a hero complex—too much time spent with you, Captain. What a sap!"

"Explain."

"You know, if that counts as a question, there will be consequences—"

"Explain or get shot. Your call."

"You do seem to like violence, don't you? Rhetorical, by the way, not a real question. All right, don't look at me like that!

"Back when you were a little captain, someone probably explained to you that we don't live forever. For empaths, though, it's a bit different—particularly if Dr. Wright has his claws in us, so to speak."

"You're asking about Bastian."

"Astounding deduction. Truly, you are—"

"That was before he came back to the compound. The part where his power was hurting him. It's different now."

"Is it, though? He's told you he's been augmented again, I assume, which means he's using his power beyond what's natural. You've probably already seen the signs."

The nosebleeds. And he seems like he's in pain more, though of course he doesn't talk about it. "It's not that bad," Henry says lamely. "As long as he doesn't overdo it, he'll be fine."

"Hmm, if you say so. But you're intending to stick it to Valentine at some point, I assume. Do you really think Bastian wouldn't use everything in his arsenal against her if it meant keeping you safe?"

Of course he would, dammit. He's already tried to, making a deal with John Doe and not telling them about it. Henry hadn't even considered that that deal would be more than just Bastian putting himself in harm's way—that his own power could kill him just as easily as a murderer could.

"Then we'll think of something," Henry says. "At the compound. Find a way to help him."

"You think Valentine would get behind that? I suppose she might, if she thinks she can keep herself an empath who would follow orders. But Bastian and I have pretty much disabused her of that notion, don't you think? Better for her to get rid of us and start over."

"Anyone with any decency would want to keep assets from getting sick—or heal them if they did."

"Anyone with any decency. So not Valentine." John Doe pauses. Then a slow, wide grin spreads across his face. "Why, Captain! Are you perhaps planning to…take over the compound? Install your own medical staff? Redirect mission objectives and resources? I believe they call that mutiny. You can get court-martialed for that, right?"

"Yes," says a voice on their left. "You can."

Henry grabs John Doe's arm so he can't run away. He doesn't bother to use his gun, though, because he knows exactly whose voice it is, and a gun would only make things worse.

"Gentlemen," says Major Valentine, stepping through the trees.

Chapter 33

BASTIAN AND LAUREL read the file together, sitting by the pool as it gets gradually lighter out. The notes aren't entirely clear on some points, but it's easy to see what Henry must have seen: the twenty-one assets were spliced with each other's abilities, the intention being to create an even more powerful empath. Using Bastian's blood.

Laurel stares at the last page, her face—and, far more alarmingly, her emotions—completely blank. After a moment, she says slowly, "I didn't realize they had already gotten this stuff. We'd only just started talking about doing it. We can probably use it to link Dr. Wright to the experiments, but there's no evidence of your John Doe. Or that the major had anything to do with what happened here."

She's suddenly alight with anger. "She *did*, though. I *saw* her. Andrew said sometimes she *watched*, like from behind the glass. And Dr. Wright would never do anything without her okay. There must be *something* in this compound with her name on it, some way we can connect her with what happened here, because I won't let her get away with what she did to us, I *won't*—"

He could tell her the truth: that people get away with this sort of thing all the time, and just because something horrible happened to you, doesn't mean you're owed any sort of justice.

On the other hand, death by plantspeaker doesn't sound very appealing.

"We'll find something," Bastian says instead. "You've seen everything on Level 1, right? And Henry found these on Level 5, if the notations are any indication. So we'll just…start looking."

Laurel sighs. "I suppose. Level 5 is the bottom, so that should be—"

"Wait. There are only five levels?"

"Secret extra compound, remember? They just wanted a space for experiments they couldn't perform anywhere else."

Bastian gets to his feet. "Well, five levels will be easier to search than hundreds. Let's get started."

As they head back to the compound, he asks, "Why paper files? Weren't they worried about not having backups, especially with a firestarter around?"

"We had a cyberreader, and she kept hacking into the compound database and going through files when she got bored. So they had to switch to paper."

Bastian laughs. "I know a hacker who would love to meet her. Uh. Who would've loved to…I'm just going to shut up."

It doesn't seem like Laurel's paying much attention, though. She's stopped in front of the compound entrance and is just standing there, tapping her chin. "You know…there were rumors. I thought it was just a joke, but a lot of people said they heard it…."

"Heard what?"

"Banging in the pipes. Things behind walls. Footsteps where there shouldn't be any. People made it into ghost stories and stuff, but it wouldn't be the first time a compound kept secrets, right?"

"Was it in any particular location?"

Laurel shrugs. "All over. I can show you, if you like." Her face brightens. "Oh! Maybe it's a secret passage. I always wanted to find one of those. We can look behind a wardrobe. I mean. If there are any wardrobes left. Did we even have any to begin with? I can't remember."

"Laurel. You were going to show me?"

"Right. Come on."

They go back inside, Bastian making sure his shield is as strong as possible. It's still bad, but now that he knows what to expect, he can focus on shielding to the exclusion of pretty much everything else, and that helps.

(It would be better to have a negator and not have to feel anything at all. It would be better to have Henry, full stop. Never mind, can't think about that.)

She takes him around the corner to a room that's a little smaller than the ones where they slept. Other than size, it looks pretty much exactly like Bastian's except that the furniture is in slightly better condition.

"They had us sleep on the opposite side of the officers," Laurel explains. "I guess to keep us from getting into trouble, although of course we did anyway. This was Xavier's room."

"And this is where you heard the noises?"

"I didn't, but Xavier said he did sometimes. Behind the dresser."

"Any of the other rooms?"

"Everyone's, I think. Now and then."

They go to the dresser and move it out of the way so the charred wall is easy to access. He starts to take off one of his gloves.

"Bastian, you don't have to—"

"We can't just walk around and hope we run into something useful. If there really is some sort of secret passage, you know that's what Valentine and Wright used to sneak around, and it'll lead us to any sensitive information. A read is the best way to figure out if anything's there. Unless you have a sledgehammer and want to smash all the walls in this place."

She looks at him dubiously, then nods. "All right. But if it hurts, you stop, okay? I mean it."

Of course he's not going to do anything of the sort, but she's fixing him with an intense gaze, so he nods once. Then he finishes taking off his glove, lowers his shield, and touches his bare palm to the wall.

He's immediately kicked in the face with a splitting headache and a bombardment of curiosity-fear-hate-pain-worry and enough other things that he has to struggle not to retch. He grits his teeth and pushes past it, trying to determine where it's coming from.

Mostly from the hall behind them, it turns out, although some of the fear-sad-loneliness is in the room itself. A good portion of the overall cloud of emotions, however, is coming from behind the dresser. Well. Not exactly right behind it, but stretched out either way behind it.

"There's something back there?" Laurel asks.

"I think so. It's…." He runs his hand along the wall, following it over to the other side of the room.

"Secret passage?" Laurel says hopefully.

Bastian half-smiles. "Secret passage. I think. But since we don't have that sledgehammer, we're going to have to follow it a while and see if there's a place where the wall is thinner so we can get inside."

With Laurel following close behind, he walks carefully down the halls, his hand still on the wall. He tries shielding a bit more, but that just cuts off his connection entirely. So he clamps his jaw shut against the extraneous stuff and tries to focus on what he's feeling from behind the wall.

When they get to the stairwell, Bastian stops. "Are the rest of the levels still in one piece?"

"I'm not sure. I tried to get into some of them, but the doors were mostly stuck shut. The stairs should be safe enough if you don't fall over the side or anything. The railings are pretty fragile."

It's a bit like being in a maze, Bastian thinks as they go through the levels they can access. If you keep bearing right, eventually you'll get out. But there are obstacles here: huge piles of debris that block their way, broken glass covering the floors, charred remains it's probably best not to think about. The stairwell is bad, but the levels are worse.

It doesn't help that Laurel's sadness-fear-anxiety gets louder the further down they go. With that constantly at his back and the rest of the emotions sticking to everything else, it's all he can do to focus on the dim stuff coming from the secret passage.

They're on Level 4 in one of the training rooms when Bastian suddenly stops. The read feels a bit different here, but more than that, the wall is thinner. He raps his knuckles against it. Hollow.

"Oh! There!" Laurel points up near the ceiling where there's a slight discoloration in the brick.

Bastian hesitates. "With all the damage, it's not necessarily—"

"It is." She looks around the room, which is mostly destroyed exercise equipment, for something to stand on. Not finding anything, she turns back to Bastian. "Okay, lift me up."

"Um. That might not be a good—"

"We're on a timeline here! I promise I'm not too heavy. I know you're scrawny, but I think even you can—"

"All right, fine."

He does manage to lift her, thank you very much, although it's harder than he thought it would be (and he's distracted by thinking about how easy Henry made it look, except of course he's not distracted because he's not thinking about Henry).

Laurel peers at the stained portion of the wall and taps it a few times, getting no result. Then she feels around outside of it and around the outside of the adjacent bricks, tapping and pushing. Nothing works.

"Laurel," Bastian says, trying to ignore his protesting arms, "I don't think we're getting anywhere. Maybe you should—"

He can feel her frustration level spike a moment before she smacks the discolored wall so hard, he stumbles back and drops her. She grabs his arm as she goes down, and between the two of them, they manage to beat gravity before she can hit the ground and hurt herself.

Meanwhile, the wall is slowly sliding open.

"See?" She grins. "Secret passage!" And she barrels through it before Bastian can respond.

It's dim inside, but there are occasional lights on the ceiling and walls. The main passage continues forward, with an additional hallway heading to the left and another to the right, back the way they came.

Bastian can hear Laurel's footsteps moving forward, so he follows, putting his hand back on the wall. The muddle of emotions is intense in here as well, with one change: he recognizes an overwhelmingly omnipresent signature.

Dr. Wright.

He feels something up ahead that can't be good, and when he catches up with Laurel, he sees why.

The hall ends in a doorway, where Laurel is standing, very still. Over her shoulder, Bastian can see it's an experimentation room that looks like every other one he's ever seen, only this one has more machines and instruments. Maybe because it was hidden behind a wall, most of it is still intact.

Including the body.

"Intact" might not be the word, actually. There's obviously been some decay—enough that Bastian and Laurel have to cover their mouths and noses with their sleeves. But it hasn't been burned. From this far away, it looks like it just fell off the gurney and lay there, its back to the door.

Laurel moves toward it, her feet shuffling a bit, like she can't make up her mind whether or not she wants to get closer. Bastian tries to follow her but stumbles first, a wave of fear-loathing-anger threatening to knock him over. It's far worse than anywhere else in the compound.

(He remembers a room like this, hidden away in the lowest levels, remembers being hooked up to machines and cut and burned and drained, passing out from it and coming to again, Wright saying soothing things Bastian stopped believing when he was still a child, and at one point, it was too much, he knew he was dying, so he waited until Wright left him alone, and then he ripped out the needles and used every last bit of strength he had to crawl across the floor and—)

"Vanessa," Laurel says. "She was here when James….She was trapped. No one came back for her."

Laurel shakes her head slowly. "This must be where they took us. We could never remember, even when Alice tried to help. Maybe we didn't really want to. So there wasn't anyone who would've known where to find her even if they'd had time to…."

He sees the angry tears in her eyes and doesn't know what to do.

"They're just stones outside, you know," she says. "I couldn't find their bodies. I overheard Dr. Wright saying no one survived when he and the major came back to look at the wreckage. But he wasn't here when it happened, so I thought maybe…I mean, I survived, right? But no one else ever came out. I just put those stupid stones out there, and I fixed up a few rooms, and…."

He opens his mouth to say something, no idea what, but it turns out it doesn't matter. She suddenly throws her arms around him, shaking, and he hugs her without even thinking.

The room smells foul, and he knows they need to be searching for evidence, but he keeps himself still and holds her and wishes there were something else he could do. He doesn't move until she's ready.

"Sorry," she mumbles, not looking at him as he lets her go. She sounds congested, and his shirt is damp.

"Don't worry about it." He looks around the room, then frowns when he feels a particular sad-furious-pain. Covering his nose and mouth again, he goes over to the body and steps around to the other side. There's a piece of paper partially hidden underneath Vanessa's hip, like she fell over onto it.

Bastian looks up at Laurel, who hasn't moved. "Can you…?"

She comes over, though she's obviously not happy about it. When she sees what he's looking at, though, she nods. "I'll get her shoulders."

Between the two of them, they move Vanessa enough to make the paper accessible. There's also a pen near her chest.

"I always thought Vanessa had such pretty handwriting," Laurel says in a low voice, picking up the note. "She did calligraphy, too. It's all over her room. Or was."

Together they look at the note (Laurel's not wrong about the handwriting):

I don't know who will find this, but you should know who we were and what happened here.

We were subjects for experiments performed by Dr. Wright with approval from Major Valentine and some sort of special committee—I never heard much about that, except I think the major reported to them. They were looking for something, but I don't think they ever found it.

There were twenty-one of us. We must have had families and homes at some point, but Major Valentine came for us, and we forgot most of it.

They called us assets, like we were property. Like we were things, not people. Since we were things, Dr. Wright could do whatever he wanted to us in this room and not have to care about it.

I don't know what's happening out there in the rest of the compound. It doesn't sound good. I don't have the strength to get out, but I saw Dr. Wright put something in one of the cabinets before he left.

Find it. Use it to make them pay.

It ends with a list of the names of the twenty-one assets, including Laurel's.

"We have to find it. Whatever it is." Laurel straightens up and starts going through things. She moves beakers and instruments with a little too much force, but Bastian doesn't think it's a good idea to disturb her while she's at it, given the mood she's in.

He pockets the note and feels out again. Sorting through this much emotional residue means pushing harder than he probably should, but it's worth it: there's something unusual coming from the other side of the room. He goes over and starts with a collection of drawers, but they seem normal, full of the usual experimentation room supplies.

The last drawer isn't the same as the others. He can feel Wright's interested-thoughtful-calculating coming from it.

Bastian takes everything out of the drawer, then takes the drawer itself out of the cabinet and turns it over. It's heavier than it should be, and it makes a strange noise when he knocks on it—a bit like the secret passageway entrance.

"False bottom," Laurel says, appearing behind him. "Let me see."

He hands it over. Laurel gets her fingernails underneath the bottom of the drawer and yanks up to reveal a space beneath filled with files and notebooks.

Bastian takes the drawer back, sets it on the counter, and removes the papers. They look at them together: similar notes to the ones Henry found, though these are far more intensive experiments, like what Vanessa alluded to. The important part, though, is what's contained on the last page of one of the files: official authorization from Major Valentine, complete with signature.

"This must be what Vanessa saw. Will it be enough?" Laurel asks.

Bastian frowns. "I don't know. The signature helps, but Valentine could argue it was forged. And there's no mention of John Doe. It might be enough for the Council to open an investigation, at least."

He looks grimly around the room. "I can do a read on this place, too. Get Michaels to record it. Match emotional signatures to Valentine and Wright."

Laurel looks at him for a moment. "Thank you. I know this isn't easy for you, being down here with all this…everything."

"Yeah, well." He shrugs awkwardly. "I mean. You're—" He pauses, seeing the slowly growing smile on her face. "What?"

"It's okay, Bastian. You can say it."

He sighs. "You're my friend. Obviously I'm going to help you."

"Twice in one day!" she crows. "You're going soft!"

"Can we please get out of here now?"

"Yes." She turns and looks at the body on the floor, all humor gone. "But I can't…we can't leave her here."

"Laurel, I'm sorry, but we have to hurry. Henry's out there alone with a killer, and we need to get this information into the Council's hands before Valentine comes up with some way to cover her ass."

"I know." She tears her eyes away from the floor and looks at Bastian. "Will you come back after and help me with…this?"

"Yeah. Of course."
She nods, then slips her arm through his as they walk all the way back up.

Chapter 34

"I WAS…CONFUSED when I realized you were no longer in the compound, Captain," says Major Valentine. "I'd hoped you wouldn't fall for Sebastian's conspiracy theories, but"—she sighs—"you *have* shown yourself to be quite gullible. I suppose I should have expected this would happen."

"Which conspiracy theories are those, Major?" Henry asks. "The ones where Bastian was repeatedly experimented on and nearly killed? Or the ones where those experiments led to the creation of a murderer you used to kill five people?"

"Hey, leave me out of this!" John Doe whines.

"Captain, I assure you, I have no idea who this person is," Major Valentine says, looking at John Doe with distaste. "I *do* know that one of my assets is missing, and you were the last person to see him."

She smiles slightly. "Incidentally, I do hope your friend here was joking about you trying to mutiny. That's a very serious offense, as I'm sure you know. With your record already tarnished, I doubt it would survive a court-martial."

"What's the penalty for gross misconduct involving unsanctioned experiments on live subjects?"

Major Valentine raises her eyebrows. "How is that relevant?"

The officers behind her shuffle their feet uncomfortably, probably in response to the accusation. *They're* not trying to be coy, at least.

"Five people are dead, Major," Henry reminds her. "And there's paperwork implying you had a hand in creating the instrument that did it."

"I'm an instrument now? Does that mean someone's playing me?" John Doe frowns. "I don't think I like this analogy."

"Paperwork?" Major Valentine says. "I'm afraid I don't understand, Captain."

"The compound in the clearing. It was created for secret experimentation performed by Dr. Wright, including splicing assets' powers to enhance and modify them. Are you going to tell me you knew nothing about it? Particularly the part where these experiments ended with the subjects being injected with Bastian's blood so you could create another empath?"

He jerks a thumb at John Doe. "It worked. After your original experiments killed twenty assets and destroyed an entire compound and all of its staff and officers."

"That's a very…interesting accusation. Do you have anything to back it up? Like this paperwork you spoke of?"

"Yes. Not with me, but—"

"I see." She looks extremely unimpressed. "Perhaps you'll have found a way to produce it by the time we get back to the compound. I'd very much like to sort this out. Just as soon as you tell me where Sebastian is."

"Here."

Every officer—including Michaels, Henry notes—reaches for their weapon. Major Valentine holds up a hand to stop them, turning to an opening in the trees where Bastian and Laurel are standing. Laurel is holding several file folders and looking at the major with murderous intent.

(Henry wants to say something but can't get his head on straight, just wonders if you can actually drown from relief and anger and longing when you see someone because he hasn't forgotten Bastian's idiocy, but that doesn't mean it isn't all he can do to keep from running over there and kissing him and saying something important like—)

"How did you get here so fast?"

(Okay, maybe not that.)

Bastian doesn't look at him, eyes on Major Valentine instead. "Shortcut. Laurel's trees helped us out."

Laurel takes that moment to shove the files at Bastian, storm over to the major, and slap her face.

"*You*," she snarls. "They're all dead because of *you*, because of what you did! I'm going to set every wasp and every bee in existence on you, I'm going to have every oak branch hit you over the head, I'm going to—"

"Laurel." Bastian is next to her, touching her shoulder with his free hand. She falls silent.

Henry notes the look on the major's face: shock. She really didn't know Laurel was still alive.

Major Valentine recovers quickly. "I see you've made a friend, Sebastian. The girl from the clearing, I presume?"

"You know exactly who I am, you—"

Bastian's hand tightens on Laurel's shoulder. She bites her lip as if she has to physically force herself to stop talking.

Bastian looks back at the major. "Playtime's over. We have enough evidence here to link you to the experiments and open a Council inquiry."

Major Valentine is quiet for a moment. Then she suddenly looks extremely concerned. "I'm so sorry, Sebastian. You're obviously very ill. Please let me take you back to the compound, where you can get some help."

"No."

Bastian and the major both turn, startled, to Henry.

Major Valentine blinks. "I'm sorry, Captain, did you just—?"

He surprises himself by how calm he feels. "You think you can just drag Bastian back, have everything be the way it was, but you're wrong. If he doesn't want to go, he isn't going. Certainly not with you."

The major's face hits a strange note somewhere between irritated and mock-worried. "Captain, excuse me, but are you injured? I'm your superior officer, and—"

"No, you're not."

He takes his ID badge off of his jacket and drops it to the ground. After a pause, he says, "I'm quitting. In case that wasn't obvious. The people in back look a little confused, so I thought I'd clarify."

Major Valentine stares at him. "Why would you—?"

"Because I'm tired of you lying about everything. I'm tired of people getting hurt because you have some ulterior motive that helps you and no one else. I'm tired of being denied the right to make my own choices.

"I'm pretty sure you're the worst boss I've ever had," he adds. "And that was before I knew you killed all those assets."

That pitying look again, like the one she gave Bastian. "Captain, compound officers don't just *quit*. That's not how it works."

"Like assets escaping isn't how it works? That's funny, since Bastian's done it twice now."

Major Valentine's pity turns to anger. "Need I remind you of everything the compound has done for you? Not to mention the uncertain state of your team? You took an oath to lead and protect them, didn't you? I'm not sure I understand how abandoning them fits in with that." She shakes her head. "I'd expect this kind of behavior from Sebastian, but you...."

"I know," Henry says. "You expect me to shut up and follow orders. And I did, for a long time. But now I think that's not the best way to protect my team or anyone else I care about. I'm not sure it ever was, really."

"This is all very touching, but what about me?" John Doe turns to Bastian. "You know, between the two of us, we could probably take all of these guys out and be done with the long-winded speeches. Want to try?"

"Not particularly." Bastian glares at the scouting party. "Well? Were you even listening? If one of you is going to cuff her, now's the time."

Major Valentine smiles thinly. "Just because the captain's loyalty is in question, doesn't mean any of these other hardworking officers will—"

The tracker asset steps forward, looking between Bastian, Henry, and Laurel. "Did you mean that?" she asks. "Twenty assets dead?"

Laurel gives a jerky nod.

"You have proof?"

Another nod.

The asset sneaks a glance at the major, then looks away quickly. "I don't have cuffs, but I can get us back to the compound faster if you think that would help."

Major Valentine stares at her. "You—"

"I have cuffs." Michaels comes to the head of the group and makes a move toward the major, who steps back.

"Officer Michaels, this is very disappointing. You of all people should know not to believe these lies. You worked with Sebastian and the captain, so you know—"

"I know that Captain Mortimer and Mr. Lucas are dedicated to the truth. I also know I've let my doubts keep me from fully appreciating that."

She hesitates, then says, "If there's nothing to these accusations, Major, you'll be free to pursue action against Mr. Lucas and the captain. If, on the other hand, the accusations *are* true, I know you'll want to act in the best interest of the compound you've sworn to protect."

Henry realizes it a moment before the major does it: she's going to run. He drops John Doe's arm and levels his gun at her. "Major. Don't."

She turns slowly back toward him, face pale with rage.

"Pointing a gun at a superior officer is *definitely* a court-martial offense," says John Doe helpfully.

"You have no idea what you're doing, Captain," the major hisses. "Everything I've done has been for the good of the compound. To protect assets and help them reach their full potential. The committee didn't understand that. I shouldn't have expected you to understand, either—a mediocre captain who plays at being more than just a glorified gofer. If you think I'm going to let a pathetic, low-ranking officer stop my important work, everything I've spent years—"

"Shut up."

Bastian's voice is so low, Henry's not sure he actually heard it.

"Whatever you think you're doing, it's none of that," Bastian continues. "You've experimented on people without their consent. You've *killed* them. You're behind everything John Doe's done—probably ordered him to tamper with my reads and delete security footage, too. Not that you'll admit it. So let's stop wasting time."

He nods to Michaels. "Cuff her. Or let Henry shoot her. I'm for shooting, myself."

"All right, well, I'm bored. Is anyone else bored?" John Doe looks around. "No? Really? I'm beginning to seriously question your taste in entertainment. Here, let me just—"

It happens too quickly for Henry to even think about shoring up his negation field. John Doe projects a wave of…something, and it slices through Henry's chest, a hot disc of fury. He stumbles and drops his gun, vaguely aware that everyone else around him is staggering, too.

Then there's someone at his side, putting an arm around him and helping him stand. "I need you to negate for the others," Bastian murmurs.

Henry struggles to find his voice. "Bastian—"

"I've got a plan." His mouth twitches. "I can't say it won't put you in danger, since we're all in danger right now, but this is me, telling you about it and then executing it."

"You realize you're not actually telling me anything, right?" Henry pauses. "It's a really stupid plan, isn't it?"

"Completely."

"I should negate both of you on principle."

"I need you to negate around the others instead. Make sure his power can't get through. Or mine. If either of us loses focus—" Bastian shakes his head. "Please just do it. We don't have time to—"

"To argue. I know." Henry swallows, then leans forward and kisses Bastian with more desperation that he intended to. It doesn't seem to bother Bastian in the slightest, though he does pull away first.

"Go."

Henry nods, picks up his gun, and goes over to where Laurel and the others are slowly coming back to themselves after the attack. Laurel takes his hand wordlessly as he puts up the strongest negation field he can manage and hopes it'll hold.

Chapter 35

"MUCH BETTER." JOHN Doe is shaking out his arms—or rather, his arm, since one of them still has a bullet in it. "On to the real show."

He looks over at Valentine. "Don't worry; I'll deal with you after. But first I'm going to take this guy out. That's what you wanted, right? Anyway, we have a deal, don't we, Bastian?"

Bastian manages not to shoot a glance at Henry and Laurel, who he's pretty sure would join John Doe in cracking open his skull if they knew the precise terms of said deal. "Get on with it."

"Eager, are we?" John Doe tips his head to one side like he's listening to something only he can hear. "Hmm, interesting. The captain thinks he can protect the others? Because he did such a good job keeping me in line during our little forest trek."

He grins at Bastian. "He's wrong, though. I've been saving something special just for you. That trick I did a minute ago was kinda like the one in your mind with the fear, right? I told you that's the reason you're going to lose, but that's just *part* of the reason. It's also because you actually care about all of these people. And I know so many ways to pick them off. Check this out."

Bastian suddenly feels cold and sluggish. It's not a physical thing, exactly; his arms just go limp at his sides, and he doesn't feel like doing anything. He thinks there's something going on right now that he ought to care about, but he can't remember what.

There's something else to it, too: a feeling like someone's leeching off his energy, keeping him quiet and dull. He tries to push against it, but he only makes a half-hearted effort before he can't be bothered.

John Doe smiles at him. "Ever wonder what it felt like, Bastian? For all those people you killed? The numbing of the mind, like nothing matters anymore, like you could just curl up and go to sleep on the ground?"

In the part of his mind that's still working, Bastian realizes he *is* on the ground, feeling tired and thinking about taking a nap. He's pretty sure that's not what he's supposed to be doing, but it's hard to think about anything else.

There's someone yelling close by, and Bastian thinks he'd really like to know what they're saying, but the cold, sapping feeling keeps happening. Then he feels a sharp, heavy force go past (glee-smugness-amusement), and the yelling stops.

He can barely move his head, but he manages to do it, just far enough that he can see a jumble of people on the forest floor to his left. They're all very still, which makes Bastian inexplicably anxious. Does he care? *Should* he care? He doesn't think so, except....

The man in front. Who looks like he was trying to protect everyone. Who isn't moving anymore.

Henry.

"Thanks for the help," John Doe says, rubbing his temples like he's got a headache. There's a sheen of sweat on his forehead. "Couldn't have done it without you."

Bastian forces himself to sit up and focus as his head starts to clear. "What... did you do?"

"My final augmentation. Neat, right? I can siphon off other assets' powers and combine them with mine. A little tougher with your captain hanging around, but we got there in the end, didn't we?" He smiles conspiratorially. "I wanted to do the last bit just the two of us. It's an empath thing."

Bastian drags himself slowly to his feet. "It isn't an empath thing," he says. "It's a you thing. Something in you got messed up when Valentine and Wright did those experiments. You're not strong; you're pathetic."

There's a glint in John Doe's eye. "You're the one who was just on the ground, but *I'm* pathetic?"

"Yeah. You have this power, and all you use it for is to kill whoever Valentine tells you to."

"That's—"

"You act like you're some big deal, like you're independent and dangerous, but you're just the same as the rest of us: following Valentine's orders. Doing what she wants you to do for the compound." He snorts. "You're not even very good at it."

"Excuse you, I'm—"

"I mean, we knew from the start who you were, right? One read, and it was obvious that an empath killed those senators. All we needed to do was figure out where you came from. And now we know that. So all that's left is to lock you up."

"You know," John Doe says after a moment, "I really don't appreciate you implying that you're better than me. Leaving aside the fact that I'm much stronger, let's not forget that you killed on orders, too. Probably more people than I have."

"You're right."

"Well, then. This isn't even a real argument, is it?"

"No. It's stalling."

Bastian sees out of the corner of his eye that Henry has managed to get back to his feet. He locks gazes with Bastian for a moment, nods very slightly, and puts his negation field back up. It's wobbly, but it's holding. For now.

"I think we've played long enough, don't you?" says John Doe, an edge creeping into his voice.

"Yes," Bastian agrees. "I do."

He thinks of Laurel's compound, the anger-fear-hate that permeated the walls and floors and secret passage, the way Laurel exuded a gut-wrenching wave of sadness when they found Vanessa on the floor, too weak from the experiment to do anything other than lie there and wait to die.

He thinks of the dull minds of the senators as they killed themselves, the aide who died just because she saw something she shouldn't have, the amount of sheer self-importance it must take to think your own work is worth more than the lives of five human beings.

He thinks of Snyder in the jail cell, mind completely destroyed, making Bastian realize all the harm his power has done, all the people he's inadvertently hurt, all the lives he took without even realizing it.

He thinks of Henry, who only ever wanted to protect the people in his care and was made to think that was a weakness to be manipulated, that his work was never enough, that someone was always going to be hurt because of him no matter what sort of ridiculous, heroic thing he tried to do, all because that kept him from ever knowing or understanding what he was really capable of.

He thinks of Valentine. Someone he trusted, someone who promised to look after him. Someone who always wanted something from him. Who didn't care if he died so long as she got what she needed from him first.

That's what really does it, in the end.

It's not just anger, like it was in the interrogation room; it's all the fear and loathing and rage and frustration, everything since he ran away and maybe before then, more than just what he's consciously admitted to himself. Stronger than what he threw at Henry during their match. Stronger than anything he's ever allowed himself to feel.

It's hot and dark and terrifying, rising up from his gut and into his chest and exploding out of him before he can even consider whether or not it's a good idea to do this. (Probably isn't.) It's like someone else is thinking with his brain. Not John Doe using his power; more like a part of himself that's angrier than he ever knew, someone who wants to *hurt* and *break* and—

John Doe drops to the ground, curling up and holding his stomach. He's white in the face and staring at Bastian. "That's…what kind of augmentation is *that?*"

"It isn't."

Bastian and John Doe turn sharply toward Valentine, who's standing—with the help of a tree trunk—within the negation field. She looks awed and startled and…pleased.

"Wright did this to me," Bastian growls at her. "Wright and your stupid experiments. You had him—"

"I didn't." Valentine looks oddly proud. "Sebastian, you haven't been augmented since you came back to the compound. We only did tests. Pushed things along a little. This is just…your power. What an empath is supposed to do."

Bastian stares at her. "You're lying. I got stronger. I—"

"That's nothing special! I just did it, too!" John Doe tries to get to his feet but only makes it to his knees.

"Not like Sebastian did." Valentine's eyes are shining. "You had to siphon power. Sebastian never did. We realized he didn't need the augmentations. We only sped up what was happening naturally. In the end, we didn't even need the empath project; we just needed to wait until Sebastian was ready."

She looks over at John Doe. "You're a pale imitation compared to him. You shouldn't even exist."

John Doe goes very still. Then he slowly stands, glaring at Bastian as he does it. "So you do one trick better than me? Fine. Good for you. Doesn't mean I can't still take you out, along with everyone else here."

That's quite enough of that.

Bastian stumbles over to him, grabs him by the shirt collar, and punches him in the face. John Doe falls to the ground and lies still.

That's when the pain starts.

First, it's Bastian's knuckles, bruised from his excellent choice about where to hit someone. After that, it's everywhere all at once: a splitting headache that makes him gasp out loud; a sharp pain in his stomach that's so much worse than anything he's ever felt from using his power before; a throbbing behind his eyes that makes the world spin.

He's vaguely aware of a shout and movement toward him. Someone is cuffing John Doe even though he's still on the ground making groggy, incoherent noises. Someone else sounds like they're having an argument with

Valentine, who's speaking sternly about her project and the obvious evidence that it worked. Laurel is talking soothingly to the tracker asset, who seems to be panicking.

But the best part, the part Bastian tries to focus on as his brain comes back online, is that Henry's nothing-nothing-nothing is all around him, probably because Henry is on the ground next to him (when did he fall over again?). Doesn't matter because Henry has his arms around Bastian, saying something that sounds like, "You're an idiot."

"Worked, didn't it?" Bastian mumbles into Henry's shirt.

Henry pulls away slightly and cups Bastian's face, looking intense. "Are you all right?"

Bastian wants to lie, to not look weak and pathetic, but—"Everything hurts. A lot."

"Well. Maybe don't go for the face next time. You can break your hand."

Bastian manages to look up at Henry, who's smiling. Something tightens in Bastian's chest, and he's suddenly babbling. "What I said—what I always say—it's not—"

"Bastian—"

"I'm not trying to be—but you never let anyone else do it."

"Do what?"

"Protect people. Protect you."

Henry stares at him. "You don't have to—"

"I know. I *want* to. I mean, obviously you don't actually need it, but—"

"How bad would you say your pain is right now?"

Bastian blinks. "Um. What?"

"I need to know whether kissing you is going to cause you to pass out from anything other than my incredible prowess."

"Don't make me laugh. Hurts."

"Now I'm insulted, but I'm still going to kiss you."

"Then shut up and do it."

He does, but it lasts for significantly less time that it should due to an interruption.

"What," says a booming voice, "is going on here?"

Bastian looks over his shoulder to find a small group walking toward them. Booming Voice isn't anyone he knows, but some of the others….

"Smith." Henry stares at her and at the other officers following behind, all of whom must be part of his team, given the way he's looking at them. "What are you—?"

"You didn't think we'd let you have all the fun, did you, Captain?" Smith grins. "The general said he needed an escort, so we volunteered."

"After I let them out of their cells," Catherine adds.

"And after I got the general here in the first place," Kent says.

"I think we're all missing the most important point here," says General Booming Voice. "What. Is. Going. On!" He looks over at Valentine, now in cuffs, with Michaels beside her. "Major?"

"Mutiny, I'm afraid, General Carter," Valentine says, her best sad-and-disappointed face on. "I'm sorry you had to come all the way from Council headquarters to see this, but I assure you, the situation is completely under control."

Carter raises an eyebrow. "There's a young man collapsed on the ground, another one who looks like he's been hit over the head too many times, and you're in cuffs. That hardly constitutes 'under control,' Major."

"Nevertheless—"

"Excuse me, General. There's something you should see." Henry exchanges glances with Laurel, who hurries over to Bastian's side to help him get to his feet. Henry takes the files from where Bastian dropped them and hands them to the general.

"Who are you?" Carter demands.

"Cap—uh, Henry Mortimer, sir. You'll want to look at these files."

Carter flips through them, very quickly at first, more slowly toward the end, his frown deepening. Then he shuts the folders and looks up. "This is extremely irregular, you all realize. As I told the team behind me when I got to your compound, the proper method of contacting the Council is to go through your commanding officer. Not to hack into the Council mainframe and leave repeated urgent messages accompanied by icons that look like little faces."

Kent grins and shrugs. "My way's faster."

Carter pointedly ignores him. "I came here under the impression that there was something catastrophic happening related to the Council's murder investigation request. That impression hasn't been lessened by running into all of you cavorting in the middle of the forest instead of doing your jobs."

He looks at Henry and taps the files with his forefinger. "I'll be looking at these in far more depth, but am I to understand you want to charge Major Valentine and Dr. Wright with some sort of misconduct?"

"Yes, sir."

Henry's let down the negation field enough that Bastian can feel the calm-determined-focused coming off him. He's a little nervous about being in front of this guy, but he's not about to back down.

The general looks him up and down, assessing him. "That's a very serious accusation. What did you say your rank is?"

"I...was a captain until about twenty minutes ago."

"What happened twenty minutes ago?"

"Captain Mortimer attempted to abandon his team and his post," Valentine says. "Accusations from a disgraced officer are hardly worth giving any credence to, General, as I'm sure you'll agree—"

"Stop talking," Bastian says irritably. "Someone take us back to the compound. Read those files. Put people on trial. Get this sorted out somewhere other than here with all of us just standing around like idiots." He pauses. "And someone get me a *lot* of painkillers."

The general turns to him, obviously expecting Bastian to be cowed. But the advantage of not being an officer is that Bastian doesn't have to give a damn just because someone has a fancy title.

"Who is this rude young man?" the general demands.

"See? I've told you, everyone thinks you're totally rude!" Laurel says, poking him in the arm and making him cringe. "Sorry."

Carter is still looking at him. "Name and rank. Now."

Bastian snorts (which hurts; bad idea).

"His name's Bastian Lucas," Henry says quickly. "He doesn't have a rank because he's an asset."

"Is this just a thing you do?" Bastian demands. "Glowering at people until they give you their name and rank? Good for you, keeping yourself so busy you didn't have time to notice all the illegal experiments going on right under your nose."

Carter looks at him silently for such a long time, Bastian can hear people start to shuffle their feet awkwardly.

"You must be the empath," Carter says at last. "I've heard about you."

"Can you maybe hear about me back at the compound? We're still a day and a half away, and I wasn't kidding about those painkillers." To be fair, the pain is starting to fade, except in his hand. Hopefully, Henry was wrong about that whole breaking-your-hand thing.

Carter continues to look at Bastian, obviously sizing him up like he did Henry. Then he looks over at John Doe, who's now being held up by another officer.

"This is about that empath experiment, isn't it, Valentine?" Carter says. "The one the Council vetoed? The one under investigation right now because somehow, an unauthorized liaison committee between the compounds and the city government managed to get the experiments going anyway? Or am I mistaken?"

Valentine goes pale. "General—"

"Our most recent intel noted that all but one of these murders have been senators believed to have had connections with this experimental committee. Interesting coincidence."

"That's hardly—"

"The Council will be expecting a thorough account of your actions in this matter, Major. I anticipate many long and irritating meetings, culminating in a trial for which I recommend you prepare extensively."

He turns to Smith and her team. "We need to return to the compound immediately so we can greet the rest of the Council when they arrive. Direct everyone here to the vehicles we brought. We hardly need to waste the day and a half Lucas mentioned. Particularly when there are...insects." He makes a face and swats at his arm.

"Yes, sir," Smith says.

"I can get the plants to make something for your hand before we go," Laurel says to Bastian as the others jump into action. "I'll have to let go of you, though. Can you stand on your own?"

"Yes."

Michaels shuffles past as Laurel moves off. It's a good thing Bastian thinks to strengthen his shield as Valentine gets closer, since she's sending (carefully modulated) venom his way.

"A moment, Michaels." They stop, Michaels wary and uncomfortable.

"This won't work, you know," Valentine says to Bastian. "And I'm extremely disappointed in you. I've spent so much time and effort doing everything I could for you, and this is how you repay me?"

"How would you prefer I repay you? By letting Wright bleed me dry? By agreeing to be a murderer who gets rid of your enemies whenever you say? By dying with twenty other assets when you make a selfish mistake that costs other people their lives?"

Valentine shakes her head. "You're mistaken if that's what you believe happened. I've always been working to—"

"Not anymore." He nods to Michaels. "We're done."

"Yes, sir." Michaels herds Valentine away. Bastian feels oddly hollow watching it.

Henry, having spoken briefly to his team, comes back over to Bastian projecting enough relief-happiness-thankfulness that it goes straight to Bastian's stomach. It's sort of pleasant, filling the hollowness up with something warm.

"Are you all right?" Henry asks, eyeing Michaels and Valentine walking away.

"Definitely not. I'll need lots of help getting to the vehicles."

"That wasn't what I meant." Henry turns back and looks at him. "Wait, really? I just heard you tell Laurel you were fine standing on your own."

"I lied. Didn't want to worry her. I'll have to lean on you a lot or I won't make it."

Henry does something with his mouth that looks an awful lot like smirking. "You sure you don't want me to carry you instead?"

Bastian makes a face. "Actually, never mind. Forget I said anything."

"You know I can hear you from over here, right?" Laurel calls. "Also, you're both disgusting. By which I mean cute. And Henry, I definitely want to see you carry Bastian around."

In the end, Henry does *not* carry him around. Henry does hold his uninjured hand the whole way to the vehicles, though. Bastian considers being embarrassed by this until he realizes he doesn't really care.

Epilogue

One month later

IT'S NOT REALLY a good day for the beach, but that's why Bastian likes it—no one else around and a bit of ominous cloudiness to boot. It means he can listen to the waves in peace.

He sits down where the dry sand starts turning wet and looks out over the water at the sun, which is just about to set. It goes behind a cloud, tinting it yellow orange around the edges. He takes off his gloves so he can run his hand through the sand while he watches the sunset.

He feels Henry coming up before hearing him. The calm-peaceful-happy is undercut a little by the anxiety, but that's to be expected, given why they're here.

"I told Valentine once that being an empath is like this," Bastian says as Henry sits down next to him. "The waves going in and out, big and small, never stopping. Like getting pummeled by other people's emotions all the time." He shrugs. "I was sort of melodramatic as a kid."

"Just as a kid?"

Bastian considers throwing sand at him but decides to be the mature one and refrains. "I like the water, though," he continues. "If it's dangerous, that's only because people are idiots. Water itself is just water."

They watch the ocean for a while in silence before Henry speaks again. "You're really all right with it? Reading the major tomorrow for the Council meeting?"

"I don't know if 'all right' is exactly…accurate. But it has to be done. So I'll do it."

"If she says anything, does anything that makes you—"

Bastian gives him an exasperated smile. "As much as I'd like to see you shoot her in front of the entire Compound Council, I don't think it'll be necessary."

Rather than come up with some suitable response to that, Henry falls silent again. Since he isn't negating at the moment, Bastian gets the full force of his hesitation.

"There's something else," Henry says. "I finished reading the book."

Bastian grins. "Wow, you found time between all of your rigorous duties, Major? Very impressive."

"Okay, let's not get ahead of ourselves with the temporary title. The trial isn't until next month, and that's only if this meeting goes well. And even then—"

"Interim leaders tend to get stuck as permanent leaders. Particularly when they're competent. Anyway, this is a dream come true, right? You *did* say something about taking over the compound."

Henry rolls his eyes. "This is all your fault, you know. If you hadn't suggested it to General Carter—"

"—your entire team and half the compound would have done it instead. You're stuck. Major."

"*Anyway.* What I *meant* to say was, I finished the book. And there's something you should know."

Bastian eyes him warily. "What's that?"

"There's a negation skill. I mean, it's really advanced, so there's no way I could do it now, and I don't even really know if it's possible, but…."

He pauses for so long, Bastian's not sure he's going to continue. "I could negate your power," he says at last.

"You already—"

"Permanently."

Bastian blinks. "You could…take away an asset's power. For good."

"If the book is right, yes." Henry runs a hand through his hair. "I mean, I could never tell anyone I can do it. Especially if I ever officially ran the compound. A ranking officer who could destroy assets' powers? Never mind an officer—anyone. Too dangerous. Too easy to let it get out of control."

He looks at Bastian. "But if you wanted me to, I—"

"This is because of my file, isn't it? And what John Doe said about my power killing me?"

"Bastian—"

"I said I'd go through all your tests after we get everything sorted out, didn't I? And Laurel said if we need any sort of healing help, she's game. And we already know I've survived longer than my file said I would."

He waves a hand. "Anyway, it's all conjecture right now. My power isn't like John Doe's, and my augmentations are different, too. Obviously, it was bad for me before, when Wright was doing all those experiments. But that's over. It's fine now."

"This is about more than just a few nosebleeds, Bastian. I saw you—"

"Okay, maybe it *was* hurting me. But it hasn't since then. And it's not like I'm the only one who ever got a nosebleed."

"Yeah? How about the way you looked after you did that thing in the forest that knocked out John Doe? You told me—"

Bastian opens his mouth to protest, but Henry shakes his head and sighs. "No, I get it. You're right that we don't really know anything for certain yet, so it's pointless to speculate. I just…wanted you to know about this. That it's an option."

Bastian looks back out at the water, Henry sitting silently beside him.

"Would you want to?" Bastian asks.

"To save you? Absolutely."

"No, I mean—would you want to use your power like that? Because of me?"

Henry frowns. "How is that different?"

"Assets use their powers the way we're told to. I did what Valentine said, more or less. But you don't have to do that. You get to choose how and when you use it. That's how it *should* be."

"Unless an asset uses their power to set a tsunami on a city. Or to send psionic shocks through everyone in a ten-mile radius. Or to convince senators to kill themselves."

"Okay, fine, there are limits. What I'm saying is, if this negation power is actually possible, I wouldn't want you to, I don't know, use it in a way you're not comfortable with just because you think you should."

Henry takes his hand (anxious but also patient-concerned-loving—that last one's always better, and more terrifying, on skin instead of through gloves).

"I appreciate that," Henry says. "But I wouldn't have offered if I weren't willing to do it. And the real question is—would you want that? To get rid of your power?"

Bastian looks at their hands, then back out at the waves. "No," he says quietly. "It hurts sometimes, feeling everything, and there was definitely a time when I would've wanted to. But now I want to know what it's like when I use my power for *me*. Not for Valentine or anyone else."

He pauses. "Although I might be willing to use my power to help a major in charge of reworking the compound's structure and programs. I mean. If he were extremely attractive and asked very nicely."

Henry grins. "What if that major put you in charge of the asset program?"

"*What?*"

"Well, Dr. Wright's obviously no longer available, being incarcerated and all, so—"

"Henry, I'm not a scientist. Or a doctor. Or anything."

"No, but you can read people. You could put together a decent support staff to advise you on ethical experimentation procedures and what we still need to know about assets and their powers."

"And you think people would actually be okay with me—an escaped asset and former interrogator—?"

"You know what it's like. More importantly, you've been through these experiments when they're…done the wrong way." His voice gets quieter. "You'd know how to not make the same mistakes. How to treat assets like people. How to get it right."

Bastian purses his lips. "Would there be meetings?"

"Loads."

"Then forget it."

"Some of those meetings could be one-on-one dinner meetings with the major the night before very important Council hearings."

"When you say 'dinner,' do you mean 'energy bar in a tree,' or…?"

Henry grins and kisses Bastian's hand. "I was thinking more like the reservation I made at an actual restaurant a few blocks from here. I hear they have actual food at actual restaurants."

He leans over and kisses Bastian's neck for good measure. Helpful that they're already sitting down because this sort of thing makes Bastian's knees inconveniently stop working. Which, of course, Henry knows. Jerk.

"I also thought," Henry says in his ear, "that we have a nice hotel room and the whole evening after dinner to think of something not boring to do."

"We could skip dinner," Bastian says quickly.

"Nope. There are rules."

"Isn't the point of being a major that you make the rules? And can unmake them?"

Henry pulls back and frowns. "That's not really how—"

Never underestimate the effectiveness of distracting a military man with talk of ranks, Bastian thinks smugly. Henry's now at the perfect angle for Bastian to kiss him on the mouth.

Henry starts to pull away after a while but doesn't get any farther than resting his forehead against Bastian's. "We should really—the reservation is in half an hour—"

Rather than let him continue sneaking kisses and distracting Henry, Bastian's stomach rumbles very loudly, which is completely traitorous and not part of the plan.

Henry laughs and gets to his feet. "Come on."

"Wait. I'm supposed to get postcards for Laurel. And Kent. And Catherine." Bastian frowns. "And I think Michaels, but it's always hard to tell with her."

"Souvenirs tomorrow, assuming we survive the Council hearing. Dinner tonight." Henry holds out a hand to help Bastian up.

Bastian looks one last time at the ocean waves coming in and going out.

Then he takes Henry's hand.

About the Author

Katy Morgan is an indie fantasy author and fiction editor with an eye for detail and a heart for supporting the creative community. When she's not writing or editing, she can be found cross-stitching something sassy, daydreaming about hedgehogs, or drinking far too many mochas, usually all at once.

Keep up with Katy on BardicFool.com.

***

Thanks for reading *Dark Empathy*!

If you enjoyed this book, please consider letting others know by leaving a review on Amazon and/or Goodreads. Reviews are one of the best ways to help new readers find indie work--and we can't do it without you!

www.ingramcontent.com/pod-product-compliance
Lightning Source LLC
Chambersburg PA
CBHW021122110726
47900CB00007B/2307